I0776938

SUN EYE MOON EYE

Vincent Czyz

SPUYTEN DUYVIL
New York City

ACKNOWLEDGEMENTS

It's been a long strange trip, and I'm deeply grateful for the help I received along the way—bottles of water, sage advice, pages so marked up they looked like impromptu maps, spending money, ham-and-cheese sandwiches, and the like. Accordingly, I want to thank Mitch Tave, who gave me a great deal of insight into societal views on the mentally ill as well as life in a state psychiatric hospital, and Stephen R. Pallucca—aspects of whom are preserved in the character of Jim Lee—for leading the way during my descent into the southeast corner of Kansas. I'd also like to thank Paul West, Samuel R. Delany, and Mary Jo Phelps for their incisive comments on early drafts of the novel (extra thanks to Mary Jo for suffering through the early years of the publication process); also Jeremy M. Davies for his editorial guidance vis a vis the opening chapters. Thanks to *Quiddity*, *Cold Mountain Review*, *Taint Taint Taint*, *Litro*, *Archaeopteryx*, *Nisi Shawl* (*Stories for Chip*), and *On the Seawall* for publishing excerpts from *Sun Eye Moon Eye*; here I have to single out Rob Cook and Stephanie Dickinson, who published three full chapters in separate issues of *Skidrow Penthouse* and have been unwavering in their support for the writing. Thanks as well to the NJ Council on the Arts for a generous fellowship. Finally, I'm deeply grateful to Tod Thilleman, who understood the "archeo sense" in which the novel was written and at long last gave it a home.

© 2024 Vincent Czyz
ISBN 978-1-959556-83-1

Library of Congress Cataloging-in-Publication Data

Names: Czyz, Vincent, 1963- author.
Title: Sun eye moon eye / Vincent Czyz.
Description: New York City : Spuyten Duyvil, 2024.
Identifiers: LCCN 2023039864 | ISBN 9781959556831 (paperback)
Subjects: LCGFT: Bildungsromans. | Novels.
Classification: LCC PS3553.Z98 S86 2024 | DDC 813/.54--dc23/eng/20230830
LC record available at https://lccn.loc.gov/2023039864

Q. Who must do the hard things?

A. He who can.

—proverb

For Robert E. Czyz, Sr.

"Phenomena intersect; to see but one is to see nothing."

—Victor Hugo

"There are three places left for an individual in America—
jail, a psychiatric hospital, and the cemetery."

—Mitch Tave (in conversation)

BOOK I

TOKPELA

"The First World was *Tokpela*. It was assigned a direction, a color, a mineral, and certain animal chiefs. It is said that it was destroyed by fire."
—Frank Waters, *Book of the Hopi*

THE SMILING AZTEC

He heard a faint chorus of birds and insects in the brush, singing, buzzing, chirping. As constant, as lasting, as the shivering of starlight. Dimly he remembered his grandfather squatting in the dark, humming. He'd lain awake, listening.

Fall was just beginning, but in the desert who could tell? Someone who lived here maybe, who could dig his fingers into the sandy soil and come up with a fair idea of when it'd rained last.

In the beginning there was no beginning. And no end. No time and no direction. Time floated on the silence, an unawakened moment.

In perfect silence a breath is a symphony.

In perfect darkness, a candle a sun.

Wind whirled dust in his face. He didn't bother to brush at the bridge of his nose or the swells of his cheekbones. A little powdered-down desert might keep the sun off some while he walked.

Against the horizon the land looked flat. Up close it was rough, unfinished, as though the Earth had once been beaten with a fairy tale–sized hammer. Each place mallet and earth had collided color was a shade off—tawny, yellow, ocher, sienna, rust, oxblood. There was nowhere the hammer hadn't fallen, nowhere that hadn't been dented, shallowed out, gouged. A god working out a lumpy tortilla. The whole strewn with stones, bits that flew off during the pounding.

He palmed one now and then, balanced its weight in his hand before throwing it. Sometimes to see it arc against sky, sometimes just to disturb what had lain for who knew how long. His grandfather would've shaken his head. *Qua'ah* sided with the way things had settled, considered each moment the culmination of a process too hard to fathom to be tampered with. The same one that'd brought him to the mellowness of his last years. *Sorry,* Qua'ah, *but you shouldn't have told all those tall tales with me on your knee, the endless on-and-on of what never happened.*

His hand went to what had been a dampness on his head, over that little dip that's still soft when you're a baby. A bird had shit right on it—payback for the stones he'd thrown at their kind since he was a child. Maybe a Navajo in its last life, here to remind him of the animosity between their tribes. The sun had turned the warm dollop to a greasy paste that he'd rubbed out as best he could, leaving his hair with the dried-out feel of the things that grew here.

The world had no name, only a syllable waiting to be spoken.
All of Endless Space a yawning ache
(imagine)
a mouth without beginning or end, stretched in all directions.
(There was no direction.)
A silence on the threshold of hearing.
Listen.
There were no words, no syllables, only a faint, only a distant
only what might be
Humming
in the emptiness in the stillness
there was something

He kept an even pace, his boots crunching gravel along the side of the road. The sky was a sheet of cool blue metal except in the west, where a hot glow was steadily fading and a few clouds lay in photographic stillness.

He turned at the sound of a car. Walking backward, thumb out, his arm went up like a gate at a railroad crossing.

The driver, hunched over the steering wheel, didn't slow, didn't even crane for a better look.

Pirouetting on a boot heel, he tried to remember how long it'd been since he'd slept in a bed: three days? Four? He didn't know the day of the week either. Without a calendar to grid the year, he couldn't keep track. Not surprising, he thought, if you took into account that he was descended from the Hopi, a tribe that had at best a hazy sense of time. Up on their mesas they'd found a way to ignore it, to get by without self-winding watches, without bells or buzzers.

His boots resumed their metronomic tapping against the road. Two-toners he'd gotten back in Kansas, their stitching a kind of script trying to tell him something. *Closer, lean a little closer.* About which way to point the scuffed toes. How much farther he needed to go. He shifted the position of the leather bag against his hip. A bedroll in his left hand counterweighted the bag.

An emergence.

The Sun, a star that warms a system of planets, would have been a hundred thousand times brighter at the core of this emptiness. And still it would have been less than a spark, hardly a bright pinhole against the unmoving changeless forever.

Somewhere a tension gathered. A tightness strung through Endless Space trembled.

A sound?

A perfect surface, a sterile symmetry shifted, broke.

A hum.

A sameness that had always been, splintered

(an endless silence left striated).

Something had given motion to what moved.

The hum drizzled through the emptiness, moved toward

Evening, just falling.

A snake holding its oversized head aloft disappeared in the brush. Reminded him of the need to keep moving. He was tempted to ignore the implied warning: When was the last time he'd made a good decision? Why not let the desert finish the job? Leave him a strip of desiccated meat that would keep for years. He'd already been cleaned out for embalming.

The same wind that had scoured rock into layered pancakes, eroded it into towering fingers pointing at the empty blue, whistled through his hollowed-out chest cavity. With no liver to send bile to the top of his throat, there was no bitter taste in his mouth. His liver had been sun-dried, ground to brownish dust. No desire or ache either—what'd been his heart was a bright streak through rust-red rock. No hunger, no pit of stomach left to hold fear or anxiety (stomach and intestine had been spread for yellow). The rest had been cauterized by a burning wind, had hardened into sandstone.

He abandoned the road and slid a strap down his arm, let his leather bag drop. Dust came up in tiny puffs. Then he dumped his ass like a load of rocks. Jeans worn through in places to white threads, face and hair and shoulders veiled with road dust, he must've looked like a photograph paling with age.

He pulled his collar out with a forefinger. If more of a wind kicked up, maybe it'd hum across the gap. Play him like a flute.

Thick veins formed a crooked *H* on the back of his right hand. Like the lump of ground he was sitting on, the water had gone out of his hands. They almost got in the way when he went to use them.

Straightening a leg, he slid fingers into a pocket and pulled out a butterfly knife. A few flicks and twists of his wrist and the blade flipped gracefully out from between the steel handles. The guy who'd given him the knife, an ex-Green Beret, used to make a show of it.

He dug his boot heels into the ground, felt the little horseshoe indentations he'd leave when he got up. Zeroing in on a callus, he sank the point of the blade. He pressed on bone, and his pulse throbbed in the twin handles. The pain that spread up his arm was oddly gratifying, something meaty and raw for his brain to chew on. He thought about sinking the blade deeper, drawing blood.

He jumped up. A few frantic strides and he was on sun-softened asphalt.

The dusty gold pickup didn't slow.

He still had the knife in his hand. *Goddamn.* Tucking it into a pocket, he looked at his palm. A red pearl had formed just beneath his ring finger.

When he went back for his things, he saw a four-leafed plant that had been trapped under his bedroll trying to right itself. Familiar, it might've been an herb his grandfather had once pointed out to him. With a shrug for the plant's bad luck, he headed west again.

Evening drifted down, a chafing of bruise-colored sky.

Two more cars passed. One disappeared behind him, the

other in front. Bird twitters and the soft whirring of insects filled in their wakes.

Under the chalky sickle of a moon, something neither bird nor insect rose like a spate of palm-sized whirlwinds. He looked but saw nothing. Restless, tribeless, they wanted to return. To the time before the land was fenced in. Before billboards went up to advertise as souvenirs objects no less commonplace than pots and pans. A time before interstates cut through the land and the future held one evil wonder after another. Before cities—cold and crystalline, without plazas for the dances—invented a new horizon.

He'd wandered through Chaco Canyon a few days ago. What passed for a city way-back-when, now a labyrinth of collapsing walls and empty doorways had. He'd stood in the droning wind, looking over the sandstone boxes and round kivas sunk into the earth. Roof timbers rotted away, the kivas lay like dusty cavities where monstrous teeth had fallen out.

The kivas presented a mystery: There were far too many, at least by mesa standards. Perhaps, a park pamphlet conjectured, Chaco Canyon hadn't been a city at all but a ceremonial center. Whatever the case, Chaco was neither city nor shrine anymore; it was a national park where for a few dollars you could unhitch your trailer or put up a tent for the night.

Picking his way among the ruins, he came across the oddness of a single window framing a rectangle of sky and its scrap of cloud. Set in the dull stone of a ragged wall. (The other three had reverted to rubble.) It'd once had a cool sheltered side and another sanded down by an endless procession of grainy dawns. Useless as it seemed, the window in that lone wall still had something to say, aligned as it was—so the pamphlet claimed—with the movements of the Moon.

He climbed a ridge overlooking the canyon, saw Chaco as an interrupted rhythm. Realized the permanence of stone was an illusion he leaned against to get through a hard week. The dead builders? Another mystery. The Navajo called them *Anasazi—Ancient Strangers*. Rumored to be ancestors of the Hopi. Their cities already abandoned by the time the Navajos encountered them.

He studied the ruins, their enigmatic geometry, hoping for a sense of familiarity, but when he stood at the bottom of a kiva cutting a rough-edged circle out of the sky, he was conscious mainly of his machine-woven jeans, his factory-made boots. Though his father had been a mason, a layer of foundations, though his grandfather might've had a soul that mirrored the layout of that once-upon-a-time place, he had no inkling of the cadence that would solve the crumbling maze.

Now he was stuck in an everlasting present marked only by ritual shifts in light, morning to evening. The vital part of him gone, there was a place for him among Chaco Canyon's eroded walls, among its kivas, where no fires burned.

The night he'd slept there he'd dreamed of fire: whole cities aflame, rivers sizzling, lakes boiling off, Earth burning like a feeble star. Not a forest or a town, not a tree or a shanty left standing, and he'd woken up with the smell of smoke in his nostrils.

A car? He turned with his thumb out, tried to fix the driver with his eyes.

The Mustang pulled over, kicking up gravel. A convertible

with the top down. The yellow paint paled almost to white in places. Rust had eaten through the fenders.

He trotted over, pulled the door open, and slid onto the leather seat.

The driver, a young woman whose hair was dark as loam, wanted to know how far he was going.

When he tried to answer, all that came out was a sandpaper-on-wood noise and "—running water." As if that were his name. He cleared his throat. "Anyplace with running water."

"You look like … I mean, you must've been walking all day."

She wore a tie-dyed cutoff for a shirt. Maybe half a dozen braided bracelets ringed one wrist. A gold bracelet circled the other. She looked like a college-age hippie.

She held out a hand. "Debbie."

His instinct was to pull back, but he took the expectant hand. "Logan."

Debbie looked nervous. Probably he was her first hitchhiker. Below her peeling nose, splotched with pink, was a wisp of a mustache she hadn't bothered to bleach. Her face, wide and angular, brought it off well enough. Just as he began to pick up her scent, she pulled out and there was wind.

What had it been? Ginger root? Sage? He didn't know herb names, but the smell was green. No makeup, maybe she put bags of herbal tea under her arms instead of deodorant—almond sunset for road trips, mint magic for a night out on the town. Probably didn't shave her armpits either. A rainforest climate with a fecund smell.

He had no room to talk, washing up in rest-stop sinks. She'd catch wind of him across a room if he took off his shirt.

She lowered the radio and Jim Morrison's voice, singing about a swim to the Moon, faded.

"What's your last name? I mean, if you don't mind."

Her voice was whittled to a pitch higher than it should've been.

"Blackfeather." Anglicized, maybe shortened, it wasn't a Hopi name anymore.

"I guess you're Indian." Strands of hair blew across her face, waved past her mouth.

"Hopi. On my father's side." His eyes were fixed on a jagged crack in the dashboard where peeling vinyl had exposed yellowish foam. He stuck a fingertip in the crack and followed it.

"You're pretty tall."

For an Indian? For a Hopi? "My old man was taller."

"Do you live up on the mesa?"

I'm not that kind of Indian, he wanted to say, *I'm the kind you find in front of a store, holding cigars.* "No, never did." Though *Qua'ah* had had a house up on First Mesa. Well, a shanty. "I grew up in Kansas." He started to pick, as discreetly as he could, at the dashboard.

"Kansas, like Dorothy and Toto?"

Splaying his hand on the dashboard, he pictured a knife blade pinning it there.

"I'm from Phoenix." She glanced over at him.

"I was born there."

"I *thought* it was kind of weird that you're Hopi and lived out in Kansas." There was something like relief in her voice. "I'm still there—Tempe. I'm at ASU trying to figure out a major."

Grateful Dead looked like her major to him. He pictured her 12-by-12 dorm room with a bunk bed in it, a cigar box crammed with junk jewelry on her desk, Jimi Hendrix and Dead posters on the walls, a lava lamp throwing off amber light, wine bottles covered with wax drippings, a bong on the coffee table.

A crystal, anchored by a coil of gold, dangled from a chain around her neck. He wondered what might be caught in its amber-tinted angles.

"What?" A self-conscious hand went to the necklace. "You're staring like I'm some kind of New Age flake. I mean, I don't wear it because I think I'm tapping into *hidden energies*. I just like the way it looks. I like that it comes out of the ground this way."

He turned to the landscape blurring by. He hadn't realized he was staring.

By the time town was in sight, a cluster of luminous specks on a flat void, the yellowy-white Moon was a pair of horns tilted at an odd angle and the car's roof was up.

A sign for a motel advertising the cheapest single whizzed by. He tried to fix the name.

"What about stopping for a beer or something? There's a bar I went to once … somewhere around here."

She was a shadowy profile. Her nose, a gentle slope roughened by peeling skin, was slightly upturned, giving it the prettiness of a comic-book heroine.

A beer sounded almost as good as a shower. "Why not?" He marveled at how much she trusted him already.

Gas-station signs rose sixty feet or more on poles, reassuring ovals, rectangles, and shells of light. Everything lined up along the road as if it were a dark river cutting through the desert, supporting a glowing oasis.

She turned off the main drag of what was more an oversized truck stop than a town: rows of gas stations, cheap all-night restaurants, corner bars, motels with cracking whitewashed walls and peeling signs.

The bar that made Debbie slow down was called the Smiling Aztec. Timbers poked through the top of an adobe wall. Next to the name, an Aztec calendar had been painted in black—a half-assed rendition of those imitations every tourist brings back from Tijuana. At the center was a demonic face, its mouth open and its pointed tongue like the triangular blade of a flint knife. All around it were rows of glyphs that had grown mysterious over time but for all he knew advertised Montezuma's favorite brand of coffee bean.

"I *think* this is it ..."

Looking at the gravel lot taken up mostly by pickups with crooked bumpers, cracked tail lights, and spider-webbed windshields, he didn't think it was.

He stepped out of the car, his bag hanging from a shoulder, and saw that Debbie was a head shorter. Maybe five-four.

She pulled on the plank door and held it for him.

He'd never set foot in the Smiling Aztec, but he knew the place.

A man rubbed his unshaven chin with his knuckles. One of his oversized hands cradling a beer bottle, he looked as if he worked in a tar pit. His arm bore dark tattoos that could've been dried muck. The woman across from him was a short-haired blonde with a little knob of a nose that made her look belligerent. Her face puffy and rounded, her breasts sagging in a yellow tube top, she dragged on a cigarette then rested her chin in a hand.

Logan could've been in The Windjammer or the Pan Club back in Kansas. The drinkers were mostly men, anchoring themselves to a stool instead of a couch, a beer in front of them instead of a tv. They didn't want to go home because home brought them that much closer to bed. They didn't want to go to bed because when they woke up, they'd have to go back to the garage, the shop, the road.

"I think it has character." Debbie looked up at a ceiling supported by beams thick as railroad ties. A thin haze hung there—cigarette smoke robbed of the long ascent to heaven.

He tucked his bag under the bar while Debbie went to the ladies' room. Her hips were a little too wide by magazine standards but pretty much in keeping with his. He didn't feel anything, though. At all. Probably had something to do with having no heart, no liver, no innards. A collection of old habits, he glanced at a man growing agitated a few stools away.

"I got my own tools." His hair curly and his beard ragged, he jerked a crooked thumb at himself. "I ain't lookin' for no handout."

"What can I getchya?" Hands planted on the counter, the bartender was like a bird flaunting its plumage, only what he had were tattoos that started at his wrists and crept unbroken up to his elbows.

"Beer. A long-neck."

"Taste better, don't they?" His smile was missing an eyetooth; the rest were large and grayish. "Somethin' different about the way they bottle 'em."

While he hustled to the other end of the bar, Logan's gaze swept around the room. Dull light polished bottles wrapped in hands with gritty nails and permanently swollen knuckles.

Outside, a flaking, open-mouthed Indian god was rubber-stamped on a wall. A roadside dead-end where you couldn't go forward but you could still back out, the Smiling Aztec exchanged bill and coin for drink, played music on a jukebox, echoed with sporadic laughter. Farther north and east, Chaco Canyon, laid out according to the secrets of the still-obscure Anasazi soul, eroded in wind and dry starlight.

The heel of a beer bottle clunked loudly on the bar. "I don't give a shit *what* Lamont says. I ain't lookin' for no handout. Whadda you wanna lissen to a nigger for anyway?"

When Debbie showed up, she ordered a screwdriver. She'd brushed her hair back from her face. He caught her herbal-tea scent again.

Narrow and long, the Aztec reminded him of an army barrack. On a small stage at the back, musicians tested their instruments, sent out isolated notes, truncated riffs.

Logan took a long appreciative swallow of beer then put the cold bottle to his forehead. Debbie was watching the band set up.

"You know, when I first picked you up, I was a little scared." She forced a laugh. "I mean, you never know, right? Now I'm curious. Something about you doesn't fit."

"What's that?"

"I don't know. How old are you?"

"How old d'you think?"

"Twenty-eight? Twenty-nine?"

"Close enough." People always took him for older than he

was. He found something exhilarating in how easily he'd begun to invent a new identity.

No, he said, he'd never gotten a degree although he'd taken a few courses at Pittsburg State.

Debbie's cheeks collapsed around a petite straw as she drank. "We're the same in a way. I don't have a major, I don't know what I'm going to do when I get out, and I feel like, kind of like I'm waiting for something—"

"Everybody's waiting for something."

She shook her head. "Not you. Half the bar looks up whenever that door opens. You haven't glanced at it once."

His beer gone, he was dry-mouthed. He looked at the empty bottle as if it were Yorick's skull, as if there were still something of use in it that he might've overlooked.

The bartender pointed at the bottle. "'Nother one?"

"Yeah." Debbie smiled at Logan. "On me." Before he could protest, she turned on her stool, her bare knee bumping to a stop against his denimed one. "No biggie. My parents ..." She waved a hand as if she were about to admit something she'd rather forget. "Bucks deluxe."

"Thanks." He stood up. "Be back in a minute."

A few heads cocked as he walked toward the stage.

The dull yellow paint on the bathroom door had been worn to the wood where countless hands had pressed. A squeaky spring closed it behind him. He flipped the latch.

The bathroom was so small his ass almost hit the door when he bent over the sink. He lathered his hands and face with soap. The water swirled filthy gray against the white porcelain. The bridge of his nose—long and narrow, faintly curved—was a little burned. Creased flesh under his eyes made two upturned crescents, like twin fallen moons that had settled at exactly the same level.

Somebody pushed on the door, rattled the hook in its eyelet, pushed again, harder. Logan shook his head. *Didn't your mama teach you to knock?*

Leaning toward the mirror, he rubbed his chin, rough with a few days' growth. Only the chin and his upper lip were fertile. He might grow a goatee someday, but that was about it. His jaw was square enough, but he envied Debbie, the width to her face. He'd waited patiently for the years to fill him out, but his mother's side had kept him willowy.

He reached for the latch but his finger stopped short.

What's the difference between a nigger and an Indian? One's imported and the other's domestic. Written in black marker on the door, it was accompanied by the cartoon head of a bird scowling and smoking a cigar like some kind of '40s tough guy.

He flicked the hook out of the eyelet, pushed open the door, and almost bumped into someone. In a brief exchange of looks, Logan saw that the man—burly and bearded, dirty blond hair sticking out from under a cap—didn't like him. Because he had a hoop in his ear or long hair or Indian looks or because the guy was just an ornery fucker. Edging out sideways, Logan grazed the leather holster on the man's hip. Bikers and truckers carried knives that way; that made it legal in most states. The knife concealed in his pocket usually wasn't.

Debbie had a shine in her eye, an easy smile on her face. The crystal around her neck gleamed like hardened light.

"So what do you think of the Ax Handlers?"

The band was just starting on some country tune. The singer, wearing a leather Outback hat with a feather in it, played lead guitar. Behind him, the drummer had a bandanna skullcap, an enormous belly, a sleeveless T-shirt. All that weight to him, he must've been the band's anchor. The bass player was a scrawny guy with blond hair. Long and straight, it flew up every time the song he was playing made him jerk his head like he'd gotten a shock. Sometimes he let the guitar hang on its strap while he played a synthesizer. He should've stuck to bass.

Logan shrugged. "They're all right."

When he picked up his beer, she tapped his bottle with the rim of her glass and smiled at him.

His smile was a sterile reflection.

A year ago he would've been grinning when she asked him about the band. *Buncha hicks can't even tune their strings right.* The grin had been replaced by a dust devil. Whatever he'd been up to with a keyboard backbone to the sound, it hadn't worked. The lake had long since dried up. What was left was stuck in the mud at odd angles. All he wanted now was a hot shower and a room where he could cocoon himself away, lie on the darkness till the maid's vacuum hummed outside his door and knocked into the woodwork.

"Hel-*LO*-oh, anybody home?" Debbie was waving a hand in front of his face.

He flicked his fingers toward the stage. "I used to play."

"You were in a band?'

Now why did he—? He nodded.

"What instrument?"

With the label picked away, he began turning the bottle as if he were getting a little planet going on its axis. "Anything with keys really." These days what he did with his fingers didn't amount to much more than weeding bird shit out of his hair, pulling up his zipper, picking his teeth after a chewy burger at one of those sloppy roadside grills.

"I *knew* there was something about you that didn't go with being a … you frame houses, right?"

He pushed aside the blank bottle, nodded.

"You want another beer?"

Pulling a ten-dollar bill out of his pocket, he laid it on the bar, but she pushed it back to him. "Keep it."

He didn't argue.

She rapped the air about a foot in from his face as if she were knocking on an invisible door. "You've got this …" She used her hands to outline an indeterminate shape. "This shell around you, don't you?"

She probably thought it was her responsibility to work a metal edge in somewhere and pry him open. Probably why she kept buying him beers, hoping he'd slide out like a slab of warm butter. "Logan Hermit Crab. Yeah, that's me. Logan Tortoiseshell."

"And you're looking to pick up work framing, right? I always think of paintings instead of construction."

That was a fiction. He was a moth, sense of direction wrecked, spiraling around the Southwest. Digging around in eviscerated ruins, from cliff dwellings to abandoned gas stations. How was he supposed to tell her he didn't know what he was looking for? For all he knew he'd already found it, and it was sitting in his pocket along with some desert grit. He might've held it in his hand, looked right at it, and been unable to decipher it. So he had to wait, carry it until he met someone who could tell him what he had—an ancient coin set before a dealer and his cyclopean loupe. Or he learned a new language.

The bartender put a fresh beer in front of him, a dull gleam coming off the bottle's shoulder. As Logan reached for it, he caught sight of the guy who'd tried pushing his way into the bathroom. *Mochney Freight* was written in big letters on the stained yellow of his T-shirt. The logo was a runaway rig, like something that had exploded through his ribs, menacing whoever happened to be standing in front of him.

Logan tipped the bottle back, slugging hard. Debbie, still talking, was like a light rain he didn't bother to get out of.

A man brushed against him and he realized the bar had gotten crowded. His hands tightened on the edge of the bar counter. He wasn't dizzy but some part of him that his hands couldn't help was unsteady. Christ he was *hot*.

"What happened?"

The veins in his hands were swollen with trapped blood; the crooked *H* of his right one looked like a sinister rune.

"Why aren't you in a band anymore?"

"Tough to make money that way."

She couldn't possibly know how much had gone into making those words come out clearly. As if his mouth were filled with gold and he'd had to bite off hunks of metal to shape the syllables properly. Worse, when he spoke, it sounded tinny and detached, like it was coming from a loudspeaker somewhere behind him. Over the music and conversations, he thought he heard the rush of his blood.

"But it only takes one song. If just one song hits …"

He eased his hold on the bar as a drop of sweat fell from the back of his jaw. For a moment everything seemed to go flat as if he'd suddenly lost vision in one eye. Trapping him inside a modernist painting, perspective steamrolled so that even if you were looking at a table edge-on, you could still see the surface.

He smiled. Not because she'd managed to instill in him some optimism but because he felt better.

"Hey, I'm going up there to talk to them."

Talk to …? A little earthquake had just rumbled through him, and somehow she'd missed the whole thing.

When she came back, her large brown eyes were a little glassy, her smile close-mouthed.

"You're on."

"I'm … *what*?"

"They're gonna let you play."

His eyes cut back to the stage, which sat at the end of a tunnel crudely carved out of smoke and dark by spare lighting.

"We got a little s'prise tonight …" The singer's voice was loud, edged in metallic echo. "We got an honorary member who's gonna play the electric piana so Bobby here can pay more mind t'his guitar for a tune or two. Come on up here, Logan." He looked around to see who would stand up.

Logan stood up but didn't move. Then he looked down at his beer bottle and walked toward the door.

"Where are you—?"

People turned to watch him, a few clapping uncertainly, as he made his way out of the bar.

"Oh hey now, fella, nothin' up here to catch fright of—"

Logan bumped square into a solid chest and pushed past.

"What the *fuck*!"

"Sorry." He doubted it was loud enough, on-time enough, to make a difference.

The night air was cool, lighter than the smokiness inside the Aztec.

The spring-rigged door opened behind him with a high-pitched *awww-uhh.*

"What the *fuck* is your problem?"

It was the trucker he'd almost run into outside the bathroom, cowboy boots bent outward by what seemed like his weight but must have been his bow-legged stance. On his cap was the head of a mean-looking bird.

"I *said* sorry."

"You didn't say *shit.*"

"You didn't hear maybe." His heart kicked up (he had one after all), and electricity rippled through his fingertips.

Noise from the bar became loud again. Two men come out of the open door and—one hand each on a shoulder, another on an arm—started tugging. "Come on, Tom—"

Tom pulled loose. "Aw what the *fuck*—"

They were persistent, one guy wrapping an arm around Tom's neck and hauling him backward.

"He's kinda drunk …" The man smiled apologetically.

"Fuckin' longhair—"

The door swung shut behind them.

Debbie had slipped outside behind Tom's friends. She and Logan were left in a strange insect quiet, the music from the bar a muffled throb.

"I didn't mean to put you on the spot like that. I'm *really* sorry."

"Forget about it."

"I guess … we should get going."

"You don't have to take me." Walking to her Mustang, he looked in a window. "I'm staying somewhere here tonight anyway."

She nodded, her head down.

"But I have to ..." He tipped his head toward the bar. "I should get my bag." Why had he even brought it in there?

"I'll wait for you." Backing up against a fender of the Mustang, Debbie pushed onto the hood with her palms, bouncing a little under her T-shirt. "I just want to sit out here for a minute and clear my head." She pulled her knees together.

He glanced back at her before stepping through the door of the Smiling Aztec.

BOOK II
TOKPA

The Second World was called *Tokpa*, Dark Midnight. Its direction was south.

1. The Gray Zone

An attendant holding a key ring that once might've belonged to a medieval dungeon-keeper opened the door. "There you go, doc."

No matter how many times he went through it, Dr. Manolakos was never prepared for the smell—an olfactory symphony composed of failed antiseptic, bodies sour for lack of bathing, clothes that had gone weeks without washing, breath stained by unbrushed teeth, and, overlapping everything, cigarette smoke. In winter the mélange was headier still because there were no open windows.

Patients who weren't sitting in a solitary daze watched tv or flipped through magazines with cigarettes smoldering between yellowed fingers. Through one kind of inattention or another—whether watching a game show or daydreaming or hallucinating—they had a habit of letting them burn down to the filter. Startled, they'd flick the butts onto the floor and massage their scorched fingers.

Dr. Manolakos sighed. He'd forgotten how little he missed this place. His former supervisor, however, had cajoled him into taking on one of his "gray-zone" clients, and it was a little late to back out.

Dr. Harry Schifferly, in a plaid sports coat, a slouch to his stance and a clipboard under his arm, was waiting for him. "How are you, Aris?"

They shook hands. Not without affection.

It had only been a couple of years, but to look at Harry, Aristotle would've guessed more like ten. His forehead was beginning to sag as though it were made of warm wax. His hair was whiter and his complexion had sallowed (the result of long hours spent indoors). In addition to his caseload, Harry was burdened with administrative meetings and stacks of paperwork. Little wonder his dark eyes seemed to have retreated, as if from some unpleasant stimulus, farther back into his head.

Harry led the way down the hall. On top of everything else, he'd gained weight and the bulge at his waistline gave him an awkward shape. Harry stopped at the door to his office. "You look like you've been taking care of yourself."

He was apologizing for his own appearance.

The office had pastel-blue walls acid-washed by fluorescent light. A leafless branch pressed against the only window, which afforded a view of the winter-brown lawns. A pair of generic flower prints gazed across the room at each other from opposite walls.

A leather chair groaned under Harry's weight. "Have a seat." He waved a hand. "Well, to sum up, your client is a collection of symptoms I'm not sure add up to a clear-cut diagnosis. No self-harm, though—except in fits of rage—and one incident of violent behavior. Here."

Here. Harry was alluding to incidents outside the hospital. At the very least to the fatal stabbing of a man in Arizona.

"But he's also exceptionally bright. And I doubt you were ever in therapy with a gray-zone client who didn't reaffirm your career choice." Harry patted a loose-leaf binder. "I'll let you take it from here. Try not to enjoy yourself too much." He stood up.

To his credit, Harry didn't really care about a diagnostic label except as a way of getting a handle on a patient. And he was right: Aris did gravitate toward the unclassifiables. The problem was that, for Harry, changing "inappropriate" behavior was the focus of therapy. To Aristotle behaviorism was wrestling with symptoms without dealing with the disease. Harry, of course, argued that the symptoms *were* the disease. Their differences regarding psychotherapy had pushed Aristotle off the hospital's staff.

Downstairs, in the rec room, an attendant named Palmer was waiting for Dr. Manalokos. Behind Palmer the center of attention was a pool table. A man leaned over to line up his shot, strands of greasy hair hanging over his forehead. "*Fuck* this shit!" He lunged with the cue, and the sheet of dark hair flipped forward.

Palmer lifted his chin. "Your guy's standing in front of the tube."

His back was to them, arms folded across his chest. His matted, shoulder-length hair looked as though it could defeat a rake. Aristotle couldn't see much more than a profile—hard cheekbone, sharp nose, skin a brown he gauged to be almond-colored. The cheek was a little sunken as if drawn inward by some lack.

"Sometimes he just stands there and stares," Palmer said. "Not a catatonic, though. You knock on the door when he's like that, he answers."

The mane of black hair was given a shifting aura by the television bolted to the wall. Aristotle had an impression of volcanic rock stranded in a silvery tidal pool. Unnaturally still, he seemed almost to have an antagonistic relationship with light. Or maybe it was more that he was a negative of sorts stranded among colors.

"Sometimes, you'd never think he belonged here. Other times ..." Palmer shrugged. "Put two of us in the hospital once. Broke my nose." His finger went over the curving bridge as if searching for proof of what had happened. "Reads everything we got— *National Geographics*, five-and-dime junk, Dickens novels …."

Aristotle watched his new client—*client, not patient,* was the preferred term—watch a nature documentary: Rock-clinging iguanas, washed by the sea, were statuesquely there after each wave receded. The unbuttoned sleeves of his shirt were rolled up, and the hands, which hung at his sides now, looked forlorn without something to hold. A bottle, even an empty one, might have done the trick—just to lend some weight, some contour to empty space.

He turned his head far enough to take in Aristotle, but his eyes didn't spend any time on him, perhaps didn't even see him, and returned to the television. In the space of that indifferent glance, Aristotle noted how much older he looked than he actually was. The dark crescents under his eyes didn't help. Maybe what that empty hand wanted was a white flag to wave.

2. WPSY

The tv wasn't doing much to distract him from the noise and smoke. The smoke was like a katsina that couldn't materialize, disintegrating even as it was forming, unable to cut a discernible figure or even disappear entirely. A hard-luck katsina who stagnated near the ceiling. No way to return to its home among the San Francisco Peaks.

"Hey, Logan ...."

He turned.

"Someone here to see you." Palmer jerked a thumb over his shoulder.

They walked past Mitch, whose jaw was moving rapidly, contorting his whole bearded face as if he were trying to fit words *in* instead of get them out. He was mumbling one of his soliloquies with bits of Nietzsche and the Talmud showing through like faces in a distorting mirror. No one complained. They tuned in or out whenever they felt like it. For most of them, the dial was set at WPSY, where the DJ was a woman with a breathy voice. *WPSY, for music no one else can hear.* Logan laughed. Harder because Palmer had no idea what was so funny and was too scared to ask. But when he saw his new doctor—goddamn blue binder and posture as if he had a pole stuck in his underwear—he sobered up. Tall, olive-complected, he looked like he could model for an Eddie Bauer catalog.

"Hello, Logan." A hand reached for his. "I'm Dr. Manolakos."

Logan took the hand. Kind of bony, good resistance.

"You can call me Aristotle. You feel like talking today?"

Logan cast a glance around the room. He nodded.

"Great. Let's head upstairs ..."

The room Dr. Manolakos took him to was small, sparsely furnished. There were a couple of prints, each of a flower so big it took up the entire frame. A sloppy stack of filters crowned a coffee machine that needed a good wipe-down. The cinderblock walls had been sprayed a soft blue. The only window wasn't covered with the usual heavy-gauge wire. Open a crack, it let in a cool stream of air that cut through the stale heat of the steam radiator. A skeletal branch scratched the glass when a breeze swayed the tree. A friend who wanted to be let in.

Shrink Number Four smiled and told him to make himself comfortable.

Logan had spent most of his life looking to do that without making much headway. He took the edge of a small couch upholstered in something rough as burlap.

"How about a little more air in here?" Aristotle squeaked the window up a few more inches. "Well …" He pulled a swivel chair noisily out from behind a desk. "Where shall we begin?"

Logan wondered what showed on his face. It had taken on an inertness all its own over the months, a mask chiseled from his inability to believe he could be talked out of the hospital.

"Perhaps you'd like *me* to begin …?"

Logan looked at the cinderblock walls. No graffitoed aphorisms. Nothing but those flower prints with their oversized petals. He studied the face across from him and wondered how long Shrink Number Four would let the silence go on.

"Maybe you want to hear about ... what happened with the trucker?" Hearing his own voice was an eye-opener. Like a bicycle going by without anyone riding it. Maybe his mouth would go the whole way without the rest of him.

"If you feel it's important."

Looking hard at Dr. Manolakos, he noticed a few grays

twisting among the black curls. "I didn't have to tell anyone, you know. I was acquitted."

"Nonetheless, it *is* a disturbing incident."

"I mean, the guy's own friend testified against him."

"Dr. Schifferly made a note of that in your file."

When Aristotle wrote something down, he used a pencil and what looked like a blue legal pad.

"That was a bad time for me." Bending his head to rub his eyes (of course his mouth had quit on him), Logan tried to remember—down to the sweat glistening on Debbie's upper lip, where she had that wispy mustache—what had happened that night. He went back into the Smiling Aztec to get his bag, but they wound up outside again, he and the trucker.

In the parking lot, the trucker—Tom, his name had been Tom—led with a haymaker of a right. Logan slid back on the balls of his feet, and the punch missed. By a lot. Tom's eyes were on Logan, his chin up, his face exposed. Logan cracked him a left hook. A clean shot just below the eye. All of Logan's weight behind it, it should've dropped him. The cap with that stupid bird on it flew off his head though the hair underneath held its shape. Straightened him up all right but didn't slow him down much.

"Hope you can do better'n that." Trucker Tom bulled forward, thick forearms up.

What Tom didn't know was that this had all been rehearsed in Bill Tarp's basement back in Kansas. There were grooves in the air—no, pipes. Invisible pipes delivered Logan's fists like two stones pressured into flight. He punished that greasy-haired motherfucker for every wild miss then danced out of range.

"Stand still you faggot."

Bill, ex-Green Beret, would've said the same thing—*get in*

close, elbow strikes, palm heels, end it quick. But Logan was afraid he'd get grabbed and tangled up. He slid in and out on the balls of his feet. One-two, ratta-tat. Hurt his hands on that hard head. Circled and sidestepped, leading the trucker in a sort of brutal ballet. One-two-*three.* Ratta-tat-*tat.*

One eye about swollen shut, breath rasping between bloody lips, Tom was a tough ol' boy who wasn't about to give Logan the satisfaction of seeing him go down. Feinting, he nailed Logan under the eye with a looping right. Hard as a horse hoof and the night trembled. Logan danced back to clear his head, timed a kick as Tom rushed in to finish him off, and Tom finally hit gravel. Breathing hard, he stayed on elbows and knees, his shirt yanked out of his jeans, jeans themselves pulled down tight along the top of his pale ass.

Logan was surprised to see him push back to his feet, something glinting in his hand.

A reflection of the trucker, Logan reached into his pocket, and the blade of the balisong flipped out from between flying handles. He held the knife the way Bill had taught him, like the point was the head of the hammer and he was going to sink a few nails. Leading with the right side of his body, he eyed the strange silhouette circling him.

He saw that Trucker Tom was holding his knife the same way, had taken up about the same stance. Which meant he might've had a little training. Or a lot.

It wasn't like the fistfight. It was careful, deliberate. Tom made a few feints then lunged. Logan stepped back, and the knife missed by so little he'd expected to feel the blade lodge between his ribs. As Tom's arm went past, Logan pivoted on the ball of his foot and drove his knife in with a moist thump that felt as if he'd hit a wet phone book. Tom jerked back, but as his knife hand came up, Logan caught his wrist and yanked on it to keep him off balance. With the other hand, he sank the balisong again. Tom grabbed Logan's wrist with alarming strength, but Logan twisted free—*always turn to the thumb*—and shuffled back.

Tom was still up, his knife in front of him. This time Logan feinted. Tom overreacted, and Logan's blade thumped into him a third time. Tom's knife fell with a clatter. He looked at Logan as if he were just waking up from a nap and wasn't sure whether he knew him. Stumbling forward, he reached for him, a kid learning to walk, lurching toward his mother.

In a moment of strange intimacy, Logan stood with his forehead pressed against a sweaty temple, the unshaven face close enough to kiss. He inhaled the trucker's rotted breath, stole it as if to soothe some sickening addiction, and took a step back. Tom dropped to his hands and knees, his head down, drawing a bead, maybe, on some last tiny detail of existence.

Dark spots on Logan's T-shirt were sticky and warm against his skin. He backed away from the trucker, who was still on his hands and knees, his breathing rapid and horribly ragged.

Omigod, omigod …

Logan looked at Debbie.

I can't believe, omigod I can't believe …

In a moment of extraordinary clarity, Logan heard the humming of the streetlamp in the parking lot, saw the little cloud of insects around it (glowing specks as they caught the light, darkening and disappearing as they ventured into shadow).

He couldn't believe it either. No lightning had struck, the earth hadn't yawned open. There were only the silent insects and the humming light.

"You didn't have to—"

Debbie, Trucker Tom, became shades that would fade by morning.

She started backing away from him.

Voices and music floated out from the Smiling Aztec as if nothing had happened.

"I'm going to call an ambulance," she said.

The face on the Aztec calendar was laughing. If only he'd been able to read those glyphs, to understand what'd been written on that flaking adobe wall.

After Debbie went into the bar, he thought he smelled smoke. Not from a cigarette. The black, billowy kind that came from a burning house. Or did he … was he smelling that now?

Aristotle was scribbling. He must've been talking.

"How did you feel about what happened?"

He'd been moving through silence and the trucker had forced him to speak.

"Why do you think you brought this incident up?"

He was hoping, maybe, Aristotle would help him understand. As fast as it had happened, his mind had already moved ahead in time and inhabited a place where he stood over a fallen body. It hadn't recoiled in disgust; it had moved forward in fascination.

"Do you feel guilty about what happened? It was, of course, self-defense, but it's quite a thing to be responsible for the death of another human being—even when it's accidental."

"If things could've happened any other way, they would have."

Aristotle looked up from his pad and smiled. "Spinoza, right? But that doesn't leave much room for remorse, does it?"

3. Blood Moon

What is presaged by the full orange moon of deep summer? Another hot day—real hot—is what they'll tell you in Kansas. Then again, might be a moon reflecting some dire event.

And what of the night Crazy Horse was killed? Had an orange moon smoldered over the plains while he lay on the floor of a prison cell dying from bayonet wounds? Although the history books don't say, they do record that he was held for the soldiers by one of his own people, an Ogallala named Little Big Man. Unlike Brutus and Judas Iscariot, Little Big Man was mostly forgotten while the Lakota grieved. Men slashed their arms and chests, women drew blades across their foreheads, and the blood mixed with tears. The keening rose like a flock of birds into the deepening evening.

And the next night, did the moon go silver again? Did it forget so soon?

Maybe it'd been silver all along.

But maybe a fire-colored moon rose had risen over Phoenix the night his father was killed.

4. The Permanent Fixture

The funk. Raised his lip when he'd first shown up. You got used to it after a while, but then you'd tilt your head a certain way, inhale too quick, and there it was. Enough to tip your stomach on end. A few months back, it'd been cut with the acrid odor of a skunk. Goddamn if that skunk hadn't smelled almost decent by comparison, a piney reek trying to teach the hospital the right way to stink.

He tried to remember the last time he'd taken a shower. He sniffed an armpit through his flannel shirt. Stank like chicken soup with too much onion. He'd worn the same shirt with these jeans yesterday. And the day before. Hadn't changed his underwear either.

Last week, he hadn't cared how he smelled.

Now he wanted to strip down and scrub with pine needles till his skin went numb. Except they'd take away his ground privileges for baring his ass like that. He'd be stuck in the rec room, where they didn't unlock the windows, another Hard-Luck Katsina with no shot at getting out.

Could've been worse. He could've stayed in that jail in Arizona. He'd known as soon as he walked into the Smiling Aztec that something in the floorboards was rotten. Turned out Trucker Tom was something of an Indian hater. Tatum, one of the guys who'd dragged Tom out of the parking lot the first time they'd squared off, had honored his Bible-backed oath to be honest.

I knew it would come to no good. Tom was always lookin' to start another war with the Indian population 'round here. He seen,

When the trial was over, Logan had gone back to the Smiling
Aztec, curious after hearing it had burned down the same
night he'd been there. Whoever had closed up left something
smoldering in the kitchen. As if what flared up in the parking
lot hadn't been enough.

The Burning Aztec joined Chaco Canyon as a memento of a
world that no longer existed. The walls were still standing, but
the building had been gutted. A walk-in ashtray holding the
cremated echoes of who knew what other tragedies, dramas,
under-the-table dealings now safely beyond being stirred up out
of the charred timber, the melted wires marbling dark cinders
like shiny veins, the glass furnaced into unheard-of shapes.
A two-bit apocalypse that had left the job vastly unfinished
though no one had died in the bar while it lit up the night.
A few memories had lost their moorings was all—shadows set
free of walls or scenes in a movie, projected without a screen,
disappearing somewhere over the desert.

The Aztec face painted on an outside wall, the centerpiece of
a defunct calendar, had survived. Its blade of a tongue stuck out
at him, mocking the whole business of time and its monotonous
cycles, not even bitter anymore about what had happened to

Tenochtitlan, the Aztec capital, which hadn't been accorded the dignified funeral of Chaco Canyon but lay smothered beneath Mexico City. Maybe, turning now and then like a restless corpse, the buried city's sense of injustice showed up on the front pages of newspapers, along with a body count and a damage estimate in dollars (only to be explained away by scientists as shifting geological plates).

Logan grabbed the vinyl jacket the state had given him and stood at the door pushing an arm into the padded tunnel of a sleeve.

Palmer hurried over, head bent as he fumbled with the keys clipped onto his waist. Logan saw white scalp through black curls, a bald spot in the making.

He held open the door to the cottage (that's what staff called these brick boxes).

The day had already sunk, a pearl tossed into a tar pit. Diffused among a haze of clouds, the light had gone a stale blue-gray.

The grounds resembled nothing so much as his idea of a country club: trimmed grass, rows of hedges, towering spruces and maples, park benches, and beyond the hospital fences meadows like farmland lying fallow. No barbed wire, nothing electrified. It wouldn't have taken much to climb the chain-link fence, head up the road to the Phoenix Diner (nicknamed the *Penis* because the neon H had burned out), grab a burger and some greasy fries. But no one did. They stood around with their arms folded across their chests or sat on benches listening to WPSY.

"Open up!" Fists that looked gouged out of stone hammered at a cottage door. "Open up you cocksuckers!" His shoulder-length hair tangled as the exposed end of an uprooted tree, he hurled his voice like another blocky fist. "Why the *FUCK* are we locked out?" The stained jacket he wore was too small for him, exposed wrists that broadened into forearms dark with swirls of hair. Veins and muscles in his neck corded as he launched himself at the door again. "GIVE me liberty or GIVE me death!"

Logan laughed. They should all give the staff so much shit. Just to give it to them.

"Open this *fucking* door!" More pounding. The black hair waved like seaweed.

The door opened and the patient's arms fell to his sides. Docile now, he pushed his huge hands into his jacket pockets and disappeared inside.

Logan felt as if he'd lost a friend. As if he'd never had one.

Only the Earth and sky last forever, only the Earth and sky and brick walls.

He remembered a night in New York City, fog drifting like smoke falling from a burning sky. When the haze disappeared, he expected the sky to be gone with it. His face pressed against glass, he was ... singing? Chanting? There was mist and cloud. There was calm. The storm was somewhere else.

He remembered the déjà vu brought on by a streetlamp submerged in mist, the uncanny familiarity in the smeared light. He banged on a store window with a palm. Not to break it, to measure the silence.

"Yo, buddy!"

A distant stone plunking in the middle of a lake.

"Yo!"

This syllable came through more clearly. He stopped and listened. Hands took him by the shoulders, turned him around.

"Is Alice doped up?" The man was big, uniformed, his head as heavy as a cave bear's. "Is Alice in Wondaland?"

Logan just stared at the cop, at the push-broom mustache.

When they found out he wasn't on anything, they sentenced him to three days of observation.

He went on staring, his face pressed against a cool plaster wall, his fingers splayed. Singing or humming the way he had when the cop had found him, slapping at the flatness to remind himself that it ended *here*; the place beyond the last star was a plaster wall. Infinitely thick.

The store window … ah, the window had been more deceptive. See-through but still reflecting—his blank face, a parked car, the hazed light overhead. He'd wanted to cross over, to be on the other side, but it would've been no good to heft a rock because then he'd have destroyed the meeting place of carpeted climate control and the city pressing in like a hungry beggar. He'd have squeezed a lover so hard she wasn't breathing anymore.

Instead, he slammed a fist into the window in the door of the observation room. Cracked the glass. But it was crosshatched with wire and held together. Could've kicked it out, maybe, but he contented himself with watching blood drip to the dirty floor.

Since the city hospital was overcrowded, they shipped him just north of Manhattan. Everyone called it "upstate" although upstate New York was a lot closer to Canada. On his first day he met an old man wrapped in a fraying bathrobe. He kept gawking and smiling, his eyes chips of bright blue, his thin face worn parchment on the verge of tearing where wrinkles ran the deepest. His skinny ankles, lumpy with veins, poked out of his pajamas like sticks.

Logan smiled back. "Is this the Island of Misfit Toys?"

The old man laughed, dry leaves crunching underfoot. He lifted a finger. "No man is an asylum unto himself." More leaves crunching.

His wit unnerved Logan.

"Don't pay any attention to him," Palmer said. "He's a permanent fixture here."

Palmer had been wrong.

Logan should've taken notes on what to do if he didn't want to become a permanent fixture. He could've been out in a week, but weeks had turned into months. Months were threatening to turn into a year. Mainly because Jackson had leaned on him. Grinning all the time because he had a key to every door. Logan couldn't even do his laundry unless somebody like Jackson was there to open up.

"Whaddya say?" Jackson would taunt him with a smile.

"Thank you." Logan's smile was just as fake.

One winter morning, the sky a gray weave overhead, the light as brittle as ice jackets on tree branches, Logan hadn't wanted to get out of bed. Not for breakfast or anything else. Sure as shit not for Jackson. The dormitory was empty for once. Quiet. He wanted to be alone. Nothing was more upsetting to him at that moment than the thought of a cafeteria loud with voices and clattering dishware, crowded with men and women inept in one way or another, one of them talking to you with jelly smeared across the corner of his mouth so you're not even listening, you just wish he'd wipe his face.

"Hey, get your ass up or I'll *make* you."

He went on staring at the white expanse of the ceiling, at a cobweb hanging down from it, a thread snaking in slow curves, caught in some current too subtle to feel. If he could just float like that (his hand rose lazily in sympathy), drift above his lumpy mattress—

Jackson took him by the wrist, but Logan snapped up and twisted free. A right against Jackson's cheek sounded like a baseball hitting mud, sent fist and head bouncing away from each other. It felt so good to finally have an outlet, a stand-in for the legalities keeping him locked up, for whatever it was that kept him from sleeping at night—it felt so good to crack something solid he let go with another right. Jackson's head snapped so far back he thought it might've detached itself.

Adrenaline ballooning his veins, feeling more alive than he had in weeks, Logan put his whole left side into a hook that sank into Jackson's stomach, all the air—"Huh!"—coming out of him as he crumpled into a sitting position against a wall. Logan kicked him in the chest, angry that it was over already, that there was no one else to hit.

Palmer showed up just as Logan had begun to decompress and made an inept attempt at a tackle. Logan popped him once, a palm heel, without malice. He felt something give, heard the snap. A few patients drawn by the ruckus cheered and clapped while Palmer, cupping his nose, was on his knees, blood running in sticky strings from between his fingers.

The Permanent Fixture brandished a crooked index finger. "You'll never be a doctor in this place. You don't have the patience."

Logan was thrown in with the hardcores, his privileges revoked. It had taken him a few months, but he'd worked his way back to where he'd started, same cottage, except for Jackson. He wasn't on staff anymore.

"Curfew time!" Palmer was standing in the doorway. "Curfew time, boys!"

Heads down, hands in pockets, patients started back.

A moan went up inside one of the cottages, rose from a deep resonant note to a high-pitched shriek. Logan glanced at windows set in a brick face like false hope.

A few hours later, he was on the other side, fingers curled around the heavy-gauge mesh covering a window.

Beds were lined up in neat rows along two walls.

Over each of the room's two doors, a bulb glowed such a dull blue it was almost gray as if blood that needed to be revived in a pair of lungs had been electrified. A metal hood sealed off the upper half; sturdy wires curved around the belly. A kind of darkroom lighting as though their dreams were in danger of being overexposed.

He looked up. A coyote might howl at this moon.

A reluctant Prometheus, the Moon had no use for light, would be just as happy with two unseen sides. The glow it turned back? That was the Sun's way of letting us know we're *not* mad, there *is* something overhead with its own pull—the Sun's Parthian shot, a bit of magic dust flung back from the dark rim of the world.

He stared at his rectangular cutout of Cartesian sky, remembering Kansas, where the night was wider, the stars thicker. He held onto images of the past because forgetting was easy. They made things easy for you here the way an actor has his lines scripted for him—laid out your meals, did your wash if you weren't up to it, handed out medication at the same time every day. On Tuesdays and Thursdays, Palmer and Carl shuttled you off to the gym. Friday was movie night.

It made for a kind of poisonous contentment running under your skin. Made you a blue-lipped catatonic (translucent skin marbled by inky veins), holding whatever position they'd left you in.

If only there were a hole in the foam-board ceiling. To let the universe in. Babies were born like that, with a tiny skylight in their skulls. *Kopavi* the Hopi called it, *trap door.* Or was it *open door*? The old-timers warned you not to let it close up. How else were you going to orient yourself in the world? With two fingers he rubbed a shallow depression in his crown where that opening used to be and waited for sleep.

5. WISH

Even after all these years, he couldn't believe it'd happened while he was asleep. Curled up under the sheets, knees tucked. He never heard the screech of brakes, the impact of bone against glass, steel, whatever else. The shallow rhythm of his breathing unbroken, he went on sleeping, dreaming, while his father crossed that yawning gulf. Alone.

The death of his father should've been like the lowering of another world. He should've sensed the sky had been swallowed, should've felt that second world settling like another night. Its magnetic poles should've pricked up the hairs on the back of his neck, stiffened them into cactus needles. The added gravity should've squeezed the breath out of him. A small, dark world pressed against his dreaming as though sinking into the mud of the just-created, tracking itself, scarring the surface—proof of the casual forces loose in the universe: a collision at an intersection where two trucks mangled themselves as if one had expected to win. Their shiny grills caught like sets of teeth, both had stopped dead trying to take a hunk out of one another. No witnesses, both drivers killed, both drunk, police had never ruled on who'd run the signal.

It had happened without waking him, without a nightmare sticking to him like blood, without so much as an off-color moon. No guardian katsina had intervened, no bird friendly to their tribe had whispered a warning. He hadn't tried picking out the night's events in a cloud formation. Hadn't divined anything from the shape of the scar on the back of his father's neck. From milling ants that had welled up like a dark stain from a crack in the sidewalk.

When his mother woke him, he clutched at whatever he'd been dreaming like a startled spider trying to leg up a ruined web. He hadn't understood why she'd been crying, couldn't grasp what she meant when she said his father had been in an accident. Sniffling and wiping at her nose, she pulled the sheets over him and turned out the light.

He should have known. Six years old or not, he should've rooted his feet and held out his hand, ballasted his father like a basket of rocks on a blanket. Kept him on *this* side. It must've been his father's wish to go off like that. Not to die but with dying imminent to go it alone. Even if as a grown man Logan had been able to take his father's hand in his own, he'd have been yanked up like a weed, loose clods of earth trailing. So it was a safe bet that anything that could push his father so far in a direction he didn't want to go in wasn't going to be offset by a stubborn child.

6. NUMERICAL ALCHEMY

Something inside him felt like a slowly expanding pocket of gas. He exhaled to release a little pressure. He wanted out of the hospital, sure, but—

He shifted on his haunches and moved closer to the end of the couch, the rough material clawing at his jeans. But he still felt that internal pocket of hot gas, a skin to it, like a balloon or that airy organ fish have to make their bodies buoyant.

—the problem, yes, here was the rub—he wasn't all that excited about what was outside the hospital either.

"I never feel ..." He crossed his legs. "Mostly I feel out of place." If he were a fish, his swollen air bladder would've had him bobbing on the surface, floating on his side, his scales exposed as if he wanted to sun himself when what he was after were cooler depths and an even keel.

Aristotle didn't answer.

Making Logan feel obligated to go on. He sighed and hoped the unquiet breath would make it to the window, cracked open a few inches. Wherever he was, he told Aristotle, he felt like he should be somewhere else. No matter what he was doing, he felt like he should be doing something else. Even music. Wasn't there something more useful he could ply himself to? Weren't farmers and priests being murdered in El Salvador? (The air bladder was so big now it was hard to breathe.) Would a song do even one of them any good?

His friends tried to help out, usually by way of buying him a beer. He'd thank them and smile, but most of the time there were two conversations going on—one about a football game or some county-record fish somebody had caught or the new waitress over at Bootlegger's, and another with himself. And sometimes he mixed them up. Which made him try to explain what he'd been thinking about. But one thought led to six others until he was as distant from the starting point of the conversation as the three destroyed worlds of the Hopi. His mind never caught up with what it was chasing, his mouth never caught up with his mind, and Jim Lee was the only one who bothered to keep up with his mouth.

"So you and your friends don't really share the same interests. Does that make you feel left out?"

"More like … I'm missing something." The air bladder deflated, left behind more space than it should have as if his vitals had gone flaccid along with it.

He spent a lot of time fighting off a sense of worthlessness—he'd be grateful to abdicate the space he was taking up. Somehow he'd gotten sidetracked from the things that should've had him talking casually, a smile on his face, a beer in his hand. Someone had thrown him a curveball, and he'd gotten the idea that the distractions he spent his time tracking down were worth missing the Superbowl, another excursion to a titty bar downtown, hunting season, volunteer work in El Salvador.

Had Aristotle caught that? Had he *said* it? He felt sure he had but there was a sound like wind in his ears, and he was afraid someone had turned the volume all the way down. He heard a fist go through a window. Glass fell in a hard rain. Blood slicked his arm, warm and cold in different places. A gaping wound (but not in his arm). Familiarity burned away, a covering of dead leaves, blackened and curling. The filmy negatives were sucked out through the hole. He wanted to fix it, but the glass

… there were too many pieces. He didn't know how they fit, and there was nothing to cover the hole.

Aris was saying something over the windy roar, asking if he was all right.

The wind subsided.

"Sometimes it feels like … like what's inside me's gone. I have trouble breathing, thinking. Then there's this fist in my chest."

"How often do these episodes occur?"

He shrugged. "Couple times a month."

Aristotle scribbled on his blue pad and looked up. "Anxiety attacks."

"Just … anxiety attacks?" Logan couldn't help a childish grin.

"They can lead to something more serious, like an ulcer, but most likely, yes. It's also likely they're related to the reason you stopped playing music. They're warnings that the problem is still there—whether or not you play."

Aristotle made it sound so simple. As though he had a Pythagorean understanding of the math governing the mind, and he was going to rearrange quantities on either side of the equals sign, perform the numerical alchemy that would free him from the hospital. From his year-long silence.

7. Moon Bones

Uncle Cal had never brought Logan a thing Logan's mother hadn't put him up to. Unless it was something he'd killed. Nothing Cal liked better than a hunting trip, which usually meant a drive up to Flagstaff. But every now and then, he brought down a hare outside Phoenix. He'd slap the animal on the kitchen table belly up, spread the hind legs, and poke the hide below the ribcage with a wicked-looking hunting knife. The hide split with a soft pop, and the gash widened as Cal worked the knife upward.

He made Logan stick his hand in the red hole he'd opened up and scoop out the entrails. Still warm. Blood and a sulfurous stink from the wet foundry of the intestines stung his sinuses. No wonder it was rumored to be the reek of the underworld.

"No, not like that." Cal pulled Logan's hand away. "Two fingers." Cal held up two of his own, thick enough, strong enough to break tiny furrows winter earth. He told Logan to start up near the breastbone, scrape out everything soft with those two fingers. Then he put something small and slippery in Logan's hand—the heart, like a tiny pyramid. He looked up, afraid to tell his uncle he didn't want to feel around inside a dead animal, but Cal saw it on his face.

Cal shook his head as he wiped off the blade. "Bushmen in Africa squeeze the water out of animal guts they got it so hard. Be grateful you don't have to stick your nose in there and suck a handful of innards when you want a drink."

All Hopi, Cal was short and squat. His head hung low on his stocky body as if he'd been made to carry heavy things over long distances. His forearms were thick, his face wide and marked-up from fighting. One scar made a seam in his lip. The other was a jagged streak through an eyebrow.

About the only thing Logan had ever asked Cal for was the beak of a game bird. But Cal broke it off too short with his impetuous over-goddamn-sized fingers. Long and elegant on the bird, it ended up in his palm in pieces, hardly recognizable. Cal had given it a try, though, he really had. It just wasn't in him. There wasn't any sympathy, no innate feel for the rest of the four-leggeds, two-leggeds, wingeds, no-leggeds sharing the planet. The Maker, maybe, had been running out of earth when shaping Cal, had had to reach up high for some moon dust to mix in. Cal couldn't be blamed; his bones were heavy not with calcium, but with memories of a waterless, airless, heatless expanse that stretched across his whole life, from nebulous conception to that long walk toward the last hill in the distance.

What was it like to be held up by bones filled with elemental knowing, *knowing* that the whole goddamn shebang is mostly empty space, from atom on up to galaxy, with suns spread so far apart goddamn centuries would pass if you tried to reach one, and what ain't empty space is 99 percent helium and just-waitin'-for-an-excuse-to-explode hydrogen? So here we are in the middle of more emptiness and burning gas than the human mind could even begin to gander at and when you had a little moon dust instead of marrow in your bones, you knew a little better how it felt when not one living breathing thing, not a stone, not one airy, masked katsina gave a goddamn what desert you disappeared into, what vacuum freeze-dried you. You weren't quite so bewildered when you got stranded where there wasn't another voice to speak your name, when you were left gasping for air or a little fatherly take-notice—it was all the goddamn same to the ground you wound up stuck in.

After Logan's father died, Uncle Cal was always over the house, reeking of the moon desolation some part of him must have dropped out of. Always with the excuse of checking up on them. *Anything I can do to help?*

Logan had never seen his uncle so neighborly. There got to be long goodbyes, the screen door creaking as Logan's mother let it close but opening again because Cal thought of something else to say. He started coming over for dinner straight from the garage where he worked. Logan would sit next to him for an awkward minute or two. Cal would turn and say something like, "How was school today?"

Hands held stiffly on his thighs, he'd say, "Pretty good." He'd try not to sit too close because when Cal talked he got a whiff of something sweet as rotting fruit, sour as old blood. Maybe cigarettes had done that. Maybe secretly Cal had been eating the scraped-out offal he was supposed to have thrown away.

Logan left the room while Cal sat in front of the tv drinking beer, his eyes as still and concentrated as a snake's. He liked to wear a sleeveless T-shirt around the house, and Logan got used to seeing the skull grinning between a pair of outstretched wings tattooed on his left arm. A dull tattoo that didn't show up all that well on Cal's dark skin. Logan had been in the room the day his mother asked him what he'd gotten it for.

"After death you take flight," was all he said. Then he bent down and shoved an arm bumpy with muscles—like a sack of rocks—in Logan's face.

The tattoo on his right arm was just the number 13. Logan never asked him what it meant.

He avoided Cal as much as he could. Hung from the monkey bars in the schoolyard or sketched in the dirt with a stick. Got himself invited to Manny's house or Ramon's. The door to his room closed, he read library books with his chin on his hands, his elbows on the floor, and his crossed feet hovering over him like the tip of a scorpion's tail.

When he knew Cal wouldn't be around, he played his mother's piano. She'd started him on it before he'd gotten out of kindergarten, and every now and then she'd teach him something new. He'd nod a little stiffly and then try it out on the keys. *Yes, that's it, you got it the first time. Aren't you proud of yourself?*

He kept the grooves of the piano clean with a cloth over his fingernail. Woodgrain patterns became familiar faces—a little inhuman, frozen in odd expressions. The calm tension of the keys reassured him. Lured by the mystery of music beneath the smooth jointed case, he rarely walked past the instrument without stopping to put his hand on the polished wood. No matter that with his big hands Cal could've squeezed his skull till it cracked, Cal would never have the gift of playing three notes in a row with any kind of harmony. No matter the heaps of guts he made Logan scrape out of ribcages, Logan could whistle for music any time he wanted.

Sometimes Cal would walk in while he was playing and for a moment, they'd look at each other across a distance both of them knew would never be crossed. What showed up on Cal's face most of the time might have been the look of a man vaguely aware he'd lost something but unable to remember what. Cal would lean against the wall between the living room and what was supposed to be a dining room, a beer in his hand, half in a world he couldn't leave, half in a world he couldn't enter, something making the white scar that split an eyebrow roughly down the middle a little paler. Logan would play for a few minutes, pretending he didn't mind Cal being there. Then, without a word, he'd settle the wooden cover over the keys and go to his room.

Cal got to be around the house as often as not. Usually in the living room where there were no doors to close, no way to avoid Cal's motionless stare. He left empty beer cans lying wherever he finished them. Never more than one or two a night. Logan's mother collected them after he was gone. Cal filled up ashtrays and wasn't above a spill of beer to dowse a butt that kept burning after being stubbed—as if he couldn't stand that little display of will, as if he wanted to make sure every bit of smoldering orange knew who was boss. No matter how much his mother vacuumed, the living room got to be stale with old cigarette smoke.

Cal started sleeping on the couch. A long one, a sort of tarnished gold, like spicy mustard, with cushions that soaked up the sweat after he'd passed out, got blotched where he'd mishandled beer or coffee, slopped gravy from a frozen dinner he'd forked into his mouth without taking his eyes off the tv. Cal moved in on that mustard-gold couch and pretty soon it got to smell like him. He could sit there with the tv on for an hour or more without moving, not even a twitch of his head. Part reptile maybe. Logan would imagine he'd quietly died, sitting up straight in the dark, flickering tv light on him—weird things like that happened sometimes, corpses didn't always keel over. Unexpectedly, Cal would light a cigarette—as startling as a statue coming down off its pedestal—and shake the daydream to pieces.

Logan lay awake at night staring at the ceiling, as broad as the Great Plains of the Dakotas. Crazy Horse had been a feared warrior by the time he was 17. By the time Logan was 17, Cal wouldn't be able to push him around anymore.

Sometimes he looked up at the ceiling and saw the deserts of Egypt—vaster than any in Arizona. He held the reins of a chariot in the pharaoh's army. One day he would request permission from the pharaoh to challenge Cal, and the other soldiers encircling them would form the arena. They would swing their swords at one another until Cal's blood ran into the sand. He would bow to Pharaoh.

He'd get on a boat, proud of what he'd done, and stand at the prow, watching the Nile flow under him, his robes snapping in the wind, while men rowed to the throb of a drum. The ship would take him out to sea, to colder lands where he'd be a Viking. A dark Viking, outcast because of his color but feared because he'd killed his uncle with his sword when he was only 17. Or maybe with his hunting knife.

Then Cal stopped sleeping on the couch.

Logan slept less after that. He heard them at night sometimes, his mother's harsh whispering and what Cal said back because Cal was always loud.

"Hell I won't. He got to learn to act like a man. Besides, he ain't gonna start payin' the bills around here is 'ee? We're goin' to Kansas and that thing's too goddamn big to take."

His mother's voice was an urgent hiss.

"We all got to make sacrifices," Cal growled. "I didn't have no tv in my house. I lived on a goddamn reservation. I'll send the little bastard up there. That'll make him act grateful. He wouldn't have nothin' if it wasn't for me."

The argument ended with a slap. Logan shivered in his bed, a tingling gathering behind his groin, and he knew he'd have peed under the covers if Cal had come into his room then. He pretended to be asleep when he heard Cal's big footsteps going past. A door slammed, and he knew he was safe for the night. But it took a long time before he fell asleep.

He prayed in those days to be older, to grow up with the broad shoulders his father had had, to have a head that brushed doorways, hands that could palm a cement block. Cal had hydraulics in him sturdy enough that he once maneuvered a refrigerator onto his back then carried it up two flights of stairs. Logan didn't care. Every time he looked at Cal he wished he were 17. By then he'd be grown enough to manhandle Cal the same way Cal had manhandled that fridge. He thought about it at dinner when Cal asked for the salt. He thought about it on holidays when everybody was forcing a smile.

Two days before they moved to Kansas, his mother was watching for him on his way home from school. He caught her looking out the window just before the curtain fell back. When he got to the living room, he pulled up short as if he'd bumped into a piece of furniture he hadn't noticed or run into a glass door so clean it could pass for a sheet of air. A space yawned where the piano had been, widened while he stood there blinking. His mother had a hand over her mouth as if terrified of the sound it might make.

8. Go Back, Jack

A soap opera was being acted out to Pink Floyd: Someone had turned the sound all the way down on the tv, but a boombox filled the vacuum. A woman on-screen cried tears black with mascara while becoming increasingly frantic with a man who looked like he should've been holding up a can of shaving cream and smiling. Their mouths moved improbably to *Hel-looooh, is there anybody INNN there? Just nod if you can HEAR me …*

Mr. Spenser, whom Logan used to call the Permanent Fixture, was squatting on his haunches and silently conversing with himself.

Is there aaaaaannee-one at home?

Ankles poked out of pajamas dirty at the hems. So spindly they probably ended in eagle talons (hidden by a pair of worn slippers). Biting unvoiced syllables out of the air, he looked to be concentrating on a floor tile.

Jack drifted over to the silently soliloquizing old man. Graying hair even longer than Logan's, Jack offered a yellow-toothed smile as though he wanted to embrace Spenser with all the brotherly love of his generation. "How ya doin' today, man?"

"Aroint thee witch!" Mr. Spenser didn't look up.

Jack crouched down, tilted his head to one side—his unwashed hair nearly touching the floor—and scrutinized the same tile. A little put off that he'd been beaten out by a square of linoleum, he stood and headed toward Logan.

"What's up, man?" He scratched his head and three earrings swung from an ear. His milky blue eyes were opened too wide, like a pop-eyed goldfish—the kind that swam with an awkward waddle of its body rather than an elegant flick of its tail—as though he were amazed at everything he came across. "Hey, you ever say how you got here?"

Logan rolled his eyes. Jack had asked him this a dozen times.

"No, don't tell me." Jack pulled back and put up his hands as if he were pushing off an invisible wall in front of him. "I know." He leaned a little closer and bounced an index finger. "Karma. It's all karma."

He had the kind of cigarette breath that smelled like he'd roasted horse manure in his mouth.

"It means *action*. But in Sanskrit."

Aum was written in Sanskrit curves on Jack's denim jacket, a general confusion of symbols, signs, and sayings—buttons of Janis Joplin and Malcolm X; a silver ankh; a silkscreen of Martin Luther King, Jr.; *chanti chanti chanti* made a train three words long on a sleeve; Mr. Mojo Risin in some kind of gothic stencil just below the collar. The jacket was like a cast, once pure white, now so inked up there was barely enough room for the name of one more well-wisher. Jack was a shade of a man, of the flesh and bones zipped up and shipped back in bags from the inferno of Southeast Asia, a miracle traveler who'd tried to cheat time by backtracking two decades.

"Somma my actions musta been pretty bad." Jack fingered a peace sign big enough to be a hood ornament. Carved out of wood and hung from a chain around his neck.

When he spoke, Logan turned a cheek to deflect his breath.

"I didn't even have to do them in *this* life, I could be makin' up for my *last* one."

Go back, Jack, do it again.

"You too, I guess."

Desire, Jack told him, wore out the body like a pair of boots. Drew us back, like tugging on a new pair when it wanted to keep walking.

"It's all there, you know? Like in a cosmic computer?"

It was a little disconcerting, the wide-eyed way he looked at Logan, as if Jack's future were engraved in the lines on Logan's face or he'd turned a color that didn't belong to the rainbow.

"Everything you do, whatever you say, even what you're *thinking*." Jack reached into his jacket and pulled out a cigarette.

His hands shook so much it made lighting up difficult. From the antipsychotic they kept him on. Haldol probably. Or a side effect of the drug they used to counteract some other side effect of the Haldol.

The doctors had him pegged for drug-induced psychosis. Logan had once peeked in the blue binder they kept on Jack, read in the police report how he'd been picked up one night for boiling peanuts in his own urine on a sidewalk. He'd set up a tuna can over a tiny fire he fed with candy bar wrappers, cigarette boxes, and whatnot. Logan pictured Jack crouched down next to a parking meter, squatting in the neon glow from a women's clothing shop, the mannequins refusing to turn their sculpted faces away from the stink. Jack a nutty alchemist inhaling the pungent Golden Vapors. Had he been planning to *eat* those peanuts?

Jack tapped his temple with two fingers, the cigarette burning between them. "You got to keep an open mind."

Prop open the doors of perception. Because everyday life reduced the Mansion of Many Apartments to one room (the upkeep on that one being about all you could handle). The problem with Jack was he hadn't just opened doors and poked around in other rooms; he'd knocked down walls.

"It gets harder as you get older … keepin' your mind open, keepin' it all straight in your head." Jack's eyes roved around the ceiling, the light fixtures, the blue-and-white floor tiles as if he'd found a larger audience to address. "You need to … you …" The sentence pulling a disappearing act the Hard-Luck Katsina would have envied, Jack stared with the serene aura of a catatonic.

Logan wondered whether he should do something to jump-start him, slap him on the back or maybe take a lighter and curl back the tufts in his nostrils.

Jack came out of the trance on his own: "You need something you can hold on to."

It was a little eerie the way Jack traveled dimensions roundtrip, returned within inches of where he'd started.

"Keep you from getting mixed up. You know?"

Logan nodded.

"I'm writin' a book." He broke into a smile. "A travel journal with, kind of philosophy and poetry mixed in. When I get outa here, I got some friends in Canada who said they'd let me crash at their place."

Jack had crashed and burned a long time ago. Staff were just trying to pat-a-cake the ashes back into shape, put a ripcord in the back so when someone pulled he squeaked *My name is Jack*. A big old Jack doll with scraggly salt-and-pepper hair.

"Goin' on up …" Jack broke into breathy, nearly whispered song. "Goin' on up to the spirit in the sky …" He looked at Logan. "What do Indians believe? I mean, what happens when you die?"

The centerpiece of Jack's graffitoed-over jacket, airbrushed on the back, was a Grateful Dead skull with flowing hair: Jack worried too much about the hereafter and not enough about here. Logan shrugged. "Different tribes believe different things."

Remembering his cigarette, Jack took a puff. "What about reincarnation?"

"I don't know. But the Hopi believe in different worlds. This is the fourth."

"What happened to the other three?"

"Destroyed."

"Yeah? Like the Flood and Noah's Ark, huh?"

"Fire the first time, I think. A flood wiped out the second world. No, the second world was ice. Third World drowned."

"Ahhhhhhh," came from Jack as though this were the syllable that had set the universe in motion. "Hmmmmmmmm." A way to solidify the newborn cosmos.

Nodding, bouncing his head rhythmically, Jack began singing, *"Goin' on up to the spirit in the sky ..."* As his hands got into the act—the cigarette between fingers like a tiny conductor's baton tracing wavering arcs of smoke—Jack shuffled off. *"That's where I'm gonna go ... when I die ..."*

Jack had told Logan about the night the stars had reached right through the ceiling he'd been staring at and yanked him into the sky, pulled him in a hundred different directions at once. Each had its own voice. Crucified on the constellations, he'd splintered in more ways than Christ, *but it didn't hurt at all, man. I just ... kept stretching and stretching, you know? And all the different pieces of me kept goin' toward all those twinkling voices.*

Spread across light years, Jack realized that breathing had belonged to another Jack—a lone, presumptuous, prejudiced, narrow-minded individual. The stars had twisted his ego out of existence as though wringing a washrag dry.

Smoking and waving his arms as he sang, Jack invited Mr. Spenser on up—

"Furies! Legions of foul fiends! Get thee hence!"

Is there anybody IN there?

—to the Spirit in the Sky.

9. Death Mask

Remembering, he couldn't sleep. nights in Phoenix heated like lizard's blood the desert breeze a rake through hair clumped with sweat. passing a bottle around in the dark. throat burned, belly warmed. sitting on the pulverized ground, grit getting everywhere— shoes hair underwear. everything in Arizona sticks you stings you is poisonous is hard prickly granular. it was worth it to drink with her, watch her stomach suck itself in when she laughed, a tan flat stomach with a life of its own he could stay up and watch it all night no one there to tell him when to go to bed. faces orange by firelight the sweetness of perfume rubbing off, sweat-rinsed away, sitting on the pebbled ground dragging smoke into his lungs holding it there as if he were underwater. kisses like ash, breath smoky, skin sliding over skin, pushing himself into a slippery gullet, the night wavering like the road at midday

Tall for 15 (just about 16), he had long arms and big hands everyone said he'd grow into. He'd gone back to Phoenix to work a construction job and get away from Cal for the summer. A friend of his father's who had his own crew, said he'd even find him a place to stay. First day on the job he met a Navajo named Sonny.

"Sonny? Is that short for something?"

Navajos had a second name, something traditional, but they kept it wrapped up like an old medicine bundle, only brought it out on ceremonial occasions.

"Nope. Just Sonny. Mom insisted on it. Figured the old man owed her that much for nine months' hard labor."

There were those Navajos and Hopis who kept up the animosity between their tribes as if they were raising a crop but not Sonny. "Hell, somma my best friends are Hopi. Even let a few white guys hang out with me." He smiled as he looked over at their boss.

Sonny's father was a banker who'd done well for himself off the rez. Although he spoke two languages, he had no use for Dine. *English is the language of commerce*, he told Sonny. *It's an Anglo world. Get used to it.*

Between semesters at UCLA, Sonny worked construction.

"The old man wanted me in an office." Sonny unwound a blue chalk line, dust coming off it like turquoise smoke. "But paperwork all year round is hard on the head. And there's something about air conditioning that makes me sick."

He wanted to be on-site while it was still dark, buzzing through joists as the stars faded out, watch the city slowly come into focus through the lens of the breaking day. Sky overhead instead of a ceiling lined with fluorescent tubes, dry morning air scented with fresh-cut pine instead of machined air exhaled from tinny lungs. By the time the heat really set in, the crew would be packing up. Then he'd pop open a beer and sit back while rush hour got into gear. No suit, no tie.

Logan learned the routine. You were unloading the truck at four in the morning. Sonny, wearing a faded bandanna and a cut-off T-shirt, was unwinding a coil of orange cord. You packed a leather pouch hanging from your hips good and heavy with nails, went back to where you'd left off the day before, started hammering.

The second-story floor—just sheets of plywood dotted with tiny dunes of sawdust—was a roof because that was as high as you'd built. You pulled a nail out of your leather pouch and tried to drive it in in three swings: set, sink, finish. (Always took him four.) And when you reached in your pouch for another nail, you tapped the flat nose of the hammer on the plywood to keep your rhythm, made sawdust dance. Sweat starting to run, you tried not to break your rhythm, hardly giving the glowing pink trails in the sky a glance.

By now Sonny had turned on a radio to help your hammer keep time, *tap-tap-tap*. You adjusted your swing a little bit maybe to take in the song. If you looked two stories down, Sonny winked up at you while he cut two-by-sixteens along a penciled line—a gift he had, a pact with the saw, not to move a millimeter off what was straight, his hands so steady they looked like they could do it without the saw. Logan watched his triceps tighten as he gripped the plank and guided the blurry blade.

On weekends they got out of Phoenix. All the way to San Diego sometimes. Logan gandered at the Pacific as if some Medusa's touch of the ocean had brushed his face.

"Whatsa matter? Never seen the ocean before?"

Logan shook his head.

"Damn, boy, where the hell you been all your life?"

The southeast corner of Kansas.

He stood watching the waves spread themselves over the sand and tried to understand how something so vast, so old and alive, hadn't kept him awake at night with its far-off voice. Hadn't added to the erosion of sleep even though he was in the middle of the continent, hadn't pounded his complacency into granules he could've spread until he had a dry beach. He'd seen plains rolling toward the curve of the Earth, but he'd never taken in anything of this magnitude that was *moving*—not a breeze pushing aside prairie grass but movement rooted in depths in which light dissolved. As if here the Earth kept time, and here he stood, bobbing on the flow.

He woke up on the sand, a cold breeze coming off the ocean, whipping Sonny's long hair around his face. Four years older, Sonny was a full-blood. He put his forearm, plumped by gripping tools and handling hunks of wood, against Logan's. "You're about caught up to my winter coat."

Logan, who'd never heard of a soffit or a dormer before he'd started swinging a hammer, who'd spun himself in circles when Sonny told him to grab a box of eights ("Eights?" "Eight-penny nails!"), had been the only one in the crew who wasn't old enough to buy a six-pack. But whenever they went out, they'd bring him along and sit him at a table while one of them did the ordering. *You don't look no sixteen anyway.*

Back in Frontenac, you watched the same girls you'd been seeing since kindergarten grow up with you. You chased one, then another, town full of the same people switching on and off with each other. In San Diego, in Phoenix, there was no end to the girls he'd never seen before—beauty after beauty flashing a beguiling smile (though not for him), that simple gesture enough to slide continents of ununderstood emotion into one another, broken edges piling up a mountain range he'd never climb or cross though it'd only been a street separating them or a few feet—maybe a matter of brushing elbows—but he never came up with the words, never found the spell to cast, always gave himself over to the unrequited bitterness of watching her walk out of his life.

Sometimes he and Sonny drove into the desert. Sonny would

pack his Bronco with climbing gear and loan Logan climbing shoes, which looked like goofy sneakers.

"Never mind how they look, they might be the only thing keeps this from bein' a trip to the hospital."

Sonny prospected for the right cascades of stone. He introduced Logan to mountains and canyons between Phoenix and Flagstaff, taught him what it was like to walk around where eagles glided on invisible currents, leisurely as could be. Took a while, though, before you noticed anything but the rock face you were breathing into, inspecting it so close up you might find yourself looking into the five black eyes of a spider tucked in his crevice.

At first you were like a nervous cat sinking your claws into anything that couldn't shake you loose, sweating with the simple thought of going any higher while Sonny was yelling at you from down below not to worry, "You're all roped up!" But you didn't trust the rope—what if something unhooked? What would it feel like to have a blunt rock push up through your back, snap your spine, turn you inside out? And that bastard down there saying, "Goin' up's the easy part!"

Coming down, you had to go feet first, feeling with toes meant for walking, not monkey-climbing. Covered by goofy-looking shoes, those stubs, which maybe once were fingers, couldn't grab onto a thing anyway. Blind and backward, you came back.

Sometimes, on what was supposed to be a fairly easy climb, you lost your concentration, forgot where you were, and let your mind go soaring out. If you slipped, every muscle in your body strained to hold on to the tiniest irregularity in the rock. You flattened out against the stony face and wished for fingers like steel claws. The rock kept pushing you backward, hoping you'd fall, annoyance that you were.

Sonny taught him how to keep his concentration, how to hug the rock like a close friend, talk to it, ask it the easiest way up. Speaking to the stone, listening for a reply, his hands and feet slipped less. Placebo effect or no, he found the handhold he'd thought wasn't there. His cheek up against a cheek colder than death, harder than bone, he felt the silent heartbeat a thousand feet in, muffled by all that petrified earth, same as he was able to feel there was a way up. By finding every fault, every bump, every crack that had opened over time. Whatever hadn't been worn smooth was a gift of the spirit sleeping a thousand feet within, a giveaway to his cramping fingers and half-numb toes.

By the time he'd gotten back to Kansas, he was a couple inches taller and twenty pounds heavier. His muscles had gained something of the angularity of the rock he'd forced them to cling to. He'd let his hair grow out and tied it into a ponytail.

"Looks like you did some growin' up, boy." Cal gave him a playful tap on the jaw. "Couple more years and you might give me a run for my money." He smiled, the scar splitting his lower lip like a seam that went against the grain.

Logan saw the opening, watched his leg whip out like a cobra but yanked back the daydream as though it were an overexcited puppy. Even if he'd let go with that kick, all he'd have done was snap Cal's head back. It'd take Cal half a second to shake off his surprise then he'd take those mallet-sized fists of his and crack Logan's ribs like slats of dry wood.

Logan's mother came between them, hugging him, saying how much he looked like a man.

"Shit. Not till he can kick *my* ass."

He looked at Cal, at the thick arm tattooed with a winged skull. Logan was taller but not as stocky, nowhere near as strong. Little Big Man they called Cal at the garage. A bull's neck almost as wide as his head, and a head that hung low as if anger and resentment and frustration had knotted up the muscles of his back, made it seem almost as if he had a hump. Cal didn't have any training, though. He'd rely on his reckless strength. He'd be slow and overconfident. One of these days that cockiness was going to cost him. One day Logan was going to surprise the shit out of him.

Alone, practicing what Bill Tarp had taught him in a self-defense class he ran out of his basement—kicking, blocking, countering—Logan would beat Cal by his own faults, the way he and Sonny beat rock faces. He thought that way unless Cal was standing in front of him. Then he knew better. Cal had shrunk him inside too often. He didn't even know how many times he'd taken a slap across the face from Cal. Saw it coming but stood there, Cal's palm like a plank of wet wood. The world suddenly blurred and his hearing went numb. He took the blow the way water swallowed a stone.

His mother would show the same passive indifference, but Logan could tell, as she rubbed a cheek, that something inside her had crumpled. He couldn't handle Cal in a fight, but Cal sensed that something had changed after Logan came back from Arizona, that he was going to wake up to a baseball bat about to homerun his head if he put his hands on either of them again.

Logan never got the chance. He walked in on him late one night, Cal sitting in the dark on that mustardy couch he'd lugged from Arizona. He looked at his uncle across a distance scoured by a silent wind—widening as Cal walked toward that mountain range, the one no one ever crossed back over no matter what legends said. Cal sat there with a half-grin on his face as if he'd struck a pocket of crude instead of a vein. He slumped against the couch, his head tipped back, his gaze slanted innocently up—a drop of rain had just landed on his nose, maybe, and he was curious about how much more the sky might send his way.

Logan watched, the way he'd watched the back of a hand, riveted with knuckles, sail toward him (recalled how thunder broke in his head and the room pitched). Same as he'd watched Cal trap his mother against the hard angle of the kitchen counter before he hit her. He watched the life run out of Cal, his wrists leaking like rusted-through pipes, palms up as if he expected mercy or understanding or an answer to drop into them. The stain spread through the factory-dyed fabric, glinted in light from the street. The tv for a change was off. Probably Cal didn't want some laundry-detergent salesman with a crafty smile and a smooth voice to affect his concentration. Logan thought about sitting down next to him and putting a neighborly arm around his uncle.

Instead, he watched his eyes become balls of glass, still and milky. Lightless. That was how he knew Cal had died—no living thing had eyes like the dusty ones on an old merry-go-round horse. Logan finally made a friendly move, felt the couch under him squeegee. But instead of comforting the dead by patting a hand or closing the eyes or planting a kiss on Cal's forehead, he dipped his fingers in his blood. The smell was faintly rusty, slightly sickening. He rubbed between his fingers what had carried Cal's life. Sticky and viscous, it'd been strong enough to mix with beer and Jack Daniels, the death of a brother, motor oil and ball-bearing grease, the tar of cigarette smoke, and an abiding melancholy Logan had sensed but never understood. And still his blood had remained loyal to its own hue, had—like the tribe Cal had renounced but belonged to anyway—steadfastly refused change.

Taking great care, Logan lined the bridge of his nose then streaked his forehead with three red rays as if a star were rising from between his eyebrows. Next, a finger-width line down his upper lip and chin, creating a bloody axis. He lengthened his eyebrows, tiger-striped his jawline, boot-blacked himself like a ballplayer with the warm lifestuff of his dead uncle. The slashes of gore went cold and hard quickly, smelled not of death but of life. How vulnerable once out of the veins, once spilled onto an old couch. What a mess his mother was going to wake up to, and her son a bloody beast—had such a thing sprung from her loins?

In the bathroom mirror—no light but a candle burning on the vanity—he looked as if he'd burrowed through Cal's entrails. Beneath his ribs he was a being of smoke (everything that should've been human gone), a glow in his eyes from his smoldering guts. Masked in Cal's blood—where was the carver to make a likeness of him now? Surely he'd passed into another realm, become a demon katsina. Surely he was hollow inside, hovering above any feelings for his father's brother, above any sorrow or pity for what had eaten away at Cal all those years.

Leaning on the vanity, suffused in a hot glow as though an orange moon were rising through the floor, he stared at a face made of blood-soaked shadow, a face that should've been haunting an underworld. Eyes like embers, conscience burned off, emotions cauterized: half-breed, if they only knew what you were half of.

Dawn scratching away the dark as if it were film negative stretched across the sky, he was still sitting up with Cal's body, a bottle of Cal's beer in his hand. *Here's to you, Unc.* Finally having a happy sit-down with Uncle Cal.

Strangely, he didn't want Cal touched, especially not by cops, who'd want to start right in on taking pictures, cataloguing, and getting medical procedures going. He wanted Cal to stiffen like that, let the body's new set of laws set in while the rest of Cal was on that long walk toward a shadowy mountain range on the horizon. Logan wanted to be able to reach out and tap a cold hard forearm, feel the strangeness—the miracle that'd once moved his uncle's thick arm invisibly gone.

The scar splitting Cal's eyebrow was white as hot iron. The one in his lip seemed delicate, like spider webbing. His head was still tipped up and a little crookedly to one side, a smile about to sprout, *Fuck you* his last expression.

Thirteen's unlucky.

Fuck you.

You don't treat that family you commandeered too well.

Fuck you.

The eyes of a merry-go-round horse, dull and dusty.

Cal had endured the worst that could be done to him—had done it himself. Looked it in the face, spit in it, and hissed, *Fuck you.*

The path his father had traveled had been broad and smooth as an avenue. Sprinkled with fine-ground cornmeal, it led him to an underworld where the Sun shone during the night of the upper world, where the nighttime sky held different constellations. His father joined his ancestors in a village whose walls were as white as a sheet of memory. They lived as they always had, their kilts immaculate as billowy clouds, their moccasins made from albino buckskin. The carpets they wove were patterned like those in the upper world, but the colors were shades of white—ivory, eggshell, bone, seashell, cotton—so that what they depicted was exquisitely subtle, nearly invisible to the eyes of the living (could they have peeked in). Food was never in short supply although they didn't chew or swallow, simply inhaled the aroma. When they became clouds, they'd rise over the Hopi mesas, not even skeletons anymore but shadows of skeletons, dropping rain on their relatives.

Cal had been assigned a different fate. He'd gotten off his final *Fuck you*, but he wouldn't be coming back. Even as a cloud. Not only had Cal's route to the Skeleton House been squeezed down to a torturous path among mountain crags, not only were cactus pads stuck to his feet like burrs clinging to corduroys, but, after a good start, he'd find himself slowed to one step a year. A single step while his throat cracked with thirst like the bottom of a lake exposed to sun. A single step as he watched, not so far off, another ghost glide along the corn-meal path. He'd beg that ghost for a drink, to spit in his mouth. Strapped to his back with bow string, across his chest and forehead, was the blood-sopped couch, the underworld having its irony, the couch on *him* now, the bowstring cutting into his flesh, and though he'd bled himself dry in life, he'd bleed again as he took his lone annual step.

Even in death his father was one up on Cal.

Even in death Cal was one up on him. No one had ever told Cal when to go to bed or hit him with a curfew or cut off his beers. Cal had insisted even on his freedom to slash himself up and bleed into another existence.

Remembering Uncle Cal made Logan want to tear off his thin blanket and start running. Run until the hospital was as far behind him as his childhood. Over those meadows beyond the fences, his lungs filled with cool night, his legs as untiring as a horse's. Except they had the keys. He had to smile and nod at them and get out of bed on time. And if they knew about the O-negative death mask he'd worn, they'd never let him out.

10. Grandfather Saguaro

The day was overcast. Its weak light warmed nothing. As if the Earth were sheathed in smoked glass.

With all the offerings to the Hard-Luck Katsina burning in the rec room, Logan wouldn't have minded putting a few out. On shirt sleeves, on palms. Make them think twice about lighting up. Some of them were wearing jackets even though the thermostat had to be up around eighty.

The door creaking on its hinges turned Logan's head. He was surprised by the fluttering lightness—gut to throat—when he saw Aristotle. Unbuttoning his trench coat, Aristotle said something to Palmer that made him laugh. Logan watched Aris fold the coat over his arm. He wanted to smile, but the right muscles wouldn't contract.

"Good to see you, Logan." Aristotle shook his hand, looking him over as if he were a new car he was thinking of buying. "I like the new hairstyle."

Logan was confused for a second then he remembered: he'd tied his hair in a ponytail.

"Shaved too. Doing a magazine cover today?" He smiled to soften the irony.

Logan wondered how Aris did it, always looked as if he'd just come from some uplifting experience—a family dinner where the men tore apart a loaf of home-baked bread between their hairy hands, polished off a few bottles of wine while telling each other earthy jokes, used the bread to sop up the meat juices— and here he was now, cleaned up, professional-looking, still able to feel the brush of his mother's lips against his cheek where she'd kissed him before he left as if we could all live this way if we'd just stop being obstinate about it.

He followed Aris up the stairs, thinking *he* was the magazine cover. Or maybe a statue that had escaped its museum. He had the straight Greek nose that had predisposed sculptors toward marble, a jaw like the edge of a table, tightly curled hair. Always clean-shaven though you could see he could grow a beard down to his knees if he wanted to. His complexion wasn't as dark as Logan's, but beside Dr. Harry's it was warm as freshly fired terra cotta. (Sallow skin, sagging gut, trampled brow, eyes receding like smoker's gums, pretty soon Dr. Harry was going to need snail stalks just to look around.)

In the office Aristotle poured himself a cup of coffee, offered one to Logan. Wearing hiking boots and a navy-blue turtleneck tucked into his crisp new jeans, he looked as though he might go off to build a log cabin after he was done shrinking heads for the day.

"So ..." Aristotle sank into vinyl. "Why don't you tell me a little about your music?"

Logan rubbed his chin with a knuckle. "Haven't done any for ... gotta be better than a year now."

"Why do you think you stopped playing?"

Logan perched on the edge of the small couch. "Loss of, uh ..." He shrugged. "Belief, I guess. In music."

"Maybe in yourself too?"

"Maybe."

Aristotle nodded, jotted a note. "Any idea what brought it on? Was it a sudden thing or, say, gradual disillusionment?"

The air left his mouth as if he's just taken an elbow to the gut. "Sudden." About as much time as it took to realize that the kid playing marbles down the block was using the ones you'd lost last week for his game. Like tiny crystal balls, each foretelling a different future. "Just … stopped playing."

Aristotle sat quietly as if he were patiently waiting to turn into a slab of stone.

After a full minute Logan sighed. "I tried mescaline a few times, acid. I quit those too."

Aristotle scratched away with his pencil.

Logan imagined the shiny gray trail of graphite on the lined paper: *Drug-induced psychosis. Same as Jack.* He rubbed a hand over the cloudy blue denim covering a thigh. "Look, the thing is, I didn't …" His laugh was a shriek of tearing metal. "I'm not crazy."

"I didn't say you were."

"I mean … Mr. Spenser?" Logan gestured with a hand as if lightly backhanding the memory of the old man. "*He's* nuts. He can't separate what's in here … " Logan tapped his temple. "… from what's out there."

"Is that what constitutes insanity?"

"I don't know, but …"

The pencil's eraser dug into Aristotle's chin.

"Sometimes, I can't either."

"Make that separation?"

"Yes!" He startled himself by shouting.

"Well, I have a feeling sanity isn't so much a difference of kind as it is of degree." His expression became puzzled. "I'm not sure who Mr. Spenser is …?"

"The old actor, always spouting Shakespeare lines …?"

"Oh, yes, him. Anyway, this confusion you mentioned happens to most of us to one extent or another. But with the clients here, it's more that some aspect of an interior reality has overridden the exterior one. It's a defense mechanism, a response to some threat or trauma. They generally aren't even aware that it's happened. Your concern is a good sign, to say the least."

Logan tried to suppress a stupid grin, making his face feel lopsided.

"Now about the hallucinogens …"

The desire to smile evaporated like wet spots on a chalkboard, and Logan was faced with a smooth clean stretch of fear.

"I quit them. About the same time I stopped playing."

"For the same reason?"

He shrugged. "The last trip …" His hand went to rake his hair but, finding it neatly tied back, fell to his lap.

"What about the last trip?" Aristotle leaned forward almost imperceptibly.

The desert cold, his back against the towering night masquerading as a grandfather of a saguaro, needles long enough to puncture a lung, their prick reminding him he was lying across the other side of the familiar. The sky gone because he'd walked a path that led to a hole in things, the stone shapes he'd seen in the distance calling to him but he was afraid to answer because loneliness was their voice, the lament of stone like the embrace of the vacuum, a keening below the threshold of hearing.

"I don't remember anymore." What happened after the stone had called to him. It was there, silver-blue tv flickerings in a dark doorway, but for some reason he couldn't go in to see what was on the screen. "All I remember is being depressed afterward." The kind of depression that left no vision of the future desirable, left only an awareness that you wanted to want *something*.

"Do you think the drugs had something to do with why you're here?"

Something on the desert's edge had taken away his voice, left him trapped outside of things, sitting at the bottom of things, his back against the finger-long needles of a saguaro that wasn't really there (that was just how Grandfather Night's beard had felt).

He sat up straighter. "You know, there're a lot of things I can't remember. I mean, I'm not even sure about ... *yesterday*." He suddenly couldn't remember whether his name had been given to him at birth or he'd taken it off a tombstone in some graveyard he'd slept in. Maybe out of the phonebook. Made it up. His fist closed and something in his chest tightened. "I just can't remember ... what I did yesterday." His hand opened and closed faster.

Aristotle's voice was sure-footed among loose stones. "If you don't do anything of much importance or significantly different from one day to the next, you'll tend not to remember it. Your mind is pretty efficient. It tends to dispense with what it doesn't need. One day in the hospital is very much like another, isn't it? It's fairly common for the days to run together."

Logan laughed nervously. "Dispenses with what it doesn't need." A chant to ward off evil.

"And try not to get worked up about it. If there's something specific you need to recall, read a book, play a game of pool, watch tv. It'll come to you."

Logan smiled awkwardly.

"What got you started on hallucinogens in the first place?"

He could've told Aris about how, as a boy in Kansas, he was sometimes awake in the stillness before the Sun was even a hint in the sky, how the minutes spun themselves out, twisted like lava tubes branching beneath the ground. Leaves on the sidewalk along their quiet street danced in the breeze. The wind chimes on the porch *tink-tinkled,* wavered just beyond understanding. You had to tilt your head the right way, get the sound of yourself pinging off things you couldn't see in the silences. *You never know, Qua'ah* used to say, *what's tryin' to talk you.*

From his bedroom he looked down on the street lined with mailboxes and telephone-pole crosses. If he could find that stillness in himself, join it to the black that buoyed up the stars and floated this whole Earth with its one boy in a single room in a quiet town, if he could let himself surround all those things that seemed to be streets, telephone poles, trees, mailboxes, they'd break their silence, they'd say something no one expected to hear.

He shrugged. "I thought mesc would help me … get underneath."

"Open up the reducing valve a little?"

"Uh, yeah," he stammered, surprised Aris had read Huxley. "I got to thinking things have a dark side, like the Moon. I wanted to get a look."

The office was drawn up into the funnel-vision of a Kansas twister, swept round with cornhusks, a scarecrow's stickbones, yesterday's newspaper. Sitting on front porches, watching evening set in, the old timers tell the story, how *a whole roof went up like a, you know, a Frisbee. Darndest thing you ever saw.* The old men who sometimes depended on a reliable paperboy to deliver them from boredom. They could tell you how every road in town got its name. Some of them had put up the signs. Aristotle, pad in hand, was among them.

11. Night's Undertow

Memory is a city like St. Louis piled along the flow of night, twinkling from a distance as it's carried downriver, lost in a heartland flooded black—a flat-out sprawl somewhere below the threshold of notice waiting for a switch to be flicked on, a star to go nova.

Jim Lee on the event horizon, one of his nasty-smelling cigars between his teeth that is, out in the fields with his telescope magnifying circles of sky, never able to take it all in. Fedora, jeans with clip-on suspenders, a pair of scuffed-up cowboy boots, he looked like a cross between a rodeo rider and a Chicago hit man. Always called his nose a beak—*Caught a ball on the beak that game*—a Roman nose if he was in the mood to classify. Better than two hundred pounds though not that tall, he'd give his gut a friendly slap. *Never know when you'll hafta be the anchor in a tug-a-war.* His fleshy face was wide and his black hair sprouted without regard to direction, the fedora there to keep it corralled.

Jim Lee, who'd taken it upon himself to school Logan in everything from cheating at poker to pointing a telescope proper, who'd spent hours amidst water-stained UFO magazines and dime-store paperbacks (*The Book That Shatters the Wall of Official Silence!*), scouring photos of hubcaps thrown in the air and tinfoil-wrapped aliens for one that might be genuine.

Teacup to go with that saucer, Jim?

Jimmy hemmed in by a stack of singles permanently borrowed from Billy Boy's near-infinite 45-caliber collection, by empty beer cans and filmy glasses, by pillars of books he'd read and reread—the Bible everpresent among them—by rusted doodads of farm machinery and toy banks with mechanical cutesy ways of nabbing money (a skeleton that sits up out of a coffin, scoops in a nickel with a bony hand), by Robby the Robot, made of that 1950s near-indestructible plastic (missing a green arm nonetheless), big as a small child, invading planet Earth, a takeover of Jim Lee's farmhouse kitchen the first step in the Master Plan.

One particular June night, whose evening had floated a full moon over the fields, simmered it orange, bloated it near twice its normal size, Logan was with Jimmy among his collectible clutter listening to an antique radio, its broad face framed in wood, glossy-tube insides lit up by Spanish guitar music that for all Logan knew had circled the Earth halfway before staining the Kansas night blue. The singer's voice a shade more sorrowful than his guitar, it made you feel you were on a street in an empty downtown soaked to your boot soles by summer rain, then out the kitchen window they went, the blue Spanish voice and the weeping guitar, through the screen easy as a breeze, wandering like horse and rider over the dark fields, but there was nothing to echo off of, no place to rest, to keep them from dissipating at the speed of sound (the fate of all prayer however fervently chanted).

James Lee took a cold cigar stump out of his mouth. "Jim Thorpe's real name was Wa-tho-huck—Bright Path. That's a good'un, ain't it?" Bent over his work, his forehead glistening with sweat, Jim Lee handled the razor with the expertise of a Japanese chef, separating heaps of white into lines, the edge-on blade nearly invisible between his thick fingers. "An Oklahoma boy. Wasn't born all that far from here."

The nights hot that June, humid as the collective breath of all those weed-chewing insects outnumbering by thousands the stars over the fields.

"This here's the stuff that made the Incan empire what it is today—ruins." Jim Lee snorted hard through a rolled-up dollar bill then handed over the hollowed greenery. "Gift to the white man from the Incan in return for abusing his women, knocking down his religion, and putting him on welfare."

Logan's nose burned, the familiar taste slid down the back of his throat like a color that wouldn't stick to the canvas. White as ground-up angel bones, a sparkle to it like radiance dried and fallen away, it fevered Logan's blood, numbed the sting at the back of his neck where there was a welt roughened by an oozing scab. A keepsake from riding a mare that hadn't much cared to be ridden.

Hugh had shaken his big head. "Never saw that horse act up that way."

Logan wasn't much of a rider, just a little run around Hugh's farm he'd been thinking, felt like a conquistador in the saddle, all that animal strength bunched up under him. Never saw what spooked the mare, but she took off so sudden he about lost a stirrup, caught a low branch across the face, then he was falling forward in the saddle as she took a steep dry creek bed. Pinching the sides of the horse between his knees, his groin stiffening up from squeezing so hard, he thought for sure he was going to get spilled when they came to that falling-apart fence Hugh had never cleared away, but the horse clean leaped it, and— just like that—pulled up short, breathing hard, her heaving ribs pushing out his shaky legs, and a good thing he was sitting—he wouldn't've been able to stand.

She walked calmly back to the barn, all the fight gone out of her he thought, but she jumped again, effortlessly, unexpectedly, through a side doorway too low for horse and rider—just blind instinct that he buried his face in her mane. The lintel, big as a railroad tie, cracked the back of his head, scraped up his neck.

Hugh came running up, belly bouncing under his denim shirt. "You all right? Goddamn. Never seen 'er do that. You okay?" He shook his head. "Damn but I never seen 'er do that."

Weirdest thing was, when the machined edge of that seasoned lumber scraped against his skull, a hole wormed through the past and he switched places with his dead father, whose head had shattered the windshield of a truck 12 years before. He couldn't help but think the horse had gotten away from him same as the truck had gotten away from his old man.

The collar of his shirt kept sticking, pulling free, bleeding again when he turned his head.

"How 'bout a little viewin'?"

Night in the old farmhouse just beginning to smolder, Jimmy wanted to pull out his telescope though what he was prospecting the sky for was likely as nonexistent as his *oofoes*.

Whether nuclear furnaces light years distant or poker chips on the table or apples in the grass, there's no divinity at work, Jim, just physics. They fell out that way is all. You might as well send your Galileo-tube back to 16th-century Holland or wherever it came from.

Later that night, it was the numbers that fell out, insisted it hadn't been an accident that had killed his father 12 years ago, hadn't been providence, it had been his father's brother.

Two more dusty lines disappeared through rolled-up legal tender.

Jim Lee rounded up the last of the cocaine with a wet finger, stuck it in his mouth. "That'd put a little zing in yer toothpaste."

The screen door hissed closed behind them.

There was a kind of sanctity in the Kansas sky, clear and deep, constellations invisibly hung like bright mobiles.

The streetlamp at the edge of Jimmy's yard attracted all manner of insects, the moths among them bumping against the hot glass that sealed them off from a mercury-vapor heaven. A cloud of wingbeats like a swarm of thoughts with no skull to pen them in. Bats flapped in strobe-light movements, swooping swerving veering off with uncanny precision.

Jimmy looked up at the bright lure. "The amount a motion here an' everywhere else is as never-changing as Superman's uniform—if Descartes is to be believed. But the soul can alter direction. Will has some say."

"I can't see that wishing gets figured in to the equation."

"Does seem to be a flaw in theory somewhere."

Parked underneath the light, Jimmy's truck was a yellow somewhere between banana and bumblebee, *The Hog* painted in fancy script on a bug-shield peppered with kills.

Streetlamps spaced half a mile or so apart marked the way to town.

Jim Lee put a hand on his fedora, forced a cough, and spat out the window. Claiming to have once knocked a kid off a bicycle like that, he reached down and turned a country tune up loud.

The Round-Up, when they got to it, was already filled with body heat, walled-in smoke, idle conversation no more intelligible than a flock of chittering birds. What with the music, Logan could barely hear his own boots clumping on the wooden floor.

"Whaddaya say, Jim Lee ...?"

Hands reached out to slap the broad back Y-ed over by suspenders. Logan a couple steps behind, always at Jim's heels, still three years away from the 21 you needed to be to drink anything harder than wine or beer.

Larry behind the bar and behind Larry black-and-whites of the town at the turn of the century, of him during his rodeo days, #27 plastered on his back, the bull's ass six feet in the air in one.

"How's the neck feelin'?" Larry's big hand, gloved in the old days before it was shoved under a rope wound around the bull's chest and humped back, came over the bar and squeezed Logan's. Rough as a grindstone.

"'S'alright." Instinctively he put two fingers to the swelling under his collar, the scab still bloodying his shirt.

Jimmy Lee leaned over the bar. "Nothin' wrong with the boy a beer won't fix."

"Hugh tol' me what happened ..." Larry popped open a couple of bottles, shook his head. Jesus God, lucky you ducked when you did."

Logan's head was full of coke and the woodgrain patterns under his bottle.

Jimmy—talking nonstop to him, to Larry, yelling to the guys a few stools away—was already motioning for another beer.

Larry switched out the empty for a fresh bottle, its shine dulled by a dewy film.

Don Moody, a third-year law student, was leaning against the wall, posed like some movie-poster icon. "Who do I luck lack?"

"Truman Capote." Jimmy motioned impatiently with a hand. "Now get over here an' buy a round."

Age notwithstanding, Logan lifted a tumbler, bottom soaked in a little puddle of sour mash that Larry's rag would sop up in a swipe, touched rims with Jimmy and Don and Larry. Burned going down, the fumes clearing his nose.

Broncobuster, bullrider, Larry could've handled that mare without a saddle. He had scars under his T-shirt from the time a bull had walked all over him, stomped him good. Nobody expected him to be breathing after that much less back up on a muscled hump in a year's time. Wasn't any riled bull or even a bucking stallion that'd clipped Logan's head, just a broken-in mare. He'd seen a bunch of Cherokees in Oklahoma too lazy to go through the hoo-ha of putting on saddles gallop past him as though he were whiter than the Anglos standing next to him.

"How was Mexico, bud?" Don with that baby face of his that was never going to grow much of a beard, round as the spare tire circling his waist—no good for hula-hooping but jiggled if he took off at a run. "They got pyramids like they say?"

"Lots of 'em."

"Ain't that something?"

Grander than anything in Kansas, built by distant cousins long before that mixed-up Italian with a Ptolemaic map as misconceived as his Atlantic Ocean crossing was ever born.

Billy Boy shouldered between Logan and Don. Thick hair greased back, Elvis Presley sideburns, black on his fingers where engine gunk had settled into tiny cracks in the skin, Billy looked at Logan with glossy pupils big as hubcaps.

He was saying something, but Logan's head was bouncing to a song on the jukebox. Fueled by powdered angel bones, alcohol mist settling over his better judgment the way clouds could gang up and blur the Moon, he knew he could do better, just wouldn't make it to any station in Frontenac. The over-and-over beat was background for Don wishing for grazing rights to the grand majority of women who walked by, Jim Lee's open-mouthed laughter, Billy Boy's out-loud figuring a system to hit the lottery.

"Ah'm tired a standin' on concrete ten hours a day, breathin' in exhaust, an' comin' out smelling like a grease pit." Billy slowed down enough for a sip from his bottle.

The end of a cigar twisted as a tree root glowed brighter as Jim Lee drew on it. "Comfert yersaylf fraynd ..." The voice of a tv preacher produced out of a pocket jingling with coins, Jim Lee put a reassuring hand on Billy. "The Lord will shoorly reward you with etur-ni-tay for suffreeng as you do in this vayle of tayres."

But Billy wasn't listening. A blonde who'd walked in threw a switch on the tracks and Billy's attention careened off in her direction. "If she ain't gonna change my life, who the hell is?"

Don waved his hand. "One hole's as good as another."

Billy pointed at Don with the long-necked bottle. "Anybody says that's only been in one."

The midnight freight Logan had been riding slowed suddenly, brakes shaving a squeal off the metal they were pressed against, curled in his ear while his body took on the weight the engine had been hauling. Suddenly he was afraid the legs of his stool were about to splinter and he was going to go through the floorboards ass-first.

Larry waved him and Jim Lee behind the bar, hustled them to the back room he used as an office. Jim Lee pushed aside receipts, bills, letters, invoices, cleared a corner of Larry's 1940s desk stolen from some private-eye movie set. Pulling out his razor, Jim Lee sliced lines like clean white scars on the desktop, a couple of them snapping Larry's head back as though he'd taken twin jabs from a boxer.

"Hoo-ee!" He shook his head once, quick as a twitch, sniffed, wiped at his nose, then the rag in his back pocket was flapping up and down as he hurried out to tend bar.

Jim handed Logan the tubular dollar bill. "Oughta keep you up for a while."

Logan pushed open the door to the bar. Voices, music, bad lighting, nodding heads, smiling faces all came together, fused like the tiny continents of bone that make up a skull—a fugue waiting to be composed, one that would take in even the wispy fleeting shapes the smoke wove itself into. He couldn't have been as almighty as he felt, though, because Jim Lee's arms made his look skinny and smooth. A wake-up call, a hey-hello—wasn't only his arms that needed work.

Friday night in southeastern Kansas. No hills to speak of, no lakes thereabouts, just strip-mine pits filled by rain, the ocean a long haul as it happened and Chicago a good six hours' drive. Things showed up newer on the broad boulevards of a city, phrases like freshly minted coins, the shine already gone by the time they reached the callused hands of awkward farm boys, this and that talked about while beer labels worked on by nails chewed to nubs came away in sticky balls dropped into ashtrays crowded with cigarette butts.

Billy Boy pulled a comb out of a T-shirt pocket and styled his oiled hair as if a little more wave to it and he'd've gotten a conversation going with that blonde.

Jim Lee dragged on his gnarled cigar, smoke softening the pinball machine's yellow flashes. A kid across the room leaned into the game as if the shiny ball were tracing out his fate in its pinging odyssey. Moans went up over missed shots at clacking pool tables, bets were collected, grins broadened, heads shook.

Jim Lee's stinking Italian stogie somehow helped restore a lost balance, as if there were too much down here, too much to take in, and some of it needed to be burned off.

Why not? See how high the smoke went. Snort it, shoot it, pop it, climb a mountain, add a few stories to that skyscraper, aim a hollow arrow through a tube of gravity, send a dog a monkey a man to penetrate the starry mysteries that only come out at night when it's dark enough to see what's melted in the white-hot glow, what's trapped in a miraculous net of bone and sinew. They were a bunch of cast-outs, wing-broke and unhaloed, trying to return to some forever-breaking dawn. Same as the moth willing to die for its immortal moment immolated. Combustible wings. Fluttering against a calcified dome sutured with cracks (skylight sealed up), lacquered with consciousness. Everything in it turned to ash in the short-circuit where old lumber and vulnerable bone collided.

Jim Lee's eyes narrowed to slits above his smoldering cigar. "This two-door town parked in the middle a nowhere had its heyday once. Used to get men of ill repute from Chicago, St. Louis, Kay Cee. Once in a great while even a black sedan turned gray by the dust of half the Midwest but you could still see the New York plates when it pulled up in front of our very ownly pool hall. Took their shots an' downed 'em right across the street at Stobart's." He jerked his thumb over his shoulder. "Boarded up now, but Sto's used t'hop, back then, a bit before I was a regular. A shiner in days a yore, Old Sto was rumored to deal on an' off with Lucy Furr, crazy old witchy kinda woman who it was they said sold him his firewater. That's a joke, son. Truth a the matter is, Sto had a still under his barn in the event the revenue men came pokin' around. They wouldn't find a thing 'cause it was all stowed belowground, see?"

Look close enough at Jim Lee's eyes alight with the bygone, awash with beer, you might see in the dark irises tiny twins of Stobart's Poolhall just as he remembered it.

"No hustlin' in Sto's, no stakes was the unwritten rule, which is why I think they came here."

Only the talk was loaded. Billiard balls knocking into each other like punctuation for wise-guy remarks falling from as great a height as heaven on eager adolescent ears. *Clack. Clackety-clack.*

Keep your ashes off the green, it unsettles m'shot. Old Stobart, hair gone white, liked the plunk in a pocket as much as the next guy. Eyes sharp enough to pick up a smudge of chalkdust on the cue, he died at eighty-something but never wore glasses. *I got a remedy for every virtue*, Stoey used to brag and the men in guinea-tees and fedoras laughed. *Boy, if you don't quit chewin' yer gum like a cow munchin' cud*—clack-plunk—*ground hog's gonna be deliverin' yer mail.*

"Used to come from all over …" Jimmy Lee's hand circled over the bar like a bird about to set down. "Right here." His finger whitened at the tip where he pressed on the bar.

Jimmy a freckled kid on the black-and-white streets of yesteryears, a cigarette poking out the corner of his mouth, a pack rolled in a T-sleeve. Then at 17, leaning on his cue stick, freckles about gone, a white guinea-tee showing a weightlifter's arms. Not too arrogant to smile, a Lone Star in his hand, fingers pressing a smoldering butt to the cold-sweating can.

Theme and variation. How many other teenagers looked just like him? Even went to Joplin and got tattooed. Smoked the same brand of cigarettes, drank the same beer in Stobart's.

"Those days I was so cool when I stepped outside, temperature dropped." His cigar a smokeless cinder, he looked at what was left as if he were missing something. "Left home sweet home to become one of Uncle Sam's Misguided Children—Yoo, Ess, Em, Cee. For the free scuba lessons. Damn near broke an' eardrum." He tipped up his bottle. "You can go down to the same spot two, three days in a row an' it's different and unfamiliar every time."

Jimmy down there in the water-dark, sinking and lost, following the beam of his flashlight, eyes peeled just in case those rumors about a sunken civilization were true. His undersea excavations maybe a way to be that buoyant all the time, that wonderstruck, that close to the sound of his own breathing, to the ocean's breath sweeping things along, making kelp forests wave like the hair of old man Oceanos long forgotten, his temples gone to ruin, half-buried face-down in the sand now, too at ease ever to move again, a natural formation on the bottom giving off a little greenish smolder in the sea night, a smidgen of glow that maybe caught Jimmy's eye as he wove through those kelp strands—why'd he come back to Frontenac?

The only waves Logan saw were in the lapping woodgrain patterns on the bar. A kind of motion, as if the wood were breathing.

"Hey buddy, what're you starin' at so hard?"

The woodgrain pattern shifting, trembling under Logan's fingertips, the vibrato of mothwings.

"You don't wanna know." Jimmy squeezed his eyes closed,

massaged his wrinkled brow. "Good God, Logan, if I had a head like yours, it'd hurt all the time."

"Here's t'gettin stupid." Billy Boy raised his bottle.

Don bumped Logan with a shoulder. "He's about as stupid as you can get and still stand."

Somebody tugged on Jimmy's suspenders on his way out.

"Awright, awright, g'bye." Jimmy adjusted his braces with a thumb under each. "Can't unnerstan why they gotta mess with a man's apparel."

Bottles and glasses were lifted to the US Armed Forces, Larry's rodeo days, good will toward men.

A little later, Jim Lee's head was bowed, and his back slumped like he was feeling the weight of those oversized volumes he read, or maybe the weight of the dead, his mother's slow leaving, cancer of some kind. Maybe that's what made him look old and worn, defeated, all three.

"I drink …" Jimmy lifted his bottle. "Therefore I am."

An old joke. Was that all he'd managed to distill from his dusty stacks of books? Was that all that'd come of sitting up late amidst the holy clutter of his collectibles, pouring out whiskey meditations on Will Blake, wrestling with the sometimes insufferable often impenetrable verses of the Bible by candlelight and cigar glow till sleep slipped up behind him, left him face-down on the table beside a hardened puddle of wax?

"They toll me philosophy'd help me pass the L-SAT, the logic an' all, but I don't hardly remember none of it." Don sounded like he wanted his money back.

"Logic leads t'Aristotle, not t'God." Jimmy finished off what was in his bottle. "Plato wiped his ass with it."

"Heard he was a fag."

"I'll tell you this for nothin', Donalbain m'boy, you couldn't be a waiter in Aristotle's Diner."

"Shit." Don's face curdled. "Philosophy about as good as forchin-tellin' ..."

Logan massaged his forehead, his fingers slipping in sweat. Who to look for in the insect buzz around a streetlamp? In the smoke-swirl conversations around them? Descartes? Or a higher-up?

"You ever been to one a those prayer meetings?" Don pointed at Logan with his bottle. "One with snakes? Those hillbillies pick up handfuls a the poisonous suckers at a time an' never get bit. Straighten 'em out like a fistful a arrows, stand 'em up like shocked hair."

Billy Boy nodded. "The spirit is in them. Amen."

Jimmy shrugged. "Whaddya expect a farmers who drink their corn?"

"They thank thay're saints from the Bable. Reincarnayted or somethin'."

Not reincarnated, Logan thought, something else, the soul a song composed of a certain number of elements already there in the ancient Sumerians and their drumbeat songs, just got reshuffled over the years till you got a Kansas farmboy blowing his harmonica blues. Old as the hills in Oklahoma. No one ever really comes back, it's all odds, theme and variation. Some things that look like others are bound to show up.

"You and Jim Lee read too many bucks, I can't hardly keep up."

Had Logan said that out loud? Or was Don reading minds?

"The Lord works in mysterious ways all right." Billy nodded

confidently. "The night old Stobart died of a heart attack I dreamed he was drowning and callin' out for help."

Why had there been no owl screech, no ominous dream, no fire alarm, no fire-colored moon in the sky the night his father died? Why hadn't he at least woken up?

The back of Logan's neck felt swollen and hot under his collar. There was sweat and the sting of opened flesh. Blood oozing between cracks in the scab, running hot, drowning the throbbing.

Fingers bent with gripping, cramped and tangled in horsehair, holding onto the bristling mane of night. Veins rippled across taut skin. Mane of the constellation Horse. Bright pain as the windows of the skull fogged with frost.

Jim Lee glanced around the room, sifting the haze of voices and exhausted cigarettes as if waiting in some dust-infested corner was the very thing he'd been scouring the sky for with his tripodded magnifying glass. Sitting there as though it might sidle up next to him, take a seat on one of Larry's stools (electrical tape sealing a split in the leather). Waiting for a vision to visit. Weren't they all? A moment different from any other, that would make sense of every other? That would make this long night of disappointment breathable, bearable? Why else look at the door every time it opened? Jim Lee, who'd seen the submerged bottom of the world, stared forlornly at the unplugged jukebox. Might as well have another beer, see what it brought on, most likely that economy-size headache he'd been saving up for.

Caught in the night's undertow, his flashlight lost and something of the cool shadows cast by tombstones in his eyes, Jim Lee had a question to put to the dead, possessed of oracular knowledge as they were rumored to be, having circumnavigated this side and that, seen the darkest of places—what he wanted to know, his ass half hanging off the stool, was why he could blow things up two or three times lifesize but not see any clearer. Was how to keep night after night from etching unwanted tattoos on memory's skin. How could it be that he was looking out on things and still wondering about the order to put them in? Does death really come before dishonor (the price of those free scuba lessons)? If forced to choose, would he take another line of poetry or a line of coke? A little sky scanning or another gander from his bar-stool outpost at the sweaty faces and smoky voices? Where exactly was he supposed to be standing (or sitting) in relation to everything else? Deep-sea diver into the early morning hours, what was all that down there on the sunless end of the ocean floor? And what have we got here on the gritty floorboards we've never noticed by day? Light chases the mystery outa things though pure darkness makes the exact whereabouts a your hand in fronta your face fairly enigmatic. A Beethoven symphony or the endless nightchant of insects in the fields? The *Epic of Gilgamesh* or another excursion to one of Pittsburg's titty bars? A little more living or a peek at the secrets of the dead?

They finished their beers while Larry cleaned off tables and put chairs on top of them, Billy dozing in a corner, the pinball lights making him look cartoonish, odd shadows shifting on his face as yellow hopped haphazardly from bulb to bulb.

Jim Lee, the white wizard, the last of his magic powder gone to Billy, slid off his stool, tucked his shirt in around his suspenders. "We're outa here." He put another bill on the bar. "An' we're laughin.'"

Larry at the handle of a push broom waving them off.

Billy Boy wobbly on his feet (even with the spell of wakefulness cast on him), Jim tossed him in the back of Don's Chevy.

Downtown was silent except for the tiny bows of insect legs scraping cellophane wings.

Don aimed tobacco juice and spat.

Nothing but coke-flecked phlegm to offer the nascent day, Logan looked up at the telephone-pole crosses, like solid shadows cast on the sky. The bank on the corner across from the Apco station sat quiet and dark, only its light-bulb display of time and temperature still plugged in, showing the first numbers of the night: 3:33, a biblical sum split down the middle.

Logan kneeled under a streetlamp. A moth skimmed the sidewalk, a gray-white blur that couldn't lift off no matter the hum of wings scorched by a close encounter. He held up a finger to the streetlight (a low-floating, electrified moon), blotted it out, and it seemed the attraction was his fingernail, now given a buzzing, shape-volatile corona.

Billy Boy was passed out in the Chevy, boots out hanging over the back seat till Jimmy went around to the other side, yanked on Billy, and the boots disappeared like the withering feet of the wicked witch under Dorothy's house after Glenda lifted her ruby slippers.

"See you boys t'marra night." Don slammed the door, rolled down his window. "Same Bat tam, same Bat channel."

Don's Chevy rumbled off, wheels indifferent to the insect multitudes they crushed.

Moth wings throbbed at Logan's feet like a feathery heart, dragged themselves over a cracked sidewalk scoured by sodium-vapor light. The concrete porous, expanding and contracting ... breathing?

He laughed. Ebb and flow, yawn and squeeze, in breath and out breath right there under his feet. The Earth as alive as he was. Put your ear to the ground and listen. Could be a thousand buffalo or a single iron horse. Could be the Earth's heart.

The Hog pulled up next to him, shivering with the engine's rough idle, a moveable beast exhaling carbon monoxide.

Logan's skin felt stretched, tingled, pressed itself against humid air pollenous with something waiting to take root.

There's providence even in the fall of a moth.

Jim Lee made his open fist into a megaphone. "This is your tour guide speakin' ... this vehicle has three speeds: first, second, and hyperspace. We'll be traveling through several dimensions so don't be alarmed. And don't bother with your seatbelt—we ain't got none."

Jimmy weaving back and forth across the yellow line, wind rushing through the open windows like a breathable flood. Logan pictured the wreck—a fireball, scrap metal scattered over the highway, some clipboard-carrying anthropologist a century from now examining the bone cinders with the same care a hunter takes looking over deer turds. *Remains of* Homo Reckless, unmistakably.

The black overhead magically no closer no matter how fast Jimmy drove.

Nerve endings spread out over the dark fields, Logan stared ahead. The road was empty and straight.

Back in the farmhouse kitchen, sleep not about to set in, Jim Lee picked up a Bible lying open on the table. "Lemmee see, whadda we got here? Sirach 6. *Let one in a thousand be your confidant.*" Jimmy's brow creased and he held the book up. "Wouldja look at the page it was flopped open to?"

Six-sixty-six. Logan frowned. "Wait. Wait here …"

He took stairs two at a time, might have been a blur in Jimmy's eyes, Duchamp's nude, except he was headed *up* the sagging farmhouse steps.

He rummaged through a leather bag he'd just bought in Mexico, snatched a book out of it. A hapless toad caught in a heron's beak. The heels of his boots drummed up a staccato racket as he dropped down the stairs.

"I picked this up in Mexico. Just for something to read on the bus."

"Hm." Jim Lee let go a plume of smoke.

The cover showed a demonic creature as vast as a nebula— look, those are stars that were its eyes—looming over a spaceship. Jim Lee pulled a bit of paper out from between the pages. "What'sis? Ticket stub?" He flipped it around so Logan could see.

The number on the top of the stub was 60606.

Logan took the book from Jimmy. "That's not my ticket. This is for seat 30. I was in 29." Logan pulled another ticket out of the book, ticket number 60605. "*This* is my ticket."

"So who sat next to you?"

"That seat was empty."

"Judas got 30 pieces of silver." Jimmy relit his cigar, threw the matchbook at Logan. "You gave me these matches, didn'tcha?"

Cheap advertising for The Zuni Bar, *right on Route 666, just outside of Zuni, New Mexico.*

"I stopped in there about a month ago. On my way to the border."

"Exactly a month ago?" Jimmy asked.

"What's today?"

"Since it's about four in the morning, the twelfth."

"So I was there May 12th. Yeah, maybe." Logan's scalp suddenly went electric, and his hair lifted itself off his head as if realizing the evil thing it was rooted to.

He fell.

He'd lost feeling in his legs and they'd given way. He landed on his ass, a solid *whump* against the linoleum floor. He started laughing. "Twelve years ago today, Jimmy. It was Cal. Cal did it."

"Did what?"

"Killed my father."

"But … that was a car accident, wasn't it?"

Through laughter like a nerve disorder, Logan nodded. "They used to call him Little Big Man at the garage. Short but wide …"

"Yeah, I remember."

"Little Big Man was Crazy Horse's Judas. Bayoneted him in the kidney. And you—you're the friend, Jim, the one in a thousand. And Cal was born on the ides of March, the 15th. He's Brutus. And Judas. I don't know how, but somehow he made that accident happen. He disconnected the brakes. Took out the seat belt. I don't know, but it was Cal. Had to have been Cal—"

"The primal eldest curse—"

"*That's* why Cal couldn't live with himself." Logan made a sudden fist in the air as though he'd caught a fly. "And the numbers all coming up now … the matchbook and the bus ticket that belonged to the ghost … that science fiction novel and … a dream. I remember it now. I dreamed I was in a store in Mexico and some guys came in to rob it. One of them had a gun, the other a baseball bat. I wanted to run but my feet froze, and the guy with the bat whacked me. I fell on my ass, just like I am now. I fell and thought my skull was cracked. It's just like now, just like the horse, the numbers ..."

"Ticket's dated May 12th . Thought you said you were in Zuniland about then?"

"I was."

Jimmy brought the ticket for a Mexican bus closer to his face. "There it is. Date was rubberstamped, see? He musta reversed it. Musta been May 21st you rode that bus."

His father killed the 12th day of the sixth month—18. Three sixes. The house in Phoenix had been 12 Madero Street. The one in Frontenac, 66 Cayuga Street.

"And that 13 on Cal's arm ..."

Jimmy flipped through the pages of the Bible. "Revelation 13 ... *Then I saw another beast coming up out of the earth, and he had two horns like a lamb and spoke like a dragon.*"

"I'm 18 now," Logan said. "Three times six. Today is 12 years after my father's death. On the 12th. Killed when I was six."

"Jesus ..." Jimmy shook his head, the cigar between his fingers cold.

The amount of motion in the universe is constant, only direction changes, acted on by the soul's desire.

Logan knew now why his head had scraped against that railroad-tie doorway. But what was that whisper running along the bone like a prayer rounding the dome of a cathedral? His father's voice prodding his conscience? Like the rumble of way-off thunder, hard to tell when it started, when it had ended.

12. The Song Katsina

He got out of bed because he thought he'd heard something. Dreamed it maybe. He didn't remember falling asleep, but how could he have heard singing? Coming from outside?

His forehead pressed against cool glass, his breath leaving a shrinking ghost on the windowpane, he expected to see a face turned up to his, to the scattering of flakes drifting down out of the icy black. He expected someone half-naked in the tinny sheets of moonlight, his song mist as it left his mouth.

There was no singer. And nothing to hear other than breath scraping against teeth or whistling through nostrils. At the end of one row of beds, Mr. Spenser slept on his back, stiff as the metal frame under him, his mouth open like a Venus flytrap. The blanket tucked under his chin stretched as though over a grave. On the other side of the room, Jack's breathing could have been a quietly humming machine.

The blue bulb over the door, crosshatched with steel, glared back at Logan as if he were an equation to be graphed. He fell onto his bed, a metallic squeal coming from the straps and the springs. Staring up at the foam-board ceiling, he heard the voice again, like wind through a hollow. Too far away to make out the words.

He got up and pressed his forehead against the window again.

The singer was closer now, his voice a kind of tension, as if he were using it to string stars together, to bridge the home of the *katsinam* to the lower realm, and they—in their woven kilts and impenetrable masks—would come sliding down its silvery pitch easy as gliding down a girder of moonlight.

No words in any language he recognized, just a voice pushing into crevices and holes, over humps and peaks, singing to shadowy accretions that melted each morning like frost on grass. (Imagine the continents forming and reforming, all the maps of the world obsolete faster than they could be drawn.) The voice, lying against this hidden geography, knew no two nights were the same, that darkness worked new magic nightly.

Logan looked for him in the weak moonlight (granulated by a few slow-falling snowflakes). He looked for someone roaming the manicured hospital grounds in stained undershorts and a T-shirt, a phantom that wasn't a vague phosphorescence but a voice.

He saw no one.

But the voice went on singing the night's contours into a dialect meant for anyone blind to the mysteries of echolocation.

Out of the corner of his eye, Logan saw Jack and some of the other patients sitting up, staring at him. They heard it too.

Then it stopped.

A key scraped in a lock.

"A'right, who's got the boombox?" Billings's face was tinted blue by the bulb over the door. Wiry, a couple of inches shorter than Logan, Billings got by on the suggestion in his voice that a thread, about to snap, was the only thing keeping him from using the haft of his flashlight like a nightstick.

Two of the patients fell back on their beds and lay still as if their hearts had suddenly stopped.

Jack shook his head. "We don't got a boombox in here."

"C'mon man, don't fuck with me. I know what I heard."

Aiming his flashlight at Logan's face, Billings disappeared in the glare.

"What're you doin' outa bed, Blackfeather?"

One hand shielding his eyes, Logan tapped on the window. "It was outside."

"Yeah all right, lookin' time's over." Billings walked toward him. "Back in the sack." He jerked a thumb.

Logan stood in the space between getting back in bed like a good patient and waiting for Billings with all his keys to come closer. He sat down on the edge of the mattress, watched Billings search under and between the beds. Lying down, Logan locked his fingers behind his head as if he were about to tell the ceiling a good story. "We told you—isn't any stereo."

Billings dusted off his knees as he headed for the door. "Yeah, well, one thing for sure—none a yous can sing like that."

13. First Mesa

We're not going to get very far, we're not going to put this thing to rest if we don't go back to that last trip of yours. we have to dig a little deeper you have to trust me we'll work through it together. now you were saying you remember, let's see, you remember waking up

On the floor. One side of his face numb, his neck stiff. He'd used a pile of clothes for a pillow. Hadn't bothered to undress except for his sneakers. The sun, even through shades, hurt his eyes, mingled with the pain at the back of his head. Already the air in the room felt viscous with dry heat. Running his fingers over the side of his face, he found a gully (from a belt loop maybe), a ridge from something folded over, a dent made by a shirt button.

Lightheaded, still running fingertips over this numb terra incognita, he reached out with his free arm to the wall and made his way down the hall. It was some kind of evil miracle that he was awake but part of his face wasn't; his fingers couldn't help being fascinated.

Not until he was back in Sonny's room, bladder empty, did he notice the smell: piles of unwashed clothes, beer soaked into the floorboards, the sour honey of hangover breath. While Sonny slept face-down on the bed, boots and all, Logan pulled clothes off the floor and stuffed them into his bag. Sonny breathed hard into the pillow as if he'd just finished a long climb or was about to heave something arm-trembling over his head. Sun sliced beneath the shade, blued a narrow rectangle of his long black hair.

The flimsy aluminum door hissed closed, and Logan stood in blinding heat. Enough to make him dizzy. Color had been scorched into a washed-out white. The road shimmered and telephone poles wavered like reflections on water.

He walked while Phoenix thinned and diminished, a dirty wave pulling back into the sea. Hard sunlight, incubating a heap of old tires, set a nauseating smell adrift in his empty stomach. Cars and trucks whizzed past, drivers taking no notice of the flesh-and-blood detail along the side of the highway.

Somewhere past the city's shabby edge, mostly flat-roofed plywood shacks that looked like brown cinders, something lumbered against his peripheral vision. At first he thought the guy pulling over in a dusty white van just wanted to see whether he could breathe in the cloud it kicked up. Then he realized it was a ride. A faded peace sign maybe a foot across was stenciled on the passenger-side door.

Logan yanked it open.

"Where you headed?" the driver asked.

"Up to the mesas."

Reconnecting with Sonny couldn't have gone worse.

"I can get you as far as Flagstaff. Hop in."

The van smelled of musty carpeting, the kind that'd had soda and coffee spilled on it, had been waterlogged from a leak. Two feathers, their stems covered in beadwork, hung from the rearview mirror.

Thirtyish and weathered, the guy behind the wheel was bald from forehead to crown. The half a head of hair left was blond and curled at the ends. His face was oddly complemented by the smooth pate and a gold hoop in his ear. One rectangular lens of the sunglasses he wore was cracked down the middle.

"Looks like water, don't it? That road shimmer?"

Bruce seemed to be talking to the highway.

"I always liked the sea."

He'd worked on shrimpers in the Gulf of Mexico, seiners in the waters around Washington and Alaska.

"Even as a kid I was a water bug. Born on an island. St. Croix."

Maybe a pirate, Logan thought, that scar along his jaw from a hook where a hand should've been.

The scar, he said, had come from two hustlers he'd beaten at pool. "Back on St. Croix. The only white guy in the bar." One of them had swung at Bruce with a chair leg, and a screw had cut an arc across his jaw.

"A few nights later I caught up with 'em." A smirk spread across Bruce's face. "Went after 'em with a machete."

But the blade had been blocked by a pool cue and had gone down the stick like a groove carved in the air.

"Sliced that fucker's thumb clean off." He laughed. "The other guy got away."

Bruce was on his way to Los Angeles via Flagstaff.

"I guess you been up to the reservation …?"

"Not since I was five or six."

"Depressing as hell." He looked at Logan, back to the road, back at Logan. "You got relatives up there?"

"Not anymore. Not really."

Logan didn't need Bruce to tell him how depressing the reservations were. He may have been born in a hospital in Phoenix, but part of him was stuck on one of those mesas, in a pit dug into the cool dark. Bruce was a tourist. Logan would notice things up there Bruce hadn't, understand intuitively where Bruce had been puzzled.

I had it in my pocket the whole time a little rectangle of tin foil a couple beads of mesc. I had this idea I'd pick up something from being on the mesa, get closer to who I am you know? if you asked me back then I'd have told you I thought I'ld come across some leftover, nothing as obvious as those petroglyphs every guidebook has a picture of but none of them can explain, I was going to dance without putting on a mask without a get-up without my body. I used to think stupid shit like that.

Logan gandered out the window at tawny hills dotted with creeping bushes, clumps of coarse grass, squat trees stunted by the permanent water shortage. Not the saguaros, though. Some were just tall poles with budding bumps. Others were old, sagely, crowned by tangles of blunt tentacles reaching for sky.

"You like Credence?" Bruce pushed a tape into the cassette player. "Cassette player's the only thing in this van worth a shit."

Bruce reached into the glove compartment without taking his eyes off the road. The hair on the heavy forearm across Logan's lap looked brassy enough to scour away rust. Bruce shook out a cluster of sunglasses. He handed a pair to Logan. "Best of the bunch I think."

As round as John Lennon's, they sat crookedly across his nose, turned the day a few shades toward evening.

"If there's a smell in the room," Bruce said out of nowhere, "you stop noticing it after a while. Same with your eyes. If you hold your eyes still and what you're looking at is perfectly still, it disappears. That's how you meditate."

Hard to do it, though. Logan had tried. If it wasn't the flick of a thought, it was a twitch of an eye. Or he fell asleep.

"I don't like the disappearing act. It's not like I'm bored. It's just … there're lotsa places to go. When I'm older, maybe, I'll bring some of it back before autumn shakes the rest of the leaves from my head." He ran a palm over his smooth scalp and laughed, looking half-crazed with the cracked lens over one eye. "You ain't got much at the end a your life if you don't got a few stories to tell."

Bruce was a piece of driftwood with faith in the tide, no fear that whatever shore it left him on would be a place where he couldn't live with himself.

"Ever been to New York?"

Logan shook his head.

"Can't say you've seen America if you ain't been to the Big Apple. If you're a good boy, drink all your beer, and give a cigarette to a bum every now and then, that's where you go after you die. But don't wait till then." He laughed.

The van climbed steadily up the winding highway, up to clear-sky country, where the stars were so thick they looked like a bright trail through space.

By the time they made it to a national park, there was no ranger around to collect the $6 fee.

"Just the way I like it." Bruce grinned. "This is America an' I'm an American. I shouldn't have to pay six bucks to park on my own land."

Logan stepped out into cool air that smelled of cedar and pine, a hard-edged clarity to it.

Hunched over in the dark, they scrounged around for wood and got a small blaze going. Bruce pulled a package of hot dogs out of a cooler, and they fired them on a gritty black grill set over a cement-and-stone hearth.

Munching his hot dog, Bruce stared into the fire.

Logan listened to it crackle.

"When I was a kid, I never thought much about gettin' a job." Bruce prodded the fire, and it sent up a shower of sparks. "I used to think I could just go off into *the wilderness*—whatever that was. Yessir, live off the land. Set down somewheres and build me a cabin near a lake." He looked over at Logan. "Fucked up thing is I'm a grownup, and basically, I still think the same way."

Bruce's eyes were black caverns.

"Next best thing to livin' off the land is livin' off the water. Few more trips for shrimp down in the gulf and me an' a buddy'll have enough for our own boat. Thinkin' about a houseboat." He tossed Logan a can of beer that had broken out in a cold sweat. Bruce burped and patted his stomach. "Nothin' like sunrises and sunsets on the water. Pretty as hell."

Logan had seen his first ocean sunset with Sonny. The summer they'd worked construction together and Sonny had been pre-med at UCLA.

From the moment Logan had shown up unexpectedly, Sonny had surprised him into helpless silence. He'd answered the door drunk though it had been late afternoon, his eyes puffy, his waist gone flabby. Sonny pounded him on the back, asking where he'd been.

Logan stood that Sonny next to the one whose arms had guided a saw with the concentration of a praying mantis, had always kept the rest of them buoyed up with long stories he concocted to set up a joke. This other Sonny drank so much night after night he could barely speak. *Ahluvya Logan, know that? Like uh brother. Ahluvya like uh brother.* He'd quit school and was working construction full-time. He laughed and held up a finger like it was a war wound. The tip was missing. A diagonal cut so clean—through the nail, grazing bone—it looked intentional.

Logan thought about the album he'd put out with the band he'd joined in LA. An indie label. Oh, it'd been a stir among his friends back in Kansas. Wasn't the kind of music they listened to, but they bought it anyway. Some of them. No doubt his record had come to rest in an unremembered corner of the room, a once-in-a-while conversation piece. *Nice cover ain't it? I went to high school with him.* A few years from now, it would be a curiosity on a rickety card table, selling for 25 cents at a yard sale. Or left in an attic to warp in a parallelogram of sunlight.

Bruce, his crown a sea-smoothed stone in the firelight, stared off into the sky's ghostly white heart. "I hear they still got tribes along the Amazon never seen white men."

"Too bad there aren't more tribes like that."

Bruce stripped a peal of laughter off the darkness.

Morning was cold. Logan had gotten up first, his back stiff because his sleeping bag hadn't been much cushion for the hard ground.

Bruce had slept in the van. Climbing out, he jerked his thumb over a shoulder. "Let's get outa here before Ranger Rick decides to collect the rent."

Bruce drove to a breakfast place he knew in Flagstaff. The Gold Spoon. Its name written in gold letters on plate glass.

The Spoon was long and narrow, a mineshaft sunk into the raw sunrise. They sat near the front window, gold script casting a shadow on their table. On a shelf above the first booth was a white katsina doll with a saffron kilt, a snout and painted teeth.

Logan watched steam catch the sunlight as it curled off his coffee. He'd always been drawn to these evanescent shapes rising in slow twists—a soul letting go of the material world. Cal had caught him once. "What the hell you doin'? You never saw a spoon before?" Logan had lowered it back into his bowl of oatmeal.

After a couple cups of coffee, after letting the breakfast special settle, after Bruce had read yesterday's paper (filched from a garbage can), Bruce dropped him off on Interstate 40.

"Sure you don't wanna come out to the coast for a while? Circle back later?" Bruce smiled, jagged as the crack in his lens, and Logan was reminded not so much of a pirate as of a Viking.

"Nah. Gotta get to the rez."

See by then that's where all the answers were, the rez the mesas my holy of holies where I'd figure out what to do with half of me. all I had to do was get there never mind I didn't speak Hopi I'd missed the ceremonies I'd lived Anglo my whole life, I had the shortcut in my pocket

He missed Bruce as soon as his van pulled away.

Some college kids heading east on the interstate squeezed him into the back seat for a good 60 miles, but getting a lift on 87, a local highway, was a little trickier. He walked a couple miles north and watched car after car zoom past before a station wagon finally stopped for him.

The guy driving had a wife as quiet as a still life. Between the two of them, you would've thought God never said *Let there be conversation.* She looked out the window, a thinness to her as if she had to dig through trash cans for her meals. Straight hair, she sat with a two-by-four for a spine, turning her head now and then so that he glimpsed the long wedge of her nose. He caught little more of the driver than the back of his head (thinning hair, pink scalp). Most of the time, he watched the road.

The ride came to an abrupt end when the man realized he was going the wrong way and had to turn around. He left Logan among shriveled hills—eroded, gullied mounds of earth, really. Nothing growing on them. Oxidation had colored them in layers: off-whites, rusted reds, blue grays. A landscape more desolate than most of the other deserts he'd seen.

The silence was the kind he couldn't break with his voice. He tried. It was a neat trick the way the best howl he could manage got swallowed up. Just like that. The kind of silence that made you take notice of yourself, what you added to the world: a footstep, a breath, a thought. The land and its sterile colors sat calmly all around you, inhumanly old.

A lizard with yellow stripes and a pointed head was as good as a tv channel if it didn't dart under a rock. Even though, aside from its barely perceptible breathing, it might not move for an hour. If you weren't careful, you'd watch him for that long. It was then you discovered that the tiniest movement—the blink of a lizard's eye—was something miraculous. The smallest sound (the twittering of an unseen bird, a scrap of insect buzz). Proof that time still existed, that the world hadn't quietly ended.

It didn't surprise Logan that, living on the mesas, Hopis had the patience of stone. That sometimes they smiled like the week-long sprouting of a seed. They understood there was a strict pattern of life that sustained all other life, ensured that the seasons kept turning, rain kept falling, corn kept growing. Their faith was as ever-present, as evenly distributed as the sky.

Cars whispered past him every now and then. The drivers didn't even slow. Pricks.

Just as well. He got to like it out there. His senses sharpened. The breeze became noisy. If an insect moved, he heard its needle-thin legs disturb the sandy earth. His own footsteps became loud and clunky, not of the desert. He began to walk more softly. He began to wonder about fading. Like the smell in a room.

A college kid intent on mapping out Mormon cosmology while Logan stared out the window dropped him off in front of an old gas station: two pumps and a shack covered with peeling clapboard. Across the street was a small shopping center. A plaza for shopping instead of masked dancing, it looked out of place. Like the mesas in the distance wouldn't stand for it. Like it would be gone next week, swept away by a fierce wind.

"Hey, brother, how much will you give me for it?" An old Navajo slapped the fender of a beat-to-shit El Camino parked in the gas station's lot. He wore a cowboy hat as battered as the car. "Fifty dollars is all I'm askin'."

Logan looked over the El Camino. The wheel wells were ragged with rust. The muffler had lost a bracket, which had been replaced by a twisted-up clothes hanger. Under the hood the hoses were dried and webbed with fine cracks. The air-filter cover was missing, and the choke was propped open by a broken-off stub of pencil. Logan smiled; he'd used the same trick for hard starts. The leather seats were held together by duct tape, and the air-filter cover sat on the back seat.

"Been sittin' here for a month. No money for gas." The words came out as if the old Navajo had to contend with a clutch of small rocks in his mouth. "What good's a car that won't go?" Missing most of his teeth, he had a monstrosity of a tongue—so swollen he didn't seem able to get it to stay completely in his mouth. It hung out the way a dog's did, looked like a third lip while he wheezed through his mouth. Every now and then he'd pull it back in to wet it.

Logan knew that even if the old-timer had the money, he wouldn't spend it on gas. He knew he wasn't doing him anything like a favor, that he'd descended on that one-gas-station town with a bullwhip in his hand, that the money he pulled out of his pocket for the car hadn't been sent by heaven but gift-wrapped in the underworld. He was one of the Whipping Katsinas, missing his mask, who wasn't initiating a boy into the mysteries but teaching an old Navajo in a cowboy hat a lesson he should've learned by now.

Logan bought four gallons of gas—the Navajo had pulled a long-necked gas can out of the trunk—doused the carburetor, and put the rest in the tank. After a nasty coughing fit, black smoke blew out of the tail pipe and the engine turned over.

The bill of sale was a note written out by Logan.

"Thank you, brother, thank you." A curve to his `spine making him a little hunched, the old man walked hurriedly on short legs toward the shopping center.

After the money ran out, and gramps—he was *some*body's grandfather, wasn't he?—had sobered up, he'd sit on the curb, a bottle at his feet, wind whistling through them both.

Logan thought about laying aside the bullwhip, tearing up the bill of sale, and leaving the car at the station when he was done with his mesa tour. A little surprise for the old-timer. Or maybe that's what he told himself to make it easier to put the gas station and shopping center in the El Camino's rearview mirror.

The car's interior smelled of sun-aged leather and dust. The AC didn't work. He pulled the shifter on the steering column, put the car in gear, and pointed it north.

"Fifty bucks," he muttered, as a hot wind blew back his hair, "is about all he'd have gotten to junk it."

The pavement eventually gave way to a chewed-up dirt track that pummeled the car's suspension as it wound tortuously uphill. Surprisingly enough, the El Camino triumphed over its rutted adversary, and Logan's ass survived the spring-shot seat.

He parked outside Old Oraibi and got out. A cluster of flat-roofed shanties rumored to be the oldest continuously inhabited place on the continent. Now that he was on one of the mesas and not leafing through hazy childhood memories or daydreaming, he felt like a tourist. No, worse. A tourist wasn't supposed to have any connection to this place.

An old man glaring at him knew it. He had a square face, thick-lensed, horn-rimmed glasses, and he looked as if he wasn't sure quite where he was at any given moment, but he knew it. They looked at each other across a distance that had widened each year Logan had stayed away from the mesas. It may as well have been a stretch of black desert separating stars, a vacuum-bitten distance that a katsina found breathable, a man in a katsina mask found crossable, but this old man, sitting out on his stoop, squinting in the midday sun, didn't get up to bridge. He made no gesture of welcome, no offer of taking a stray back into the fold.

Logan was half-glad. He didn't want him poking around

in his past with his old man's walking stick, asking why he'd missed so many ceremonies, why he'd never bothered to learn a language formed by whatever had heaved these mesas out of the earth. Too late, too much of the cities in him. Too caught up in signing with a big label, writing a hit song, cutting a smash album. He saw it in the impenetrable face, in the dark eyes that, even behind their glass rectangles, saw farther than his. He was a blot on the light reflected by those lenses, like an ulcerous black spot on the Sun's skin. The downturned mouth, Logan could tell, had formed the names of things he'd never known existed.

He walked on, following a dirt road. Houses were one-story, rectangular boxes made of sandstone, cinderblock, sometimes brick. A few had earthen roofs. Others had wooden roofs patched a dozen times. Some had even been fitted with the thirsty black of solar panels.

He was the only one walking around. No children playing, no women walking by, no men talking. Somewhere, though, was the sound of scraping. A carver at work maybe. And somewhere—direction seemed a made-up thing, as hard to find as the side of a circle—a radio was playing Frampton's *Show me the Way*.

Don't touch anything a brochure he'd picked up warned, not a rock, not a castoff G.I. Joe's head, not that spent .410 shotgun shell lying in the dirt. From this it seemed the Anglos had gotten the idea that everything was sacred to the Hopi. Either that or it was like being in a blind woman's home, the position of every object necessary to her sense of her surroundings. And if you took something that the Hopi expected to be there—because they'd seen it there yesterday, the day before that and last year—it threw off their sense of balance.

That yellow shotgun shell, anchored by a brass bottom, might've been a clue to the bespectacled old Hopi, to his life atop a mesa poking up into a dusty sky filled with silence. His thick lenses had congealed out of technology too, but they'd taken on the quality of a mask—not that you couldn't see through them. Just that those glasses were as forever as a mask and would always find another nose to sit on, another pair of eyes to befriend.

Would the mesa always find another people? Maybe. But not a people whose prayers would spill down its sides like runoff, shape it like wind, raise it up to scrape against the swirly edge of a nebula. Chance and luck, disguised as the favor of the gods (rain an overflow of divine gratitude), held a place in the villages. Fear of extinction had kept the ceremonies pure, harsh equation though that entailed.

On his way back to the El Camino, Logan saw a long-haired Hopi, about his age, walking toward him in faded California shorts and a baseball cap. He smiled like an old friend.

"What's up?"

A greeting, not a question. Somehow he'd found a way to navigate the living ruins of Oraibi and the shop-lined streets of LA. *What's up* had come as naturally as a breeze; who would've guessed he was among those upholding Oraibi's claim to being inhabited?

Before Logan got back to the El Camino, he thought he heard the rhythmic squeaking of bedsprings. *Well I'll be.* Announcing it like that in that near-silence burned white at the edges, in the middle of the day. Life goes on in the dust, in the stillness, something older than instinct deciding where those G.I. Joe heads and .410 shotgun shells came to rest, a rhythm carrying things along. The mesa, the desert, the universe were never as still, never as empty as they might seem. And that drone radio astronomers picked up with their billion-dollar satellite dishes was just the distress of worn bedsprings. They'd spend years trying to decipher it, an inexplicable hum making static a permanent part of radio reception. A year or two younger than the tick-tock march of time, it was just life getting on with its business.

Outside the gift shop in Shongopavi, he picked up a free newspaper and read a story about a Navajo medicine man, a *hitali*, who'd seen the land when it'd been gouged by wagon ruts.

It was a beautiful gift.

The *hitali* had sung a medicine song for her and the reporter had written *It was a beautiful gift.* Had he done it for *her*? This song the old man had had in him since the afternoon his parents rolled on the dirt floor of their hogan and created a spitball of mud with breath at the center. *A gift.* What did she know about its beauty, ugliness, grace, magic, evil? What did she know about the place it had come out of? What did Logan?

Sliding across the lumpy seat of the El Camino, Logan turned the key and toyed with the accelerator till he got the engine to cough into a rough idle. Pulling out, he caught sight of a dirty yellow puppy on a hump of road. Eating the mangled remains of another puppy that must have come from the same litter. Likely to end up the same way.

There's a gift for you, Miss Reporter.

He drove along roads that climbed in sharp bends and switchbacks to First Mesa where hefound himself among the same flat houses. Mostly brick. One of them used to belong to his grandfather. He walked through the quiet streets, looking at bundles of corn hanging from eaves, trying to remember. Stovepipes poked out of the roofs. Crooked antennas might've been trained on distant galaxies. The rusted-out hulks of cars, stripped of parts, sat on blocks.

He walked slowly, half remembering. Bundles of firewood had been piled up for winter. Fenced-in junkyards were filled with old washing machines, broken pottery, chairs missing legs, boots without soles, obsolete refrigerators. He used to dig around in these heaps until dark. If he showed his mother what he'd found—a cracked watch that still ticked when he shook it, a silvery tube from a tv set—she'd make a face. *Oh you don't really want that do you*? He prospected anyway, deciding it was all around better to keep his finds hidden, a sly lump in his pocket on the long ride home.

An old woman with a mane of white hair sat on a stoop. The brown fingers that worked at braiding it had no stiffness in them as they went about their work. She could probably have greeted him with a grip firm enough to make him wince. Her eyes, glinting slits squeezed by soaring cheekbones, followed him as if he were another antenna come distant, good for an evening's diversion but not about to last as long as a properly baked clay bowl. Did her slash of a mouth know English? Did she have a son or a grandson? Did she want one? Who'd listen to all her stories of Way Back When?

In winter, snow whited everything over. The village smelled of smoke. Stacks of firewood dwindled, and women covered themselves with shawls and blankets when they came outside to the kilns. Hands smelled of corn and clay and split-open trees.

Looking out over the mesa, an eagle's eye view of the world, he imagined he knew what it was like to be untouchable, to be beyond the reach of rising food prices, ill-tempered uncle-stepfathers, failings as a son. He'd finally found the place the old Sonny had talked about, the one inside him that stretched from horizon to horizon. Where he'd stop hitching or driving or walking and stay a while.

Only it was temporary, a little euphoria brought on by the dying amber light the grand view maybe too the frybread and beans I had for lunch. I waited for night to take my two hits of mescaline, find out what I was missing, something I couldn't rub between my fingers roll on my tongue put into words something I was trying to chase down. a month or two later the slow unraveling I was going through finished up in the parking lot of the Smiling Aztec. I know you want to get at what happened on that trip well I remember my back against a big saguaro but there aren't any that far north I hallucinated it I'm beating around the saguaro I know but Old Man Night's beard was prickly enough to pierce my heart and the sky was gone but I still can't put my finger on what happened I still can't

14. Pills

"Come on, god *dammit*! You can't *do* that." Pete knotted the collar of his T-shirt in a fist.

Jack studied the chessboard, his eyebrows stuck together, his chin resting on a palm. "But a knight can move in an *L*."

Pete reached over the board and took back his pawn, a plastic stem with a knob on the end. "Yeah, but not *any* size *L*."

That was the trick, Logan thought, you had to know when you could move sideways, when it was okay to cut in a diagonal, when to leapfrog somebody.

"Have at you!" Mr. Spenser shouted over Jack's shoulder.

"Yeah, have at me." Pete put the knight back. "Just move somewhere else."

"Line up boys!" A tall attendant clapped his hands. "Time for medication! Pop y'pills and ease y'ills."

The nurse poked her head out of her office and pushed her glasses a little higher on her nose. "Medication is sufficient explanation, thank you, Carl."

"Yes, Ma'am." Carl grinned and clapped his hands again. "You heard Mrs. Wilson! Medication!"

Better than half the patients shuffled over to Mrs. Wilson and formed a scatter-shot line.

Carl pointed with a long, dark arm. "You too, Mr. Spenser."

Spenser was still staring at the chessboard, a senile god standing over the tiny clashing armies frozen in position. He'd forgotten, it seemed, how to set it all in motion again.

Carl took the old man's arm gently, but Mr. Spenser jerked away. "The bow is bent and drawn. Make from the shaft."

Carl looked like he wanted to grab his crotch and say, *Shaft this.* Instead he smiled gently. "Now what's that supposed to mean?"

"I'll put an arrow up your ass, that's what!"

Carl, a whole head taller, tugged on a spindly arm. "Come on now, Mr. Spenser ..."

"Moorish heathen! I don't want any!"

From behind, Carl steered Mr. Spenser by his narrow shoulders. "It'll make you feel better."

"Oh Humanity stinks to heaven!" Spenser's head was thrown back against Carl's chest. "The Lord shit and we are the likeness of His excrement!"

Logan didn't know whether the medication made them better, but it made them easier to deal with. It spread their thoughts out until there was enough empty space between them to put a simple thing like a daydream out of reach. Until a memory floated overhead, leaving them looking hopelessly up. They didn't have much to say anymore because putting together a sentence demanded the kind of effort that usually went into putting up an apartment building. By the time they'd traveled the distances and gathered the building materials, the need had disappeared. The sentence went unsaid and things began to scatter themselves again. Give them enough medication, they probably wouldn't even dream. A flat sleep, smooth as stone.

If Logan spoke Hopi instead of English, he'd have regarded the key-janglers from the loftiness of the mesas. They'd have looked at him as if he were a standing lamp or a coat rack. Staff would have no more expectations of him beyond the occasional nod or grunt.

Something in his back pocket poke his belt. He reached for it, and a square of paper whispered against denim.

Mouth scorched, breath smoke, you wind up picking through ashes for answers. Or stooping to superstition, trying to read cracks in blackened bone.

The paper curved to the roundness of a butt cheek and the ink blurred, it was a forget-me-not from a previous existence, the one in which the Burning Aztec had still been smiling. From his last mescaline trip, which had flash-burned a silhouette of him onto some desert rock. The trip Aristotle kept after like a hound on the trail of a fugitive who just wanted to be flushed into a catch basin of anonymity and forget why they wanted to lock him up.

Logan refolded the paper and tossed it on the floor for somebody's broom.

Jack, who'd once been stretched to his melting point by the gravity of his past lives (until his thimbleful of ego had been dumped into a skyful of stars), was staring at the chessboard. His eyes bulged as if he'd once seen a good friend rise from the dead and never been able to rid himself of the sight. He glanced up at Logan. "We think we're the ones makin' the moves but it's not us ..."

Pete sat back down.

Jack took the pawn he was after with a bishop instead of a knight.

Pete smiled and moved his queen. "Check."

Jack moved a rook.

"You can't DOOOO that!" Pete threw his head back, his fingers cramping into claws around his collar. "You're in check."

Mr. Spenser peered over Jack's shoulder. "Chocolate is good for trances."

"You lose the game if you don't move your fuckin' *king*." Pete put the rook back with one hand while his other latched onto his shirt collar as if he were strangling Jack through some kind of sympathetic magic. "It's the rules."

"The king rules!"

"Oh yeah ... right." Jack had a *silly me* smile on his face. "Check!"

"Make like a bowel and *move*," Mr. Spenser suggested.

Jack seemed suddenly confused. "My king?"

"Chocolate is good for trances."

"Your *king*."

"The king rules!"

Predictably, Pete's miniature black army crushed Jack's little white one.

"You're next, Tonto." Pete grinned at Logan and his small eyes nearly disappeared.

Logan lifted an eyebrow. "Won't be anything left a that shirt if you play me."

Jack stroked his chin, the salt-and-pepper stubble giving off an occasional glint as if some of the bristles were metal. "Let me try again. I'm startin' to remember."

"Have at thee!"

Pete looked down at the tortured collar of his shirt, his chin stabbing him in the chest. "One more game before I throw Tonto a beatin'."

Staring at Mr. Spenser, Jack began to finger his jumbo peace sign.

"Sir, do you bite your thumb at me?"

Jack's fingers let go of the sixties memento to ransack the pockets of his denim jacket for a cigarette.

"Do you bite your thumb at me, sir?"

A brown hand gripped Logan's shoulder, shook him slowly back and forth. A greeting. Paul was the only one who felt that neighborly toward him.

"What's up fellas?" Paul put a hand on Jack's shoulder. "If it ain't the psychedelic relic. Whaddya say Jack Be Quick? How 'bout some cards after Pete whups your ass all over the chessboard?"

About the same height as Logan, Paul had an afro that made him look a little taller.

"I don't like cards that much." Graying hair tied with a beaded headband, Jack kept his eyes on the chessboard while his fingers roamed pockets that had just come up empty.

"C'mon, man. I even got a special deck—one two-eyed jack, two one-eyed jacks, and one pop-eyed Jack."

Jack was about to be checkmated again.

"That's game." Pete pushed back his chair and stood up. "I'll getch you later, Blackfeather."

"Can't wait."

"You sure you don't wanna play cards, Jack? You ain't no good at chess."

Jack seemed lost in a metaphysical quandary. Instead of answering Paul, he creased his brow and concentrated harder on the chessboard.

"Look at this dude." Paul tipped his head toward Jack, but his eyes were on Logan. "Boheme to the extreme. A lean, mean, dope-smokin' machine."

Jack patted his pockets absentmindedly.

"Jack be nimble, Jack be quick, Jack's gonna bum another cancer stick."

"But I'm out. I swear."

"You believe that shit, Blackfeather?" Paul winked at Logan. "Let's just check the threads ..." He dipped a hand in Jack's pocket and came up with a cigarette.

It'd been in Paul's hand, Logan noticed, before it had gotten to Jack's pocket.

"What kinda shit you tryin' to pull, Popeye?" He put the cigarette under Jack's nose.

"Nothin' man, I swear, I didn't know I had it ..."

"Aw take the shit and quit your goddamn whinin'."

Paul leaned closer to Logan and overdid a southern accent. "Ain't never picked no cotton, but I sho can pick pockets." Pulling up his sleeve, he modeled an expensive-looking watch. "Like it?"

"Whose is it?"

Paul laughed. "Dr. Harry's. Peckerwood still ain't figured out where it got to." Paul turned it a couple of times. "I'm a clepto-fuckin-maniac. Can't help myself."

"Seems like you help yourself all the time—mostly to everybody else's shit."

"You quick, Blackfeather, you quick. Right on too. What's mine is mine and what's yours is mine."

Logan liked Paul's straight-out way of doing things, liked to see what he could get away with. He hassled other patients because the truth was they needed hassling. After a while you got used to your regular meals in a cafeteria where the mess you made was confined to a tray you could leave on the table. You got used to being handed the state pittance so you could buy your smokes, a few slices of pizza, a six-pack of soda. To seeing a movie Friday night when they set up a little screen in the gym. With the days scheduled, the week planned out for them, nothing scared some of these guys more than the thought of *outside*. As unreal a place after a while as Middle Earth.

"Uh-oh."

Paul grabbed Logan by the backs of his arms, his long fingers, cable-like. He Peeked from behind Logan, his head about even with the other man's shoulder. His woolly hair gave off a musky odor.

"I think Bible Mike's headin' right up our alley."

Like crosshairs added to his field of vision, the name fixed Logan's eyes on a patient wearing a stained University of Michigan sweatshirt and a wooden cross as big as Jack's peace sign. Mikey's pants had a habit of sliding down because even though he had a little pot he had no ass. He was taking baby steps toward them as if a more forceful stride would scare them off.

"I am the resurrection and the *life*!" A goofy smile on his aging college-student's face, Mikey lifted a hand in absolution.

Paul pushed away from Logan and, tilting his head, cocked an eyebrow at Mikey. "If you the Second Comin', I got to be goin'."

Although Paul had let go of Logan's arms, a shallow depression, like a footprint disappearing in creeping mud, had been squeezed into the nerve endings.

Bible Mike waved goodbye, that silly smile still on his strangely aged face (he had to be in his mid-forties). "Go, brother. Go do your appointed homework." His yellow smoker's teeth were tiny and straight, as if a doll-maker had put them in.

He turned to Logan. "Welcome to Upstate University." (Logan might as well have been visiting for the first time.) "To our temple of learning." Mikey spread his arms and panned his gaze to take in the room. *"Everything a man does is for his mouth, but still his soul is not satisfied."* His voice falling, he cited his source for Logan's benefit: "Ecclesiastes."

Back home, Jim Lee, a Bible-quoter himself, might've had a nice sit-down with Mikey.

Except there was a hollowness around Mikey's eyes and dark smudges underneath them. As if huge hands had grabbed him by the head and the thumbs had pressed the eyes deeper into his skull, leaving ashy imprints behind. Making his open-mouthed smile a little disconcerting.

"It's almost here," Mikey said conspiratorially.

"What's almost here?"

"The Resurrection."

"Easter?"

"You can't keep a good man down." Impressed by his own wit, he showed those neatly aligned little teeth again.

"Still a couple months to go."

"Yes, but it's closer than Christmas."

Mikey walked halls that reeked of musty books. When he sat down with pen and paper, it was a time-consuming affair. The guardian of the hospital's vaults of knowledge, he wrote letters home in careful ornate script as if the words would carry farther with their forms perfected. He used a calligraphy pen that he kept in a lacquered black case and dipped in an inkwell. Took him half an hour to write *Dear Mom, how are you?* But there was no shortage of time. Scratching paper with his fancy pen, he could use up most of a day.

Maybe more patients needed this lesson in concentration, this innocuous obsession that made it easy to ignore the setting of another season, the procession of minutes that passed so unbearably slowly you could hear it. That's why they left the tv and the radio on—to distract themselves from the hum. Older than any of the gods blown up and let go like balloons to colonize the firmament, the same hum would watch the last of them, deflated and downwardly adrift, land in a lump of gray daylight dense as glass, preside over chess games in which the demoted deity couldn't move a pawn. Faintly, almost below the threshold of hearing, the drone would still be there, the inevitable thrum toward which everything was sinking as slowly as a continent dissolved. Or a will faded beyond color, a shade of transparent you could walk through, vaguely aware that something less substantial than a spider's web once had been there.

"He's *coming*." Mikey's voice had taken on a sudden urgency. "He'll come for the spring semester. But only if this place gets its standards up. Ivy League! We have to make it Ivy League before He gets here!"

Vacillating between reclusive scribbling and rah-rah recruiting, Mikey was a child's robot banging from one wall to the other and back again. Already he'd moved on to the pool table, informing the players he was the resurrection and the life—qualifications enough to pick up one of the balls. "They look like Easter eggs, don't they? Only more round."

"If you don't put it back, your head's gonna be flat." Pete pulled the ball out of Mikey's hand.

Logan looked up at the clock. Dragging ass like it was hauling a lead cross, humming the whole way. It would drone on when the earth had spun down to dust, would watch the dust dance again into a new world. Ceaseless, it had never begun. It could not be bargained with, was only what it was, could only be, now and again, ignored.

He still had almost two hours till he'd see Aristotle.

133

15. Ghost Hitcher

A long straight road, a paved rut through cornfields. The corn as thick as dark as old-growth forest. No street lamps, just the car's high beams and a moon to see by. No rush either, doing 30, maybe 35 miles an hour.

Up the road a ways a shadow detaches itself from the corn, a shade of a man, a look to him as though he's been drifting around for years, stained with the rainwater that washed him over the fields, grayed by prairie winds blowing him in from somewhere distant, his hat the kind a farmer might put on a scarecrow.

A sickle of ice skewers soft organs, a cold rib growing through his vitals, a frozen horn. He knows whatever he does he shouldn't stop the car to pick up this scarecrow of a man (who knows what cross he came down off of?). He needs to speed up so the wind of the car roaring past makes him hang onto his hat. Run him off the road, run him over if need be, let him go tumbling over the hood and bounce off the windshield—anything but slow down. Only he can't stop his foot from pressing on the brake.

The car stops just shy of where the hitcher is standing, casual as waiting for the bus.

A fist of ice squeezes his heart. He doesn't know how it keeps its rhythm how it can bear the hitcher's head hovering in the passenger window how it keeps beating through the icy fist why it doesn't stop cold at the sight of the gray skin, the eyes bright in the moon-smeared dark, the face cuneiformed with tattoos. He can't move. His chest frozen solid he can't lean over and lock the door. He watches as the door opens, drawing a rush of wind through the car drawing fear out of his mouth like an arctic breeze.

"That's it, that's when I woke up." A horde of invisible, weightless spiders crawled up his spine, poured out from under his shirt collar.

He and Aristotle were sitting on a bench, its slats painted over so many times the wood underneath was a dim memory. The other patients were mostly sprawled on the lawn, squinting in the sunlight.

Aristotle, who'd scribbled a padful while Logan was talking about his dream, looked up. "Any idea why you were so afraid?"

Logan shook his head. Underneath the padded vinyl jacket and his flannel shirt, he felt a drop of perspiration slip down his armpit and lost track of it somewhere past the bump of a rib.

Aristotle leaned back against the hard wooden slats of the bench. "What else can you tell me about the hitchhiker?" The eraser of the pencil found its way into Aristotle's chin right about where he had a shallow cleft.

"He seemed old, but he didn't look it. No wrinkles on his face, just those tattoos." He studied Aristotle's face for a moment, saw only a life-like bust—*Study in Patience* would've been a good title—the whole head balanced on that pencil. "It was, you know, just a feeling."

"You didn't recognize this man at all?" The eraser of the pencil started tapping gently against his chin.

Logan shook his head. The markings on the hitcher's face were like no tattoos he'd ever seen, his skin the gray of rain-washed slate, his eyes somehow visible in the dark, as if they held pale fragments of moon.

"Well, let me ask you ... do you know anyone who hitchhikes?"

"*Besides me.*"

"And you said this was a farm road. What do you associate with farms?"

"Kansas."

"How many hitchhikers do you know from Kansas?"

Logan smiled. "One."

Aristotle nodded. "What can you tell me about the markings on the hitchhiker's face?"

A gray doppelganger blown through an unlit labyrinth by a chill ghostwind. On his face, a map of the soul's wanderings.

"They weren't anything I recognized, I just know they were … somehow they were important."

"Then it's safe to say that there was literally hidden meaning in your dream, something either that you've been looking for or perhaps have been overlooking in your waking state."

"What do you mean?"

"Dreams are complementary to what goes on when you're awake. You probably know Freud thought that one of the primary functions of a dream was to protect sleep. I think something like the reverse is also true—we dream to preserve consciousness. Dreams channel off excess mental energy, which sometimes appears as simple wish fulfillment, and as I said, they're complementary. If you think too highly of yourself or you're striving for unrealistic goals, you may have dreams of falling from a great height. That's a dream making up for poor judgment while you're awake."

A cold breeze set the branches of a nearby tree waving.

"So what've I been overlooking?"

Aristotle shrugged. "Could be any of a number of things. If you're too confident in what you think you know about yourself, the dream may be reminding you that there's still unmapped territory. It could be telling you that there's a part of yourself that's frightening not only to others, but to you too if, as in the dream, you could see it."

Having been made of things older than cities or language, having been designed by an indifferent wisdom innate to whatever pushed us to evolve in the first place, we were strangers to ourselves. Which meant that if he was carrying inside him a homunculus with his own face, its gray skin stitched with indecipherable tattoos, it was nothing out of the ordinary.

"A part of myself I'm not willing to admit is there?"

Aristotle uncrossed his legs. "An aspect of yourself that you don't want to acknowledge *is* part of you. But the fact that you couldn't stop the door from opening seems to me the dream's way of telling you that you can't completely shut this aspect of yourself out."

He nodded. But what was he supposed to do knowing that a cellar—its ill-fitting stones hardly different from the wet earth they held back—had been scooped out underneath the floor he was standing on? A whole cavern maybe. As old as the field of corn the hitcher had come out of. That night at the Burning Aztec, had it been the gray-skinned wanderer who'd held the knife?

Logan could see from the way the eraser was pushed into Aristotle's chin that he wanted to say something else. He wanted to tell him they were going to have to stave in a door or two, poke their heads into that damp, rooty cellar, flick a lighter.

Some of the territory would be forever unmapped.

16. Turned It All Back

"Hi. Mind if I sit down?"

She stood in front of him, blue-eyed and blue-jeaned, strands of sandy hair dancing on a puff of wind around her head. Pretty in a rough way, she held a notebook in one hand.

"Sure." He slid over on the bench. The breeze carried the smell of mud and dead grass, sap oozing from winter-split pines, shampooed hair.

She leaned toward him. "What I really need …" An expression of anxiety wavered on her face, a candle about to go out. "What I really need is to find out what today is."

"You mean … the date?"

She nodded.

He didn't know either. One of those things he'd gradually lost track of as the days and weeks slushed together. He made a gesture of helplessness with his hands (the novel he held turned up like a wing flap to slow acceleration that wasn't there).

"It doesn't matter." Her voice was perky. "It's not the real one anyway. They turned it all back." She blinked. So hard that it wasn't a blink but a twitch.

His face must have shown his confusion.

"They had to." Her forehead creased. "If they didn't, that would mean I'm only 24. That can't be right. So much has happened in my life." She blinked again, jerking her head back as if something had splashed in her face. She bent down and twirled grass around her fingers, tugged until a few blades softly snapped. She stopped twirling and sat up again. "If they didn't turn everything back ... then I'm only 24." Her gaze fell to her feet.

Her puffy white high-tops with their powder-blue laces reminded him of baby shoes.

"What happened to your hand?" she asked.

Pale scratches—scars—laced the knuckles. Two had come from teeth. Some from a glass door when he was seven. Others from a wire-reinforced window—why the hell hadn't he *kicked* it?—in the city hospital.

"Hey, would you do something for me?" She snatched up her notebook and handed it to him. Bluebells or something wallpapering the cover, it had a little strap with a buckle and a lock. "I have a hundred of them now, but they don't let me keep them here. They're in a secret place because once, once my father threw them out. He said there wasn't any room for them. But if history wasn't written down, it would be just like it never happened, wouldn't it? We'd never know." She giggled. "Isn't that funny?"

His weak smile felt like something tearing.

"Here ..." She pulled a pen from a back pocket. "Write your name and the date. I mean, just February whatever, you know? Not the year, it's not the real one anyway. And say *Today I met Linda O. Feehly*—my middle name's Olivia—and whatever else you want to write."

On a warm February day, I met Linda O.— "How do you spell your last name?" *Feehly. She's the friendliest person I've met here. I hope I see her again soon.*

"Make sure you sign it." She was leaning over, watching him write. "That way people will know I didn't make it up."

He closed the diary and handed it back to her along with the pen.

She smiled as she took it, the corners of her eyes crinkling up.

"Hey man …" Jack had two fingers in a pocket, hoping to scissor a cigarette that probably wasn't there. "What's goin' on?"

Linda's smile disappeared as if someone had ironed it away.

Jack's smile showed yellow teeth, the spaces between them caulked with something yellower.

"Man, I didn't know you could sing like that."

Jack had been saying this every day since the night Billings had come into the dormitory looking for a boombox.

"It wasn't me, Jack."

"I'm Linda." Linda seemed more relaxed now.

"How ya doin'?" Standing in front of them with the beginnings of a beard and his long hair, he looked like a nervous Christ. The front of his denim jacket had been decorated like a soldier's uniform but with buttons and patches instead of medals, a collage of pin-on or sew-on collectibles from a couple of decades back. For some reason, the denim showing through the flak embedded in it looked like blue smoke, vaguely in motion, without anything as definite as a stitch or fiber pattern. "You got a cigarette?"

Linda shook her head. "I don't smoke."

Jack's fingers were running up and down a chain that ended in his hood ornament of a peace sign. "I know this is America, and everyone has the right to be an asshole and all, but too many guys in Seven are exercising their right. That's why I came outside."

Linda lifted her arms over her head and stretched.

Logan looked away. With her tics and non-sequiturs, with her confusion about the year of Our Lord and her age, with that smell of hers and the soft swellings under her shirt, Linda made a spreading puddle of warmth in his groin. Instinct didn't disappear in the hospital, it just slept less, burrowed underground. An arched back roused it. An open mouth. Shampooed hair.

"Bad karma," Jack muttered, his gaze still fixed on Seven. He turned to Linda. "We should stop eating meat too."

But they'd made it too easy. Nowadays you didn't need to look a chicken in the eye. You didn't say a prayer as you lifted up rows of skinned thighs strapped down with cellophane to a little Styrofoam tray. You weren't the one who had to clear out coils of intestines with their swampy reek, the brown bump of liver—slippery between your thumb and forefinger—the tiny pyramid of the heart, the limp sacks of the lungs. Unless you were Cal. Unless someone like Cal forced you to.

He let them do the talking. Especially Jack, who had stories from the days he was crisscrossing the country in a van full of flower children.

Logan wasn't with Jack in his van. He was on First Mesa. A ghost town almost it was so quiet. A little wind piled dust and sand up against the sides of flat-roofed houses with bundles of peppers and corn hanging from the eaves. He could barely hear them anymore. Jack's voice, Linda's voice were swept up, carried away, and became the wind.

17. Aristotle's Box

Aristotle was sitting beside him on a bench, and for once he was talking without jabbing, pressing, or hitting himself with the eraser-end of his pencil. Probably because the session was pretty much over, the hard thinking done. Now came the half-time pep talk, Aristotle telling him how even the director had noticed his improvement.

Maybe because he tucked in his shirt nowadays, kept his hair brushed or tied up, a gold star had shown up next to his name. Maybe they wrote in his file that he smiled more often. (That was tricky: You smile and you haven't brushed your teeth in a while, might lose a star.) A couple of stars for not beating up on the hired help lately. Shaved regularly—half a star.

Pushing off his knees, Aristotle stood up. "Be right back."

Never a suit or a tie, Aris wore a jacket once in a while but with jeans so he could slip out of formality with a shrug. Hiking boots for winter mud, a belt that held up his pants—not a sagging gut—he looked like you could rely on him to lead you through a mountain pass or chop wood if the hospital were snowed in. You could put faith in Aris. You could hang onto his hand and trust it to haul you in from the window you'd planned to leap out of.

Dropping the truck's tailgate with a metal squeal, Aris pulled a box out of the bed, waddled back with it like he was pregnant with a calf. The box landed with a solid *whump* on the bench. "Wooh. Heavier than I remembered."

Logan stared at the box as if it were unearthed treasure.

"You're always complaining you don't have anything to read, so I hit a library sale."

"Can't beat that at Sears."

"Just try to be discreet about where you got these. I don't want other patients to feel shortchanged by their therapists."

Nodding, Logan pulled back a flap and looked down cautiously as if a book might rise up and go flapping all over the grounds. A thin paperback called *Rat Man of Paris* lay on top.

"One other thing ... I don't think you should be out of therapy, whether or not you're out of the hospital, until we've gone back to that last acid trip of yours."

Logan rubbed his chin. "Mesc."

"Sorry, mescaline. The point is, unless we retrace what happened that night, I think we'll be leaving something in there that might show up again one day."

Logan pursed his lips, nodded absently. The last thing he wanted to do go back to that night in the desert. Better to leave it buried. Send flowers if Aristotle insisted he mark the occasion.

Aristotle took a deep breath. "All right then ..."

They shook hands.

"Remember ..." Aristotle started walking toward the cottage, a blue binder under an arm. "We're getting there."

A student of the *psykhe*, Aristotle had the oversized intellect of his famous namesake, was going to read Logan's soul as if it were a relief map and he were blind. A laying on of hands. A translation of the bumps, depressions, protuberances, gullies. Maybe his pad wasn't just for scribbling. Maybe the mind was like a gravestone, and by holding a pale blue sheet of lined paper up to it, Aris could get a murky rubbing with a lead pencil.

Sometimes all Logan cared about was Aris's smile. Invited

your Sisyphean tendencies to lay aside their boulder, unburden themselves like an overworked donkey. A smile that was a smack on the rump to send you running off to frolic in a sunny glade, enjoy the coolness of your sweat-soaked hide, munch sweet grass, swish away bees that had mistaken the brown pucker under your tail for a flower—no sense of smell, some bees—toss your mane in the breeze.

Aristotle came back out of the cottage, put the tailgate of his truck up with a solid k-*chunk,* and waved before driving off.

Logan pulled back the flaps on the box again and glanced inside. The hairs on the back of his neck stiffened. It wasn't the comic-book cover showing a spaceship dwarfed by a demon as grand as a nebula; it wasn't the brightness filling the eye sockets as though stars peered out of them; it wasn't the ominous title—*The Number of the Beast* was just a science fiction novel. It was the fact that it'd turned up like a Tarot card in Jim Lee's farmhouse kitchen. Cal was the Beast, the Brutus to his father's Caesar (if reality could be interpreted like a text), but how could Cal have arranged for a drunk kid to run a stop light—Logan knew it was the kid's fault—and kill his father? Not to mention killing himself in the process? The more he thought about it, the more certain he was Cal had figured a way, but the *how* of it remained tucked away, a grub curled inside a log.

18. Night Visit

From the row of beds lined up along the south wall came Mr. Spenser's open-mouthed wheeze. Straight across from Logan, Paul ground his teeth (like a metal joint that needed to be oiled). Pete, not far from Paul, might've been the source of a faint trickle, his bladder emptying itself like a poorly knotted water balloon (happened twice last week). Three beds over from where Logan slept, there was urgent mumbling that sometimes collapsed into soft moaning—Bible Mike sweating through a vision of an angel. Not one of those chubby-faced cherubim Raphael painted, but the kind who, when Muhammad asked to be able to look upon him, burned away the horizon with his aspect and sent the blinded prophet reeling into bright oblivion.

Tonight, there was no moon beyond the Cartesian windows, only the oblique glare of an outside light and the leaden glow of the bulbs over the doors. Logan lay on his side, eyes unfocused, his thoughts as featureless as egg-shaped stones in a stream bed. He'd been woken by a tingling in his scalp and in the pit of his stomach an uneasy feeling as if he'd swallowed something still squirming. Fear surfaced on his skin as gooseflesh and made the hair on the back of his neck rise. He sat up, tried to sharpen his vision on a whetstone of feeble light.

Someone was walking toward him.

He sensed something familiar about the silhouette moving silently down the bed-lined aisle. About the set of the shoulders, the walk that treated the air almost as if it needed to be plowed through. Or as if it would have taken something as dense as lead to stop him.

Logan's father sat down at the foot of the bed, the mattress sinking under his weight. He wore a sleeveless-shirt as he had around the house, especially Sunday mornings when he sat in the kitchen reading the paper. Logan remembered the expanse of his back, the shoulders bent forward over the table.

His father held a tire iron in one hand as if he'd just changed a flat. Four arms for the four seasons, the four directions, four different lug sizes. A piece of leather secured four long feathers, all of them blue, to the wrist of his other arm.

"You—" Logan's voice broke off. He swallowed to grease the machinery of his throat. "You came to visit?"

His father nodded. There was a hint of a smile on his broad face.

Logan remembered being shaken awake in the middle of the night, his mother's eyes and nose red from crying, remembered her telling him in a shaky voice his father had been in an accident.

"You can't be here now, you're dead." He said it hoping to be contradicted, hoping some miracle had occurred.

This didn't seem to affect his father anymore than the accident Logan thought had killed him.

"Where've you been all this time? Why did you leave us with Uncle Cal?"

His father didn't seem to be ... breathing?

"I'm glad he died," Logan said. He wanted his father to agree with him. He wanted to hear his father say his name. Or call him by the nickname they'd used for each other ever since Logan, a whining four-year-old, had insisted on being his father's best friend. *Okay, Buddy.* Logan's feet had flown suddenly up as his father hefted him. *You're the best.*

He wanted his father to lock his mason's arms around him, tell him that he was forgiven. For failing his mother—his father's wife—every time Cal had taken that plank of a hand to her. For having lost contact with her, given up on her as if she were the one who'd failed him (but hadn't she?). For abandoning music like a mineshaft without another hunk of coal to be dug out of it. For forgetting the old ways as though there were no cloud-topped mesa inside of him. For taking out that blade in Arizona.

"Buddy?" He leaned forward, but his father pulled back. This hurt him more than his father's silence, left a tightness in his throat that he had to loosen before he spoke. "Why don't you say something?"

His father stood up.

He wasn't forgiven.

Each of Logan's stomach muscles became a dense lump in a body shrinking around it. His lungs squeezed, but the opening in his throat was so small he could only hiss. "You're leaving again?" No one could have heard that.

His father—why was he walking away? His father was wearing a kilt hung with a horse tail. The tail was dotted with white as if it'd been repeatedly poked by a finger that had leached color on contact. Below the kilt he was bare, but white dots ran in rows up his legs. The tire iron was gone.

Logan slid out of bed to follow his father, but his scalp went electric, the hair rose off his scalp, and he couldn't move.

When his father looked back, he saw that his face was covered with strange markings. He knew then that it wasn't his father, that he shouldn't follow him. The heavy-boned face was etched with an elaborate maze of swirls and dots that turned his features into shadows cast by natural formations. One eye glimmered with a mottled full moon, pale-burning and silvery. The other iris was a crescent moon—maybe what lit the underworld he'd come from. A bit of rock that carried dead light beneath the surface. The two moon eyes, out of phase, flashed at the foot of Mikey's bed. Mikey whined in his sleep, twitched at the presence near the foot poking out from under the sheet.

Logan was the only one awake.

He listened.

Paul's teeth-grinding. Jack's dull snore, Mr. Spenser's wheeze. Blending with the uneven chorus of drawn and expelled breaths.

"You're not here, are you?" As if he the air might answer. He wiped at a warm tickle on his cheek. It hadn't even been a real ghost.

19. The Commandments

Logan didn't know why he didn't tell Aristotle about his moon-eyed father. Might be he didn't want the dream dissected like a cadaver. Might be his father wouldn't come back if he and Aristotle appointed a meaning to it. It was the first time he'd dreamed about his father in a while. And never as a ghost. It'd always been the fantasy that he was still alive, that they could be more or less eye-level when they talked—though his father still had him by a couple inches—that for once Logan could grip his hand as though they simply hadn't seen each other in a long time, and even though he couldn't match his father's mason's grip, even though he didn't have his father's bulk, his father understood, through bone and ligament and muscle and old scars, his father understood he wasn't a boy anymore.

The room Logan was in, not much more than a walk-in cinderblock closet adjacent to the rec room, used to be for staff meetings. He picked up a guitar in the hand-me-down room. No television, no boombox, no voices to compete with. Everyone was outside, like a plant uncurling new leaves to the Sun.

Tightening a key, he plucked a string, turned it into a blurry quiver. He listened to the steadily diminishing note, wondered whether the sound had faded from hearing a second or two before he actually stopped hearing it.

He improvised a riff and liked the way the air thrummed. Maybe instead of all those tests they were going to put him through before they let him out, he could play them a song.

Doubtful.

It was all outlined in blue marker on a sheet of oversized paper taped to a wall:

GOALS:

Client will not hallucinate. This includes loud discussions with himself.

Client will keep up his appearance. This includes dressing neatly in fresh clothes, showering and shaving regularly, keeping nails trimmed, hair brushed.

Client will manage his own money in a responsible manner.

Client will cooperate with staff and participate in programming.

Client will get along with other patients.

Thou shalt not hallucinate was his favorite. Some of the patients had gotten pretty crafty. What visions danced before their eyes staff couldn't be sure because although Mitch or Mikey might be mouthing a frantic soliloquy, they'd turned the volume all the way down, and the key-janglers would have to hire a lip-reader to decipher the delusion. (The dancing goes underground.)

Pulling the guitar along by the neck—a frazzle of extra lengths of string going off every which way—he yanked the cottage door open and got through before its own weight closed it.

The Hopi translation for March was something like Moon of Whispering Breezes. Couldn't spell it in Hopi, much less pronounce it, had never felt it on the mesa, not that he could remember, it was just something he'd heard. Might as well rename March Moon of Making Music.

He saw Linda lying on her side, pulling up grass. Paul was standing over her, an unbuttoned denim jacket beginning to levitate in the breeze.

Logan stopped in front of a glint in the grass. Stooping, he picked up a credit-card fragment. Nothing left but a corner holding the iridescent hologram of an eagle taking flight. For all he knew chewed up by that skunk they'd smelled one night.

Linda looked up, one eye squinted closed against the sun, her face lopsided and crinkled. "You got no manners, Paul."

"Etiquette is my special-tee." Paul made an elaborate bow and affected an upper class accent. "At the moment, howsoever, I shall be a study in hiss-toe-ree. Later, baby."

Turning, he bumped into Logan. Their eyes clicked into place for a second because they were about the same height.

"Lawd have muhsee on my black soul!" Paul took a step back with a hand splayed on his chest. "Speak of the Devil …" Paul's Southern accent faded. "And the grinnin' motherfucka shows up." He shook Logan's tied-up hair. "Tail and all." He stepped around Logan. "Seein' how I'm in the manic phase of my illness, I'm just gonna rise above this losin' proposition …" He wagged a finger as he walked away. "And you best stay off my cloud."

Linda squinted up at Logan. "He calls you Crazy Horse."

"He's all right."

"I guess. Sometimes." She waved a hand toward the southern end of the grounds. "You know there's a brook over there?"

"A brook?"

A breeze lifted sandy hair across the bridge of her nose. "Yeah, way down there. I always think about taking a walk in it. You know, with no shoes or socks. And my pants rolled up."

"Be awful cold."

"But wouldn't it feel good?"

"I s'pose."

"Are you going to play that?" She lifted her chin at the guitar.

"Gonna give it a try." He sat down, the guitar across his legs. "Got a pick right here." He held up the plastic fragment etched with the multi-hued ghost of an eagle.

Linda sat up and crossed her legs as if she were going to meditate. "It'll be like we're in Central Park."

Logan noticed that the zipper in her jeans, beneath a silver button, was open maybe an inch.

She closed her eyes and the blue disappeared from her face. "Wouldn't it be great if we were? You know, like a free concert or something?"

Probably listening too much to the Psychedelic Relic, who was always talking about *how cool it was, man*. The Age of Aquarius. When they believed that by gathering with one purpose and singing in a collective voice they could bend the ear of Universal Mind. That by mouthing a mantra they could bring on global peace as if it were a simple thing, like rain. That holding hands had something to do with brother- and sisterhood. The good old days when talking reasonably and listening thoughtfully could divert the course of events and induce guns to point harmlessly skyward. When they believed.

"Oh I know this song."

She started to sing, her voice rising and falling depending on whether or not she knew the words, crumbling into a mumble to keep the rhythm when she didn't. He almost laughed. Not because of the way she was demolishing the lyrics but because she was giggling at her mistakes. Maybe he wasn't going to help peasants in El Salvador, but someone had extended him a little credit between his thumb and two fingers, and he was glad he'd taken it.

Now you take it because I'm feelin good today and the miracle of these strings is I can take this nothin inside me this nothin-you-can-put-a-finger-to even if you put your hand to my ribs all you'll get is that bloodpump you won't know what's keepin it goin you gotta listen for that you gotta listen to what my fingers are up to with this piece of shiny plastic. you want to feel my pain I can give it to you if you want but you don't have to keep it, you can just watch it go along some evening street you've walked same as me, maybe send along some of your own pain, keep it company watch them go down the block forget which corner they turned because this is as fine a day as any since the Mahu led the way to the just-created world. isn't paradise, no brick walls in paradise, but it's one up on bein a groundhog, it's two up on bein a telephone pole. the music isn't even mine but now it's hers it's yours anyone can get in on it take it while you can who knows when we're gonna have a day like this again a blue-eyed woman singing next to me again when we're going to be alive again.

20. Mr. Spenser's Macbeth

The coffeemaker, flecked with dried coffee, was topped by a lopsided heap of filters. He wondered why Aristotle didn't clean up some, at least straighten the filters. Instead, he just lifted the clear carafe by its plastic handle and drained off the last of it.

Aris swirled what he had in his cup. "Kind of muddy. But that's closer to what we Greeks drink anyway."

Logan figured it out: if Aris wiped down and tidied up, the other doctors would think they could just go on slopping things up and a little *deus ex coffee machina* would intervene. It was his silent way of saying *clean your own mess*.

Rainy out today. A leafy branch shook against the window. Logan recalled a city half-obliterated by night and drifting mist, fog falling like smoke from a burning sky.

Today Logan had something to talk about. *Today he'd remind him—*

Aris was busy writing something on his pad, busy having his little cup of warm-me-up.

"—about what happened in New York. With the cop."

Neon, scattered and smeared, like the glow of deep-sea fishes. Streetlamps illuminating damp fallout. Buildings and shop windows and streets too slick for light to stick.

"They think—you think—it's something … something like with Jack. I know about Jack. They leave those blue binders out sometimes. Drug-induced psychosis. They think I'm the same, don't they? They think it's just one bad trip too many."

"Why do *you* think you're here?" Aristotle put the eraser of his pencil into the dimple in his chin as if he'd been born with it to rest pencils and thoughts there.

Logan's scalp felt too tight for his skull. He reached for the band tying his hair back and loosened it by a loop. He wasn't about to admit to anything that would add time to his sentence. He shook his head.

The window offered no sky, just some gray backlighting. A sudden gust of wind made leaves flutter, showered the window with drops. A single leaf stuck to the window.

Logan's forearms were on his thighs, his fingers meshed together except the thumbs, which pressed futilely against one another. "Take a guy like Jack—"

"The old hippie?"

"Yeah. They can keep him in here for … I don't know … because he sees the sidewalk breathing, right?" Logan had slipped in what *he'd* seen at 3:33 a.m., coming down from a coke high in Kansas.

"Mental illness is a lot more than a predisposition to what may or may not be hallucinating. Identical symptoms can have entirely different causes."

Logan's scalp tingled. "Glad to hear that." If the room were to fall suddenly into darkness, he wondered whether Aris would see the blue sparks dancing around his head.

"There was, for example, a behaviorist who trained one of his patients to walk around with a broomstick by rewarding her with ice cream whenever she did. Then he called in some psychoanalysts to observe her. Predictably, they saw the broomstick as a phallic symbol."

Aris shrugged under his fisherman's sweater. "Sometimes a cigar is just a cigar. The psychoanalysts were pretty embarrassed when the behaviorist published his little practical joke. While it's clear why this woman held on to the broomstick, there are going to be countless other cases in which several explanations will hold up well, and …" He held up empty palms. "We may never know for sure which one is right."

A coffee filter slipped from the coffee machine, fell to the floor. Aristotle glanced at it but made no move to put it back. It was like one of his silences and someone on staff would eventually feel compelled to speak—by picking it up.

"As for Jack, if he truly had a psychotic break with reality and is convinced the sidewalk is breathing, he won't acknowledge another explanation. For all I know, Jack saw right to some quantum-flux aspect of the concrete and *that* looked like breathing—*breathing* was the only way he could translate what he saw. To understand what's really going on, I'd need a lot more context … Jack's personal history, whatever guideposts he uses to navigate the world—"

"The Vedic philosophies," Logan offered.

"Exactly. He's got a worldview—we all do—that grew out of his upbringing, his education, his life experiences, what he's read. You need to get a handle on those things to understand a patient. A *client*."

No room in that cop's head for that kind of thinking. Or Dr. Harry's.

"But a psychotic won't admit more than one possibility—he *needs* a breathing sidewalk in order to maintain the rest of his delusional world, whatever that entails. If you explain away his breathing sidewalk, he'll have to 'rationalize' the explanation away—paradoxical as that sounds."

"I'm not sure I follow." Logan followed just fine; he wanted to hear more.

"Okay. Let's say part of someone's delusion is that he's Macbeth, and he goes around carrying a broomstick, believing it's Macbeth's sword. If I prove to him that it's just a broomstick, that doesn't end the delusion. He'll just come up with a reason why Macbeth lost his sword and had to grab a staff to defend his illegitimate claim to the throne."

Logan thought of dreams, how sometimes they incorporated an external sound—the alarm clock going off turned into a school bell—to keep sleep intact.

"Every behavior," Aristotle continued, "trivial or not, is meaningful. Similarly, every delusion is intelligible—*if* we can find a way to see it through the patient's eyes."

Logan didn't think he'd ever heard Aristotle talk so much.

"Excuse me, by the way, for not congratulating you at the beginning of the session."

"What for?"

"You played a guitar on the lawn and had a little sing-along with some of the other clients. So I heard. Welcome back."

Logan started to laugh.

"First time you played anything since you quit, right?"

Not quite done laughing, he sputtered like a motor that had been shut off but shivered as though it might start up again. "Yeah, I think so."

"There's something else I wanted to tell you—pack that old rucksack of yours. You're moving."

21. What *Really* Happened?

Was history adding up to anything? A special sum, a utopia at the end of a rainbow of wars? A Manifest Destiny? Did it repeat, like a fried burger cut with too much fat?

How do we know, Linda kept asking, what really happened? Different books say different things. And what happened to all those great empires anyway? They're all gone now and Italian moms dry their wash on the walls of the Roman Coliseum. I saw that in a magazine. They're like bed-time stories, queens and emperors and hanging gardens and slaves and pyramids. Why did we fight so many wars?

But if we forget it all, she insisted, if all those falling-down monuments disappeared, if ancient cities had all been buried like Pompeii, if the statues, the pottery, the tombs, and whatever else was cluttering museums vanished, it'd be just like it never happened.

Would it? He wasn't so sure. Might masquerade as something fancy and French like *déjà vu*. Even as an author's innocent mistake in calling his work fiction—how could he have known his vision had already come and gone, lived and died, rose and fell? Or hers.

What would Linda make of the Hopi myth of Emergence? Would she think the War Twins, who'd sent out their voices along the axis of the just-created Earth, had really lived? Would she believe that Spider Woman had thrown a cape woven of her "woman's wisdom" over some pat-a-caked mud, sung her special song over them, and just like that the first man and woman sat up, looked around, and scratched their heads? What if he told her they were true, yessir, true as two plus two is four, but no, they never happened?

I still don't know how old I really am.

The lessons of history are hard ones: Don't help starving Pilgrims. Don't accept blankets handed out by government agencies. Don't sign treaties drawn up by Anglos (no matter what doctors with stethoscopes say, they have two hearts).

One of the strangest things about Linda was a sing-song voice that almost never lost its perkiness no matter what she was talking about. *Two guys got killed in a car accident about two miles from here, did you know that?* And then she might bend forward suddenly and laugh into her hands as if to keep a bird from flying out of her mouth. *Isn't that terrible?* Dr. Schifferly would call that *inappropriate affect.* As if her voice were little girls' hair that had been curled for a special occasion but stayed tight and bouncy when she mentioned Dad putting honey on the end of—

I couldn't have been four, I must've been older, he wouldn't play a trick like that on me if I was four. He kept saying it was a lollipop and when I got to the center I would get a surprise, my mouth would fill up, it would be warm and sweet and creamy, but I didn't like it, I didn't like the way it tasted at all, I spit it out but I swallowed a little, I guess, and he said that's all right, you don't have to swallow it, but I can't remember how old I was when he was fooling me with Daddy's lollipop. I mean, of course I knew it wasn't a lollipop, and I ask him about it sometimes when he comes to visit, but he says I made it all up, none of it's true, that's why I have this diary and I have about a thousand of them because every time I ask him about something that I remember, he says I made it up but I think he's lying, that's why I write in my diary every day so I know what happened that day. I have a whole history of things and sometimes I cut out newspaper articles and paste them to prove when it all happened, like those guys who got killed in the car accident a couple miles from here, I cut that one out, I cut out the date too, only I don't know about the year because they had to turn it all back because of me. Isn't that somethin'?

I can't be 24, I just can't.

And you know? When my stepmother comes to visit with him, she says it too, that I make things up, and she wasn't even there. I imagined it, she says, or maybe it was a dream. But it wasn't a dream and how would she know anyway? She's always drinking and she wasn't even there so how would she know? Even when she comes here to visit me in the hospital you can smell her breath, god everybody must be able to smell it she drinks so much, she thinks she's smart drinking vodka, she thinks it has no smell but it does and I asked her once did I make all this up too? Am I making up the hospital and the doctors and my cottage and everything? Did I make all that up too?

22. No Future

It's a dead-end world was written in thick black marker over the pale blue of a stall partition whose bottom edge was dotted with rust. A few inches below that, *Johnny is rotten and so is his dick* had been penciled in (a shiny film of graphite he could've smudged off with a thumb). A pencil-drawn arrow, accompanied by the words *Him too,* pointed at G R E G, who'd scratched in his name with something like a nail. *Fuck you* underneath that in blue ballpoint pen (Greg, it seemed, disagreed), *I have a big cock.* The reply, again in pencil: *The one up your ass doesn't count.* Near this was a cartoon punk with wrap-around sunglasses and a mohawk that looked like a lizard's dorsal frill.

Maybe those caves painted with bison and horses and shamans wearing animals hides were just subterranean latrines, Neolithic humans doodling away while they were squatting, and scientists were knocking their heads too hard against the simple fact that all they were looking at was shithouse graffiti. (Except that some of the stuff was up so high they would've had to have been shitting off ladders.) Something about the heave and ho of the big intestine brought out the artist in some of us, art maybe nothing more than trying to leave some trace of a savage grunt, something that wouldn't be flushed down.

By way of a balloon coming out of his mouth, the doodled punk said, *I don't like Mondays OR hippies.* Next to the complaining punk, in thick black ink, rose a column in the hand of a different writer:

No future

No future

No future

No future for you

NO FUTURE

No future

No future for me

Fuck Monday, someone had agreed.

He heard the bathroom door squeak open. Sneakered feet stopped in front of the stall. The sides of the sneakers had split open, making frayed smiles in the suede. Pete.

Logan stood, pulled up his pants and flushed. A parallelogram of shadow stretched and narrowed across the white tiles as he opened the stall door and let it swing closed.

"Hey Tonto, you ever look at what you leave in the bowl?"

My feces is often black. Please answer yes or no ...

"Only when I get lonely for you, Pete."

Pete opened the rust-speckled door and Logan heard the latch click into place. "Kept it warm for me, huh?"

"The kinda guy I am."

His new home was a hallway lined with doors, closed except for one with music coming out of it (*Huuush, huuush ... I thought I heard her callin' my name now ...*). Communal bathroom, communal kitchen, roommates, it reminded him of a college dorm. The caged windows weren't to keep them in this time but to keep them from leap-frogging over a moment of despair and landing on the lawn. They could come and go pretty much as they wanted, even off-grounds.

"Basically," Aristotle had said, "it eliminates the need for a boarding house and helps clients make the transition to living outside the hospital."

Although the building was just as old as Cottage Seven, new

walls had gone up inside, sheetrock dust still in the corners. The hall still had the resiny reek of fresh paint, a blue to match the faded color of the bathroom stalls. Logan's only real worry was that that someone would get it into his head that he was the Galloping Gourmet, make a chef's hat out of a puffed-up paper bag, and turn the kitchen into Dante's Inferno through some cooking accident. Maybe it'd be Jack, resuming his alchemy experiments on a grander scale now that he had cast-iron pans to replace that tuna can. If all Jack managed to do was flood the halls with the pungency of his Golden Vapors, they'd get off lightly.

Logan had his own room. Adjacent to it, a door between them, Jack shared a bunk bed with Paul. The day they'd moved in, Paul had pointed a long dark finger at Jack. "Don't be greasin' wheezer when I'm under you, right?" Paul began bicycling his fists, like an old-time fighter. "Or Buckwheat gonna lay some *shit* on Alfalfa ..."

Jack looked confused. "Naw, man, I ain't gonna do that ..."

Paul threw a crumpled ball of paper at Jack. Jack took it in the chest, right next to his Jimi Hendrix button, then ducked to the side half-heartedly.

"God *damn* you slow." Paul whipped a jab at him, pulled up just shy of his nose.

Jack didn't even blink in time.

"Jack be nimble, Jack be slick, Jack needs t'*move* the next time I stick—" Paul threw another jab.

Jack jerked back, a batter avoiding a wild pitch.

The rooms were assigned, but Paul acted as if he'd given them out. "Go on, Blackfeather, take the room, I'm gonna be busy runnin' the floor." Right after he emptied his duffel bag, he started walking up the hall, banging on doors to see who was living where. And took to calling himself the Manic Black Cat. "Watch yourself now, don't cross my path …"

When Logan walked into their triple, Jack was lying belly-down on the top bunk, elbows and hands propping up his head, his nose in a notebook.

Logan felt like playing something, but that old six-string had disappeared as mysteriously as it had shown up.

"What's up, man?" Jack rolled over onto his side and switched to one arm to hold up his head. His long salt-and-pepper hair hung down past the thin mattress.

"Porcelain prices."

"Porcelain?" He was sitting up now, his wide eyes narrowed almost to normal.

"Yeah." Logan walked toward his room. "At the rate it's going, porcelain will be far too valuable a commodity to make toilets out of."

"No foolin?" Jack put his hands on the edge of the mattress as if he were going to jump down and do something about it.

"Just read it in the paper." Logan pushed open the door to his room with a foot.

"I wonder what we're gonna use instead."

Logan leaned back through the doorway. "Not only that, but how're we going to protect existing urinals and toilets from porcelain plunderers looking to cash in on the lucrative black market that's forming even as we speak?"

"Wow! I never even thought of that!" He was in his denim jacket, boxer shorts, and a pair of grayed white socks. "Even the crapper's not safe these days."

"You know it, Jack."

Logan looked at the clothes piled on his bed. There were two pieces of furniture in the room, a dresser being the other. He looked at the empty walls (freshly painted), at the blue-and-white floor tiles then out the window, which faced south. He had the right to hang photographs, postcards, posters or album covers, nudie magazine clip-outs, photos, love letters (if only he had any), *The Communist Manifesto*—or anything else he could get to stick. He had the right to remain in bed till he felt like getting up. He had the right to sleep with the light on. He had the right to miss breakfast. To go to the Phoenix Diner for a real breakfast. Get a job at the diner if they were hiring half-sane half-bloods. Who said there was no future?

23. The Phoenix Diner

Collapsing butt-first onto the bed like a boxer who'd taken a nasty uppercut to the chin (a squeal from the bedsprings instead of a roar from the crowd), he pulled a sneaker on over a bare foot. Once white, the canvas had dulled to a dingy gray as if they'd sat under rainy skies often enough to permanently take on that sodden hue. Yeah, they were pretty raggedy. *They are nearing nirvana,* Jim Lee would've said. But nothing knew his feet better. It would've taken a sole tearing loose to get him to throw them out. And even then, he wouldn't leave them to mix with trash. He'd find a place to leave them—next to a saguaro in Arizona, on a rooftop in New York City, in the middle of a field in Kansas—where they could gradually weather into whatever afterexistence awaited old Converses.

Lacing up the other foot, he bounced off the bed and eased open the door to his room.

Paul was flat on his back, left hand on his chest, right arm palm-up on the floor as though he'd been shot and fallen dead covering the wound.

Nearly invisible, the sheet pulled up to his ears, Jack might've been hibernating in a cocoon of flimsy cotton.

A Styrofoam container lay open on the coffee table. Leftover fries from the Phoenix Diner sat in a confused heap, slightly shriveled, the way fingertips get when they're in the water too long.

The three of them had gone off grounds yesterday, walked on the gravel spillover along the edge of a little two-lane highway.

The tops of weeds brushed against their arms when they shied from passing cars.

Jack kept looking back, sure one of the attendants was following them.

"Relax, Jack." Paul's smile was uncharacteristically reassuring. "We cool."

Roadside weeds swayed, their fuzzy blooms heavy on tall stalks, like the tufted heads of willowy children. Logan's hand reached out for their leafy presence as they walked toward the diner, the H in its neon sign gone black.

In the restaurant Paul tipped his chair back on two legs while he looked over the menu. When the waitress showed up, he glanced at her name tag. "Lila? That your real name? Or a stage name so the customers don't get too friendly?"

Lila smiled, her big glasses slipping down the bridge of her nose. The translucent frames were shaped like the wings of a butterfly, and you weren't supposed to be able to tell the lenses were bifocals. Her hair, held in big stiff curls, was mostly gray. "That's my real name." She pressed a pencil to her pad. "Have you decided yet?"

"I'm gonna have the biggest, meanest, nastiest, sloppiest, greasiest cheeseburger ya'll make. Sauteed onions and french fries on the side."

Jack took the longest to make up his mind, finally settling on lasagna. "It's got no meat, right?"

When Logan lifted his burger, catsup squeezed out over his fingers and dripped onto the heavy white plate.

"That's right, Blackfeather, you ain't eatin' right if you don't get it all over yourself."

Logan chewed.

"Tell you something else—Linda makes it to Transitional, you gonna get yourself some."

"Oh yeah?" Logan used the back of a wrist to wipe his mouth. "What about you?"

"Me? I'm already hooked up." He winked. "Ain't no patient either."

"That a fact?"

Jack, the most out of place with his graying mane and collaged jacket, was still nervous, but no one cut eyes at them as if they knew they were inmates at the hospital down the road.

Through the window beside their table, Logan watched cars go past on the quiet highway. Headlamps went on as night settled.

While Paul twisted himself around to look at a pretty Latina who'd walked in with two of her friends, college-age maybe, Jack stole one of his fries. Popping it into his mouth, he looked up at Logan and put a shushing finger to his lips.

A month ago, Jack would never have gotten up the nerve to swindle anything from Paul's plate. *What do you think of that Dr. Harry?* Did fry-grabbing rank up there with daily showers? With regularly brushed teeth? Clothes that smelled of fabric softener?

The second time Jack snatched a fry, Paul turned around just in time to catch the look on Jack's face. "You thievin' my food, Popeye?" He looked down at his plate. "Damn! You did, didn't you?"

"No, man." Jack grinned like a fool. "I didn't touch 'em."

Paul looked at Logan. "You believe this hippie leftover? I remember somethin' about free *love*, not no free french fries."

Logan laughed.

"Damn." Paul slid his plate closer and hunched over it. "You sittin' next to Blackfeather next time."

The fries sitting in the Styrofoam box on the cluttered coffee table had been Logan's.

Likely as not, Jack would pop them down for breakfast when he woke up.

Slipping quietly out the door, Logan headed down the carpeted hall, bounded down the stairs in a baggy T-shirt, cut-off sweats, no socks under his moribund sneakers.

The desk where an attendant sat was empty except for an abandoned coffee cup, a full ashtray, a newspaper. Taking a leak, maybe.

The air was brisk, the Sun—still behind the building—too weak to make him squint. Eyes fixed on a huge spruce flanking the front door, obscuring windows as it rose past the three stories of the Transitional facility, Logan spread his legs. Dropping his butt lower and lower until he'd almost managed a split, he held the position. Straightening up, he shook out his arms as if they were covered with tiny bugs he wanted gone without the cruelty of smashing them. He danced up and down, shaking his arms harder to get his blood moving.

But now that nothing was in his way, he stood breathing in the fresh scent of grass, reluctant to start, like a swimmer, drowsy and warm, unwilling to dive into water he knew would stiffen his body with cold.

A short run (a couple of miles at most), to wake his body up, remind it what it had been built for.

Pushing off a foot into a leap, he began, as he always did, at a track-meet pace. He was the first to disturb the dew on the grass. The soles of his old Converses worn close to bald, he had to be careful on turns.

It only took a few hundred yards for him to decide his legs weren't up to it. A sharp pain knifed him under the ribs, and he thought about slowing to a jog. Except that he'd inherited his father's bias against it: *Jogging was made up by white men with beer bellies.* Most days, his father used to do a five-mile run before work. Not before going to the office but before going out and laying bricks, cinderblocks, stone. When Logan was up early enough, he'd sit on the stoop and wait for his father to come back, his stride steady, his loose fists pumping as if he were an engine you could hitch to a railway car.

Back then he'd been too much a boy to keep up with his father, and maybe he was no boy anymore, but his lungs felt raw already, and there was no snap in his stride, no flow in his movements. He pushed his limbs as though they were dead weight. Right there within the first minute, he knew he wasn't going to make it.

In his day his grandfather had been able run a deer down to exhaustion. Without a special diet. Without fancy running shoes. Without a scientifically designed training program.

Logan coughed up phlegm, spit into the grass. Right in front of Linda's cottage. He was glad she wasn't awake to see him wheezing after maybe a quarter mile. He was like one of those cars in a post-apocalyptic world that had been sitting for a year or two, coughing black smoke, stuttering and hesitating instead of picking up speed.

He tried pacing himself.

Breathing more deeply, he evened out his stride.

The air was clean. It would scrub his lungs, and he'd keep

spitting out what'd been building up all these months he'd been sitting around.

Something fell away from his muscles as he broke into a sweat, a gummy coating that had been making his motion sticky. The cool morning felt like a damp cloth pressed to his face. He hawked and spat again.

Thumb and forefinger starting at the end of each eyebrow, he smoothed his hair back, away from his face. Sweat and the wind of his motion kept it off his face.

He pushed off his feet a little harder, put more twist into his trunk as he swung his arms.

Looking down at his old sneakers trampling grass, he turned them into hooves. His head pushed forward with each stride as if to break some invisible barrier. His long hair flew behind him like a mane.

Jarring his body with each step, the earth never felt so solid.

The day, fully emerged now, was going to be beautiful. He turned sharply to avoid slamming into a fence. Slipping in the dew-slicked grass, his arms flew out, as if he were imitating an eagle in flight, returned to his sides as he righted himself. The blur of the fence's chain-links gave the illusion of extraordinary speed.

His own rhythm carried him. The earth ran with him. Even the wind, pushing his hair away from his face, seemed to be at his back, urging him forward. He wouldn't tire over distance; he'd draw strength from his forward motion.

His T-shirt soaked with sweat, it alternately stuck and pulled away with each stride, each time he swung a fist. His legs stretching farther, his feet hardly touched the ground anymore, skimmed the grass lightly as if there were no ground to which it was rooted, as if the blades were the meniscus of a green lake and he had to hold his speed, touch the surface only with the balls of his feet if he didn't want to sink with a splash.

Against his body's will he slowed, heard the land groan to be so sluggish again. He let his pace wind down to a trot, giving his body time to adjust to its own heaviness, to the land's inertia.

He stopped in front of Transitional, hands on his hips, looking at the mammoth spruce that angled shaggy branches across the brick facade. A grandfather of a spruce older than the hospital. For half a second he thought he'd gotten a kind of approval from the tree. Which had needed no instruction to sink its roots, no prodding to spread its limbs for light. In a way that he couldn't explain, the tree had affirmed that, for the first time in almost a year, he'd done what his legs had been given to him for, had woken up his lungs, startled his body into remembering that, unlike the tree holding earth in place—a forest of them made an Atlas—he had more in common with wind, water, fire.

He pulled off his shirt to perspire more freely. Sweat salted his tongue. He wanted it to pour out of him, run down his body, empty him of impurities. He would let it evaporate in the morning sun and cool air. He would be clean.

24. Sun Eye, Moon Eye

Lying on his bed, he heard Jack through the closed door. "Hey man! I got a letter today! I'm going to Canada when I get out!"

Logan was looking up at the ceiling, recently painted but somehow freshly stained. A yellowish continent edged in brown, lost in a silent sea of white.

He heard Paul less clearly. "Jack be nimble, Jack be quick, Jack gonna give them shrinks the slip!"

Once upon a time, before Logan had ever done mesc, there'd been a knock on the door at an ungodly hour: Cal's tattoo and Cal's nickname, a matchbook from a bar, a pair of bus tickets from Mexico, a page in the Bible, a science fiction novel, a selection of street names and addresses. How could he know for sure his uncle had killed his father?

Candles floated in the darkness, repeated as ghostly images in a dark windowpane. Reminded him of the way memories sometimes surrounded him.

Things had flipsides, called up an unseen place—the source of dreams, where scarecrows climbed down from their crosses and hitched rides, fathers returned with riddles etched on their faces and gazed at you with moons instead of eyes.

The book on the table next to the ashtray beside the puddled blue candle (if you sighted just above the back of the chair), intimated a passage in an underworld maze. The mundane and the arcane shared a room, were double exposures: one perceived through the murky Loch Ness in which consciousness was adrift; the other entered through the doors of the senses.

We're a bit like a god whose one eye is the Moon and the other, the Sun. Vision blending somewhere at the back of the skull. The moon eye saw in grainy black and white, the sun eye in color, with clarity. The moon eye was at home in a netherworld where only the shadow of the ordinary fell. The sun eye followed every line and angle, every contour, was fascinated by shape's lovely demise—a melting candle, say.

We end up trapped between geometry and emotion, indifference and familiarity, the erosion of form and the permanence of essence. To end the confusion, we keep the moon eye shut (we want to *see* better after all). Leave it to primitives, the foolhardy, the poets, the lie-abouts, the mad, to close the sun eye, to lose themselves in fables lying just beneath a papery-thin lid.

Linda had tried to lengthen and deepen her sight in hopes of reading the text of history (still being written). Of finding the page, the paragraph, the sentence where she was mentioned.

But the next moment shows up only to be incongruent to our expectation of it.

Maybe everything he'd ever said to Linda or Jack or Paul had just been his mouth moving without any sound. Even now their voices were receding (Jack's and Paul's), lights on shore as the ship slipped away into blackness. Yes, he could hear them, but—there was some sleight of hand going on—not what they were saying.

He closed his eyes.

Ghosts, the old stories said, sometimes hovered around the living, their presence doubled in dusty mirrors or dark windowpanes. Out of loneliness. Enough to last an eternity.

Where had the tribal elder in his life been? The shaman? His grandfather? Buddy? How was he supposed to make sense?

He opened his eyes. The lost continent floating above him, a stain in a calm white sea, seemed to have moved, to be adrift.

"I never been to Canada!"

He'd dropped into a well once. Or maybe down a hole. Light dissolved into dim phosphorescence. The nadir of a dead sea where overarching stone became sky. Unless that crude dome overhead was just him looking up at his own skull. The hole at the top unsutured.

The hitcher had forced him to slow the car. On the gray face, tattoos no one could read, a map of the soul's wanderings. Logan was afraid a wrong turn and those tattoos would show up on his own face, and his voice would join a chorus of little whirlwinds. But there were no signposts.

He heard them speaking, Jack and Paul, still at a safe distance from understanding.

He heard Bible Mike, talking to him through tobacco-stained teeth, searing Revelation 21 onto his skin like a brand: *And I saw a new heaven and a new earth, for the first heaven and the first earth had passed away.* (Where oh where, revelator, were you standing to watch this?) Mikey, smiling as cheerfully as a greeting-card cherub, his face unshaven, the circles under his eyes like thumb-smudges of ash, assured Logan it was coming. And all he had to do was dance, dance and the old would pass away. When lightning came to shred the sky, the Earth would convulse, shrug off cities—cold and crystalline, with no plazas for dancing—cast them into yawning rifts. A chosen few would take refuge with the Ant People, who, the old-timers say, are at home in the deepest, most ancient places of the Earth. Where the storm will have its eye.

Only he couldn't hear the music to dance to anymore. Even the stones were silent. Not just lonely but dead and silent. (He'd searched but had not been able to find morning.)

Anthropologists, squinting at the Hopi language through a microscope, designated something they saw through its lenses an *objective component.* He knew well enough it belonged to the realm the sun eye looked down on—what had come and gone and left its mark, what'd been photographed, the that-which-had-cracked-you-across-the-head realm: a medicine man's weathered face, the smell of roasted corn, the droning wind, a branch of dry cottonwood, a lump of moist clay.

Sharing a nebulous boundary with what-might-be, what-could-only-be-imagined. Spotted by the moon eye, this was the dimension of that-which-could-be-dreamed-of, the pottery the lump of clay was set to become, tomorrow's weather, life in a distant village (where no television existed), the continuum of Maybe This, Maybe That. Time extended into space so that what had happened a long, long time ago was something far, far away. The thing to remember was that one might *become* the other. What was once only a straining desire might become What Is. A story being told beginning to happen while the teller tells it.

"Hey man!" Jack came into the room talking through a fog, his T-shirt so big it billowed out like a dress. "I'm goin' to Canada!" He sounded like he was talking underwater.

"When?" Logan tried to focus on Jack, but someone had propped open the lid to the moon eye with toothpicks. He couldn't see him clearly.

"When I get out, man."

He thought he should lift himself off the mattress, but he couldn't seem to signal his body. The connection was lost.

"You all right, Blackfeather?"

Paul's voice was like a strobe light, broken and repeating. He looked strange hovering over him, his head disappearing in the light that came from the room he bunked in with Jack.

Logan nodded and forced himself into a sitting position. Sweat plastered his shirt to his back.

"You sure, man?"

He blinked. "I'm all right." Sliding off the edge of the bed, he went into their room.

"Ain't it great?"

Jack's frog eyes widened a little more. His face looked as if it were made of wax, polished and unreal.

"Yeah." Logan grinned longer than he should have. *Do you know, Jack, that once you merge with that wonderful Oneness, there's no more Jack, just Oneness?* He laughed.

"What's so funny man?"

Sometimes, maybe, he slept with the moon eye open.

"Oh, it's an inside joke, huh?" Jack was grinning too.

Inside? Logan laughed harder. Sometimes, maybe, he was asleep while he walked around.

25. By Ice

This morning Logan had seen a skunk burrowing under the fence. The same skunk, probably, he'd smelled a few months back. Looking up every now and then to gauge its progress, he saw it flatten itself out, crawl under the fence, and come up on the other side, where, if it wasn't careful, it'd wind up a roadside attraction for flies. He should've tied himself to its tail like a prayer feather. He could go off grounds anytime he felt like it without jumping fences or digging under them, but then what? The skunk had instinct to get by on; all he had was a little bit of pocket money.

Sure, there were centers he was supposed to be able to navigate by (*Qua'ah* could've told Aristotle about them), the one at the top of his head in particular. But they were gummed up, clouded-over, vulnerable as radio reception. No, he wasn't ready to put himself to a rock face at a 90-degree angle the way Sonny had taught him when they'd rappelled down a sheer drop, wasn't ready to trust his weight to what his grandfather said he'd been born with.

The door opened and Jack came out looking a little dazed as if what was outside Transitional was hard to believe. "How'd the testing go?"

I told you yesterday, Jack. "Got a hundred, I think."

"Intense."

His teeth were a little better since Logan had shown him how to floss.

"You goin' to the movie tonight?" Jack shoved both of his hands into the pockets of his jeans.

Logan nodded.

"With Linda, huh?"

"I ain't bringing *you*."

"No, I know *that*, man."

Logan looked south, past Jack.

"A cold front's comin' down from Canada, d'jew hear?" Jack looked up as if the sky were already darkening. "It's gonna drop sleet on us. Might even snow Easter Sunday."

"I heard." *But I ain't plannin' to be here for it.*

Last night, the winds had come first, ruffling his sleep, snapping it like a flag. The Earth had been frozen in its own blue skin. The ice hard as marble, veined with shadow, like streaks of cloudy iron, and not a soul to relieve a landscape of loneliness— not a chirping bird, not a whirring insect, not a movement in the immaculate wastes of snow. Forests petrified to the last tree. No fire burned, no smoke rose, as if the Earth had somehow brushed up against its satellite and the cold of the Moon had rubbed off.

Glaciers advanced like a mountain range freed of its moorings, sheared cities away, and stood in their stead, freezing sunlight in their translucent bodies. So cold that, standing beside one, your breath would shatter against it. Rivers and lakes, oceans and seas hard as glass, solid to the bottom. Not a fish left that wasn't a frigid fossil. Suspended at various depths, betrayed by their own element.

The Earth, slipcased in ice, held still for all time, was a near-perfect, near-indestructible memory.

Except for a hole. Like someone had gone ice fishing. Only there was no lake. He knew that he was supposed to go down it even though it would've been a squeeze just get his head in.

He'd woken up shivering.

Time, he decided, for a hot shower.

Linda was waiting for him, arms crossed over her chest, eyes glistening above the swells of her cheekbones.

"What're you doin' here?" He started walking.

She shrugged. "Sneaked off. They don't care. We're all going to the movie anyway."

She caught up quickly and grabbed two of his fingers as if she had a baby's hand and that was all she could fit in her fist.

He slowed a little to make it easier on her. Letting go of his fingers, she took his hand. Making him feel like a middle-aged teacher betraying the public trust with someone's daughter. Zeus using his godly wiles to seduce a beauty whom he'd abandon long before she'd been wasted by old age. Linda's father sliding a hand under her skirt.

"You ever notice that?"

She'd already begun a conversation with herself and was just getting around to including him.

"That you can tell things about people just by looking at them? Not always, but sometimes." She squeezed his hand. "Your nose isn't as nice-looking as some people's but it's made to be out front, you know? Like a bumper on a car."

He laughed. "I got a car bumper in the middle of my face?"

"No." She giggled. "I meant it—it's like … the way when birds fly, the strong ones are out front. Everybody's nose is out front, but yours … it looks made for that. I don't know."

"If you say so."

"But I bet your whole face was made to protect your eyes.

That's your weak spot, your eyes. You can get hurt there."

"You mean like if someone pokes me in them?" He forked his fingers and stabbed at her eyes.

She turned her head away, laughing. "No! Not like *that*."

He tucked his hand in a pocket.

"I mean ... I mean that's where it shows. Not on your face."

"Huh."

"I'm missing something." Linda slid her hands into the pockets of her jacket. "I'm like my mom. My real one. Her face was smooth and round, like a baby's."

He looked at the little bump in the bridge of her nose. "You don't have a smooth face."

"But I'm soft like her. I think it has something to do with why I'm here."

He tugged on her ear but couldn't get her to smile.

"If I'm so tough, what am I doing here?"

She studied his face. "That's the part I can't figure out."

26. Night Flight

"Hey Jack, you got a piece of paper I can write on?"

Clothes lay on the floor as if a roomful of people, chatting amiably, had disintegrated and their garments had collapsed like pole-less tents. Papers were scattered as though the contents of files dumped by agents with a search warrant. Jar lids and empty cans had been used as ashtrays, books made into uneven stacks. Bottles, some not quite empty, stood like glass columns with nothing to support. Every so often, Paul would make Jack clean up (*Jack be simple, Jack be out of it, but Jack better learn to pick up his shit!*).

His head under the bed, his ass up in the air with a cut-out denim patch stitched on his falling-apart jeans, the Psychedelic Relic was looking for something. "Got a whole notebook here somewhere ..." He looked back and up. "Here." He handed Logan a sheet of paper. "You can murder on that and no one will put you away."

"Not a bad idea." Logan folded the sheet of paper in half, creased it with two fingers. "You still writin' that book?"

Jack scratched his beard, starting at his chin and working his way down to his Adam's apple. "Uh, yeah. I been takin' notes mostly. It's kinda hard to get in the mood t'write around here."

"I know what you mean." Logan left the door to his room open a crack. Kneeling in front of his bed, he used it for a desk with a book for backing.

He stayed in that position for a long time.

The steady press of the linoleum floor numbed his knees.

He heard Paul come in.

"What you up to Popeye? Ain't got your hands on no dope, do ya?"

"Nah, man, I don't smoke no more …"

The words passed through Logan's mind like light through the dusty windows of an old warehouse. He was glad Paul hadn't poked his head in, hadn't seen his leather bag, rounded out with what little he had to take with him, sitting on the floor.

There were three words written on the page Jack had given him.

It might have been three in the morning. Jack and Paul had to be asleep by now.

Jack had tried

Was there any?

Had tried to make sense.

He and Jimmy Lee in the early-morning hours trying to decode smoke rising in sine curves from the tips of cigarettes. What— wouldn't he like to know—was really burning? Coked out, fucked up, they kept drinking till the floor was a wall they had to lean against.

Broken bottles stand for skulls emptied of their contents. No deposit, no return. Dead brain cells blown out of noses and thrown away with the bloody tissues. Sprawled on the hardwood floor, inhaling dust. Breath poisoned. Beer gone sticky against skin.

Running. His body light as motion, gathered up in its own momentum, hardly touching the ground. He leaped onto the fence he'd seen the skunk burrow under, clambered up it like a squirrel. Dropping himself onto icy grass, he started running again. He looked down at his old sneakers trampling grass, turned them into hooves. His head pushed forward with each stride as if to break some invisible barrier, hair twisting behind him like a mane.

"Kiss my Buddha!" Jimmy yelled when they tried to get him off the floor. The running joke. When they finally pulled him to his feet, he said a prayer. "Dear Lord" (he wobbled) "rezzarect our pal Billy Boy, who done passed out and cannot stand. Give 'im the strength." Jimmy fell backward, Logan caught him. They both laughed. "As for me, renew this broken-down body a mine so I can do it again t'morra night. Finally, shrink Logan's cranial cavity some. It's for his own good. Amen."

Sleet bit his face, melted, ran like chill perspiration. His hair was weighted with water. The bouncing ends, braided by ice, whipped against his face like bony snakes. He sucked in cold air, blew it back out, swept past the tiny clouds he made. The Earth, jarring his body with each step, never felt so solid.

Consciousness cracked against old wood short-circuits in starry flashes. Memories spilled over bar counters collect in a puddle where tired eyes slouch forward to stare. What have they seen? Numbers and biblical allusions in Cal's tattoo—the death of his father not heaven's will but Cal's.

Katsinam are the unseen proven by gathering clouds, falling rain, growing corn.

The incandescent dust of nebulae still swirls outward at speeds outstripping thought: the faster starstuff emitting blue light while the slower glows the red of afterbirth.

His legs leaped, his lungs yawned, the Earth ran with him. Because the highway chattered with sleet, was slippery beneath his sneakers—twice he almost fell—he took up running alongside it, worn soles stirring up gravel frozen in clumps. The last frosty gasp of Old Man Winter. Cables between telephone poles were hung with dripping icicles. The poles themselves, the weeds on the side of the road, the trees, wore ice jackets.

Night would end long before the road.

It shored him up, knowing they had the same direction in mind, knowing the road kept going. Ice storm or no, so would he. His body carried by the wind—never mind its sleet teeth—by the Earth running with him, by whatever had set him in motion in the first place.

He ran without the thought of stopping, couldn't remember anymore what it was like to be still or how he could've gotten along without this motion, how the land under him could be sustained without this motion. He'd begun to lose mass the way a meteor chafes into a puff of bright dust. Space had emptied out, and he was an empty thing moving through it, a hollowness filling itself with breath, a pounding weightless heart rushing blood through him. Sweat and melted sleet dripped as he ran, a miraculous rain he shed in passing.

Raw and running, his nostrils flared to feed his lungs. The muscles in his legs coiled, sprang. His hair, frozen at the tips, swung as his head pushed forward with each stride. He was barely aware of the leather bag bouncing against his back, barely aware of the growing light. Pelted by a sky breaking up in icy chips, he headed for the Earth's cold edge, chased the glow rising behind it, emerged into the new day.

BOOK III
KUSKURZA

1. Place Of Many Sparkling Waters

Signs were lit up along the street, the street a canal flowing with light. Electric dusk. An evening made of falling shadow, a lethargic smokiness in love with its own downward inertia.

In Arizona what gave a stone finger pointing at the sky its majesty, what made tons of rock rising like a smokestack in the desert a place to set up an altar was the space it commanded. Here they were crowded together, riveted steel and sheer faces of opaque glass that cut the Sun's arc short, brought on darkness early.

If nature isn't such straight lines, he thought, *we must be the ones so full of right angles.*

Looking up at a high-rise tapering toward the sky, its windows flush with panels of polished granite, he imagined the men who stood on girders ribbing the heights, clambered along the steel skeleton—fitting frame for one of your lesser deities—wind whistling past their ears. Industrious as any ant ever admired by a kneeling Hopi.

The ice storm hadn't made it this far. Here, it had rained. Although he couldn't see the Sun or even the horizon, the sky was still light. Here they didn't dance to ensure that it showed up for dawn, didn't didn't hold any rock concerts in its honor, probably hadn't even named a nightclub after it. Why should it bother to rise for eternity?

The air outside the hospital had smelled of trees and grass, of soggy earth after a downpour. He couldn't say what the odor burning his nostrils here was: asphalt, sewer smells, something vaguely electrical carried up from the subway. The smell of urban karma, the residue of every business day. Maybe their souls were electric and moved on tracks.

He'd left the hospital without so much as a goodbye. To anyone. Linda would take it the hardest. He wished he could've promised to keep in touch, to meet her once or twice a year over dinner or drinks, laugh while they talked about what they'd gotten up to.

He'd let Linda take him by the hand after the movie, guide him to a splotch of shadow between two spruces. Her mouth tasted faintly of spearmint, as clean as a child's. He thought they could stay like that, kissing like kids behind an empty school, dark except for a few mysterious lights, an unmanned ship adrift in a night of soft insect buzz. But his hands, scarred and rough, untucked her shirt, slid up the smooth skin of her back.

How long had it been?

She unbuttoned his shirt, a breeze cold enough to stiffen his nipples making it belly out; he lifted hers up to her armpits. Arching against him like a cat, she kept both of them warm.

"I wish …" Her lips brushed against his ear. "I wish we were somewhere else."

How long—?

Rings of light that formed while his eyes were closed—some charged spillover from her skin on his—were still there when he opened them. The hard nubs of her nipples pressed against him when she moved. Her arms locked around his neck, her tongue in his mouth, he worked her pants over the hips he'd watched so often, tried not to think about where he was, tried not to think.

They used their jackets and pants to make a quilt on the grass. He pinned her arms to the ground as he pushed inside of her, barely heard the moan that fluttered up as she ground her hips against his. The bright rings became glaring.

Linda was not the awkward lover he'd expected and moved beneath him as if she knew exactly the way he wanted it to feel. Something burned away, and for the first time he thought her beautiful. Her head tipped back, each breath sucking in her stomach, her cheekbones feline and her mouth open—he was amazed *how* beautiful.

The way he remembered it, they arrived together at that strange moment when a hole seemed to have been punched through him, and something rushed in with the force of seawater. Shuddering and dizzy, he felt gauzy enough to be carried off by a breeze.

She fixed her bra and buttoned up her shirt, shoved a leg into pants with the belt buckle dangling. She'd already missed her curfew, and they'd be looking for her.

After a rushed kiss good night, a quick taste of her minty tongue, he went back to Transitional like a dog that knew its master would be waiting with a rolled-up newspaper. He was gone that same night. No assurance that, even if they weren't going to set up house together, he wouldn't forget about her. No false insistence she'd be out soon either.

Instead, he'd waited in Transitional with the patience of a stone angel keeping vigil in a cemetery. When the attendant got up to go the can or get a fresh coffee, Logan was out the door like a sudden gust, leather bag in tow.

And now he was in a city he hardly knew, a tiny square of paper with a Greenwich Village address in his wallet. He'd been on his way there when—how many months ago?—face pressed against glass, a cop had arrested him and he'd been shipped off to Upstate University.

He kept walking.

2. Carmine Street

A blade of light cuts through sleep. Hours or days? Rip Van Logan. A drunk snoring next to him. Face-down, hair a gray tangle of curls, back of his neck black and gritty as asphalt. A cardboard mattress. No pillow. Compadres, Logan thinks, me and you. Shanghaied. Or maybe the whole island floated away because everyone pushing past him, crowding the sidewalk is Asian.

He sucks at the sourness coating his teeth, takes his ass off the concrete—Christ is he sore. All that running. His legs stiff as aluminum rods, he hefts his bag and covers his sidewalk buddy with the puffy vinyl jacket the state issued him.

He joins the stream of moving people, his reflection keeping pace in store windows, almost bumps into a cop. Shoulders steeled for the hand grabbing hold of them, he keeps walking, telling himself, They haven't even figured out I'm gone yet ...

With the cop blocks behind him, he stops to look over tables and blankets spread on the sidewalk. Earrings, magazines, sandals, books, bandannas, a pair of worn cowboy boots, bracelets, socks still wrapped in plastic, African figurines, reflector sunglasses. He takes the shades for two bucks.

Signs are written in Chinese characters, read right to left, right? Crowded, intimate, smelling of garbage, fish, fried food, a strange mix of the nauseating and appetizing. Centerpiece of it all a bank masquerading as a pagoda—maybe that's a Japanese word?— painted a panel of bright colors but mostly red.

Unsure at a corner. Left or right? Avenues run north-south, streets east-west. No need for a trail of bread crumbs or a thread unwound behind him.

The back of his neck exposed to the wind was a new sensation. His hand went up and down the bristles above his neck. The sides and the back shaved, on top barely enough left to comb—a Marine cut almost. His hand kept going to his head, rubbing stubble. Glancing at shop windows, he was repeatedly startled by a man with an angular cut and big reflector sunglasses looking back at him. Even Paul would have trouble picking him out of a lineup now.

He'd taken the subway too far downtown, but he wasn't too many blocks off.

The buildings became brick or brownstone as he walked. Smooth sills, jutting ledges, faces sometimes carved into the stone. Only a few narrow stories high, with fire escapes like wrought-iron balconies.

Three twentysomethings, spiked hair glowing fluorescent, shoved each other down the sidewalk. Ten of them picked at random would've drawn a parade crowd back home.

A patch of asphalt had peeled back, and cobblestones showed through like the rough skin of a land leviathan surfacing. Once upon a time, horses had pulled carriages through these streets.

A horn blared.

On the corner was a Mediterranean-looking Church, color eroded to a dull white by sun, its single tower capped by a copper dome. He turned down Carmine Street.

Stopping in front of a brick tenement, he double checked the creased paper and hoped they still lived here, hoped they were still feeling as friendly as when they'd invited him to look them up. He rang 4G.

"Hello?" The voice came through an intercom.

"Hank?"

"Yeah ...?"

"Logan." He knew he should say something else, but he just stood there looking at the little metal screen that filtered voices.

"Logan *Blackfeather*? I don't believe it! Come on up."

A buzzer rang and he pushed the door—surprisingly heavy—open.

Hank, dressed in jeans and a T-shirt, greeted him at the top of the stairs with a handshake and a slap on the shoulder. "I can't believe you're in the city. What's it been? Like two years?"

"'Bout that." He followed Hank in.

"That *haircut*—what a difference. I wouldn't have recognized you on the street."

Burgundy-colored carpeting made his sneakers feel as comfortable as when he'd first put them on. He let his bag slide down his arm and drop beside the couch.

"So what brings you to New York?"

Logan shrugged. "Had to see it, right?"

Hank nodded. "Everybody should, yeah."

The couch was a dusty red that somehow avoided being tacky. Sitting down, Logan spread his arms across the top of it, caught a whiff of his body's sourness. The place had an other-century air, its woodwork heavy and dark, a fireplace ("That doesn't work") across from the couch, no tv in sight, the living room quiet and cool.

"Pam's gonna flip out when she sees you."

A loud redhead whose urges all seemed to have escaped

repression, it was hard to picture her with Hank, a Minnesotan who still parted his light brown hair on the side and never bothered to replace his glasses with contacts. Jeans, sneakers, T-shirt, Hank's arms stuck out of the sleeves with room to spare. A lightweight, a morning push-up routine kept him tight. Logan had met them at a hostel in Santa Fe while they were driving cross-country in Hank's old Buick. Logan played tour guide and showed them around for a couple of weeks.

"So you're still floating around the country, huh?" Hank asked.

"I think I might stay a while." The city would bury him with everyone else, would spider-web his face until it was an indistinct memory—no eyes, just thumb-holes pressed into soft gray.

"Great." Hank came out of the kitchen with a tray of cheese (four kinds) and crackers (three kinds). He put a beer down in front of Logan. "I know you can drink a nice cold one."

Logan looked at the bottle as though he didn't know which end went in his mouth. He reached for it and took a pull. Bubbles scoured his mouth.

"We've got some raw vegetables and dip too if you want." Hank got up.

"Whaddayou do? Wait around with trays of food in case a party drops by?"

"Just so happens we're having a little soiree tonight. Nothing heavy-duty, just a few friends."

Logan ran a hand over the arm of the couch, watched the hue of the fabric darken slightly. He knew if slapped the round arm—it looked as if a log had been rolled inside it—he'd get a little cloud of dust. "Mind if I take a shower?"

"Where do you wanna take it? No, just kidding. Bathroom's right there." He pointed. "Towels are on the rack."

Logan untied his dingy gray sneakers, lopsided with wear, and left them by the couch. He stood up, stiff all over again from the running he'd done.

The bathroom wasn't much more than a big closet, the floor a mosaic of tiny tiles edged with years of grime. But there was a *door*, a door he could *shut*. A shower he could be alone in. Not just a curtain to draw and a bench to come out to and a key-jangler like Palmer standing around making sure nobody tried to make breakfast out of the soap. The glass door came free with a tug and a metallic clack.

Mechanical rain: the clouds have given up their secret.

His hair was soaked, but there was hardly any weight on his head. He felt bald. He turned his back to the nozzle and put his hands on the tiled wall, let the hot, hard rain pelt his back. *Goddamn.* Everything began to loosen. Pores opened like desert flowers after a thunderstorm. With all those tiny little flowery mouths all over him, he really hated—after scrubbing up—turning the water off. He stood for a second feeling the faint tickle of sliding drops. Pushing open the glass door, he stepped onto a shaggy, pink rug.

After he toweled off, he pulled his jeans on, the worn denim as much a part of him as the hair he'd left on the barber shop floor. He put on a fresh T-shirt, raked his bristles with his fingers. When he opened the door, the bathroom's rectangular mouth exhaled a swirl of steam.

Pam almost knocked him over. "Oh I can't believe you're *here!*" She squeezed his chest.

Hank called from the kitchen: "I told you!"

"God, what did you do to your hair?" She reached up to touch the wet spikes. "So how long you stayin'? Oh if you don't stay at least a week, I'll never forgive you." She locked her arms around his neck and kissed him on the mouth.

He was glad Hank was in the kitchen.

She jerked a thumb toward Hank. "I'm sure he told you we're having this little thing tonight, so pardon us if we don't pay any more attention to you. Which reminds me: Someone's coming you've just *got* to meet."

Logan was already light-headed with beer when people started to arrive. Hank's friends were mostly MBA students from Columbia. They wore plaid coats and tweedy jackets he thought had gone out of style, matched them with jeans and sneakers.

Instead of grimy Converses, he was wearing his scuffed-up cowboy boots.

Pam's friends were mostly waitresses from the bar where she worked. The one he wanted to talk to was already talking to a tall man in a checkered jacket. His hair had blond highlights.

"You can have $500,000—how old are you?—by the time you're 48. You just have to ... let me see ... interest is at 12% these days, all you need to put in is $150 a month in this annuity—"

Logan leaned against one of the arms of the couch, hoping Pam's friend was as bored as he was by the investment class.

"Oh where *is* she?" Pam hurried past with two empty bottles of wine in one hand and a tray of raw vegetables and dip in the other. "I can't believe she's not here."

Logan grabbed a broccoli head and crunched it between his teeth.

"Invention in itself hasn't been important *for years*. I mean ... the toothpick? A billion people must have invented it, starting with a cave woman who picked her gums with a splinter of mammoth bone. But whoever decided to *market* it—*that* was genius."

Logan came up on Hank from behind. He heard him arguing—in a circle of three—that the prime rate would *have* to come down if construction was going to keep its pace.

"No, it doesn't." One of the men paused to sip from his wine glass. "The Fed could probably *raise* the rate and not slow things at all. The DOW hasn't lost a point in weeks, and that means investors are optimistic. The thing is you can fuel an economy on optimism alone."

Logan stood at the edge of the circle of voices.

The man in the checkered jacket who'd been talking to the cute waitress reached a long arm over Pam's shoulder for a carrot.

"Logan, did you meet Matt—?" Pam rushed off, leaving the two of them to finish the introduction.

About six-foot four, Matt had a smile with a life of its own.

Feeling like a kid in a room full of adults, Logan took the hand Matt held out.

"This place is an antique, turn of the century." Matt swept his gaze around the room. "Buying an apartment's the way to go." Matt stabbed the air with a toothpick as if to give his statement a fine point. "You *can't* make a bad investment with an apartment in this city." Behind glasses glossed with light, Matt's eyes were alert. "Now if it's a *house* and it's out*side* the city ... I'd say pre-fab."

Logan had seen prefabricated roof gables, trucked in and placed on the house frame, each one like a triangular hat on a waiting head. They'd seemed flimsy to him.

"You cut construction costs, keep the price the same, and pocket the difference. Everybody's happy." Matt put a big hand on Logan's shoulder and moved closer. "Care for a line or two? Got a gram on me."

"Nah." He shook his head. He wasn't up for that kind of weirdness tonight. "Nice of you to invite me along for the ride, though."

"Anytime." Matt presented his broad, checkered back ("Catch you later") and headed into the bathroom.

A breeze came in through an open window, put a chill hand on the back of Logan's neck. His head was full of words he didn't understand. The prime rate sounded like a side of beef; financial instruments were nothing like the hooked metal a dentist used to dig around in your mouth; stocks were mythical abstractions traded in a place called Wall Street. A slow rain of paper, like floating ribbons of tickertape, fell in his head.

No one questioned paper's validity until an Ivan Boesky fooled you into giving up one pile of paper for another. And just like that you'd been duped out of a lifetime—the lifetime you could've done something with, gone somewhere, but you'd put it all into getting into work on time, keeping a step ahead of the boss, dressing the part, nodding and yessing when you wanted to slap him—standing there like there was a real reason he was the boss and you weren't—when you would've liked to tell him what a stupid tie he was wearing. Watching the clock and wishing it'd hurry up, the erosion of time was your friend because it got you out of the office, into traffic, and when dinner wasn't ready, god *damn* it, still not ready when you walked in, the whole day seemed to backslide. No matter how tired you were, though, you didn't want to go to sleep (you wanted to hold back the hand on the clock; time wasn't your friend anymore) because when you got up in the morning, you'd have to go back to the office. But all of it was nothing compared to your frenzy after you realized your pile of paper had been stolen, you went and put your money all in one place, and something no one should've been able to steal—a lifetime—had disappeared in a game of white-collar three-card monte.

Tipping back his beer bottle, he decided to do something about the music.

His favorite waitress was standing next to the stereo, talking to Pam.

"The whole thing about directing is you have to get work *out* there. It has to be *seen.*"

He drifted toward them then squatted down to flip through a milk crate of albums.

"I can't believe my best friend stood me up." Pam tapped his butt with a foot. "Whaddayou think you're doin'?"

"Come on Pam, it's been reggae all night." The waitress who wanted to be a filmmaker came to his defense. "You know they only have one song, they just change the lyrics."

"Fine, Rona, go ahead. If you find *chickens* strung up in your room, if you get strange unexplained pains, if the walking *dead* stop by for a visit, don't blame me."

"Pa-am, you are so lurid." Rona tucked a black curl behind an ear.

Pam made a face at Logan that he interpreted as how-dare-she-use-a-world-like-that-on-me.

"Can I help you pick?" Rona asked.

He stood up, his knees fighting him the whole way. "Sure."

Rona's back to him, he watched a polished red nail separate albums.

Pam sighed. "Where are the days when the world was my playpen?" She picked an empty beer bottle up off the floor. "I'll get you another." Lifting herself on tip-toes, she pretended to kiss him behind his ear but whispered, "Get *away* from her." Smiling over a shoulder, she headed toward the kitchen.

"She's sweet, isn't she?"

Logan nodded. "Only that's not my bottle. This is." He held it up.

Rona laughed. "Why didn't you tell her?"

"She's a bartender, she drinks her mistakes."

Rona's pumps were red and her ankles were thick. Her wine glass had smears of lipstick around the rim as if the color were draining out of her and she'd be white as alabaster by the end of the night. She held up an album. "How about this?"

He tilted his head because she was holding it sideways. A Motown compilation. "Fine with me." He admired how she'd balanced her outfit—black blouse, black skirt tied with a red sash that set off a surprisingly small waist, black stockings, red pumps, lipstick, and fingernails. A dark bloom you might expect to be cold except for fire-tipped petals.

Rona cut the reggae album in the middle of a song, put another disc on the turntable, and Logan recognized the opening notes of "Heard it through the Grapevine."

Mission accomplished, Rona combed her hair with her fingers, getting a dark wave to sit higher on her forehead. "I think it's time for me to get out of New York. I mean, the film industry's in Los Angeles …"

California, Jim Lee used to say, *is the last knot on the rope. They'da kept goin' if the Pacific weren't so wet.*

Pam showed up with a bottle of Chianti and refilled Rona's glass. Pam pointed at Logan's beer. "Where'd you get that?"

Rona was smiling, showing teeth that could have used braces.

"What are *you* grinning about? Are you two talking behind my back? Already?"

"Us?" Rona's hand made a five-legged spider on her chest just about where her blouse opened.

"No, your neighbor." Pam pushed Logan. "I knew I couldn't trust you."

"You know how it is with us Indians."

"Mmmmmm," Rona's glass covered her mouth. "So that's where you got the tan. Much better than mine." She held up her forearm. "I hear it's safer than lying out on the beach? A sun lamp?"

A sun that plugs in.

Pam put an arm around each of them, pulled them closer; Logan caught the flowery scent of Rona's hair. "Either of you feel like a couple a lines?"

"Not tonight, Pam."

Logan shook his head.

Pam let her arms slide down their shoulders. "Well, at least you guys know you were my first choice. I mean, I'm a *good* person—it's just that I'm a bad influence."

Pam pulled him down by the neck, whispered in his ear. "I only offered her some because she's *standing* there. All she's got is that rack and those blowjob lips. You know that, don't you?"

He whispered back, "I can work with that."

Pam slapped his shoulder. "Men are *toe* cheese." She headed for the bedroom, opening and closing a hand over her shoulder to say *bye-bye*.

"Hey, Logan ..."

He turned around.

("I can have a million dollars by the time I'm *how* old ...?")

Hank waved him forward with a hand. "I want you to meet a friend of mine."

"Look, I can do it right now on a calculator for you ... if we just assume interest is at 13 percent—you know it's going to hit that in six months—"

Hank was smiling and rosy-cheeked, as if he'd just come in from a snowball fight. "Logan, Rona ... this is Jeff."

Logan took his hand. Cushiony, moist with sweat.

"Jeff's gonna help me land a job at Shearson Lehman after I get my MBA."

"I'll do my best."

A little taller than Logan, Jeff had a pile of wavy black hair. A dark jacket and a white turtleneck set off what Logan figured was an Italian complexion. His oval face had a dainty nose that almost didn't fit in with the rest of his features (maybe he had a twin sister and somehow, in the womb, she'd gotten his nose and he'd gotten hers).

As they went through the preliminaries of who did what and who lived where, it turned out Jeff and Rona had both gone to Pace University.

"So ..." His hands pushed deep into his pants pockets, Jeff turned to Logan. "Are you a waiter-slash-musician?"

"Just a musician."

Jeff swirled the red wine in his glass. "Where do you play?"

Hank clanked his beer bottle against Logan's. "He just got into New York."

Jeff sipped his wine. "Did you go to school here?"

Logan wanted to tell some lies. Or maybe some truths. About how a man had been killed one perfectly ordinary night. Anything to punch a hole in Jeff's evening. "I didn't go to school."

Jeff nodded. "Oh."

"I'm the waitress with a slash—director," Rona said.

"Hi folks! What's goin on?" Pam squeezed between Jeff and Hank.

"We were just wondering why our hostess was ignoring us." Jeff smiled.

"Good thing I'm here, look at you." She brushed at Jeff's nose with a finger. "If you're going to powder up, at least take a look in the mirror when you're done."

Rubbing his nose—that small, straight, feminine nose—Jeff excused himself.

"You're bad Pam." Rona smiled.

"The worst." She leaned close to Rona, put her arms around her neck and whispered something. Both of them laughed.

"What was that all about?" Hank looked at Logan as if Logan knew.

"For Christ's sake, Hank, if I wanted you to hear I wouldn't have *whispered!*"

Hank looked up at the ceiling. "Maybe I should shave my head and join a monastery in Tibet." He put a hand to thinning hair the color of ripe wheat. "No more rent payments, no more job, no more redheads."

"No more *fun*."

"I was a Buddhist for a while." Jeff was trying to find the place where he'd been standing a moment ago.

"What kind?" Logan asked.

"What do you mean, what kind?"

"I mean, if someone asked you what kind of Christian you were, you'd say Lutheran or Catholic or Baptist ..."

Jeff put his fist to his closed mouth and cleared his throat. "Oh I don't ... I don't remember. I was young. Doing that soul-searching every college kid goes through. I gave it up because ... well, let's just say my prayers weren't answered."

Logan quoted Jim Lee: "Prayers are always answered—and sometimes the answer is *no*."

Pam giggled.

"Cute." Jeff nodded and smiled a little uncomfortably.

"So, not traditional Buddhism," Logan said. "There's no one to pray to."

"They're atheists?" Hank looked perplexed.

"Not exactly." Logan took a sip of beer.

"Really, I don't remember." Jeff pushed an empty wine glass toward Logan. "I guess you're a Buddhist."

Logan shook his head.

"Well you seem to know a lot about it. Life is all suffering, right?"

Logan smiled. Somewhere, in a vacuum sealed off by glass maybe, there was a document that entitled everyone to life, liberty, and the pursuit of the trivial.

Hank held out a hand toward Jeff's glass. "Refill?"

"As a matter of fact ..." Jeff looked at his watch. "That's the ballgame for me. I've got to be up early tomorrow."

Pam whispered in Logan's ear: "Late to bed, early to rise gives yuppie cokeheads bloodshot eyes."

Jeff and Hank shook hands. "I'll put in a word for you at the office." He held up a hand. "Night everybody." He pointed at Rona. "We should go out for lunch sometime. I know a great Thai restaurant not too far from where you work."

Pam had already opened the door. "Baa-eye, Jef-ree."

Shutting the door, she put her back to it and braced it with her arms as if someone might try to break it down. "I wish he'd take *me* out to lunch. I'd run up a tab that would make the alligator on his shirt roll over and *die*."

Jeff's leaving seemed to be the cue for everyone else. Within half an hour Rona was helping Pam collect empty bottles and glasses.

Logan and Hank were on the couch, still drinking and talking.

Pam yelled from the kitchen. "Hey! Get off your skinny ass and give me a hand."

Hank stood up and clapped.

"You know, you got rid of the orange hair, the big floppy shoes, the red nose, but you're still a clown. Get in here." She pointed from the kitchen doorway.

"Well, doing dishes is where I draw the line," Rona said.

Pam rolled her eyes. "How predictable."

Logan held up a leather jacket for Rona (it'd been the last of the outerwear on Pam and Hank's bed).

"Thanks." She used her fingers to flick black curls over the collar. "It was really nice meeting you." She put out her hand. "You should visit us at the bar."

"I will."

Rona opened the door. "Hold him to it, Pam. G'night."

After Rona left, Pam elbowed Logan in the side. "You can do better than *her*."

"Who, me?"

"No, your neighbor."

3. Ark Run Aground

"Sleep well?" Pam padded across the burgundy rug into the kitchen. A T-shirt advertising a cinnamon liqueur hung to her knees.

"Pretty good." The couch folded out into a bed, but he hadn't bothered to open it up.

Light glanced into the room from a pair of windows facing Carmine Street. He walked over to one, his bare feet silent on the thick carpeting, and opened it. He felt a puff of cool air and laughed. To be looking out a window that *opened*.

"Want some coffee?"

"Nah."

Opposite him, fire escapes zig-zagged down buildings. In the hospital, iron to keep you in; here, iron to get you out. Eyes squeezed shut, he laughed again—silently this time—his head tipped back, the flesh at the back of his neck bunched up.

"Come in here and sit with me, will you?"

The table in the kitchen could fit four people around it as long as they didn't mind bumping elbows while cutting their steaks. He pulled out a wooden chair.

"Got anything special planned today?"

He dug in the corner of his eye with a finger, wiped away a hard granule. "Uh-uh."

"That was your chance for an excuse." She stood up, coffee mug in hand, nipples clearly visible under her T-shirt. "I don't have to be at work until about four. Which gives me plenty of time to take you around."

She walked him past Carmine Street Guitars. The namesake instrument, floating in a window, was outlined in red neon, lit despite the fact that it was a good-looking spring day. If you were three feet tall, the guitar would've been about the right size.

Suppose you could get a soul in that glass tube and shoot electricity through it—what color would it glow?

At the end of the block was Our Lady of Pompeii, the white church he'd seen yesterday.

Across from the church, someone at Cho's Grocery had neatly arrayed apples, oranges, limes, bananas as though color had become an endangered species while he'd been in the hospital.

A horn blared, wheels screeched, a driver swore out a window.

A shoulder knocked into his. He stepped to avoid someone else, got bumped anyway. Twice he moved, twice there hadn't been enough room.

"There're too many people in the world," he complained.

"Too many on the street anyway," Pam said.

After crossing Demo Square, actually a truncated triangle, they were on Bleecker Street.

"Can you believe what they did to that Hopper?" She lifted her chin at a print in the window of a frame shop.

Elvis Presley, Marilyn Monroe, and James Dean were having a good time in a diner. Humphrey Bogart, dressed for one of his detective roles, was contemplating the smoke from his cigarette, while Elvis whipped up ice cream floats behind the counter. He wasn't sure who Hopper was.

Pam shook her head. "It should be fucking il-*legal*…"

Movie stars dug out of their constellations, like precious

stones from their settings, and dragged down from the heights. Made portable. Like photos in a wallet.

She grabbed his hand and tugged. "Let's go through the park."

The entrance was marked by a marble arch with a different George Washington flanking each side, both of his faces map-works of fine cracks.

Among the trees and benches, spread on the lawns and along the paved paths was a mix of people who looked as if they'd arrived in an ark that had run aground: a heavily made-up Filipina (he was guessing) absorbed in a novel; a guy with a bush of hair and a goatee singing in Spanish and swinging his arms as he strutted to his own music; a blond Asian balanced on a unicycle while he talked to a middle-aged woman (her red hair was dyed, and one of her arms was straightened out by a little dog straining at its leash).

The park was a kind of oasis—grassy, tree-studded, free of traffic that didn't travel on bike or foot or skateboard. Out of a boombox somewhere, Grace Slick suggested asking Alice, *when she's ten feet tall*. Another, competing with the first, he heard the Clash: *London calling to the faraway towns*.

An odd tension held it all together as if the park were intricately webbed and something going on in a far corner came to you as a faint vibration.

A red Frisbee sailed past them. It'd been tossed by a tall shirtless black—very black—whose muscles were so well defined no skin seemed to be covering them.

"*God* he's got a body." Pam shook her head. "Even if his pants do need a wash."

Following a path paved with brick-colored stones, they

passed a guy with reddish-blond hair as long as Jack's, a guitar across his lap. The woman beside him, wearing a paisley shirt, handed him the burning stub of a joint.

In the middle of park was a dry wading pool studded with cement pedestals perfect for performers. A big circle at the center of Washington Square.

A kid, his skin almost as white as the guinea-T he was wearing, his head shaved down to scalp, eyed the guy with the guitar. "Give *war* a fuckin' chance!"

The musician held up the two-fingered sign for peace.

The kid put up his middle finger and kept walking.

4. Dramarama

Amplified sound thumped in the hollow of his chest, turned his ribs into tuning forks. The Sea Beasties had stacked up so much wattage you'd think they were playing to a stadium. Hair a tangle of flaccid kelp falling over his eyes, the singer screeched at the small crowd hovering around the stage.

Except for a few guys bouncing up and down like pogo sticks—about all you could do to music this fast and hard—no one was dancing. Logan and a handful of drinkers clung to the bar.

The guy next to him, in a denim vest that ended in shreds at his waist, had stiffened his hair into a row of spikes and dyed them fluorescent red. His fatigues, tufts of frayed fabric ringing gaping holes, looked like they'd been washed in battery acid. One of the copper buttons on the vest caught the ruddy light and winked at Logan.

He thought of the coal town he'd come from, of Billy Boy with his fifties' haircut and Elvis Presley sideburns. He pictured Jim Lee elbowing Billy: *These're the kinda people take all the fun outa Hollaween.*

Women drifted by, makeup whitening faces already pale, liner to remind you where their eyes belonged.

"Did you ever see so many freaks?"

He tried to communicate telepathically: *Come with me upstate, ladies. I'll introduce you to some of the boys.* But their eyes failed even to glance off him. He wasn't part of the show: intact jeans, a black jacket he'd borrowed from Hank, a single hoop in his ear that even back home they'd gotten used to, a pair of boots with pointed toes and metal tips. "You can keep 'em," Pam had said. "Hank won't wear 'em." The boots came with harnesses that looked like Navajo concha belts in miniature.

"Piss on you!" The lead singer put his back to the audience. "Piss on alla you fuckahs!"

Some of the two dozen or so who'd crowded around the stage booed. Some screamed for another song, punching the air over their heads.

As the band's guitars kicked in, the drummer began hammering away like a preacher taking the rod to a sinner.

Swallowing a mouthful of beer, Logan burped, tasted the falafel he'd eaten for dinner. Middle Eastern spices smoldered in the pit of his gut. He drank more beer to cool the witch's brew.

"I yam an anarchist!

And I yam an anti-Christ!"

They'd decided to cover a band that had blathered to the music magazines about raw as if rock hadn't used Janis Joplin's sawed-off voice to mainline blues. As if the strings of Jimmy Hendrix's guitar hadn't snapped in metallic shrieks and Morrison's voice hadn't broken on lyrics like a galleon on shoals. As if Dylan and Springsteen were crooners, and four unemployed boys in the UK had invented angst and frustration.

"Don't know what I want but I know how to get it,

I wanna dee-stroy passers-by!"

A tall woman led his attention by reins he hadn't known were there. Her bare shoulders glittered. He didn't want to get caught gawking, dumb as a statue. He looked past her. Her hair wasn't spiked or shaved, hadn't been dyed to a glow. Her dress was elegantly out of place. There was no point approaching her, and yet he followed, turned sideways to squeeze in among the bodies creeping up the narrow staircase while an equal number pushed down.

The music on the second floor came from a DJ. The freak-count was lower. But she was gone. He searched the mix of chic and ruined fashion, of beauty heightened by shading and hairstyles savaged by razors and unnatural colors, by brutally wielded black lipstick, but didn't see her.

Darkness greasing the edges of vision, the orchestrated light and music were like the electric wash of *déjà vu*, recalled what once took place by firelight (the magic only works at night). Even if we don't get onto the dance floor, he thought, if we only ring it like a watermark, we need these images to take home with us. That woman in the leather biker's cap spangled with studs, her hips perfectly outlined by liquid pants, might be part of tonight's picture show (chosen by whoever ran the projector when we slept). And he'd see again the way the rusty light shifted on her long body, the close-mouthed smile like the emotionless grin of a reptile, her blink like the flick of a snake's tongue.

A woman who brushed against him as he walked to the bar startled him. It wasn't the woman with glittering shoulders. It wasn't a woman. Despite the dress and makeup, he could see, even in the ruddy murk, the bumps around the mouth and chin, like goose skin, where hair had been removed.

She winked as she sashayed away.

Gas gathered, pressed uncomfortably against his stomach. He patted himself and burped. The spices were still hot embers. Harsh land, harsh food.

Somebody stumbled into him.

"What the 'ell, anovuh one on the flaw." He brushed at Logan's shirt and jacket.

"On *me* is more like it."

"Sorry 'bout that, mate." His bleached hair stood on end. Chains swung from his vest of red leather. "Lemme getch you anovuh. What'll you 'ave?"

He didn't seem to realize only one drink had spilled. "A beer."

"Straight away."

The little limey pushed from person to person back to the bar. It took a few minutes, but a bottle, wet with condensation, made it to Logan's hand.

"Thanks." It was a cool swirl through the hot juice in his stomach, left a faint coffee taste in his mouth.

"You loik Freud?"

"What?"

"The music!" He leaned closer, yelling in Logan's ear and pointing up at huge speakers hung from the ceiling. "Floyd!" His breath smelled of fermented yeast.

The DJ was cutting a song from the *Dark Side of the Moon* album with an instrumental that was all percussion.

The Brit tapped his thin skull. "Center a the moind y'know. The lunatic is in me 'ead. Bit of 'im in all of us."

Logan nodded. The Brit's voice was high and clear, a spoon ringing against glass.

"Years ahead of the toimes, ay?"

The Floyd song already gone, the instrumental was receding, like a wave sliding back, while another song rushed in.

The beer was rough on his tongue.

"'Scuse me, mate, 'ave to 'ave a go on the flaw. Sorry for the wet cloves. No 'ard feelins, ay?"

They shook hands before the little guy turned to go, chains swinging across flapping red leather. The silvery-white hair disappeared among the crowd ringing the dance floor. Logan stared as if he were a cat absorbing the slender flame of a candle into its slitted pupil.

Joy Division came through the mix. He polished off the bottle and wove himself among the dancers as if he were the only body in a cemetery of celebrating spirits. He found just enough of a clearing, like an unmarked grave, in which to maneuver.

A Sisters of Mercy tune kept him going, the rhythm urging him as though he had no say. Sweat began to run, cooled a scalp that still felt exposed by the barber's razor. He danced as though music that had coagulated underfoot were holding him up. He danced not to bump into a hip that would bump him back, but because there was no thunderstorm to rush into, no angry sky he could dare to scratch him out with a crooked finger of light.

Tonight's dancing was nothing that would outlast the music, nothing that would sound the name of a katsina or gather clouds, but it was enough to float him a little above the crowd he'd joined. To simplify him, boil him down to motion, pour him full of music. The way a flute or a violin might've felt if either could feel.

It was a good half hour before a song he didn't like settled his body, turned it into a kite losing wind. Sweating, he walked briskly to the bar, picked up an unguarded drink, and slugged it. Whiskey sour, diluted by melted ice. He rammed the thick-bottomed glass onto the black counter, the sharpness ringing in his ear, and moved down the bar.

A man pushed past him, his upper body bare except for a black leather vest pinned with a swastika. Tattoos twisted and coiled from the bowl of a shoulder to a hirsute wrist. A bird of luxuriant plumage was all that Logan could make out in the reddish smolder. His eyes followed the man to the bar, held by images given a false start toward movement by the interplay of muscle beneath. Logan admired the furrowed arm as a hand in a fingerless glove went up to adjust a gray Civil War cap.

"Hey! Where's my fuckin' drink?" The Illustrated Man began looking around as if he expected someone to volunteer an answer. His face was sharply cut, looked hacked out of wood with a heavy blade. Shadow filled the gouges and ruts.

Logan imagined a creaking leather glove announcing a fist.

"Fuckin bartender." The Illustrated Man, cheekbone virtually a ball beneath his eye, slapped money loudly on the bar.

The equations that could have described the situation had shifted. The tension was gone, equilibrium re-established by solving for X where X equaled blame. If the bartender equaled X then there was no need to solve for Y where Y equaled a form of retribution.

"Fuckin' place is Deadsville." The Illustrated Man shouldered roughly past.

Logan moved back to the edge of the dance floor, dry ice fog creeping across it. A strobe light broke movement up like words in to dis tinct syl la bles. Gaps mea sured for ef fect.

There she was again, mouth wide enough to force hollows below her cheekbones, bare shoulders like asphalt flecked with glass. Smoke crawling at her feet, the light fragmentary, she didn't seem to be touching the floor. She glanced around as though she'd lost her way or maybe she couldn't find someone. Eyebrows arched as if by a taut intellect.

Her back was to him, and he caught her by the upper arm, letting go as she turned around.

"I've been looking for you."

Eyebrows arched as if by a taut intellect, she scoured his face for something she could match against a memory. Her mouth opened, but she hesitated. "Do I know you?"

"You don't recognize me?"

Dimpled at its extremities, her smile arranged her whole face around it, and he knew that this was the woman he'd spent half his life trying to avoid.

5. Wanted

Logan was sitting on the velvety couch, his forearms across his thighs, the classified section of the Sunday *Times* open on the coffee table. He studied it as though it were a map of the route to his salvation. A one-column story on the front page was a bad sign: "Suicide Rate Among Indians in Oregon Highest in Country."

The jobs he'd circled didn't look promising. He could throw boxes in a warehouse on Hudson Street. He could wash dishes or bus tables in three or four restaurants. He could park cars in a garage. He wouldn't have minded getting hired on at a construction site, even as a laborer, but in a city like New York, without a union card, there wasn't much chance of that.

He pulled out his wallet, the black leather worn gray along the spine, and dug in one of the pockets. Drawing out Aristotle's business card, he saw there was an address and a telephone number in Manhattan.

Pam came into the living room, yawning and barefoot, wearing the liqueur T-shirt that hung almost to her knees. Her mouth closed as if her jaw were hinged with elastics. "Achhh … nasty." She made a snapping sound with her tongue against the roof of her mouth.

He'd seen three different brands of mouthwash in the bathroom, all cinnamon-flavored.

"That thing folds out into a bed you know." Pam said it every day now instead of *good morning*. "Where's Hank? In the kitchen with eggs and coffee and an open notebook?"

Logan nodded.

She stifled another yawn. "Figures."

Logan pointed to a shelf of books that was nearly solid orange, a brick-like row of paperbacks. "Does he read those?"

"What're you kidding? Hank won't read a book with *people* in it. Dickens is *my* guy. She started to close the bathroom door behind but held it. "So … get a phone number last night?"

He shook his head. "Almost."

"What happened?"

"She said she had to go to the bathroom."

"Not the *bathroom* … if they ever say *bathroom*, *phone call* or *coat*, they're *gone*." She padded over and kissed him on top of his head. "Hey, there's always Rona." She smirked. "And I still have a friend or two you haven't met."

He nodded, his eyes on the *Times*. Whomever Pam had in mind wouldn't be anything like the woman he'd met last night. She'd glanced at him and he'd felt himself stretched, guts to fingertips, on the rack of her smile.

Somehow he talked her into a dance. She pulled him not by his hand, but by two fingers, using a shoulder to cut between other dancers.

Her languid movements were a marvel to him, effortless and yet just what the music called for. She was a calm, slender flame. His style threw itself off in every direction, like a spreading fire.

He came off the dance floor wiping his forehead and squeezing sweat from his eyebrows. "Can I get you something to drink?" He still hadn't gotten her name. She said no, she needed to use the ladies' room.

He laughed out loud, thinking how easily he'd been taken in.

While he was in the midst turning a page of the newspaper,

Pam pulled the whole thing away from him and tossed it on the floor.

"Never mind this. How'd you like to be the star attraction at the Copper Crow? Our keyboard player hasn't shown up for two weeks."

"Huh?"

"The bar where I work."

"I gotta audition?"

"Well, yeah, that's how it works."

He didn't have to play anything original, didn't have to go out into deep water, just splash around in the shallows with cover songs. He grinned. "Who am I to say no?"

"See?" She winked at him. "It's who you know."

6. The Copper Crow

Logan pulled up a seat behind a double-decker keyboard: a Roland on top umbilically connected by a couple of sagging cords to a Yamaha. The instrument might as well have been a dead body—he wouldn't have wanted to touch either. Didn't really want to look at it. He adjusted the height of the stool, eyes on his hands, and tried to ignore the Crow's owner.

Dave stood next to the bar, glaring.

There was a book of sheet music on a stand next to the keyboard. Unreadable as that painted-on calendar outside the Burning Aztec two worlds away. He closed it and wiped at a wet tickle on his upper lip.

Hands poised above the instrument, he let them sink in air that felt dense as mercury. Until the curves of his fingertips were just tangent to the smooth white of the keys.

Dave cleared his throat.

Logan waited. For something to flow into him. Maybe for a jump start. He lifted a hand and flicked at a key as though aiming at a fly. The surface broken, his fingers began to move on their own. A little off, sure, but with unexpected enthusiasm. Truth be told, they didn't need him all that much. A smirk spread like a stain.

The song drew him in deeper, and the space his senses occupied, opened, expanded. Deposited each at a distance, each in a place lonely enough to echo. Solidity began to waver and he broke down into a cloud of fireflies. He wondered whether they could see it in the bar's perpetual dusk, how the notes gave the swarm its flicker, how, unlike the haphazard tremble of starlight, a harmony held it together.

Good as playing made him feel, he was rusty. No matter how many knobs he adjusted, he couldn't quite get the sound he wanted.

"You can sing too, right?"

He nodded.

"I gotta take your word for it?" Dave shook his head, a crooked half-smile on his face.

Logan sang the next three songs.

Cheeks acne-pitted, oversized nose bumped in the middle, hair that looked to have been pressed out of black vinyl, Dave cut him off at the beginning of the fourth. "Okay, okay, good enough." He gave the ring on his finger a couple of twists. "I'll give you a call if I need you."

He disappeared into a back room as Logan stood up.

"You did great," Rona said. She and Pam were waiting by the door.

Logan hadn't been great and he knew it.

Before leaving Pam and Hank's apartment, he'd taken a shower but hadn't been able to find a comfortable mix of cold and hot. Every time he turned a knob, it was too far in one direction or the other. He couldn't help recalling those four-pronged shower handles while he was fiddling with the black knobs on the keyboards. An odd echo.

"C'mon," Pam tipped her head toward the door. "Let's get out of here."

The night air was warm, damp with what was left of a rainstorm. A light breeze turned cold where sweat had soaked through his shirt. A blurry sickle of a moon showed through ragged breaks in the clouds, and lingering mist.

"Well, whaddayou think?" Pam looked up at him expectantly.

He shook his head. "I don't know."

Rona put a hand on his shoulder and squeezed. "Oh you're a hundred times better than the last one."

A shiver ended in a pool of warmth in his groin.

His nose suddenly began to run. As if he'd been eating Mexican. He let the women get a step ahead of him while he wiped his nose on a shirt sleeve. Then he used the back of his thumb and the side of his forefinger until his nostrils didn't feel slick anymore.

"I'm starved." Pam was wearing a short black skirt and black boots.

An unnatural glow—the city's aura—made the hard edges of buildings hallucinatory against a still sky. Façades were mostly stacks of opaque windows and the painstakingly arranged stones in which they'd been set. Sometimes the shallow niches were brick. Each like an entrance to a separate past.

Light was the moony whiteness of streetlamps, a match flaring beneath the face of a black woman with full lips and a high forehead, what drizzled from suns so distant they were glittery debris in the sky's memory—no brighter than sparks from the first flints struck by apish, leathery hands anxious to get at the glowing secret overhead.

"Where are you going?" Pam sounded annoyed. "*This* way."

He fought a sudden urge to put his arm around Rona.

She looked at him and smiled. A generous mouth set in a Mediterranean face, teeth dulled a little by smoking, a jaw more rounded than straight. She had no idea what he was feeling, no sense of the urgency he was holding back. How could she, divided as she was from him by what might as well have been a light year or a century or a language?

The back of Pam's head was an impenetrable tangle of curls. "Here we are."

He got the door for both of them, their reflections translucent in the dark glass.

Too much light, white and sterile, flooded the next moment.

Pam took them upstairs, picked out a table next to a wall-sized window with a view of the taller buildings across the street.

The menu, a slim cardboard rectangle, listed about 20 different kinds of coffee, a dozen or so salads, a few sandwiches. He looked up at Pam and Rona. They seemed at home with it.

Closing the menu, he caught sight of a paper relic on a brick wall. An old calendar illustrated with … a buffalo hunt? A reproduction of a Russell maybe. He got out of his chair and crossed the hardwood floor, stopped on a board that creaked under his weight. Yes, Russell. *In Okeene 72 Years* the calendar announced (in case you were wondering) and beneath that, in letters that dwarfed its claim to longevity, *STATE GUARANTY BANK*. The full moon in February 1972 had fallen on the 29th. A big month for the *katsinam*, when a whole bunch who'd overslept the December ceremonies showed up on the mesas.

Above the bank's name and a statement of its resources ($6 million), a brave gripped his saddle-less horse with legs alone. His bow was drawn to the point of breaking, the hump of a buffalo an arm's length away. Nearby was the dust-hazed figure of another hunter with bow drawn.

The colors were what he liked most: red breech-clouts, ocher skin, beige grass, chestnut-brown bison, rust-tinted sky. Underneath the age-tanned February page, March was as white as a sheet of new typing paper.

Like the calendar, Logan had once been in Okeene, Oklahoma; what were the chances the two of them would meet up in New York?

"Hey, are you going to order or what?" Pam's hands were turned up as if testing for rain.

He spun around, saw the waitress looking at him expectantly. "Uh, ham and cheese?"

"Ham and mozzarella? Ham and Swiss? Ham and Monterey jack?"

"Swiss, I guess."

She marked her pad and stuck the pencil in an apron pocket.

As if connected by an invisible rope to the waitress, he walked back toward the table as she moved away from it.

"We were just talking about one of Rona's films. Ever see *City of Trams*?" Taking advantage of the fact that Rona was looking down, Pam mouthed *City of Tramps*, pressing her lips together hard to mime the *P*.

"No," Rona said, "he didn't. It was a short. Hardly anybody saw it. Twenty-two minutes."

"What's it about?"

"It's set in New Jersey in the early '60s ..."

He could tell by the way the words came out she'd pitched it before.

"A white hit man falls for a black prostitute. It's really not bad. If I could get a backer, I'd love to expand it into a feature."

The waitress brought a fruit cup for Rona, what looked like a salad sandwich for Pam, coffees for both of them. His ham-and-cheese was cold. He'd expected the cheese to be melted, the bread to be toasted. He wanted to send it back.

Looking at the candle in the middle of the table, he thought about lighting it to see what a warmer luster would do to Rona's face.

A spoon tarnished by shadow lay next to a tiny pitcher with the curves of a leaning woman.

Rona lifted the toy-like pitcher and poured white into her coffee. "New York must be a big change from Kansas."

Much as cities fascinated him, he'd never much liked living in them. He thought of a kid who waits all summer for the carnival in August, spends his whole savings on melting ice cream that keeps his hands sticky for the night, on dizzying rides that remind him his stomach is bloated with soda, on game booths where he throws balls at wooden milk bottles or shoots a stream of water into a gorilla's mouth until he's won a prize to give to a girl he's trying to impress, gangs of boys from other towns looking him over. The Kansas night stood just at the edge of the electric magic, the music of the rides dimming, fireflies rising in the warm air. Sick of it all after a few days, everything was gone soon enough, and the field was full of empty cups and wrappers, trampled by so many feet he didn't ever want to see a carnival again. Until next year.

"Carnival overload. Never heard that one before." Rona held a white grape between her slightly uneven teeth before she let it fall inward and crushed it. Which is how it goes for things small, soft, and sweet.

The hiss from an espresso machine was as loud as the air hose at a gas station.

Pam was hardly done with her sandwich when she stood up. "Well, I gotta go." She put down a few bills.

He stood up and got a hug.

"See you tomorrow, Pam …" Rona called after her.

Pam waved to them over a shoulder without looking back.

The crystalline fruit cup empty (spoon sticking out of it like a cowlick), Rona lit a cigarette.

"What was the hardest thing about making your film?"

She turned her head to the side and blew a stream of smoke. "That's a good question." Having hit on an answer, she nodded, . "Getting together a good cast—no, getting everyone to work as a team. *That* was a bitch." Her focus shifted. "Oh no … *Kevin*."

Two men in sharkskin suits stood near top of the stairs, but Logan was distracted by a man whose long hair was graying and whose back was to him. He couldn't see much of the denim jacket—the back of the guy's chair was in the way.

Rona put a hand as warm as breath on top of his. "I really don't want to talk to him. He kept saying he was going to finance a film I was doing with a friend of mine—Kevin's *loaded*—but it was all bullshit. He just liked having everyone kiss his ass."

Logan nodded, but he was still looking at the gray hair, the denim jacket.

"Is something wrong?"

He looked out the window. He felt safer with the glass expanse nearby, something to keep the night from collapsing in on them but breakable too. A promise of open space.

"Oh god, here he comes."

Angeldusted Jack. Probably the last person he wanted to see.

He looked up at Kevin but turned to Rona when she introduced him as her boyfriend. There was a pleading look on her face.

Kevin, in his shimmering suit, took his hand. "How you doin'?" He had wavy blond hair and a tan. He didn't look anything like Dave, the guy who owned the Crow, but something about them was the same, as if they were somehow related.

"So what brings you here?" Rona asked.

Logan didn't hear Kevin's answer; he was staring at the apparition of burned-out Jack, peppery hair falling down over worn denim.

Logan started toward the artfully twisted iron railing, which divided the section they were sitting in from the rest of the upstairs, leaned over it as if he were on a reeling ship. A turn of Jack's head exposed enough of a profile for him to see it wasn't Jack.

"Hey it was nice meeting you."

He faced the source of the voice and took Kevin's hand again. "You're not staying?"

"Nah, we're headed uptown." He looked at Rona. "I'll stop by the Crow when I get a chance." He turned to Logan, held his hand up like a Boy Scout taking an oath. "Strictly business."

Logan smiled. "No problem."

Kevin and his sidekick descended the stairs in their shiny suits.

"Sorry about that." Rona's hand covered his again. She smiled, swollen red lips stretched to glossy tautness. "That was your first role for me." She withdrew her hand to look at her watch. "Well, I should get going."

He looked for the waitress, but she was already on her way, tearing the check from her pad.

He left the money for both of them next to Rona's coffee cup.

Rona went down the stairs first, her wavy black hair tapering to a point between her shoulder blades.

Outside, she took his arm.

The sky had become utterly smooth: no stars, no moon, no katsinas, just an expanse of artificial orange and a receding fleck of red—a plane.

Rona stopped in front of a shop window. "That's gorgeous."

A sequined dress on a mannequin whose face was such angular perfection it was a shame she wasn't alive. Round scales of bronze and red adhered to her lean body.

"Five hundred at least," she sighed.

Where's Kevin when you need him?

"I just like to look." Her smile might have been apologetic.

Maybe she'd read the look on his face.

They turned a corner onto a street that was all tenements and stopped again. "Well, this is me." Her eye sockets were filled with dark.

He should give her a good kiss good night, he thought, but somehow didn't, sliding off her cheek into a hug. The scent of whatever she was wearing made him forget there were any such things as traffic lights, burned-out Jacks, banks that advertised themselves with buffalo hunts, sequined dresses that could suck dry the paycheck he didn't even have yet. He wanted her smell to rub off on him. That would be enough when he was falling asleep tonight. Her smell.

7. THE ECHO TWINS

He was glad he was at the back of the bar, tucked into a corner of the Copper Crow where it was easier to feel alone. Still surprised Dave had called him in for Sunday through Wednesday, he was grateful Rona wasn't working his first night.

Every time he finished a song, he had to bend down and blow the keyboard clean of the rust, like dried blood, flaking off his hands. Month after month—a whole year—he hadn't played. He was a tin man in need of an oil can. Or maybe a revival meeting. But if his playing hadn't been anything special, neither was anyone paying much attention: tie score.

He swiveled on his stool and reached over to adjust the drum machine. He tried not to look up, a little embarrassed at what he'd come to—all these synthetic sounds and watery versions of pop tunes.

A Doors song, he decided, was what he should throw into the set, loosen him up some. A one-beat drum machine would have to take John Densmore's place. For Robby Krieger's guitar he had no fill-in. He himself was going to have to double as Ray Manzarek and Morrison, both of whom he idolized though for different reasons. This would be a version of their music they might not even recognize. From a half-Hopi who'd grown up in Kansas. Who'd decided he wasn't going to sing like anyone he'd ever heard cover this song.

He wondered whether Morrison, an expert on doors, had known anything about the one at the top of his head, that soft spot on babies mothers were careful of. (*How do you think you're soul got in you? Qua'ah* hadn't been smiling.) Then the skull sealed it. You forgot it was even there unless you aum-ed and meditated it open again, made it into a skylight. Unless you dabbled in cactus extracts and turned the night into a saguaro the size of a sequoia—only to have it come crashing through the glass. Unless you remembered how to use it to sense direction, to orient yourself without map or landmark or Boy Scout compass. Unless you played music to bang-start things all over again, expand space, form new constellations throwing shadows on the bowl of your skull.

His fingers slid comfortably into Manzarek's carnival-ride grooves, his downsweeps and sudden swells. Lingering over the beginning of the song, he twisted and reshaped bars as if the song were a bit of space-time taffy between the fingers of a mischievous god (he was glad Ray wasn't listening in).

The half-interested drinkers, their elbows resting on square tables, began to fade. The lights dimmed until all he could see were silhouettes gathered around the occasional glint of a raised glass.

Opening verses sung, he let his fingers have their way. Instinct in them strong enough to leave the part of him not hitting the keys free to rub elbows with the Humpbacked Fluteplayers, who'd accompanied the Hopi into the Second World. He bumped nose-first into the midriff of one of the War Twins, whose job it had been to harden the Earth when it'd been a big ball of mud. Bare-chested, kilted, leanly muscled with streaks of red lightning painted down their bodies, they were too tall to get though the door of the Copper Crow without crouching. They'd sent their voices shivering up and down the Earth's axis—a game of telephone from one pole to the other—answered when you called out. So he'd nicknamed them the Echo Twins.

They looked over his shoulder, scrutinized what had gotten him so worked up sweat was running down the side of his face. For them it was a break from poking around in music shops, toying with the vast array of instruments that had shown up since the creation of the Fourth World, experimenting with synthesizers, thumping drums—giddy as spoiled children— blowing trumpets, floating their breath across shiny flutes such as the mesa had never seen in the old days.

The grinning Twins shrank down, grew woolly beards, and slipped into denim jackets as if into new skins, blanched as though with fear or a sudden loss of blood. They were joined by others: floury women who wore loose, tie-dyed shirts, glass beads, American Indian headbands, Asian Indian sarongs; men who were suffering from hallucinations of brotherhood and free love, who made two fingers into Vs, who refused to eat meat and basked in their stainless karma.

He opened his eyes. A woman drinking at the bar had crimson skin, green lips, violet hair. Trapped, it seemed, under a dome of many-colored glass.

Closing his eyes again, he strained to keep his voice at the depth he wanted. So what if it had the second-hand timbre of an echo chafed into silence by craggy slopes? What did they expect from a musician in a basement bar drawing pocket money? It felt good all the same, emptied his pores of soot and grime and whatever else rubbed off this decaying city.

From far away, some part of him marveled that he could play by feel while the other part did the marveling. Nothing touched him where he was now. Not even the long-haired hippie ghosts who crowded around the keyboard. On their denim jackets, like woven blue smoke, symbols of peace, emblems of love, tokens of good will, hearts the wrong red for spilling blood, flowers that gave off the scent of enlightenment, ankhs glittering with ancient wisdom, astrological stars out of Babylonian skies, crescent moons, Tibetan mandalas. As if they'd fallen into trances and come back with nothing else. Wearing them as charms to attract the serene destiny no civilization had ever been allotted these thousands of years.

The witched jackets had failed. They'd been no good at stopping bullets. Not in the jungle inferno of Southeast Asia, not in the academic sanctuary of Kent State. Not in the incendiary ghettos of Watts or Newark. Love was never free. Turn the other cheek and they truncheoned that one too. There wasn't any Woodstock Nation and there never would be. Wounded Knee hadn't happened once but twice. The buffalo weren't coming back and the Anglos weren't going away. Why not set it all on

"FIIIIIIIIII-*YUUUUUUURRRR*...."

His eyes opened, got stung by sweat. For all he knew, his skin had gone crimson too.

There was a trickle of applause, and someone, more excitable, whistled.

It hadn't come off badly, a song meant for four, meant for a different voice entirely.

"My *god*, Logan ..." Pam picked up the empty beer bottle at his feet. "How did you—I mean, you could sing *opera*." Her freckled face, her hair, were the right colors.

He stood up, not ready to re-enter the realm of two-way conversation.

Pam swung an arm heavy with beer mugs. "You goin' on break now? Perfect. Someone I'm *dying* for you to meet just walked in."

He headed for the bathroom.

Two guys in mirrored sunglasses were smiling at him, battered instrument cases in their hands. Professional courtesy. Their skin was dark enough, their straight hair black enough, to be Indian. They had on worn, outdated suits. One rust-colored, the other a little browner, closer to oxblood. He nodded to them as he went into the bathroom.

He sat on the toilet lid with the door locked, the darkness almost complete (although the soundproofing was mediocre). He wanted a smoke, maybe one of those Italian stogies Jim Lee always had between his teeth. Wanted its smoldering ember to focus on, to burn away—by some miracle of sympathy—what was keeping him from joining everyone outside, from talking about a baseball game, the office, the song he'd just played. He wanted to watch the glow brighten as he drew on the cigar, watch it arc from mouth to knee (where he'd rest his hand), and back.

Those musicians with beat-up instrument cases and old suits—Salvation Army leftovers, he'd bet, weathered by road trips city to city, bar after bar, to the tune of drinks and a few bucks here, a little applause there—had he seen them before? The first time he played at some cramped little cantina in LA? Maybe in Phoenix too. He'd never caught their act—if it was even they. False déjà vu probably, one musician for each eye.

Feeling better, he listened through the door to idle murmur streaked with loud laughter.

When he opened the door, an imaginary cloud of smoke mushrooming out, the musicians with mirrored eyes were gone. Pam was at the bar talking to a woman whose dimpled smile got his blood going in a rush. When she saw him, there was a subtle shift in her expression, like the surface of a lake roughened by a breeze, rippling from mild expectation to recognition to—disappointment? No, more like shit luck. He started to laugh.

8. 12 NEVER-BEFORE-REVEALED BEAUTY SECRETS

He took the straps off the boots Pam had given him. The lines were clean without them, the boots smooth black tipped to sharpness by metal toes. His old two-toners, the tops fallen over like a pair of collapsed lungs, sat in a corner with the look of an abandoned girlfriend. Slapping a pocket to make sure he had his keys, he headed out.

The carpet in the living room cushioned the characteristic clump of his heels.

The warm evening was lit by scripted neon, oncoming headlights, streetlamps flickering to life. He passed Our Lady of Pompeii Church, which, with its copper cupola and stony whiteness, might have been uprooted from an island in the Mediterranean.

He took Bleecker, where at one or two in the morning, people would still be buzzing in and out of bars and cafés and poster shops. No pilgrimage called for in these shops, no fasting, no tearful prayer, no sleeplessness. What you were looking for was already printed, backgrounded, bordered. Willing enough to buy an Ansel Adams photo of the desert, not quite as ready to wander in one. Infatuated with ready-mades because even if you stopped in your travels to take stock of the architecture the moment surrounds you with, there's no way to hold onto it, not without lugging around a camera or a notebook or an easel and canvas. There was something in being able to rummage around for a spectacle you might otherwise never see, something in a frame you could cart off and hang up. There was something, too, in reproductions breaking the monopoly of the museums, something that had closed the moon eye like an old diner that wasn't doing the business it used to.

A block over from Bleecker, the Copper Crow pressed up against a tiny firehouse with interlacing stone and brick that looked to have been mortared in place at the turn-of-the-century.

Down a flight of stairs.

It was comedy night. Dave had reserved the slowest nights for him: He was a spare tire.

One of the drinkers at the bar was a huge biker, his broad back covered by a leather jacket.

Pam came out from behind the bar. Her friend, the woman who'd ditched him, was sitting at a table.

"Hi, sweetie." An arm around his waist, Pam patted his chest with her free hand. "In case you haven't noticed, my bosomest buddy is all by herself. A real man would go over there and keep her company."

The dazzle of the night he'd met her in Dramarama had been unplugged. She was wearing a wine-colored sweater and a pair of jeans she might have put on to paint her apartment. Her hair, ragged with strays, looked hastily pinned up. She hadn't bothered with makeup, not that he could see. Still it seemed you'd have a better chance of getting a crow to trill like a canary than of striking up a conversation with her. And here all he had to do was walk across the bar, pull up a chair, and sit down.

He waved.

She smiled, lifted her hand and scratched the air with a couple of fingers.

He looked down at Pam. "I think I'll stay at the bar. I came to see Rona."

"God what's *wrong* with you? That's like sending back *filet mignon* so you can have meatloaf."

"I like meatloaf."

Pam mimed pulling out her hair.

He didn't tell Pam that he preferred pretty to stunning, that he sensed behind looks like her friend's a web-work of supports, like the steel girding behind a billboard. Liable to collapse if one or two stays were knocked loose.

Pam sighed. "Whaddayou want to drink?"

"A beer. Something dark."

As Pam left, Rona sat down.

"Ha-aye." She pulled out her tips, spilling crumpled bills onto the bar. Sitting diagonally from him at the rounded corner of the bar, she was smiling, but her eyes kept flicking over his shoulder. "What's up?"

He shook his head, looking down at her red nails, which had the sheen of a new car. "Just thought I'd drop by and say hello."

She sighed heavily, put her chin in her hand. "I need a drink."

"You came to the right place."

She straightened up suddenly. "How did it go?"

She was talking to someone behind him.

"Ah, a pain in the ass as usual." Dave's pale pink shirt was open at the collar, showing a carpet of black hair. He had a nose like a toucan's beak, a face as weathered as a dirt road, a gut held back by a straining belt. "What brings you by on your night off?"

Logan looked at Rona, but she was concentrating on her tips. "Thought I'd say hello to Pam."

"You don't see enough of her at the apartment?"

"I hardly see her at all." He smiled half-heartedly. "I'm out during the day, and when I get back, she's at work. Hank never sees her either."

Dave nodded.

"Well, I'm going to get going." Rona's lips stretched into a smile. "My tables are all done, and Lynn is here."

Logan watched her disappear in the direction of the ladies' room.

Dave was digging in the register like a raccoon who'd come across a garbage can without a lid.

Pam put a bottle down in front of him. "Glass?"

Logan held up the bottle. "Comes in a glass."

"What's that look on your face? You figured out Rona's no prize?" Pam was trying to keep an I-told-you-so grin to herself. "You know she's fucking Dave, right?"

Out of the corner of his eye, he saw Rona coming. She leaned toward Pam—"See you tomorrow …"—but reached down to squeeze his thigh. And she was off again, black skirt above thick calves, slim waist below a slighter body than you might expect looking at her from the bottom up.

Dave met her at the door. Maybe she was looking for a graceful way out of it …? He looked at Dave, remembered Kevin in his sharkskin suit, and his *strictly business* Boy Scout's oath. It *was* strictly business. Kevin had liked fucking Rona but not enough to pony up for her film. Dave was the new bank.

Pam was taking bottles down one by one and wiping them off. There must've been close to a hundred standing in neat rows in front of a mirror the size of a small pond, its edges trimmed by woodwork from another era. A flourish of leaf patterning dressed up the top corners and bloomed into the centerpiece of a fluted mantel. A scribble of neon below the mantel reiterated itself in the mirror, an illegible signature the pale red of iron just before it burned white.

"Hi."

Her smile showed teeth almost too big for a mouth almost too big for her face. The winey color of her sweater gave her face a ruddy cast. Or maybe that was just the moon eye.

"We haven't been able to get much past names, have we?"

He smiled weakly. Her hair was an unusual color, a reddish brown fired to coppery highlights. Dyed probably.

"And when I saw you here on your first night, you pretty much ... well, it's not that I didn't deserve to be ignored, but since you're staying with Pam, who is after all my best friend, I thought ..."

Her eyes were a milky jade.

He nodded. "It wasn't payback or anything. Just didn't want to bother you."

"Okay, well, you're not bothering me now. So why don't we start again? My name's Shawna. Glad to meet you—really."

He put his hand out. "Logan."He sipped his beer, hoping it would soften the brittle edge to his voice.

Pam clunked a bottle on the bar. "An LA woman in New York."

"I spent some time out there," Logan said.

"Like it?" Shawna asked.

"Not much."

"That makes two of us."

"Why don't you guys go sit at a table? I need the bar for *paying* customers." Pam smiled as if it were an effort to be nice to them.

As he got up, the big biker sitting at the other end of the bar held up his beer bottle and winked as though he were Logan's father quietly congratulating him. A step behind, Logan followed Shawna to her table. In Dramarama they'd been about the same height. Now, even in sneakers, she wasn't that much shorter. He turned a magazine lying on the table until it was facing him.

"I buy it mainly for the ads."

"Not the—" He looked down. "—twelve never-before-revealed beauty secrets?"

"The ads."

"Isn't that what most people complain about?"

"I'm in advertising."

"Selling?"

"Mostly selling. But I work with creative sometimes."

"What about an album cover? Ever do anything like that?"

Her eyebrows, already arched, drew themselves up a little higher. "Why, are you going to put one out?"

Caught out, he tried denial: "Just wonderin'."

"Well, no, I never did anything like that, but I'd love to. I do photography. For myself, really."

Because neither of them said anything for a few seconds, a question came out like something sliding off a tray: "You … don't sell them? The photographs?"

She pressed her lips together and shook her head. "I'm just interested in the way light falls, the way things are arranged. The way objects … relate to each other, I guess. Spatially. But at a certain moment. I'm not good at painting or drawing, so I took the easy way out." She raised her wine glass and took a sip. The knit sleeve of her sweater sagged.

He wanted to see the arm in that sleeve as if it would tell him something about her that wouldn't come out in conversation. He tried to imagine her bones, the undersymmetry intimated by the strange light in Dramarama.

"Actually, I've always been a little envious of musicians. The way music moves things around inside you. I'd like to do be able to do that with a photograph. My job, though, is moving money from one pocket to another. Of course, that presents its own challenges." She brushed a few strands of copper sunset behind an ear.

"How does it work?"

"Well, you have a target group, like businessmen or single women or suburbanites, and you get them to come to a certain conclusion … feel a certain way. About a product."

She let the bulb of the wine glass rest on the tips of her fingers.

He held his beer bottle in a fist (certainty a deity he didn't believe in).

"Pam told me you're from Kansas?"

"Arizona originally."

"Where in Arizona?"

"Phoenix."

"I was in Phoenix for a while."

"Like it?" he asked.

"Not much."

"That makes two of us."

"Well, not at the time, anyway. Maybe if I—"

"This must be a re-run." Pam turned a pair of shot glasses upside down next to their drinks. "From the nice man in leather and studs who thinks you two make a lovely couple."

Logan lifted his bottle to the biker. "That was neighborly of 'im."

Pam glanced in the direction of the bar. "Let me clue you in … with a few minor exceptions, men are toe cheese."

"I guess that's why we age so well."

Shawna smiled, her dimples deep enough to collect rainwater.

"Whatever you do, don't let her go to the bathroom."

Logan almost laughed.

The look Pam got from Shawna made her lean back from the table and cross her arms over her chest like a Hollywood vampire in her coffin. "*Teas*ing, hon."

"Does that mean I shouldn't trust her to take me out to dinner tomorrow night and show me around town?"

"Dinner...?"

"At your favorite restaurant. Isn't that what you said?" He smiled optimistically.

"Tomorrow night ...?"

"It's about time you acted civilized." Pam flicked her bar rag at Shawna.

Shawna raised an eyebrow. "This should be interesting."

9. Two Gardens, Two Fools

Shawna took him past restaurants in Chinatown he'd seen before—cramped places with dingy tile floors, peeling vinyl chairs, tablecloths with stains you noticed even from the street. The way she looked tonight, in a black dress that gave her green eyes a flinty hardness, she might've cracked their chalky lighting.

This was the fourth time he'd seen her, the third hairstyle: pulled back in a single braid and gelled to a sheen. The dress came up to her throat like a turtleneck but left her shoulders bare. Her bronzed hair and the false depth of all that black chiseled her cheeks and jaw.

Hunan Garden had a whole street corner to itself. The floor was carpeted in plush red. Paper lanterns, each with a stern black character in the center—like a warrior's ethic in calligraphy—floated in their own muted light. Screens with lacquered panels depicted wading herons, towering pagodas, mountains disappearing in mist. The flute music was the spare, dreamy stuff his mother sometimes played on an old Victorola.

Though she had never known—Grandpa hadn't stuck around to see her born—his mother always insisted she was Chinese on that side. She had Asian eyes and high cheekbones, but no one ever considered her anything but white. Didn't keep her from hoarding books on Chinese history and art, from using pennies instead of yarrow stalks to practice with the *I Ching*, from quoting out of Lao Tzu's *The Way*. She'd even learned the language to some useless extent. Lot of good it did her to practice her inflections in the southeast corner of Kansas. Though with her dread of chaos and her penchant for harmony, she might've had something of the distant East in her.

After his father had died, she'd taken up with Cal like someone casting about for something to plug a break in a dam. But water shot through a half dozen places where the fit wasn't even close. No matter how she tried to stop up and smooth over, the other side always threatened to pour through.

"You okay?"

"Just thinking," was all he meant to say but added, "about my mom."

"Is she still in Kansas?"

He shook his head. "She never much liked Kansas or small towns. She's in San Francisco now." Bought a cute little house with the insurance money after Cal died. Just outside Chinatown (where else?). She lived alone, and what social life she had was tied to outings with a church group she belonged to. "She loved Chinese things, that's all." He opened a menu bound in red leather.

A harp, lightly plucked, joined the flute, intimated cherry blossoms settling on a pond.

The waiter, wearing what could've been a white lab coat had it been a little longer, stood over them with a pencil pressed to paper. Combed to the side, his oiled hair was short and fuzzy from the temples down. "Ready to ordah?" The waiter's smile worked against a frog mouth and thick lips naturally inclined to turn down.

Logan went with the moo-shoo chicken; Shawna asked for Buddha's delight.

A moment later, another waiter set a glass of wine in front of Shawna and poured a beer for Logan. Setting his hands together, he looked over their table. Then, as if he were a master painter who was satisfied not another stroke was necessary, turned and left.

Logan remembered his mother in their yard, a slight figure in faded jeans and flannel shirt, digging, planting, rearranging. Black hair falling as she bent over. She made Cal bring truckloads of dirt so she could terrace and slope. She chose stones as though each were something she'd have to live with forever. The same flowers grew in the same places every year. She raised her little hill in the flatness, arranged a tidy cosmos she presided over with sublime beneficence, aiming a hose to bring rain, uprooting invading weeds as if sweeping away marauding armies, protecting delicate seedlings with the humped backs of stones.

"Knock, knock." Shawna crossed her hands in front of his face like a flag signaler without the flags. "Are you sure you don't want to have dinner by yourself? I wouldn't want to interrupt."

"Sorry. I used to catch hell for staring out windows in grade school too."

"Uh-*huh*. What's your sign?"

"Does that have something to do with it?"

"Just tell me."

"Slippery When Wet."

"I know it seems silly to you. A guy walking on water and getting up three days after he was tortured to death seems silly to me. When were you born?"

He took a long swallow of beer. "July."

"Cancer?"

Logan nodded. *Logan Blueclaw. Logan Bottomfeeder. Logan Sidecrawler.*

"Domestic, creative, and, yeah, a little dreamy." She pointed an accusing finger tipped by a coppery nail. "*See?*"

"Doesn't matter." He waved a hand. "The star it's measured by has shifted. It's all off."

"The *equinoxes* have shifted. A Greek mathematician figured that out about 2,000 years ago."

"The equinoxes?"

"When you look up at the sky, it looks like the constellations are rotating—the Earth is turning, of course. The axis they seem to be turning around? Well, over thousands of years that moves, which means the pole star changes."

"The North Star."

"Right. It also means that every 2,150 or so years, right at the vernal equinox, the Sun appears to be in front of a different constellation of the zodiac. It was in Pisces around the time Christ was born. Now it's just about in Aquarius. Remember the song? 'Age of Aquarius'? The whole New Age thing? That's what got it goin'."

Logan thought of Angeldusted Jack.

"Don't you think there's *some*thing to it?" Shawna asked. "I mean alignments and arrangements? It's not that far from the composition of a painting. Or architecture. Except what I'm talking about is an invisible architecture—except where stars surface."

Astrology, maybe, was looking at astronomy through the moon eye. "There's something to anything that's been around that long, I guess."

"Don't you want to know mine?"

"Your sign? I'm gonna go with Dangerous Curves Ahead."

"Oh you're funny. Scorpio."

"You look like a Scorpio."

"Yeah?" For a second her teacup hid everything except her green eyes. "What does a Scorpio look like?"

"Like you wouldn't want to step on one."

Collecting the silverware, a busboy replaced it with chopsticks and set down little bowls of rice.

The cushioned surroundings—the carpeting, the red cloths draped over the tables, the paper-shrouded light—made it seem they were inside a huge jewelry box. But the precious stones were *outside*; lift the ceiling and the sky was bedecked.

The waiter brought their entrees and with enviable skill used two spoons in each hand to roll the moo-shoo—it looked like a tangle of seaweed—into pancakes. Placing the stuffed pancakes on Logan's plate, he arranged the remainder of the moo-shoo, the bowls of rice, the plate with two more pancakes, and Shawna's Buddha's delight, until he looked pleased. "Enjoy you dinneh."

Risking the stares of those better acquainted with etiquette (Shawna in particular), Logan lifted the rolled moo-shoo as if it were a burrito. "You draw charts?"

She shook her head. "I used to do Tarot readings, though."

Swallowing a mouthful of moo-shoo, its saltiness mellowed by the bland pancake and sweetened by plum sauce, he was pretty sure he'd gotten away with his boorishness. "How about Ouija boards?"

She stopped picking around in her Buddha's delight and glared at him.

"What? It actually worked?"

"I'll tell you, but you can't laugh."

"How about I cover my mouth?"

"Just don't. This was like … three years ago? We were all on the beach getting drunk, and it was getting dark. I remember cold sand between my toes. Somebody took out a Ouija board, and I *swear* it worked. Four people had a finger on the pointer—no single person could have moved it that smoothly." A finger landed on her chest like a flagpole claiming the black territory of her dress. "I know what I felt."

"Where was this beach?"

"East Hampton."

"Where's that?"

She smiled. "You really are from Kansas. Out on Long Island. Anyway, the little plastic pointer was going around the board, and we wanted to know who was moving it."

"Don't tell me, a shipwrecked sailor."

Still chewing, she swept her head from side to side emphatically. "No." She swallowed. "Just listen. The guy was a passenger coming back from England. His own friend hit him on the head and threw him overboard—something like that. All we got were things like *hit, head, overboard, friend.* And we filled in the blanks."

He thought of his father trapped in the dream of an afterlife. His mouth was open, veins and muscles bulged in his neck, but no sound came out.

"We asked him the name of the ship, the year it happened, the captain of the ship—things like that. I went to two libraries the next day and spent hours looking through old shipping records, and I *found* it." She stabbed a finger at him. "You're thinking that one of the guys set it up, right?"

"You got me." He decided to give the chopsticks a try.

"Well, *listen.* One of the guys kept asking for a prediction. The pointer started flying around the board so fast it was hard to figure out what it was saying. It kept spelling out *death* but wouldn't give us a name. We just kept getting *watery* and *sign*. And numbers—13 and 22."

Logan remembered a coke-singed night in Kansas, a night that broke up toward dawn like a meteor finished by its fall. Numbers with biblical echoes, uncanny coincidences and parallels that intersected like sets of train tracks.

"About two months later one of the guys we were with that night drowned. He was swimming in the ocean at night, drunk, and hit his head on some rocks." She sat back in her chair and lowered her chin. You have to admit that's a little weird."

Having decided there were few things quite as demanding as eating wrapped up moo-shoo with chopsticks, he went back to using his hands. "It's a weird coincidence."

 She bounced a ringless finger at him. "There's more. The guy who died? Nicky? Was 22. He died on August 13—13 and 22. His apartment number was 22."

Logan grunted.

"Nicky was an Aquarius—the water-bearer? He was born on February 11. February is the second month."

The last calendar he'd seen, which he'd followed from Oklahoma, had been open to the second month.

"Two times 11 is 22 and 11 plus two is 13. Aquarius isn't actually a water sign, but the suggestion of water is there. And 13 is the number of the death card in the Tarot deck. Twenty-two is the Fool."

"Twenty-two or zero."

"You *do* know something about Tarot cards."

"More about fools."

"Well, get this—Nicky used to act in college and guess what

part he played in *King Lear*? The fool. He used to go around quoting the lines and calling people *nuncle*. It *fit*. Nicky had all this talent, but he didn't look where he was going. He was the kind of guy who would light a joint in class while the professor was lecturing and still get an A in the course." She pinched a tangle of vegetables with her chopsticks, shook it until a manageable amount remained.

"There's something to all of this, I guess." He glanced up at the lantern-hung ceiling. "But I don't think anybody knows enough languages to understand it."

"What do you mean?"

"Well, if you didn't know anything about Tarot, you never would've put together Shakespeare's fool with the Tarot fool. And if you didn't know anything about the Zodiac, you wouldn't have thought about Nick being an Aquarius."

The expression on her face changed. "I'll have to think about that."

"Maybe religions fall somewhere in there too. I mean—"

"So you believe in God?"

"Lot's of 'em. You know how it is with us heathens."

She frowned.

He shrugged. "Do katsinas count?"

"I have a katsina doll in my living room. A Butterfly Maiden. Don't look so surprised. I used to live in Phoenix, remember? But ... you really *believe* in them?"

He glanced at his white teacup, the single character on it matching the one on the pot. "I believe in lots of little forces at work, not one Great Spirit in the sky."

"Hm. Angels but no god." Her expression was thoughtful. "I was raised Catholic, but ..." She shook her head. "The last thing

I need is some old geezer in Rome giving me commandments about *my* body."

"What about a young guy in New York?"

She lifted an eyebrow as though it could cut him.

He turned his teacup. "Just askin'." The brush-stroked character appeared and reappeared like a sun rising and falling transversely. "Nowadays religion is mostly a list of dos and don'ts."

"What's it supposed to be?"

He reached for his beer, but it was empty. He turned the ceramic teacup instead, focusing on it as if he expected it to influence the planet's rotation. "I don't know." His sense of their surroundings had become as nebulous as the mist-wreathed mountain peaks on the lacquered screen. "I think we've made religion too artificial, pushed it too far outside ourselves." The teacup's calligraphy came around to him again, and he left the black slashes to face him like any other impenetrable mystery.

"What do you mean?" The wine had given a slight flush to her cheeks. About as dark as Aristotle, she had, not an olive complexion, more like coffee lightened with milk.

"Well, they say the stars—the galaxies—are moving apart at thousands of miles per second, separating themselves by light years. It's the same with people. We're becoming separated by more and more lifetimes. You know, from our origins." He tapped the rim of his plate with a chopstick. "We used to know things without reading them in books. We used to have religion without going to church. When we invented books, we stopped knowing, we let it get outside ourselves. We stopped telling— and knowing—the old stories. We stored it all on paper. But not everyone takes the time to read, so part of himself—" He lifted a hand in her direction. "Herself, is sitting on some library shelf, undiscovered. Pretty soon it'll all be on a microchip."

He shrugged. "We want it that way. We want defined boundaries—between church and state, business and pleasure, life and death. Straight-edged certainty. But it hardly exists. And all we're left with are the straight edges." He stopped drumming and used the chopstick to push around the last of the unrolled moo-shoo. "When the world doesn't work the way we want it to, we make it fit into our idea of it. We'd rather have a diorama, cut to scale, than deal with bad weather."

Reaching for their plates, the waiter asked whether he could bring them anything else.

Forking two fingers, Shawna slid her empty wineglass forward at the base and asked for another. Logan ordered another beer.

A moment later a bow-tied bartender took Shawna's empty glass and replaced it with a full one. He poured a fresh beer for Logan. As the bartender left, the waiter placed a plate between them. It held two fortune cookies and two slices of orange between them.

Shawna took a healthy sip of her wine and pointed to the bottle. "Tsing Tao is the best-selling beer in the world. Says so right on the label. See? Cute little advertising gimmick. It's the only beer on the Chinese market, and since there are about three-quarters of a billion drinkers—and no competition— voila. The world's best-selling beer. That's the art of advertising."

The art he admired was the opposite: driving a spike between the eye and the deceptive image.

"It was fun in the beginning, but now it's really a way to maintain an Upper West Side lifestyle."

Upper West Side meant about the same to him as East Hampton. "You can always move ..."

"I wouldn't mind a job that does something for *me*. Even designing the ads … well, they're still ads. I feel like it's time to move on—not out. Do something else.""

He pushed the fortune cookie dish over to her.

She broke a cookie in half, pulled out the ribbon of paper, and smiled. "What? Did you make a deal with the waiter?" She handed it to him.

You are in good hands tonight. He returned the bit of paper. "It's supposed to tell you something you *don't* know."

"I have my doubts." She pushed the dish toward him.

His didn't break so neatly, the pieces falling to the plate. "The woman across from you will soon renounce the world, leave all of her possessions to you, and retire to a Buddhist nunnery."

"Let me see that—"

He jerked his hand away.

"*Your mate has a surprise for you.*"

"The *waiter* has a surprise for you. It's called the check."

There was a tightening in his stomach over what kind of a tab they'd run up.

As if he'd been listening in on their conversation, the waiter—thick lips flattened by his smile—left a glossy leather book on the table.

She reached across the table and picked it up. "I was kidding."

He marveled again at the width of her mouth.

"You can get the next one." She raised her stemmed glass.

He touched the bottom of his, thick as a paperweight, to the delicate rim she held out to him. A crystalline ting worthy of music.

"To Moonchildren."

10. Raphaelesque Head Exploding

He was still sleeping, his mouth not quite closed. No teeth showing, there was just a break in the seal of his lips. She sighed. What was she doing with this man next to her? She didn't want another relationship. It wasn't a good time for one—out of season, she thought, like certain fruits.

Fingers spread, she touched her palm to his hair. Black as crow feathers, it was thick and springy, but not stiff, which was how it looked. Her finger glided down his temple so that if he was dreaming, the tickle might turn into a drop of sweat. She smiled to think she might be able to divert the course of his dreams even if it was just a little.

He had cheekbones high enough to crowd his eyes, which were such a dark brown the pupils almost disappeared into the irises. His nose, with a faint curve to it, gave his face an edge. What she liked most about his face were the crescents underlining his eyes. Once, when she was a teenager, she'd seen a photo of a boxer who'd gotten a mouse beneath his eye. Although she knew his eye was half shut from getting punched, she'd found it inexplicably attractive. She cut it out of out the newspaper and pasted it into a scrapbook.

With the childish thrill of reaching for something forbidden, she touched one of the soft pouches under his eyes. She tapped it lightly, as if this would tell her finger what was in it. Well, the same thing that was under most of his skin, of course, but why had it gathered here like this? Padding eyes already cupped by cheekbones?

With another sigh, this one inward, she conceded that he had his good points. So many men were such disappointments after they opened their mouths—*there* was the explanation for the cult of the strong, silent type. But there was something a little odd about him, a little off. Oh he drank beer and talked more as he got warmed up, he could hold up his end of a conversation, and he laughed at the usual things—he didn't have a nervous tic or anything—but he always seemed, even when his smile was at its warmest, to keep her at arm's length. She pictured him as a little boy hiding in a cemetery, regarding her from behind a tombstone, careful to keep the marker between him and her. Maybe it was just that he wasn't at home in New York. She'd wondered whether he'd brought a piece of somewhere else with him, like a charm on a necklace, something he could touch his fingers to for reassurance. She'd half expected, when his shirt came off, to see a tiny bag of earth on a leather thong around his neck. But the only thing he wore besides his clothes was that hoop in his ear.

And there was something else, something that came off him like the musky smell of an old hide—the readiness of a deer to take flight. Almost as though if the ceiling were to collapse he'd sense it just before it happened. The second night she'd seen him, she happened to be watching him from across the Copper Crow, and he suddenly became very still. She was amazed how still, as if he were one of those insects that looks exactly like a twig. His eyes were fixed on something she guessed to be on the floor about three or four feet in front of him. Maybe, with those near-black eyes, he was boring a hole in the worn floorboards so he could anchor the new axis running through his life. Or maybe some part of him, not used to the new place he was in, had fallen into a hole that wasn't there for other people. Then he moved and the spell was broken.

They hadn't made love last night. It was just that … well, she hadn't wanted him to leave. She felt a little guilty about stringing him along like that. After long kisses and the insinuations of their hips, she gently discouraged anything more, but after trying to settle comfortably into one another, he couldn't sleep. He lay with his eyes closed, and his breathing was steady, but she knew he was awake. It made her a little uneasy, and she wondered why she hadn't put him on the couch.

Now he seemed innocent, vulnerable.

This was the best time to look at a man, when there were no pretenses. His body spoke a language that had nothing to do with the one used to advertise deodorants and hair products and clothes, a language that showed up in involuntary twitches, in restless groaning or maybe in an insecure drawing of the knees into the chest. He was on his back. One leg was straight, one bent; one arm down at his side, the other thrown up past his head. Trying to be his own complement, she thought, his own reciprocal.

A spasm rippled through her and ended up as a tingling below her belly button.

He turned to her as if he'd somehow felt what'd gone through her, and she scraped her nails lightly over his scalp. He slid a hand up her back. His eyes were still closed, but he was waking. She pressed her chest against his. This was when the distance he kept between them disappeared, when he touched her. Then he became affectionate, maybe a little needy. Reaching under the sheet, she slipped a finger just beneath the waistband of his underwear, let her nail fall into the furrow whose hard bottom was his backbone. *God* she was wet.

To muffle the shiver that ran through him, he pulled her more tightly against him. Mindful of the sourness in his mouth, he let his cheek slide off hers and kissed her just below an ear.

She dug under him with a hip and pulled him on top. They maneuvered into each other until, if it hadn't been for the red silk of her panties and the wash-worn cotton of his briefs, they would've been making love. In the mirror built into an expansive headboard, he saw himself look up for half a second.

His mouth gone dry with the sudden rush of adrenaline, his hands shaking, he slipped her panties off. Surprised she didn't protest, he was more surprised when she reached up and tugged his underwear down to a knee. He lifted his leg until, positioned like a sprinter in the starting blocks, he got a leg free. He didn't bother with the other, leaving his briefs somewhere around his calf like a fallen flag.

He'd meant to settle his weight on her, to press himself between her thighs and tease her a little—and himself—but her long fingers had already closed around him. Pulling on his hip with her other hand, she guided him to a soft impasse that suddenly gave way. He cuffed the back of her neck as his stomach muscles tightened. Her little gasp as he slid inside was almost enough to finish him off. There was no place in his experience for a woman like her—how else could he explain the way *I love you* pirouetted at the back of his throat? A fragment of delirium, a hallucinated emotion that never made it to his mouth.

If she knew how close he was, he thought, she'd stop moving like that.

Eyes shut against the inevitable, he remembered Linda in the same position, and it dulled his arousal. Shawna's fingernails began to dig into him, her movements more urgent, and she cried softly each time she arched up. Hanging on like a rider with one boot in the stirrup, he felt with every bounce he was about to be thrown. When she bit his shoulder, stifling a breathy shriek and shuddered against him, his body almost went flaccid with relief.

Her head fell back against the pillow.

Infinitely satisfied with the motionless equilibrium they'd reached, he smiled down at her. She smiled back, and the valves in his heart widened.

He kissed her and they moved into a slow rhythm, her legs pulling him as insistently as gravity. Time seemed to stretch. Then dissolve. They shape-shifted into different positions until, as though she sensed how hard he was trying to keep up with her, she whispered, "You can come inside me."

Even after he did, he stayed where he was, his body lying along the length of hers. She looked even better than she had last night, her eyeliner a dark smear under her eyes, her hair a lovely wreck, with kinks worked into it from the braid she'd had it in all night.

"Hey ..." She tapped a shoulder blade. "I have to get up."

He pulled out with a grunt.

"Did that hurt?"

"Sort of. Always does." He shifted his weight off her but kept a hand on her waist. Peeling his fingers back, she pulled his hand away, and he was afraid this was the last time he'd be in her bed.

She got up and slipped into her panties with her back to him. Her legs were long but heavy with muscle, her hips a healthy width but maybe a little too wide to be one of the women in those ads she sold. Odd how that shimmery bit of red silk across her sprinter's ass was enough to keep him out—not only closing a door on his eyes as if they were a couple of salesmen peddling vacuum cleaners, but the rest of him too, uninviting him. Even after she'd gone, he watched the bedroom doorway, half hoping his gaze would bring her back sooner.

She went to the bathroom feeling a twinge of guilt for no good reason. She was 28, old enough to make her own decisions. But he was still a stranger, and this was *him* running out of her. She wiped herself with a tissue, tossed it into the toilet, and flushed the miracle of life into a sewer pipe.

She leaned toward the mirror. *God, I look like shit.* Her hair looked as if a family of squirrels had gotten to it. The black smudges under her eyes made her five years older. She used her fingers like a pick to pull her hair up and even it out a little. Dried mousse turned it to like plastic. She scrubbed her face, brushed her teeth, and pulled an ex's T-shirt out of a narrow towel closet.

Logan was sitting on the edge of the bed in his boxers. There wasn't enough fat on him to grease a frying pan.

"You want some breakfast?"

"Sure." He put out a hand.

She took his hand, but he sensed she was doing it out of politeness. He tugged her closer and hugged her waist. She squeezed back, her long fingers clamping down between shoulder and neck, but he felt the tension in her arms; she wanted to pull away. He slipped a hand under her T-shirt, which hung on her like a drape, and pressed his fingers on the small of her back, the dip just above her panties.

"Ohhh." A hiss of breath.

Using both hands and mashing an ear against her ribs, he pressed hard and slow along the twin ridges on either side of her spine.

"Oh, that's … sooooo nice." She put a hand on one of his shoulders to steady herself.

Anxious to do something for her as long as she wanted it done, he spread his fingers to other parts of her back.

"What do you want to eat?"

"Surprise me."

"A gambler, huh?" She took a step back. "Let me get started."

His hands dropped to his sides.

While she dug in a dresser drawer, his eyes skimmed over the walls: two large frames with arrays of snapshots that were probably family and friends; a corkboard with notes, postcards, and articles pinned to it; a black-and-white poster sheathed in glass—a blown-up photo of an impossibly slim building rising above trees, blurred by snow.

"Stieglitz." She was still adjusting a pair of shorts, which would disappear once she let that T-shirt fall like a stage curtain. "Everyone has the other shot of the Flatiron, the Steichen with the coachman going by." She grabbed one of his hands and tugged. "Come on—"

In the living room he stopped short, jerking her back a step. "You take these?" Eight-by-ten black-and-whites.

"Mm-hmm."

Different settings, different subjects. Ranging from an abandoned café along some desert road to a saguaro's bleached skeleton to a night shot of a diner. A single customer sat at a table, an old man, his cup of coffee in front of him like the rapidly cooling prospects in his life. Pale light seeped out onto the street where a couple kissed. Between them, the man and woman held everything the old man would never hold again.

"They're good, *really* good, but I like this one." He tapped the diner with a finger. "It's personal."

"That's probably why everyone likes the Steichen Flatiron better than the Stieglitz—you can barely see a cloaked figure in the Stieglitz, but the coachman in Steichen's shot is in the foreground."

She tugged him toward the kitchen.

Somehow guessing what he was thinking, she said, "I'd be fooling myself if I thought I could make a living as a photographer."

"We're all fooling ourselves." He pulled on his shirt—in fact, Hank's shirt—which he'd had in his hand until now. "One way or another."

"What's that supposed to mean?"

He sat down at the table. "I guess we all need to believe something. Real or not."

"I like it both ways: if I'm going to believe in it, I want it to be as real as this frying pan." She held it up.

It looked heavy enough to stop a bullet.

She put it down, turned on the gas, and butter sizzled in the pan.

Her kitchen, not to mention the rest of the apartment, had to be more than twice the size of Pam and Hank's. And newer. The table didn't threaten to keep any drawers from opening. He could see that Shawna had more use for her kitchen, that she didn't stock cans of pasty Italian food with little rubbery meatballs or soups with lumberjacks on the labels (more than once he'd seen Hank reading with a spoon handle sticking out of a can in front of him). Opposite the stove was a spice rack filled with slender jars. Half a wall was taken up by a cabinet with glass doors. Tall jars held pasta, coffee beans, rice.

Shawna broke two eggs at a time cleanly, one in each hand. She stepped over to the refrigerator; one of the plastic drawers rattled open.

"Hope you have good teeth." She held up a loaf of bread as if it were a prize. "Seeds, nuts, a piece of shell every now and then."

"I guess we'll find out."

The plate she put in front of him with a breakfast sandwich on it looked to have been baked in a kiln, white with a Southwestern motif in the red of desert rock.

Shawna pulled up a chair so that a table corner separated them.

In the first bite he tasted egg, cheese, tomato, and ... something else. Juice from the tomato ran down his fingers. Salami or pork roll was what else. "We could set you up back in Kansas. Shawna's Homecookin' Café."

She held her sandwich poised over her plate. "You ought to get out of your cave more often."

"Grunt softly and carry a big club I always say."

"Maybe Dave can use you on comedy night at the Crow too." Her fingernails, coppery with polish, looked like jewels.

"I think I better stick to music."

"What else do you do?"

Drift. Lose track of time. Waste more looking for where it went. "Poems once in a while."

"How do you know the difference between a song and a poem?"

"I guess … I think with a song you add the music later even though it might be in your head while you're writing it. With a poem the music … it's built in."

"Hm." She took a bite of her sandwich so big her nose creased on the sides; for a second she looked like a snarling cat. She chewed thoughtfully then put her sandwich down and twisted a long finger in a napkin.

She got up, pulled a carton of orange juice out of the refrigerator, and filled two glasses.

He took a long drink: sweet, acidic, cold.

The sandwiches didn't last long. Neither did the juice. He hadn't realized how thirsty he'd been.

"You want anything else?"

He shook his head. "That was great. Thanks."

The plates clinked in the sink, and there was a burst of water from the faucet.

He looked down at his feet, bare on tiles the color of baked clay. He remembered a grounded moth, its wings throbbing in a pool of light under a streetlamp. Remembered the concrete of the sidewalk ever so gently rising, falling. A crescent moon orange as fire. Bats flapping through a cloud of insects—

"... would you?"

The beginning of whatever she'd said had burned away like tissue paper, left his head aswirl with smoke.

"Sure." But he wasn't.

He got up, walked past her wall of photos, found the stereo—a high-end component system—and pushed a button. A song materialized.

"Thanks!" she called over the sound of running water.

Was that what she'd asked? *Turn on the radio, would you?* Cal used to threaten to slap the shit out of him when he didn't hear something. *Don't ignore me, boy.*

"Hey."

There were hands on his chest and she was pressed against his back.

"Your shirt smells like smoke." Her mouth was next to his ear.

From the bar they'd gone to after the restaurant.

"Maybe we should check to see what's burning," he suggested.

"Maybe you should take a cold shower."

"How about a warm one?"

He raised his arms while she peeled off his shirt, static crackling as it slid over his head. Locking her hands just over his belly button, she raised goosebumps on the backs of his arms. He didn't want the ring of her arms to open, didn't want to be turned outside.

"You smell a lot better than your shirt."

"I'm easier to wash too."

Where Hank and Pam had a phone booth with a shower nozzle in it, she had a full tub. The glass door was rough and uneven, like a pane of ice with cloudy white fish frozen in it.

A dream? Of … a sea hard as glass?

While she leaned over to turn on the water, he dropped his pants and stepped out of them.

She pulled off her shirt and motioned for him to go in first.

The spray was hard and hot on his face, made him close his eyes. He felt her bump past him—shoulder, hip—heard the door rumble closed.

"What's this?" She scratched with a fingernail at the back of his neck just below the hairline.

He couldn't see it without two mirrors, one reflecting into the other, but he knew what the scar looked like: pale fire against his dark skin. "Horse tried to scrape me off on a barn doorway." *Consciousness cracked against old wood. Numbers clustered like stars spelling out shapes. A scar that marks the spot where I found out my uncle killed my father.*

He felt soapy hands on his shoulders, a thumb on the neck he'd hurt years ago.

He turned to face her. Her drenched hair followed the contours of her head.

"I'm not done with your back."

"I'm not done with your front."

She was refined, beautiful; he was a rough beast she'd allowed to wreck her bed.

She smiled, leaned into his kiss. The taste of a summer thunderstorm in Kansas.

Sometimes he would stay out in them, shirt off, arms out to make a cross of himself, eyes half closed. Somewhere his mother was calling him, he knew, but he couldn't hear her above the rain clicking in his ears. Light flashed overhead, and the sky shook to its foundations. He imagined being connected to the sky by a jagged streak of light. The sulfur smell of burned hair, bone blackened from the inside out, nerves lit like a tiny galaxy. Gone in the same flash that had set everything in motion, his infinite instant incinerated. When he ran home, he pretended to dodge random strikes, the rain hitting harder, his shirt flapping heavily up and down. Aiming for the puddles, he went splashing through them like a clopping horse, elated to have the empty streets to himself.

"Okay, fine." Shawna put soap and cloth in his hand. "You do me."

"I'll come by every day and do you if you want."

She elbowed in the gut hard enough to force an involuntary grunt.

He lathered the cloth, admiring the V of her back as it tapered to her waist. He put a steadying hand on her trapezius, scrubbing the other side. She let her head droop.

He worked his way down her body, past tan lines slicing a pale, concave triangle out of her buttocks, all the way down to her ankles then, turning her around, started back up. Moving his free hand from her hip to her back, he massaged one breast at a time, his hand always removed from them by the rough cloth. He'd never seen anything, he was sure, as beautiful as this woman when her head was tilted back and her hair was wet.

Between the steam, the steady pattering of water on his body, and her touch, he felt himself swaying. *Promise this isn't the last time.*

Shawna turned off the water, slid open the glass door, and stepped out.

After wrapping a towel around herself, she patted him dry with another one. "Stay here."

This woman to wake up next to, to shower with, to sit across from at the table while he hummed to remind this out-of-tune city what it was supposed to sound like, he'd be too content for restlessness to take root again.

He was daydreaming.

They'd just met. The emptiness would come again—it always did. Would start to gnaw at him and he'd swallow the nearest thing—wind if there nothing more solid—to stave off the pangs. He'd feel the pull again and he'd follow. Not as predictably as a change of seasons, not for anything as sensible as warm weather, not for anything he could name.

"Here."

A light bundle slapped against his chest.

"Make yourself presentable."

She was already dressed in baggy cotton. He couldn't help wondering, as he pulled on the sweats she'd given him, who else had worn them.

She beat him to the couch because he stopped to look at a print on a wall. See-through and empty, a head and neck took up the whole frame. A woman's head, her gaze downcast, composed of fragments—the debris of a collapsed building maybe—whirling around a shaft of light. He laughed. The shaft of sunlight, cut circular by a hole, illuminated a cranium disguised as a cathedral dome. His fingers went to the dip at the top of his head.

"What did you say?"

Had he said something? "Nothing."

"Nothing seems to be the operative word—nothing but trash on the tube. How 'bout we rent a movie?"

"Sure."

He put a hand out to help her up off the couch, but with a jerk and a smile, she pulled him down. He landed on top of her, his hands sinking into the cushions. She kissed him and his skull loosened into swirling fragments.

Blue evening falls.

Red dawn rises.

He comes.

11. Between The Leaning Islands

A murky cubby-hole a few steps below street level, the Copper Crow always made her feel at home. Quaint, except for that tacky squiggle of pink neon Dave put over the bar mirror, it probably had been built when ships still needed sails. In fact, as you came down the stairs, you had to pass a painting of a schooner cutting through open sea. The paint had cracked like a dried lakebed, and the colors had been dulled by a layer of dust. Although the gilded frame made it look as if it'd been stolen out of a museum, Dave never mentioned having it restored.

She checked her watch. Fifteen minutes before he was late. She lifted her coffee cup; it was empty.

Had it been seven years already? Seven years since Joan had driven them out of Phoenix, with pretty much everything they owned packed into a Chevy Impala? Seven years ago she'd never seen the Earth's curve from the top of the Twin Towers or gone to a gallery opening in SoHo, but somehow she'd decided—as if intuition were reliable enough to mix with expectation and pour for sidewalk—that New York was where she wanted to live.

Joan's *raison d'etre* was making fun of everyone within reach. Mostly, though, she saved it for guys. "If you got *these*," she would say, expanding her chest, arching her back, and cupping herself, "you gotta deal with *them*." She wasn't all that pretty, but she was stacked, bust to hips. They'd spent senior year cutting classes and trying to figure out how far from Los Angeles they could get and how long they could stay there. The day after all the speeches were made, they hopped in Joan's car and headed for Mexico. Shawna remembered letting papers go flapping out the window—homework assignments, term papers, tests—while they drove down the freeway. Joan kept screaming and crisscrossing lanes, sinking alternate shafts of fear and hilarity into Shawna. No one knew where they were. No one had known they were leaving.

Half the fun of the trip had been looking forward to it, imagining what the postcard she sent from Mexico would say, imagining the look on her mother's face when she found it among the credit card bills, magazine subscription offers, and sweepstake entries.

After Mexico they'd gone to Phoenix and gotten associate's degrees, but then Shawna had talked Joan into New York.

SoHo was a dark maze of narrow streets that had its own current. If you stopped, you could feel it eddy around you. The gallery openings had been crowded with people who looked baroque and gritty at the same time, who all seemed to know something she didn't, to have been places she hadn't, to know how—and how far—to ride that current.

She and Joan had gone splashing into the streets. They'd plunged like high divers into the strobe-lit caverns of clubs whose owners always seemed to invite them to private rooms where they'd cut endless lines. They'd watched other women wind up under tables in those back rooms. Their dresses were no longer anything to look at—they were just in the way and too thin to protect them from anything. No matter how delicate the straps or how elegant the cuts or how glittery the sequins on their outfits, no matter the designer names they wore, they may as well have been working a street corner.

Shawna had never slept with anyone for coke, but curiosity was something else. There'd been enough of them, usually artists, who'd been something to rub against, a way of shedding adolescent skin and its persistent itch. Some of her finds had been embarrassing without clothes. One she recalled was pale and hairless, like something spit up from a whale. Another, his shoulders left in the padding of his jacket, had looked so underfed she'd backed down at the last minute. Remembering was enough to make her laugh, and her forehead fell into a hand while her shoulders shook.

Sex was worthless when it wasn't done right, and the arts we'd invented were more imperfect than anyone should be able to bear. So we smoked, tapped out lines on a mirror, shot up.

Sometimes she imagined a wind humming between two islands, two Gibraltars leaning toward each other without touching. The ocean washed through at the bottom, foaming white as it broke against the stone fists. Humans were the saddest of all things, after all, able to freely envision angelic beings but never to become one. Alone was their natural state, and the sigh between the leaning islands was their anthem. There would always be this gap to define their disappointment and remind them of their separateness.

You would think one of the men she'd been with since landing in New York would have had something to say about all this, but no, what they said rarely had roots in anything at all. Like one of those air plants growing out of a gorgeous sea shell glued with a magnet so you could put it on your refrigerator. *Hot* was always on the tips of their tongues—hot galleries, hot clubs, hot artists and their feverish movements, which had progressively shorter lifespans and sizzled away with less and less impact.

One of the things she liked about Logan was that he was half country bumpkin—maybe three fifths. He never said, *hot, happenin', down, goin' on, bad* (to mean cool), *hip*. Even if he got to know the city and adjusted to the vernacular, she had a feeling he wouldn't tie the latest catch-phrase around his tongue as if it were a gift in need of a strip of color.

Music—that he knew. He could talk about the Velvet Underground, Joy Division, the Church, or Ultravox as easily as he could about Bill Evans, Chet Baker, Robert Johnson or, for that matter, Holst, Verdi, Wagner, or Rachmaninoff.

She lifted her coffee cup but remembered it was empty and put it back on its saucer with a soft click.

Rona, who'd just come in, waved to her. Shawna smiled. Shawna watched her as she went by. She was packing a little too much in her ass and hips. In about three years she was going to be a size 14.

Shawna sighed quietly, a little nostalgic for the days when she had seven earrings in each ear, her head was shaved, and the hair still left was dyed three or four colors. Instead of making her less attractive, which had been half the point, it'd made her more attractive to a different kind of man.

Pam, wiping tables, had worked her way to Shawna's. "You want another coffee?"

Shawna pushed her cup and saucer away. "Mm-mm. He should be here any minute. Besides, after the movie we'll probably go out for a cappuccino."

"So now that you're shacking up with our piano man, does that mean Brian's out of the picture?"

She rolled her eyes. "Buried, rest in peace."

"I still can't believe you ditched Logan at Dramarama. Now me, if it weren't for Hank, I'd have fucked him silly."

"Since when has being with Hank stopped you?"

"Since the guy's *living* with us, and there's a really good chance I'll get caught, okay?"

Shawna was smiling, but she wasn't looking at Pam.

Turning, Pam glanced over her shoulder. "Oh don't get all bloated with self-importance. He's probably here to see Rona."

12. A Lump Of Inferno

Shawna was gone when he woke up again. Vaguely he remembered the alarm going off, the bed half-empty, a kiss that became part of a dream. Probably she was hanging on to a strap on a subway train by now. Beside a man smelling her perfume and wondering about *him*, about whomever she slept next to. He thought it odd to be included in the thoughts of someone he'd never met. It made him a kind of mirror, wondering right back at whoever was next to her in one of those trains rattling under the city.

Another rider, lucky enough to have snagged a seat during the morning rush, was reading a newspaper. Maybe a novel. The words, like buzzing gnats, making a cloud around his head. And maybe the author was on the same train, the cloud invisible to her though she might recognize the book's cover. Then again, the author might have passed this reader by in a station, headed for a different turnstile. A station in which a page of yesterday's newspaper was transformed into a thin welcome mat, stepped on as if the people in its photos never existed.

In Shawna's office, as she was heading up the cement steps that led out of the subway, could be that someone was just lifting his face expectantly, looking forward to saying *G'morning, Shawna,* to seeing her toothy, dimpled smile, to hearing her voice before going back to the papers spread over his desk, having gotten that bump most people get from a cigarette or a swallow of coffee.

He considered the thoughts webbing the city, strands vanishing almost as soon as they appeared, crisscrossing. What did it support, this harmony—or cacophony—of invisibly fine girders? Nothing maybe. Maybe just a little scaffolding for him, a musician slow to get out of bed.

Through the ceiling he heard a steady stream bubbling into a toilet. From the force with which it hit the water, Logan reconstructed a veiny prick bent under its own weight when held at the base, an opening like a sewer pipe.

Flipping the sheets down to his ankles, he sat up. With the ham of his thumb he took grit out of the corner of an eye.

The framed Flatiron Building, like a prow with no ship behind it, drifted in snow.

On a corkboard pinned with a collage of postcards, snapshots, and newspaper clippings, he saw a note with his name on it.

Hated to leave you this morning. Didn't want to wake you but had to give you a kiss goodbye. Pancakes in the fridge. Hugs & squeezes, Shawna Rhae

He pulled on his pants, still adjusting to a room that had nothing to do with the dream world he'd just left.

Shawna Rhae Madrepearla.

"You're Italian?"

"Well, that's my father's last name. He's got the dark skin in the family, but he was adopted so I really don't know whether I'm Italian or not."

"R-H-A-E. Where'd that come from? I never heard of it being spelled that way."

Some aunt, she'd said, but she'd never met her aunt R-H-A-E.

Logan pulled the card Aristotle had given him out of his wallet. He could stop by his Manhattan office, tell him the truth about Indian-hater Tom, walk him through that last mescaline trip (would he be holding Aristotle's hand, or would Aris be holding his?).

He left card and wallet on a nightstand. He walked to a window, put his weight on the sill. His nose nearly touched the glass. A day of rain, the city embalmed in fog. Strip away the sky's fallen breath and you'd find the river. But he'd grown afraid of peeling back, of following rivers to their underground sources, of nadirs, butterfly knives, shattered windows.

Half buried in the grainy indistinctness lay a city with a past that didn't belong to him. Even what poked through from underneath was blurred. The sun eye invited you to reconstruct according to blueprints drawn up by memory. But put a finger on the aberrations after the mist lifted, and at every imprecision you'd find the moon eye at work. A little softening of geometry and the moon eye—prone to speculation, invention, rearrangement—ascended.

The fog offered a clean page.

A streetlight on the corner recalled the long neck of an extinct lizard, mammoth bulk hidden in pearly smoke.

Open up the moon eye too wide and it'd bore straight through flesh wrapped around bone, through bone itself, so that projected on its retina would be not the soul, but a ghostly blankness. Like something lopped off from a star, a lump of inferno that'd been set inside the hollows to warm them, bound us here for an unspecified purpose, kept us moving through the world without lighting our way.

Maybe he'd done that trucker a favor, cut his star-stuff loose from the ugliness where it'd been holed up. Tom came to him clearly now, like tuned-in music, his belly slippery-easy to the knife blade. The shock of steel in there. Punctured the diaphragm maybe, wrecked breathing. Sent a gift of pure black along the nerves. After he'd fallen, one of the wounds had opened like a grin. It was still widening.

He should've been disgusted. Instead, he'd burned with a strange fever, pitch-tuned to death, which was the exact hum of the light planted in a flaking adobe wall of the Smiling Aztec— something he'd never told Aristotle. He'd wanted to wade waist-deep in it, reach into Tom's ribcage and find there was more to life than the sulfurous stink Cal had gotten him used to.

He'd lied to the police, to their machine designed to call bluffs, to Aristotle. He hadn't had time to think, he'd said; when you step on a snake, it bites you. If only that had been the way it'd happened, if only he could go through his life that way, as if he were a snake or an elementary particle. Without thinking. Without looking up to other elementary particles as role models. To be, according to his nature.

Tom had been a stand-in. Logan had gotten confused, had gone after the mute surface with a sharp blade instead of a keen moon eye.

He'd thought about it, was the point, hadn't slashed a tendon in Tom's arm to make it fall like a puppet limb with a snipped string (Bill Tarp had taught him how to do that too), hadn't kicked Tom's knife away or planted a boot in Tom's face—he probably could have. He thought it through and decided if Trucker Tom came at him, then—Logan was confusing one thing with another—he'd use the balisong to slice a hole in what seemed to him no deeper than a billboard. Surfaces, back then, were all he still believed in.

Or maybe he'd stabbed at himself, to see whether he really

was as hollowed out as he felt. Only he'd pointed the knife the wrong way.

Music, sometimes, was the spark he used to span the gap that he was. Sometimes was the only way to ground himself.

If he didn't let go of the window sill, his hands would cramp in that position.

He imagined the placid deception of the Hudson in winter. The ice heaped over by unbroken white. No ice thin or thick— until you fell through. A little like sanity.

His past had brushed against him with the sandpaper skin of a shark, left that scar on the back of his neck. That day when a horse cracked the back of his head against old wood, spilled bright stains across the backs of his eyeballs. His neck throbbing and bleeding, he'd inhaled coke as if it'd been incense, drank as though his guts were liable to catch fire otherwise.

And another thing, doc, I got this delusion Cal was the Beast, the biblical one. Got a tremble in his hands at the thought that the 13 tattooed on Cal's arm was an arrow pointing to Revelations 13: *Then I saw another beast coming up out of the earth, and he had two horns like a lamb and spoke like a dragon.*

Jim Lee could flip to the page. Bible Mike knew it by heart. Cal had picked up Little Big Man as a nickname as if someone had known he was another Judas—to his own brother. Would one day clip a brake line, unbolt the seatbelt, or ... *some*thing.

Maybe Cal hadn't killed his father in the realm presided over by courts of law, by the sun eye, maybe he'd done it by wishing it, funneled fate into the black hole dead center of the moon eye. Might've been a Two-Hearts, a witch, and what he'd done came out in the whispers of numbers, left traces on the moon eye's retina in coincidences. Maybe the fervently wished for, the devoutly desired, the persistently hoped for was as bad as the deed itself.

Would Aristotle believe any of that? Did he?

He let go of the windowsill and padded into the living room, still in his underwear.

There was Shawna's katsina doll with an end table to herself. Slits for eyes, no nose, a small mouth. A Butterfly Maiden, just like she'd said. How many other women in this city had one? A mask branching into a headdress, the face white except for the red and yellow stripes around the mouth, a few on the cheeks. Across her wooden brow, a tiny cylinder painted black and white to represent rain clouds, zigzags for lightning. Seven shapes along the perimeter, each like a triple-tiered wedding cake, might've stood in for the mesas themselves.

Go-betweens for the Hopi and their rain gods, the *katsinam* visited the mesas, danced in the plazas from December until July before returning to their home on the San Francisco peaks. Or among the stars.

Shawna's furniture was dark, had an air of age about it (shiny modern would've made him feel as if he were living inside a machine). Next to a window a Greek urn sat on a squat pillar black as onyx. A plant, its fronds overflowing the pot so that it looked like a green fountain stilled by a crease in time, sat on a table too small to be practical. The Butterfly Maiden, taking the place of a telephone, put you in touch with a rain god instead of the office.

He loved Shawna's faith in the placement of things, in an order that wouldn't keep the stars from burning out, just preserve the part of the world *she* lived in. A philosophy his mother would have admired. She had an extra sense that told her when a rock in her garden had been displaced (by her curious child) or a flowerbed had been trampled (Cal stumbling in on a drunk).

He stood in front of a glassed-in bookcase, a carpet fiber tickling him between his toes. He ran his finger along a shelf, stopped on a thick paperback by Daniel C. Geraci. Intrigued by the title, he sat down with the book. Glancing guiltily at Aris's card atop his wallet, he began to read.

Sixteen pages later, he looked up.

His father was staring down at him. One eye was a star; the other had a crescent moon where an iris should have been. Logan didn't know whether the spreading puddle of warmth in his lap was blood carrying an electrical charge or plain old piss.

13. The Silver Surfer

Some six-foot-four mannequin in a black tuxedo glanced at the invitation Shawna handed him, unhooked a velvety red rope strung between waist-high poles, and stepped aside. Smoke curled out of the top of the doorway as if it led to infernal depths.

He hadn't told Shawna about the visit from the underworld—his father looming over him with him with eyes cut from some part of the sky, a T-shirt advertising a bar, a katsina's kilt instead of pants, bare feet. Geraci's book had thudded against the carpeted floor spine-first. His father just stared. Then he walked into the kitchen. Logan leaped out of his chair, but when he got to the kitchen—he braced the door frame with his hands as though the opening might close—no one was there. No father, no ghost, no shadow that didn't match up with something in the room.

This was the first time he'd seen his father's ghost outside a dream, and it scared him.

Maybe he shouldn't have left the hospital. Maybe he shouldn't have backed out of that call to Aris. Maybe Shawna had a right to know he had a degree from Upstate University. Maybe he shouldn't have come with her to this place—not much more than a brick rectangle full of people standing around, squeezing past each other, smoking, all trying to figure out, it seemed, just what they were supposed to be doing.

But he *had* come, and a man in a plaid jacket and sneakers was taking Shawna's hand.

"So glad you could make it." Balding though baby-faced, he offered a cherubic smile. "I think this is one of our better shows."

Above a plaid shoulder was a 12-foot ... tassel? Painted clay-red, speckled with black, somehow attached to one of the walls. Neo-primitive was probably how they pitched it.

"Isn't there a Picasso here?" a woman asked.

"Probably a sketch," a man answered.

Logan looked over as many heads as he could, but the walls were mostly blocked from view. He wasn't as interested in the artwork as he was in meeting Daniel C. Geraci who, Shawna had mentioned, might show up. As if Geraci and his father were somehow connected because that novel had been in his hands at an intersection of the Upper West Side and the Hopi netherworld. As if an author he'd never met could somehow answer questions about his life.

"What does he look like?"

Shawna had shrugged. "I have no idea. All I know is he's black."

The main character in Geraci's novel thought in ways familiar to Logan as though he were an uncanny reflection, a doppelganger in print. Which in a weird way stepfathered Geraci.

Pam, in her short skirt and cowboy boots, had three drinks wedged between the fingers of her hands. "Hi guys."

He took a plastic cup by the rim, breaking up the triangle. A screwdriver heavy on the vodka.

"Freebies." Pam gave a bottoms-up salute.

The windowless brick room was air-conditioned but still stifling with the warmth of June, body heat, cigarette smoke.

The ceiling—so high you could never be on intimate terms with it—belonged in a factory. Industrial lights covered with tin Chinese hats hung from cords between enormous rafters.

While most of the women were in black and glittered with jewelry, had teased their hair up in search of the distant ceiling, wore flamboyant earrings and shocking red lipstick, Shawna was in flat-heeled sandals, a long buckskin skirt with a matching vest, and had pinned up her hair. The women she moved among would rub off against her like electroplated gold.

"Pa-am! Hi!"

She was as short as Pam, a little heavier, a lot bustier and … naked?

"Look at you!"

Everyone was.

The woman was wearing flesh-tone spandex with nipples colored in about where they should have been. There was a generous mound of fur between her legs that looked like it might have come from a rug.

She smiled as if they were aiming a camera t her. "It's part of the art."

"You remember my best friend, Shawna? This is her boyfriend, Logan."

Logan squeezed four of the pseudo-naked woman's fingers.

"Aurora's a painter. You've got something hanging up here, right?"

"In the back."

Logan wondered if Aurora was her real name or one of those single-word appellations, like Cher. *Aurora what? No dahling, just Aurora.* Her real name was probably Mildred Higginbottom.

"That's *brilliant!*" A man with a crewcut and an English

accent introduced himself to Aurora as a photographer for *Real People.* "Just fucking *bril-l-l-l-iant* ..."

Trevor, the guy in the plaid jacket, grabbed Logan by a shoulder. "I want you to meet Jules Dandridge—"

Tall, black, and elegantly dressed, Jules had a hollowed-eyed face reminiscent of Miles Davis. One side of his head was shaved, while the hair on the other side was long, wavy, and surprised the eye with a blond streak. He smiled as Logan shook his hand.

Logan eyed his coppery silk vest and felt hickish in jeans and a button-up shirt. All he had in the way of dress-up were hank's boots and an onyx bola tie, the black of the stone fractured by a vein of white.

No conversation between Jules and him ensued. Shawna acknowledged Jules with a nod, tugged Logan away by an arm.

Pam took his other arm. "Are we having fun yet?"

Logan shook his glass. Empty now except for ice cubes, it rattled like a cheap maraca.

Lips brushed against his ear. "Look at the guy on your left."

His hair was white. Pulled tightly back in a tiny tail, it had a sheen that made it look like spun metal strands. An albino? No, Logan caught a sliver of icy blue iris. He was wearing an outfit that had to run about six hundred bucks: an off-white, crinkle-leather jacket with matching pants.

Logan leaned closer to Shawna. "He looks like the fuckin' Silver Surfer."

Shawna giggled, bumped him with a shoulder. "Not so loud."

Plaid was talking to the Surfer, who must've been one of the people people came here to meet. There was a circle around him, a space he maintained with his hands in his pockets.

"Who is he?"

"A collector, I think." She rubbed her fingers together. "Big bucks."

Pam pulled on Shawna who pulled on Logan but lost him as his shirt sleeve tugged free. The women drifted into the crowd without him, and he found himself surrounded by expectant smiles, glittery eyes, and plastic cups hovering over the bare wooden floor. The cups were drained until they held only a little wetness on the bottom and a film of light along the sides in the demeaning way plastic holds light, scratches it in its passing. The paintings and collages and photographs were like planets in a stationary solar system, their rectangular orbits belonging to some cubist galaxy.

He tried sliding sideways along the wall. Below the works were labels with a bunch of names he didn't recognize—Robert Rauschenberg, Willem De Kooning, Mark Rothko, Fred Haguin.

There were so many people around the Picasso sketch, he didn't even try to get a look.A cigarette brushed his elbow. Sparks and ashes fell to the floor, twinkled orange.

"Oh I'm sorry—"

"It's all right, I'm fireproof."

"Hi, I'm Liz." She lifted the cigarette to her mouth, a dozen or so bracelets clinking and jangling along her skinny arm.

Logan put out his hand. "Fred. Fred Haguin."

"Hi, Fred."

Her fingers were as cold and moist as the soft meat of a shellfish.

"This is Michel ..."

Dirty blond hair and a T-shirt he probably should have thrown out a year ago.

Michel's painting was a solid red square that could've been

done with a roller. By a house painter.

"Very whimsical," pronounced a woman next to Liz.

"What is it?" Logan stepped a little closer.

Liz looked at him as if he had a sapling growing out of his forehead. "It's called *Atomic Sky.*"

"Not anymore." Michel corrected her. "Now it's *Le Gran Rouge.*"

Someone nearby nodded. "A study in restraint."

"The Big Red?"

Logan was thankful Liz had translated. "So it could be a radioactive sky or … a broken bottle at the blood bank?"

"Exactly!" Michel smiled.

Michel looked like he might've been gaffed out of the Hudson an hour ago, salvaged from among plastic bottles, Styrofoam cups, water-stained lumber.

He tucked hair behind an ear hooped with earrings. "I paint first. I decide what I've done later." He rubbed at his stubbly chin with the back of a pale hand. "The title's arbitrary."

What if, Logan wondered, *Le Gran Rouge* and a few other color squares were left maybe 10,000 years from now? What would the canvases say about the people who'd painted them?

"How about Red Square?" Logan asked. "Like in Moscow?" And because that's what it was.

Michel looked miffed that he hadn't thought of it first, but Liz stood back at little to glare at Logan (the sapling was growing taller by the minute).

He'd read somewhere that for Neolithic painters everything was alive—stones, mountains, clouds, the sky they floated in. (Maybe for some of the old-timers on the mesas too.)

"What if things with form are striving to be felt?" Logan

asked. "And things that're only felt are … need a form?" He waved a hand as if to dispel some smokiness obscuring his thought process.

"Sorry, I don't follow." Michel lifted his pale eyebrows impatiently.

"You've got a form here, but—"

"*Look*, you can't put limitations on art—exclude the arbitrary. You can't be so *rigid* …"

"If you put something in your painting and you don't know why, if you *like* it, okay. Serendipity, the unconscious, all that. But when it's done, you shouldn't be able to shift anything—or it's not done." Since he knew next to nothing about painting, he probably sounded hopelessly like a hayseed at his first art show.

Michel's eyes looked a little recessed in his gaunt face as if shying from the light. "I'm dealing with the *idea* of red because we live in a world that we experience through *ideas*, abstractions rather than things themselves, and I … I'm just taking it a step further, obliterating form, even light, and reducing it all to color. Color is the essence of a thing, I think—"

"So you could call it Stop Light or Big Anger or Atomic Sky or Bloody Sunday—"

"Why not?"

"In their essences, then, there's no difference between a stop light and anger …?"

"Well, the particular *shade* of red I'd use might be different …"

Logan nodded, but he didn't see how Michel was putting back some of what'd been lost over five thousand years of civilization.

"You don't like it?" Michel lifted his pale eyebrows impatiently.

Logan despised the arbitrary word, line, color, note, but

only now did it occur to him that it might be a musician's bias; harmonic structures fell apart if the progression of notes wasn't precise.

"Are you a painter?"

Liz seemed anxious to cast doubt on his authority on the subject, giving him an excuse to ignore Michel's question. "I did that one in the back, the big one ..." Logan pointed.

"Oh, *figurative* work." Michel rolled his eyes without rolling his eyes.

"Don't take everything so *seriously*, dah-leeng!" A man who seemed very comfortable in a long red dress and matching gloves touched Logan's shoulder and smiled as he went by. "He's just hitching a ride ..." His open hands shook beside his head like two tambourines. "So much easier than Daedalus lifting himself out of the labyrinth." The man waved with a single gloved hand but didn't look back as he threaded his way through the crowd.

"Daedalus...?" Liz started to ask but plugged her mouth with a cigarette.

Aris said that dreams made up for some misjudgment or misperception in waking life. Maybe art did the same. A balancing act, a complement on a societal scale, a dream coming out in fragments—one artist at a time. And those cave artists who hadn't been able to separate dream from not-dream all that well, divide the living from the inanimate or the passed-on, who'd sketched bison and aurochs and rhinos and mammoths in charcoal, fleshed them out with red ocher—wasn't entering the cave a little like being inside one of their skulls?

"Fred ..."

Startled, Logan turned.

"Come on, let's go."

He shrugged at Michel and let Shawna lead him away by the hand.

"How long have you been here?"

"The whole time pretty much. *Trés amusante*, introducing yourself as Fred Haguin."

"Hi, babe." Rona's puffy lips were drawn back in a generous smile.

Although he didn't see it, Logan felt Shawna's head cock.

"Babe?" Her breath was hot, almost liquid in his ear.

Rona waved to Shawna. "Ha-aye." Her other hand was held by the ex-Buddhist Logan had met at Pam and Hank's.

"How you doin', guy?" Jeff took Logan's hand with the same fishy grip Logan remembered.

"I didn't know you were into painting." Shawna hooked Logan's arm as she glared at Rona.

"Of course. *Images*." Rona giggled a little drunkenly.

"Not to mention potential investments," Jeff said.

Logan noticed Jeff's jaw working side to side, like an insect flexing its mandibles. Even when he spoke, it tended to slide around. "You remember my friend Matt—"

Matt extended his arm and shook Logan's hand.

Matt and Jeff both had jaws working overtime, talked too fast, and seemed way too happy about running into him.

"Well ..." Pam threw herself into the middle of things. "I hate to be the one to bring tragedy into such a perfect world, but we have to meet Hank around twelve."

Rona's back was almost to him. "See you at work." Surprised when he felt his ass squeezed then pinched, he looked at Shawna, but she was still holding his arm with both of hers and saying, "Nice meeting you" to Jeff.

Rona winked at him as they pushed back into the crowd, Jeff leading her away as though he had a horse with a race to run.

"Hallelujah. A match made in heaven." Pam pulled Shawna back to the table covered with screwdrivers.

Logan saw the Silver Surfer's head bobbing among darker knobs, a mercury-vapor streetlamp amid unpowered bulbs—except for the guy who was talking to him. Shorter and stockier, he wore a T-shirt, thick-rimmed glasses, and nondescript trousers. His hair and beard were shot through with streaks of gray, a color as distant from silver as old lead from new chrome. Without moving, the two men seemed to circle each other, and despite their contrasting appearances, something about them was similar—as though they were two engines that burned the same exotic fuel (neutrinos maybe). But while one was built for hauling tonnage, like a locomotive, the other was designed for speed. The way the shorter man dressed, he could've been blue collar, but he carried himself more like a college professor. The thick fingers ringing a plastic cup gave Logan the impression of a hollow egg held in a vice.

"Isn't that Daniel Geraci over there?"

He turned at the sound of the voice, trying to pin down the owner. Scanning the room, he expected to find a small crowd encircling the author. He pushed past people, eavesdropping on their conversations, but heard no other mention of Geraci and saw few enough blacks (all too young to be Geraci).

"Pre-fab is the way to go," someone very tall and very close to him said. "I'm telling you ..."

"Pre-fad? You mean hopping the trend before it really gets going?"

"No no no, pre-*fabb*..."

Logan recognized Matt's watch. He shouldered past and found Shawna talking to Trevor.

"I kind of see punk as a re-emergence of Dada—"

"Oh come on." Shawna was frowning. "Laurie Anderson is a lot closer to undermining harmonic progressions than any punk band. I mean their lifestyle and the nihilistic lyrics, I can see that. Really though, it's *tell*-me Dada, not *show*-me Dada. They're whining about their problems, and the Dadaists … they just put up their work and let you figure out the rest."

"Well, yes. The idea of startling the middle class mind out of routine—"

"Toiiiii-let-bowl art." Hands gloved in red were cupped to make a megaphone.

Logan wasn't sure whether he meant that's what Dada looked like or that was where it belonged.

"Sure, Dada failed." Shawna shrugged. "But it pushed back on the old limits, didn't it? Gave everything else a little breathing room."

Trevor's head invaded the bottom of a framed poster; it was just a list of aphorisms. *Meat is murder. Humor is a virtue.* Printed in black ink on white paper. *Man's insanity is heaven's sense.*

Trevor put a drink in Logan's hand and leaned into his ear. "It's pure trash but it's important to have it at a show like this because it made it to the Whitney. But then so did this 25-foot rubber curtain. I mean that's all it was, an incredibly ugly rubber curtain 25 feet long."

"Ready?" Shawna hooked one of her arms in his.

Logan took the cup she was holding and drained it as if it there were no vodka in the orange juice. He swirled shrunken chunks of ice. "Now I am."

"Come on." Pam took each of them by a hand. "We're going to Bill Bailey's, *Big* Bill Bailey's. Hank *promised* he'd meet us there after twelve." Hands on Shawna's waist now, she was pushing her out the door.

The sky, edged by cornices, was too dim to show off many stars.

Logan stopped next to a lamppost. The bottom of it a kind of mosaic, it looked as if it'd spent a century steeped in trash, and shards of blue willow plates, coffee mugs (there was even a handle), milky glass, mirrors, tiny tiles, and chips of brick, had attached themselves. It seemed random, natural, like a sunken mast that had accumulated sea life. Just as he was about to turn away, he saw bits of white that made up letters; the letters, words: *SoHo.*

"Thinking of pitching a tent?" Shawna tugged on his hand.

Pam turned and looked up at him. "*We're* on Greene Street, I don't know what *you're* on." She turned to Shawna. "Can you ever forgive me?"

"For what? Introducing us? I'm sure you'll do time in purgatory."

"Well, *I'm* not—heaven don't want me and hell ain't hot enough."

Shawna tugged on Logan's arm. "This way ..."

"Across Mercer—"

Rounding the corner, the smell of urine was overpowering.

Pam pinched her nose. "That oughta bring rents down a little ..."

Mercer was emptier, darker, than the streets they'd been walking. There were none of the gently billowing banners announcing galleries as if each were a small country. Papers and empty bottles shouldered the curb. Xeroxed pages pasted in rows over stained brick read *The Shape of Things to Come*. The accompanying image was a mushroom cloud.

What if somebody took an aluminum rib of the city—a streetlamp—and planted it in a forest? Maybe for the first time it would be seen as something distinct from the street it'd kept lubricated with light. Why not plunder the museum holding "The Starry Night," hang it on the side of a building, expose it to weather until it faded to a memory? No memory, of course, would preserve it precisely, sparking a thousand debates as to what it had actually looked like—brighter or darker or paler or more defined. Or less. Why not preserve a chunk of asphalt (embedded with bottle caps, a brass key, a key to a sardine can, a bad-luck penny, the shadow presences of the thousands of lives that had passed over it), vacuum-seal it under glass, make an offering of it to the first distant civilization that came visiting? They'd get more out of that fragment of updated tar pit than out of "Red Square."

Shawna and Pam had gotten ahead of him.

Two skinheads wearing combat boots and army fatigues sat on a stoop, drinking from paper bags. A third, on the sidewalk, swigged from a wine bottle.

"Yo man, how'd you like to get your cock in *that* yuppie pussy?"

Logan stopped.

"Logan *don't*—"

"C'mon, motherfucker …" The skinhead hefted the wine bottle by its neck as he walked toward Logan. "Come on, faggot, I'm right here …"

"Please Logan there are *three* of them—"

Pam had one of his arms, Shawna the other.

The two skinheads on the steps stood up, bagged bottles in hand.

"Come on you fuckin' yuppie faggot ..." He gestured with one hand, shook the bottle with the other.

"*Logan* ..."

Burning inside—anything was better than this burning—he couldn't make himself go forward. If he caught a bottle on the head and went down, he'd wind up in a hospital, leaving Shawna and Pam with these assholes.

He felt Pam let go of his arm but didn't see where she went, his eyes locked on the skinhead, hoping he'd take a couple more steps forward and give Logan no choice.

"Come on, come on, get in." Pam was holding open the door of a cab.

"Logan, *pleeeeease* ... "

His eye still on the leering skinhead, he let Shawna pull him toward the cab.

"You fuckin' *faggot* ..." The skinhead was on the verge of laughter as he walked with a cocky bounce toward the cab.

The door *k-chunked* closed and the driver pulled out.

The cabbie looked at Logan in the rearview mirror and glanced quickly away. Logan understood: he wanted to size him up, figure out whether he'd really wanted to stay and crack that guy or just been putting on a show for the women.

He looked down at his hands. They were shaking. He wanted to go back or at least get out and walk.

Shawna leaned into him and whispered, "Your heart's in the right place, but there were *three* of them. With *bottles*. Please, just let it go."

He nodded, but he knew that the ghost of his wavering would follow him all night, would be there all week, would put in appearances years later when he'd wonder whether it'd been cowardice or good sense.

Shawna locked her arms around his neck, pulled his ear to her mouth. "Forget about it, it's done with. Let's have a good time."

The cab pulled over to the curb, and Logan got out, shoved a hand into a back pocket for his wallet. He pulled out a few singles, his hand still a little unsteady.

"Mighty white of you." Shawna was smiling.

"Only half."

The lights in the blues club were dim red. *No Cover Charge—Ever.* The sign swung past him with the door. They got a table right next to a stage that was just a roped-off platform. A group of three was warming up. The jukebox was playing Billie Holliday, the record scratched to shit. A linebacker-sized black behind the bar just might have been Big Bill.

"You know, if Hank doesn't show up, I'm going to drag home one of the brothers and have my big black fantasy right in front of him."

"Can we watch?"

Shawna nudged him with a shoulder. "Speak for yourself."

"I *hate* being stood up." Chin up, Pam was scanning tables. "Right now if he were drowning, I'd throw him an anchor."

"Speaking of true love …" Logan tipped his head toward the door.

"Hey guys." Hank put his tweed cap on the table. He was wearing jeans, a *Banker's Make Bigger Deposits* T-shirt, and those squarish suede shoes that looked like Hush Puppies.

"Well if it isn't the love of my life …" Pam kissed Hank hello, winked at Logan. "We were just taking bets on how late you'd wander in. Can you believe your pal across the table said you wouldn't even show?"

"Thanks a lot." Hank wore half a smile. The way the skin wrinkled at the corner of his eyes, nine out ten expressions that showed up on Hank's face must've been smiles.

Logan flagged the waiter, a spindly guy with rolled-up T-shirt sleeves and fifties, slicked-back hair, and ordered for Hank.

He dropped four dollars. And the mug was *small*. "Shit." *Two* things you wouldn't find at Bill Bailey's: a cover charge and a cheap beer.

Hank lifted his mug and, like a magnet, it attracted three more. Glass k-*lanked*.

Logan emptied half of his at a gulp then stood up, his chair scraping loudly against the wooden floor. "Gotta shoot the porcelain."

"Don't expect us to be here when you get back."

He smiled, his face empty behind it. Maybe that punk and his pals would wander into Bill Bailey's. He pictured that as he made his way along the bar, turned sideways to avoid bumping into a black with the beginnings of an afro.

"You see that babe by the door?"

"Man, I been seein' her since she walked in."

Logan recognized the second voice.

"Bee, bee, bee."

"Baddest bitch breathin'."

Logan put a hand on a shoulder that was just about level with his own.

Turning, he stared at Logan for a few seconds before a look of recognition spread across his face like a slow spill. "Well I'll be sliced thin and spread for shingles. Cray-zee fuck-in Horse."

14. The People Of The Red Willow

Looking for it during the all-male ceremony the kiva dark, smoky, the drumming like breaking thunder, not his own tribe but what the hell close relatives only flashlights to see by and the glowing ends of joints going around endlessly in the damp earthdark in the press of sweaty bodies pounding on buffalo-hide drums shaped like puddles like ponds like lakes, bigger than any factory-round drum he's ever seen. never any alcohol none of the white man's shit medicine the specters of flashlight faces rutted with shadow like parched earth, he heard spanish heard the sometimes-guttural sometimes-bird-call sounds of the people of the red willow praying to a god who was there before the anglos the same god white men brought but with a different face. stripped down to shorts, sliding off each other's backs and arms, singing sweating chanting all night their voices a single prayer he doesn't always know the words doesn't always know whether there are words echoes what he hears knowing theirs is not the first voice ours won't be the last. an indian god or a man sitting next to him? the breath of both smoke. earth-and-stone smell of the kiva the air humid stifling, hot with a god's burning breath. joined by something deeper than blood a hundred heartbeats on a single buffalo-hide drum in the underground night a world without time without barbed-wire fences without boundaries a world that'll never spin down to nothing will emerge not into a simple blueing of sky and light chasing off night's ragged edges but a slow coming to wakefulness

15. Glossy Confetti

Logan was standing in front of a frame filled with glassed-in snapshots. "Hey…" he said softly. Shawna, in another room, couldn't have heard him.

He was looking at the painter he'd met last week, Jules. His hair fell in black curls—no streak of blond, none of it shorn. He had his arm around Shawna's waist in some club or a bar. *Her* hair was shaved on the sides, was platinum white in places, copper red and, as if some of the copper had corroded, green in others.

For some reason the photo sent a fragment of conversation— something Paul had said in Big Bill Bailey's—whizzing through his mind like a skipped stone: "How you get a babe like that, your head all buzzed and shit? You know she gonna drop you like a bad habit when she meets me, right?"

Paul had left the hospital a couple of weeks after he had.

"How's life on the outside?" Logan had asked.

A beer in one hand, Paul held his arms out like a vaudeville performer and started singing, bending the lyrics of a Timbuk Three song: "I'm doin' all right, gettin' good grades, gotta smile so bright, y'all should wear shades …"

"What about me? You hear anything?"

"Yeah, what a-*bout* you? Didn't say goodbye to the man who pulled your ass outa the deepest, darkest hole you ever fell into—sorry-lookin' head first."

Didn't say goodbye. The more he talked to Paul, the more obvious it became that everyone was under the impression he'd been released. Tell the cops one thing, tell patients another.

"You gonna introduce me to your babe or what?"

"Yeah, only you and I didn't meet Upstate, okay? She doesn't know about any a that."

"Not a word, bro."

"Shawna!" he called.

She came into the bedroom pulling her hair into a ponytail.

He tapped the glass covering the photographs. "Why didn't you tell me?"

She folded her arms over her T-shirt. "Don't look at me as if you don't have any ex-girlfriends."

"Hundreds. Worldwide."

"So quit moanin'."

He turned back to the photos.

Lifting herself up on her toes, she put her chin on his shoulder. They were ear to ear. "You wanna see some *really* old stuff?"

She went to a closet, slid open a door of lacquered black, and pulled out a box big enough to hold stereo equipment. Inside were albums, those packets (bulging) film developers gave out, and a shoebox from which she pulled out handfuls of loose snapshots. Black-and-white squares settled onto the carpet like glossy confetti: Shawna as a baby with huge eyes and a few wispy curls; Shawna in a bathing suit carrying a little red pale and a matching shovel, her body tiny and androgynous, her back with a little too much arch in it, her face with a little too much purpose and no smile; Shawna in high school, the homecoming queen.

He sank to his knees, picked up a photo. "This is your father?"

"Yup."

Dark hair receding so that above his forehead it was like bird fuzz, Mr. Madrepearla stood behind a grill with a spatula in his hand. Smoke blew across his waist.

"He's a sweetheart. I just can't figure out why he married my mom."

Shawna had his green eyes, the same café au lait skin. Her nose and mouth were different. Mr. Madrepearla had full lips but they lacked the arch that made Shawna's look half pursed all the time.

"That's my brother, Michael …" She pointed. "And my sister, Gina."

Shawna was in the middle, an arm around each. Taken at the same barbecue.

"I didn't get along with them too well. As my mother never tired of reminding me, I was the oddball … the only child who didn't get dark hair, the only one who wasn't an extraverted overachiever. I'm the oldest, but Michael got out of college before I did. He got a full ride—baseball and grades. Gina was editor of the school newspaper, straight-A student, captain of the field hockey team, yadda, yadda yadda. I got average grades and didn't like clubs or groups. I was pretty good at basketball, but they took all the fun out of it at the varsity level." She looked back down at the photo of the three of them. "Gina's at a magazine now, and he's at an insurance company. I hardly ever hear from them anymore."

"Does it bother you that your dad was adopted?"

"Once in a while I wonder what half of me is …" She shrugged. "My dad thinks he's North African, probably Tunisian, although he's guessing based on a couple of trips he made to North Africa."

He looked at again at Mr. Madrepearla, nodded to himself; North African was a good fit. And Shawna had a thing for Egypt.

He kissed her suddenly, hard. "I only want your body 'cause it's wrapped around your soul. You know that, right?"

"I bet that's what you told your hundreds of girlfriends, worldwide."

"So why'd you stay home from work today?"

She threw a downward-slanting punch—blurringly fast it caught him in the solar plexus, forcing a breath out of him.

"To kick your ass."

He laughed and put up his hands because her hand was still a fist. "What about the other pictures?"

"What other ones?"

He pointed to a photo showing two broken windows like empty mouths leading not to separate gullets, but to the same empty black. A white pigeon, wings blurred, was flying out of one. A streamer of shredded plastic flapped in a breeze, a wing abandoned by the power of flight. "Like that."

"Aren't there enough of them on the walls?"

"You must have more."

"Yeah, well …" She waved a finger at the walls. "That's all you get to see."

He felt the way he did when he came across a fenced off desert in the Southwest.

She stuck out her tongue and looked oddly sexy doing it. "Another time, okay?"

He grunted.

"You're pissed off." She raised her fist. "You want another shot to the gut?"

"Maybe later."

She got up and tugged on his hand. "Come on, I want to take a boat out in the park. It's warm and beautiful—I want to be outside." She slipped her arms under his and hugged him. "And I want to watch while you row."

He looked to the framed collage of family and friends and wondered if a picture of him—of them—would replace a picture of someone else. "Hey …" He bent down to pick up a photograph. "This is you, huh?"

"Minus my two front teeth."

In the eyes of this little girl with disobedient curls was the waking dream of a place that had nothing to do with the camera she was looking at—intimations, maybe, of that otherplaceness that came to her in the way light fell in a room or from a still life: a spoon tarnished by shadow, a tiny pitcher with the curves of a leaning woman, a half-full ash tray.

Gazing at the photo of this child he'd never met, could never know, he felt sure he would've fallen for her if they'd met while finger painting in kindergarten, as teenagers smoking in a parking lot, as retirees in an old age home. The smile, missing teeth and all, was already a cage for his heart, owned it from a past he'd never been part of.

"Can I have it?"

"What for?"

He shrugged. "Just to keep close."

She took the photograph by a corner and pulled it out of his hand. "Wouldn't you rather have the real thing?" She leaned forward and kissed him.

"Can't I have both?"

"We'll see."

16. They Dance

Shawna was dreaming. He knew because he could see her eyes moving beneath their lids. He sat on the edge of the mattress looking down at her, his own eyes adjusting to murk tinged red by the glow of the digital clock. She was on her side, the sheet pulled up to her neck and a hand balled underneath to anchor it there. No matter how hot the night, she needed that scrap of cover.

He stared for a long time, memorizing the slope of her nose, the slant of her puffy upper lip (the lower tucked underneath as if taking shelter), the slash of an eyebrow.

He slipped a hand under the sheet. The bony furrow between her breasts held off his fingertip. He wanted to press a shape into it, a shallow depression that might hold a flat gem or attract gazes, maybe intimate the life's star beneath. Through his finger he tried to insinuate himself under her skin, expand outward with her chest, feel what it was like to be warmed by her breath (he heard a sound like winter through a broken attic window).

The parts of him that were bristly, unrefined—hands so rough they made a rasping sound when they slid along her clothes— were smoothed away. Dissolved in her blood, he circulated through her, lodged in her heart. The part of him most in need of her would always be in one of these four chambers (soaked with dark, never still). It was here that the body remembered everything that had squeezed saltwater through the corner of an eye, forced breath into a burst of laughter, sent blood through her too fast to leave her anything but dizzy.

A double life to her, the Shawna who smiled at him during the day was off somewhere without him at night although he slept right beside her. Her body went on with its hidden chemistry—a good deal closer to the miraculous than the parlor-trick of duping lead into revising its elemental blueprints enough to be taken for gold.

Through it all, his mingling with her blood, the breaking and entering into her organs, she never stirred.

Anything woke him. The silent liquid change of a digit sometimes. Or maybe that was happenstance, the flowing number coinciding with a change somewhere else, a subtle difference in the arrangement of things. Maybe he picked it up somehow, like being on the ocean bottom and feeling a pocket of cool water drift past or a shift in the tug of the current. Maybe what he really felt was a good friend whose heart had finally given out. Or a mother's distress for the son she hadn't seen in years.

The street, the sidewalk, were slicked with rain that had fallen maybe half an hour ago. Traffic lights signaled to drivers who weren't there. The silence was amazing to him, that anything of this magnitude could be still.

They led café lives in this city, blocked out bits of the night, put a sheet of glass between themselves and the homeless woman shuffling past, sipped their coffee. Living in one compartment, working in another, shuttling back and forth between them, only ants had a greater affinity for niches and chambers.

Steam seeped around the rim and through the perforations of a manhole cover, rose across the street like fog from the underworld. The only movement there was. Or you might never know the city was hollow.

New York was Euclid's dream of space: straight lines, angles as sharp as blades, planes like smooth stretches of sky, circles and spheres as friendly to pi as fish eyes and turtle eggs.

A line of glass moons on steel posts made a long tent of pale light. At home in the brick stillness, he put his hand on a cornerstone fixed there … for how many years? For how many more? The weight of a building on it. There had been cities in the Americas before there had been Anglos. A place to come back to, something to haunt.

The mouth of a subway reeked of grease singed by electricity. The entrance grated off to keep insomniacs like him from being swallowed.

Cramped, crowded, dense as New York was, there were still vacant lots. Discarded bottles like shiny grave markers knocked over, in disarray.

Broken glass crunched underfoot.

Outside Okeene, Oklahoma, he'd come across an old rockery. Floorboards warping up to meet his foot covered with bits of plaster, shards of window, a dozen open boxes, strips of wood, papers (sales records? letters? tax documents?), calendars well past the years they marked (maybe one issued by State Guaranty Bank in 1972). The whole place a kind of stopped clock. Where you got to look at time—not at what time it was, at time.

A storefront with meticulously attired mannequins recalled the tribal dead buried in their finest regalia.

Wind swept past him from an unexpected car. He watched the red glow of the tail lights, reflected on the wet street, shrink and disappear around a corner.

No one stood still anymore.

He stood, staring.

Clouds so low they almost touch the tops of skyscrapers. Lights making bright spots on them as if tiny suns were on the rise. Katsinas dance on rooftops, stomp on the tar and gravel of these hollow buttes, parade their power—like flashes of lightning in a dry desert storm.

Above the day a desert of crystal blue.

To the north one of immaculate white and ice.

Three fifths of the world sea-misted desert where St. Elmo's fire dances on spars, winds itself like electric blue eels around masts, reminds mariners of voices older than their superstitions.

They dance.

The maskwearers, whose faces we are not allowed to see.

The firebearers, whose bodies we are not allowed to touch.

Gold-spun hair floating lazily above empty sockets, the skull of a Norwegian woman whose grave is sealed by asphalt turns to him and speaks: If only she had known this earth was restless with native dead she would've gone back to her home across the water, she would've returned to its arctic calm. This beauty, she says, is too terrifying, it will not let her lie.

Remember what it was like before cities buried horizons, he says, remember that.

A katsina with slits for eyes, kilt stitched with lightning, reaches for her withered hand. Beneath stars humming in their vacuum-bitten desert, they dance. Bones rattling, feet thumping, hair curling into flame, they dance.

By light leaking from the ceiling (how could it?), by light that seeped through the window, bled from the red digits of the clock, he saw Shawna's face. He looked up to see whether there was glass in the ceiling, a moon overhead. There was neither.

The music had gone out of time—no chime on the hour, no

melody played at midnight or midday, no cuckooing bird, no tick even to announce the passage of the night.

He heard Shawna's breathing.

He lay in bed beside her, not sure what had woken him—something pushing out or something pressing in.

He looked down. His jeans lay on the floor, belt still threaded through the loops. He remembered the leaden light of the hospital, remembered the night he'd heard his own singing coming from someone else, from outside. He lifted a sneaker off the floor; the bottom was wet. He hadn't been dreaming. Or if he had, he hadn't been sleeping.

A red convertible with its white top bunched behind the back seat came for him Thursday night at Pam and Hank's. From the fourth-floor window, the driver and Shawna were a pair of heads in the front seat.

When he got downstairs, Shawna was standing beside the open trunk. He tossed his worn leather bag in beside her shiny vinyl one and laid the black jacket he'd borrowed from Hank over the top. Zipping open a garment bag, Shawna took the double-breasted jacket and put it inside, shaking her head at him as if to say, *Men.*

"This is Wendy."

Her blond hair was short and wispy, her smile shy. A small nose slightly upturned, cute.

"Hi Wendy." He took her hand. "Nice wheels."

Wearing a pair of denim cutoffs, Shawna got in the back seat with him, her bare thigh pressed up against his pant-covered one.

When Wendy pulled out, there was a breeze.

Signs glowed, bright windows checkered dark facades, streetlights bent toward passersby on the sidewalk like parents watching over children.

After a tunnel took them out of Manhattan, they couldn't talk to Wendy without leaning between the bucket seats and yelling through a hurricane of noise. He was glad the city was shimmering behind them, glad to have warm wind in his face, sky overhead, scenery sailing past.

One of the names Shawna had mentioned (Montauk) and one he'd seen on a sign (Patchogue) settled comfortably in his ear. They should've been as foreign to him as to the English or the Dutch who'd settled this island, but they called up something, the way the overcoat of a long-gone uncle, hanging on a peg, vaguely implied his shoulders and back.

Even without traffic, it took close to an hour to reach the main street of a quiet town. Huge trees interlacing their branches formed a leafy archway.

Shawna pointed at a weathered house. "I like these old saltboxes."

"Is that what they turn into this close to the sea?"

"No, silly. They're shaped like the wooden boxes people used to keep salt in."

Wendy pulled into the driveway of a small saltbox and parked.

The ghost of wind rushing through his ears, he helped Shawna unload their bags.

Wendy didn't get out of the car.

"I'll see you two tomorrow." She backed out of the driveway and waved.

He watched her tail lights recede, lifted his arms and arched his back. "Where's she goin'?"

"To visit her parents. They have another house."

"They have *two* houses?"

She nodded and handed him a garment bag. "The other one doesn't have beachfront."

"No wonder they need two." He hooked a finger under the hangars sticking out of the top of the bag and slung it over a shoulder.

At the back of the house was a porch worth the drive out of the city. Screened in, it didn't keep out the stars. The sea was a black expanse different from the sky mainly because its surface was sheened and vaguely animated, held no constellations.

He listened to waves rush ashore.

Lose a bit of flesh and you could put an ounce of seawater in its place, let it take on the heat of your blood, coagulate there—you're so close to walking seawater your body would hardly know the difference, life having crawled out of the ocean so the ocean could get a peek at what the land was up to. So the ocean could cross a desert with booted feet, fill veins just beneath sunburned skin with saline. But there was a price: a drink of water every day or you'd become as dry as the hostile dust at your feet. What else had he been a year and a half ago but an oversized drop of seawater on the verge of evaporating in the Southwest?

He looked up. The ocean had climbed there too. *The Eagle has landed.* A lonely world that prayed in silence. For a dolphin to swim its seas (seas in Latin only, deserts in any other language). To leap up, sleekness arched against airless sky, before gliding in a graceful parabola back into a plain of silvery talcum.

Shawna hugged him from behind.

They made love on the tiled floor of the porch, on newspapers they knocked from a stack, rolling over headlines about the invasion of an island called Grenada and the firing, en masse, of striking air traffic controllers.

Shawna peeled a page off his sweaty back. "I hope they weren't planning on saving any of these ..."

18. Prayer Smoke

Shawna was up early, her bathing suit already on under a long-sleeve shirt. She'd pinned up her hair, and wore no makeup other than white lipstick.

"Go without me." Warm, his body stiff with fatigue, he didn't want to get out of bed. "The beach'll still be there when I get up."

"Oh, come on."

Groaning, he pulled himself to a sitting position. A shirt hit him in the face, fell onto the bed. A whiff of laundry detergent brought back her apartment.

"Let's go," she said. "Get some clothes on."

"I left my loincloth back at the wigwam." He shouted because she'd left the room. "Do I have permission to leave it wavin' in the wind?"

She poked her head back through the doorway. "No. And hurry up."

He looked down. "You hear that soldier? You're outa uniform."

Early as it was, there were already a few people on the beach, the kind on which a painter might've set up an easel: dunes heaped by wind, reeds and long grass sprouting in clumps.

The breeze coming off the water had a clean tang to it.

Wearing a knee-length bathing suit that Pam had helped him pick out, he was a little self-conscious about his legs, which were skinny and slightly bowed and not as generously proportioned as hers. Two steps behind, he carried a folded-up chair in each hand. The shirt she wore billowed up and floated in the breeze. He admired the slim V of her back, the strength implied by her hips. Ice rattled in the miniature keg she carried.

"Quit staring at my ass and walk next to me, will you?" She stopped and gazed out at the water.

It looked like ruffled tin.

"Good place to set up camp?"

"Sure." He stacked the chairs on the sand and helped her spread a blanket.

She weighed down one corner with a compact boombox, another with the keg of ice tea. She opened up the beach chairs (aluminum tubing crisscrossed with canvas straps), sank the rails so they faced the water.

He pulled off his T-shirt.

Shawna sat on the blanket, a white one rough with balled lint. "Here." She handed him a bottle of oil, put her back to him, and leaned over her knees.

He squirted a clear pool into his cupped hand, and a coconut scent flowered in his palm. He greased between her shoulder blades, rubbing in widening circles.

"Mmmmmmmm." Her forehead fell against her knees.

Pouring a shiny squiggle of oil on her back, he worked his hand under the strap of her bathing suit, used his thumb on the base of her neck.

"Ohhhhhhhh, right *there*—ohhh …" Her head tilted back against his chest.

He lowered himself and kissed her behind an ear, his chin slipping against a greased shoulder. Her skin was hot. A few stray hairs against his lips felt like threads. Working over her trapezius muscles with his thumbs, he glanced at the sky. Its color had mostly been burned away, leaving a hot white haze.

"Are you still reading that Geraci novel?"

"I'm half way through a second reading." He squinted, trying to separate where sea blurred into sky.

She sprawled forward on her side. "I guess you liked it."

"The main character's kind of like looking at a reflection, but certain things are reversed."

"What do you mean?"

"He's half Indian but on his mother's side. He's a poet with an ear for music. I'm a musician who dabbles in poetry." He left out the part about their both doing time in a psychiatric hospital, about their inability to navigate the world for similar reasons: landmarks just wouldn't stay put.

"Hmm." Almost a moan. "I'm sorry we missed him at the art show. Geraci, I mean."

"Yeah." Though what would he have said to him?

Removing the prop of her arm, she settled onto her belly, her arms at her sides as if she'd fainted and fallen forward.

He remembered how he'd once hung onto Jack's glass words. Remembered how hollowed out he'd been the night he and Debbie had walked into the Smiling Aztec. He'd had a breakdown. He'd lost his bearings. He was better now. But who sees katsinas dancing on rooftops? A dead father with celestial bodies where his eyes were supposed to be? Or were those just dreams bulling their way in where they didn't belong?

He wanted to relax for the next three days. He didn't want to think about his father's ghost in Shawna's living room, his uncle-stepfather, whatever kept him up at night. For three days he wanted to feel like everyone else.

His gaze wandered down the beach. Only property owners allowed. They didn't own the ocean, just the sand leading up to it. Like the Southwest, where miles of fencing let you know you weren't wanted. What did it matter that you'd walked the hard-packed silence for half a lifetime, that your tribe came from those dry, mostly flat lands, where they'd left the dusty ruins of their accomplishments along with etchings of hovering horned beings to watch over them—what did any of it matter beside a chain-link fence he could've jumped without burning a whole calorie?

Shawna stirred, careful to re-hook her bathing suit top before rolling onto her side.

He stood up, sweat slipping from his armpits down his sides, bumping over ribs.

"Where're you goin?" Her voice was rough.

"Swimming."

A run in the ocean. A dance on the waves.

She watched him become a tapering shadow against bright water. He broke into a sprint, kicking up spray before falling into a wave. Settling into an even stroke, he rose and fell on the swells.

Wrinkles on the blanket had creased the side of her face and left it a little numb. She rubbed at sand clinging to an oily flank.

Out on the water, Logan was growing smaller. He looked so tiny in all that ocean, tiny and vulnerable. Remembering the Ouija-board séance, she got anxious.

He was still swimming out. Lost in the noise of the ocean and his own breathing, he wouldn't have heard her even if she screamed. "Where does he think he's going?" she muttered.

She walked down to the water's edge, her arms folded across

the top of her breasts. He was almost out of sight, just a speck in all that shifting shine. Fear hollowed out her stomach.

A lifeguard blew a whistle. Standing on his towering white chair, he waved Logan in.

Finally.

He was swimming toward shore now.

Relieved, Shawna walked back to the blanket and picked up *Psychology Today*. She got so absorbed in article about depression that when the sun suddenly dimmed she was surprised. "Hey—!"

He was strong and wet and salty on top of her.

"Get off! Oh you're *cold*!"

Pinning her to the blanket, he tried to kiss her. She kept turning her head, fighting to get him off, but he was too heavy. His face teetered on the brink of laughter.

"Quit slobbering on me, you animal."

She was laughing too hard to put up a real fight.

He rolled to the side.

"Look what you did." She threw the magazine at him. "Now help me fix the blanket."

Wendy showed up in the afternoon. Her blond hair was boyishly short. Older than Shawna, she hadn't bothered to powder the lines webbing the corners of her eyes. She wore a terrycloth outfit—a bright red he'd never pick out for anything but an M&M—had an angular jaw, an arch to her eyebrows, and skin as pale as cream. Cute in a prudish way. She offered Logan beer from a cooler. He turned it down.

"Glad to be out of the city?" The way Wendy had smeared her nose with white sunblock, it looked like a tribal marking.

He glanced around. "The water, the open space … kind of like sky to the part of you that's bird."

Wendy glanced at Shawna. "She says the same thing."

"Yup." Shawna didn't look up from her magazine. "We're pretty packed in in the city."

"But you like a few things about Manhattan, don't you?"

When Shawna didn't say anything, Logan realized Wendy was talking to him. He lifted his chin toward Shawna. "Her."

Shawna slapped a page flat. "I put an ad in the paper for someone tall, dark, and obnoxious. There he is."

Wendy, Shawna had told him, had majored in anthropology but had become a social worker.

Shawna stood up, pulling the bottom of her bathing suit to keep it from riding up. "I'm going in."

Neither of them offered to go with her.

She looked at them critically. "Okay. So stay here and sweat."

Logan watched wind sweep her hair over a shoulder as she walked toward the water.

Here the Sun was not the one that dried the ocean out of things, left airy husks to be whisked across the grit. Here it was more like a tyrannical father whose disposition had been softened by a disapproving mother.

Wendy was drawing circles in the sand with her finger. "Shawna told me … well I can see you're Indian. Hopi, right?" Her blond bangs touched the top of her sunglasses.

For the first time it occurred to him that he was on exhibit.

"I'm sorry I didn't mean …" She laughed. "I guess I belong in the Outback with nobody to offend."

"The Outback? Was that where you—"

"I can tell you a lot about Aboriginal culture. More about the Aranda tribe."

"You got a thing for Australia?"

"Always did. I spent a summer there and loved it. I thought about moving there, but I guess I'm just a scaredy cat. I'd be so *far* from everything … from everyone I know."

He nodded.

"And I do like my job. Mostly. My clients don't have to understand me, I have to understand *them*. And that I'm good at, I'm a great listener." Her white nose and dark glasses made a strange mask of her face.

She was a good looker too—she was talking to him but watching Shawna splash in the waves.

"She loves the ocean," Wendy said, "but she misses the desert."

"I've seen some of the photographs."

Wendy nodded. "She's crazy about all those red rock formations, saguaros, the colors. I think she wants to be Georgia O'Keeffe with a camera."

He didn't need to know who O'Keeffe was to get the point. "You think she'll go back? To Phoenix?"

"She talks about it, but I don't know how serious she is. I know she's bored with her job, but, well … hard to just pick up and start all over somewhere else."

"Wendy!" Shawna was walking toward them, her hair plastered flat with water. "Why don't you take off that bathrobe and stay a while?" Dripping, she pulled Wendy to her feet by her shirt. "Come on, take it off."

"*Shawna!*" Wendy grabbed at the terrycloth and tugged back.

While she was readjusting the top of her beachwear, Logan crawled forward and wrapped his arms around her knees.

"Hey …!"

He pushed a shoulder into her waist and as he stood, she folded over it.

"My sunglasses!"

She struggled, but he had a tight hold on her as he walked toward the water.

"Put me down!"

Shawna was pushing them, one hand on his back, one on Wendy's rump. "Dump her!"

"Don't—!"

All three of them went in in a pile.

Wendy came up coughing. "Oh you two!" She squeezed water from her eyes.

Dishes were piled in the sink. The last bottle of wine was on the living room floor. He was next to it, his back propped against the couch. Shawna, showered and fragrant. was above him. Bronze flakes glinted when she turned her head.

Wendy, her legs stretched out behind Shawna, was talking about the Moon, how landing on it had unnerved a tribe of traditional Maya. They didn't understand how men could show up in a realm reserved for beings made of less vulnerable stuff, so they made up a myth. The astronauts, they assured each other, had had to ask permission of the Moon Goddess, who stayed locked away in a great mountain to which the astronauts were refused entry. Day after day she commanded the guardian of the entrance to turn them away—just to let them know who was boss—before finally giving her consent.

"The Maya are like the wine." Shawna's knees were tucked up against her chest and her arms were holding them there. "They're not going to last much longer without becoming something else."

"I hit a restaurant on the Moon last week," Logan said, a verse behind. "The food was good, but it had no atmosphere."

Shawna pushed his shoulder with the heel of her foot.

Wendy, still wearing that M&M–red beach outfit, got up, kicking Logan in the back of his head ("Sorry"), padded over to the light switch, and turned off the overhead. She stuck a cassette in the tape deck. "I'll be right back."

They saw the glow of the candle first, Wendy behind it, her face ruddy. Something else was burning, giving off a familiar smell. Wendy put the candle on an end table, handed him a stone pipe.

Standing up, he took a puff, held the pipe out at arm's length, blew smoke. He turned, faced another direction, repeated the ritual. The wallpaper in front of him hazed over.

"Hey, don't hog the pipe." Shawna held out her hand.

Ignoring her, he did it twice more. Small puffs.

"What was that all about?"

Wendy was smiling. "I know."

A practice popularized by Native Americans writing books to show Anglos where they'd gone wrong. But Anglos held only the empty bag of the ceremony (and wondered why it was so light). They'd been told what was behind the motions they were going through, but they didn't believe, not as they believed there were 109 elements, as they believed that for every action there was an equal and opposite reaction. They *hoped*, tied wishes to pouches of tobacco as the Hopi tied prayers to eagle feathers. So did he.

"I made an offering." One for each direction.

"Oh yeah? Whadjew you offer?"

"Smoke."

"Big spender."

Shawna drew on the stem of the pipe, the bowl cupping a glow. She held her breath, her mouth tightening into a puffy seam, her face crinkling up, her eyebrows looking like they were waving white flags. Eyes watery, she handed the pipe to Wendy.

By the time the pipe had made a few circuits and Shawna had tapped black residue into an ashtray and refilled the little bowl, Wendy was lying on the couch looking at the room sideways. Her head was pressed up against Shawna's thigh at an angle that looked uncomfortable.

Shawna had the pipe going again.

He saw a flake pattern to the clay-red stone as she handed it to him. His breath, mingled with smoke, leaked out of his body like fog crawling down a mountainside.

There was a moment of Tangerine Dream shot through with the synthesized cries of gulls.

Logan took another hit of the pipe, the burning in his lungs strangely pleasant now. As if nerves reserved only for rare sensations had been exposed by the abrasive smoke.

He tried his voice but nothing came out.

"Remember ... my hair?" Shawna rubbed at her nose. "Shaved? And those ... *colors?*"

A way of startling the middle class mind out of routine.

Wendy shifted on the couch. "Aging hippies are okay. Punks I can't stand."

He leaned back against the couch, the pale ceiling descending like mist. He heard Shawna drag on the pipe (wind through a tunnel). His head filled with space. Thoughts zipped around in so much emptiness there was of any two colliding, hardly a chance of retrieving one.

"How did that slogan go?" Shawna smacked the pipe on the heel of her hand. "You know, from May 1968? Paris?" She rubbed cinders of hash off, let them fall beside the misshapen remains of the candle. "Better to die of starvation than boredom?"

Mikey had said something like that. From *Ecclesiastes*. But he couldn't remember what. He was stuck listening to Shawna's voice echo softly in the helium-filled cavern his mind used to inhabit.

"Punks don't like the choices they have, so they choose *nothing*. They want to look *nothing* like the society that created them ..." Shawna's words formed a cloud as she spoke.

It was fun to pull down statues of Caesar, overthrow a state, smash department-store windows—but then what?

"Cowards," Wendy said.

"Sure they're afraid." Shawna sat up a little straighter against the couch. "Of the future. Afraid there *is* no future."

Voices in the dark now, the three of them, their bodies and the space they enclosed melted down, like the candle.

Shawna moved back up to the couch so that one leg rested against his shoulder, tucked the foot of the other under her thigh.

Five snakes writhed along the back of his neck, wrapped

themselves around the tightness there, found their way under his skin, invaded the muscle.

Wendy yawned. "All I can say is things were never worse."

It was all falling apart, like Rome. Hadn't he just thought that?

A New World is coming...

But you must dance. And not stop dancing...

He moved his foot because the knob of his anklebone had gone numb against the linoleum. It felt as if a metal disc had been implanted under the skin.

When the music's over ...

"Samuel Beckett is snickering in his Paris flat right now."

Shawna's voice, behind him. He imagined Beckett sitting in a room with the lights off, his white smile disembodied in the darkness. To see people walking around in plastic garbage bags with holes cut out for their arms and heads, syringes through their nipples, safety pins through their ears and noses.

Turn out the lights ...

Gangs of kids, Indian-shaved and fluorescently plumaged, circling the cities, eager to speed the dying world on its way—get rid of traffic lights more regular than the sunrise, smash wonderfully vulnerable display windows peopled by mannequins, serve up Molotov cocktails in five-star hotels.

Turn out the lights,

Turn out the lights ...

"Heyyyy ..." Wendy lifted her head from the couch. "*2010* is on tonight. That's suuuuch a good film to watch when you're stoned."

The movie wouldn't go on for an hour.

In an hour Wendy was asleep.

Logan was on the floor, Shawna on top of him.

She stopped kissing him and pulled off her T-shirt. Then she jumped up and thumped across the floor.

He heard the screen door batted open, the soft hiss as it eased itself closed. A warm breeze slid along his bare chest. Pushing off the linoleum with his knuckles as if he were a lower primate, he got up and swatted the door open with a palm.

The edge of a shell scraped the ball of his foot as he ran. He saw her ahead of him, saw her drop her something. As she ran toward the water—an animated silhouette—he realized it had been her shorts. He looked up at the houses along the beach with their porch lights on. Laughter and voices floated out to him.

He heard a splash.

Running after her, he didn't register the water until the weight of it slowed his legs. He toppled forward, the seawater embrace surprisingly cold. When he came up, he stripped off his shorts, flung them toward shore. A dark shape arced briefly past stars.

There was still a cloud of smoke in his head; his thoughts played hide and seek in it.

The Moon, many-faced enchantress, floated elegantly over the water. While he was gawking at the sky, waiting for the water softly sucking at his body to dissolve him like a sugary lozenge, arms locked around his chest. He maneuvered himself until he was facing her.

Something inside him rippled. He liked to inhale ever so slightly when he kissed her. This must have been how the first man had been created—warm glass with breath blown into the hollow part of him.

She turned abruptly and kicked away from him. He chased her into deeper water. When she turned to face him, he saw the endless waters—ghosted by moonlight—in motion around the island of her head. She disappeared beneath the surface. A few seconds later hands yanked him under. His outstretched toes brushed the sandy bottom.

They tried kissing in the strange sea-quiet. Below the surface, another existence. He knew he was in love with her, this woman opening his mouth with hers (tasting of salt), this shadowy, underwater shape. But he couldn't breathe. Or stay.

After they kicked up toward the surface, hauled in air in gasps, she put a hand on his chest and pushed off. Laughing, she churned water into foam as she swam.

She stood and waded ashore, a wave breaking lethargically against the backs of her knees. Her hair was a dark waterfall down her back. She sprinted up the beach.

He watched her, his breath coming hard, seawater washing against his calves.

Long-legged, an animal's strength in her leaping stride, she looked almost as though she were shoving ground behind her, sliding earth under the balls of her feet. The secret of her strength was in her hips, her lower body carrying the slender V of her torso almost the way a horse carries a rider. He saw the dent in a muscular cheek above her thigh before she melted into shadow.

He wondered that she didn't leave a trail. Or maybe she did, a streak beyond his range of vision, something that rubbed off her like the talcum of butterfly wings.

The screen door opened and closed.

He looked at the beads of water on his body, small pearls under the Moon.

She was coming back toward him, a bundle in her arms. He shushed through the water to meet her.

She spread a blanket on the sand then spread herself on the blanket, her breasts flattening against her ribs, her stomach sucking itself toward the pelvic bones. "What the hell are you standing there for?"

He fell on his knees, sand gnawing at his skin as he covered her body with his. While they were making love, he couldn't bring himself to tell her it was love he felt.

19. Prisms

The wind. The sea. The dawndusk before the Sun has risen. His nostrils flared, sucked in air. The sand his bare feet kicked up pelted his ass. At the water's edge his legs turned a wave into spray across his chest and face—a coolness like chilled sweat. His heels thumped solidly, ball and toes slapping wet sand. Firm as flesh. He felt the sudden furrows that separated thigh muscles with each stride, felt them fill back in.

Wind hummed in his chest and throat. Waves broke against his ribs and rushed through. Overhead, gulls screamed as if afraid for him, a wingless cousin weighed down by the earth inside him. He could've spoken to them if he'd wanted, told them he wasn't quite touching the Earth anymore, that the salt wind in his ears was his own breath, that he could just as easily have been churning up sky as sand on this empty beach, that the calm inside him stretched as far as his eye could see.

Sweat streaking his face mingled with sea spray. The movement of his arms meshed with his legs, and his head pushed forward with each stride as if to break some invisible barrier.

Caught up in his own motion, a gull's wing riding the wind, he was airy as an atom, was scattered along blades of light cutting into the sky, amounted to hardly anything.

The Sun would rise out of the water, plying the horizon with light. A sleeping rainbow in each ray. But we needed prisms to see the colors: a little cactus extract, a dream falling in a thin drizzle, a retina cracked like van Gogh's, a good run before daybreak.

20. Dawn Rider

He lifted his beer mug. It left a wet ring on the table. The thickly varnished planks looked like timbers recovered from a shipwreck. Wendy and Shawna were still in the ladies' room. An awning, stretched protectively over tables and chairs, blocked out most of the sky.

They'd spent the afternoon at the beach and, after a seafood ladled over with a sauce so rich he felt like he'd swallowed ribbons of silk, had driven to see fireworks over the water.

Shawna had put on a white zip-up outfit that was shorts and shirt all in one. Her lipstick matched. In spite of the heat, he'd worn jeans with his old two-toners.

"Boots? In July?" Wendy had looked at him as if he were a vase she was sure had a crack.

"Indians have a special gene for it."

By the time they got to the waterfront, they had to squeeze and elbow and push their way through the crowd. There was a sudden boom like a thunderclap then dozens of runaway stars. They slowed rapidly, fell as bright dust.

Ohhhhhhhh.

Heads tipped back to take in the harmless re-enactment of war.

There was another explosion, and a flower of red light bloomed, died, faded away.

On the Hopi calendar, July Fourth was just another day.

He glanced at Shawna, saw her upturned face suddenly illuminated. Her profile was marblesque, as if, like Lot's wife, she'd become landscape.

After the sound and light show, smoke drifting lazily toward the water, Shawna and Wendy had wanted to go for a drink.

He stared at the lagoon lapping softly against a wall of railroad ties. Lights atop metal posts were cold wavering flames in a dark moving mirror. The Moon made a rough trail of light all the way to the world behind the world. His grandfather had taken it for granted. Not behind, below. And above. Three below, at least one above (what else would there be to look forward to?). A universe built in succession, history laid to rest in layers. He didn't know how it was supposed to work—destroyed worlds that still existed in the general direction cactus roots took were also havens for the dead. Mirror images somehow, the Sun rising there as it set here. Were they side by side, these netherrealms? End to end? Flat and square like the Earth before Columbus?

He'd once asked his grandfather—the story was so farfetched he couldn't help it—"Did that really happen?"

His grandfather, looking irritated, shrugged. "Maybe it didn't. Maybe it did but not the way you think. Anyway, it was a long time ago. Before you were born. Or me. Even before the Anglos were here." He tapped the bowl of his pipe on a stone. "But don't get the idea that things happen once and that's it. They go on happening."

A cheek brushed against his, arms crossed over his chest. Shawna kissed him behind an ear. There was wine on her breath.

The men at the next table were dressed as brightly as boys on the first day of school.

He looked at his beer, something watery and domestic, with a stale aftertaste from the tap lines. He lifted the mug. "Whaddaya think, half empty or half full?"

"Sometimes I ask myself the same thing about your skull."

Wendy coughed on her bay breeze and patted her chest. In spite of all the sunscreen, there were red semicircles under her eyes. She wore two pink buttons in her ears, which matched her barrettes.

"That's no way to treat the birthday boy," he said.

"Today's your *birthday*?"

He nodded.

"Thanks for the advance warning." Shawna looked at Wendy. "Half empty."

Wendy's blond eyebrows pushed together. "Why didn't you say something?"

He shrugged. "I kept forgetting." By the rockets' red glare, he'd remembered.

"So how old are you birthday boy?"

"Twenty-four."

"*What*?" Shawna leaned closer as if she'd had difficulty understanding him.

"Twenty ... *four*."

"I was so sure, I mean ... I was *sure* you were older. Twenty-*four*?"

"Shawna get *over* it. So you hooked up with a younger guy." Reaching for her glass, Wendy knocked it over. A shapeless chunk of ice sat sparkling in a tiny puddle.

"You're tilted young lady." Shawna's hair rested on her shoulders in weak waves, indolently beautiful.

Wendy put her elbow on the table, tucked her fist into a cheek, and looked out over the water. "I wish I could go."

"We can." Logan took a hurried swallow of beer.

Wendy lifted her face off her fist. "I meant to Australia."

"You can." He finished off his beer. "In fact, I'd say the first step to Australia is to get back to the house."

Shawna leaned close to Wendy and spoke so softly it was easier for him to overhear a woman at another table: "Awright, who wantsa do a few lines?"

Logan stood up. "Are we going?"

Wendy held up a finger. "Just let Shawna finish her story—"

Logan slapped the table, startling Wendy. "Tell ya a story 'bout a man named *Jiimmm* …" He sang it to the tune of *The Beverly Hillbillies.* "Ain't nobody quite like *hiimmm.* Makes a clean livin off 'is own *laaaaaaaaand*—" He lowered his voice to bass— "meaner than *rat shit* rolled in sand." He thwacked the table again and glasses jumped.

Wendy peeked from behind the blinders of her hands to see who was looking.

"Come on. Let's get outa here."

"We have to pay for our—"

"Fuckit." He pulled her up by her hand. "The prices they charge here, they won't miss it."

"We can't just walk out."

Shawna was already weaving between tables, hooped earrings swinging.

Inside the bar Wendy was looking around desperately, the pink button in the ear he could see like another eye, wide and unblinking.

"Criminals!" Wendy called after them in the parking lot.

Logan and Shawna were sprinting for the car, Shawna's wood-soled sandals clopping on the asphalt. They all shoved into the front seat, Logan at the wheel. Shawna handed him the keys, and he backed out between a Mercedes Benz and a Corvette. He pulled onto the road with a screech of tires.

Lined with huge leafy trees, the road was illuminated every so often by a lamp fixed to a pole stiff with boredom.

"Do you have any idea where you are?" Wendy sounded peeved.

"On a long, long island inhabited by people with big, big bank accounts, driving a car owned by a woman with a short, short temper."

"Pull over."

He let go of the wheel and squeezed the accelerator. "You wanna drive?"

Shawna grabbed the wheel.

A cluster of lights ahead signaled they'd come to a town. Logan threw his hands over his head as if he were on a roller coaster. Shawna laughed as she steered.

"That'sa red light!"

The light turned green before they got to it.

"Oh God."

Wendy looked a little green herself.

The light was weak, leaden. Not meant to illuminate anything.

Static from an electrical storm raging across the screen scoured his ears.

Shawna was asleep on the couch.

He squatted in front of the tv. The snow didn't fall, traced no pattern he could follow. Was simply a brightness in which imagery had dissolved. Would it bother her that he was mesmerized by these tiny rectangles of light (never still for a second)?

In his mind he made them still. Or if not still at least not random. A dance at the core of the television's being. He reached slowly with an outstretched finger. The shifting light edged his hand, lent it extraordinary solidity.

He turned to Shawna, studied the spectral glow on her face, the way a strand of hair fell across a cheek. She was walking her dreamland again. Without him. He traced a curve from an ear to the corner of her mouth with two fingers.

Snapping off the television, he padded barefoot to the porch and pushed open the screen door.

The sand was cool under his feet, ground gently between his toes.

Having gone running before dawn, he'd been awake almost 24 hours.

He walked to the ragged waterline, watched waves curl, break, foam. As they had for the first Americans. Intuitively they'd known that the Earth could be tipped, and these waters could be poured into their veins. Oceans sounded inside them. When they made fires on the shore, they were comforted by the sea's rhythm, by the solidity of their hands against a wavering background of firelight.

He stood under a distant shore of sky dotted with faraway campfires, silent and white. That was where they'd gone. Those were the fires they clustered around now.

In a single night he'd wandered from the clinking of silverware and gourmet sauces smothering cravings for burned flesh to exploding flowers of light. From perfumed bodies and hungry mouths politely lipsticked to syllables spoken in echolocation.

Wondering whether, like water, the soul took the shape of its container. And when the container was broken ...?

A stone observatory built long before Columbus bumbled his way to Hispaniola rose out of jungle in southern Mexico—The Mouth of the Well of the Itza People. Home to heavenly seismologists who, doubling as priests, tracked an invisible fault seaming the sky. Thunder murmured the sky's distress, intimated apocalypse.

Logan held up a finger. As if he could feel the flaw behind a roving cloud, the zigzagging fault line you see on a skull. At death the closed-over hole opened again, an escape hatch for the soul. That's what *Qua'ah* had told him. Or he'd read. Or made up.

A rush of wind drowned out the sound of breaking waves. Overhead, the sky wheeled.

A shape loping away from dawn blotting out stars threatening to overshadow the Moon. a presence the eye cannot catch clearly cannot hold any more than it can curves of dancing flame. hooves, he thinks, a plumed lance and shield. night-black hair immune to gravity's pull, tied with feathers, waving lazily above flickering red that might be shoulders. the Moon, whole constellations, a swath of sky swept away by the twisting apparition of horse and rider. reining in his mount, lance held in a fist, he speaks in a voice made of lightning and the dry desert storm. from the flared nostrils of his beast—chest bluegray and neck spangled with white—comes pure wind.

21. Night's Undertow

Red. Bright and glowing.

He stirred. Squinting, he turned his head away from the overcast sky. The ground shifted against his back when he moved. Sand. He rolled to an elbow, pushed himself to his feet. He brushed at his hair, swatted at his jeans, his shirt, as he walked to the house.

The gray line of the roof made a seam against the lighter gray of clouds. He wondered when they'd come in. Last night there'd only been one or two, wind-driven past ... the Moon? He remembered a dark shape given a sudden silvery corona, backlit by the world floating behind it. The last thing he'd seen before crashiing on the beach.

What would Wendy the anthropologist say if she caught him adding the hallucination of a Plains horseman to the katsinas dancing across the tops of buildings in Manhattan? The wrong tribal delusion, she'd note down in her field book. Might be crazy after all. But why didn't it bother her that Anglos a hundred times removed from the Middle East had visions of a bearded Semite hung on crossbeam, shivering as if he'd come down with a fever? And what did she expect, anyway, of a Hopi who'd grown up in Cheyenne country, in the land of the Kansa and the Pawnee? The dream of the land, swaying the corn and wheat stalks, was bound to get under your skin.

He let the screen door hiss closed.

"Hey. How's the birthday boy?" Wendy was sitting at the kitchen table, one of her fingers looped through the handle of a coffee mug.

He grunted.

Her hair sticking up in stubborn tufts, her eyes bloodshot, Wendy looked like she'd rather be in bed.

"You have a good time last night?" She was in her terrycloth outfit.

A pattern of leaves running along the top of the wallpaper crowned the room in autumn red.

"The harder it is to get out of bed, the more fun you had." His voice was gravelly.

She cocked an eyebrow at him. "You didn't even *make* it to bed. You look a little ridiculous standing there barefoot in your clothes from last night."

He didn't mention that she looked like she was wrapped in old towels. Or the way the sun had broken through her lotion defenses. Nor did he bring up her resemblance to a raccoon.

"You want a cup of coffee?"

"Sure." As he sat down, she got up. Counterweights.

Her flip-flops slapped the floor. She slid the glass pot out of the coffee machine. "How do you take it?"

"Like a man."

"Cute." She put the cup in front of him. "Milk, sugar?"

"I like my medicine black."

Wendy sat down across from him. "So what're you doing sleeping with the sand crabs? Shawna kick you out of bed?"

"Nah. I was workin' on a new a song and just … fell asleep."

"Got enough for an album?"

He stopped blowing on his coffee and straightened up. "Already put one out."

"Sure."

He smiled, amused that he'd coated himself in the slipperiness he'd always aimed for. "I did."

Wendy tucked her chin into her neck as if he'd flicked water at her face. "What? A collection of Tibetan chants for the dead?"

He shook his head. "Never mind."

"You really *did*? When …?"

"'Bout three years ago. Little indie label in LA." He shrugged. "Didn't sell."

"Oh." She seemed disheartened but anxious not to let her pessimism spread. "What's the name of your band?"

Burnt Offering had been the first one, four fifteen-year-olds playing in a barn. Brass on White Silk had lasted almost a year. Crisis Cult came close to having the sound he wanted, but he had to get rid of a couple of people, including the guy who'd come up with the name. Then he decided to go it alone.

"Moon Eye. Which was just me, an acquaintance doing me a favor, and a couple musicians the label loaned me." Jorge Gitano—he could charm a dance out of ghosts the way he played the flute—was the only one who wasn't replaceable.

"*Moon Eye*? I've *heard* of you. They're playing one of your songs on the alternative station out here. It's kind of hard to get in Manhattan—the reception—but it's a great station."

He slid his bare feet across linoleum tiles rough as alligator skin, tucked them under the chair. "One of *my* songs? Are you sure …?"

"'Wind Canyon,' right?"

"'Wind *Rock*.'"

"*That's* it."

"That *is* me. And Jorge." This weekend morning in the

kitchen of an old saltbox had taken a turn toward the surreal. "I don't know why—"

"I *love* that song."

He sipped his coffee and calmed himself. *One* alternative station on Long Island was playing *one* of his songs. Which probably meant that *one* DJ, just out of college, with no friends and no social life, had gotten overly excited after picking up his album at a garage sale.

"I mean, I've only heard it a few times, but it's … yeah, it's different."

His face broke into a helpless grin. "I have to call Harvey. Maybe he knows something about it."

"Harvey?"

"My old manager."

She rocked forward suddenly in her chair and leaned half way across the table. "Oh I can't be*lieve* this! Shawna never even *told* me."

"She doesn't know."

Wendy's pale eyebrows crinkled like tiny trains crashing in slow motion. "She doesn't *know*?"

He shook his head.

She sagged back against her chair. "Why didn't you tell her?"

He looked into the dark liquid oracle of his cup. "You wouldn't believe how many bands put out albums—even on big labels—make it to the radio, then burn up in the airwaves, and they're gone." He shook his head again. "I'm not gonna be one of those guys selling his records out of the trunk of his car."

"You should at least let them put a few on display in the Copper Crow."

"I don't know. But why is it getting airtime *now*? Why not three years ago when the album came out?"

Wendy looked at him, ready to be surprised again. "I don't know. I still don't get why you didn't tell Shawna."

He held his breath. Then expelled it as if he'd just kicked up from the bottom of a lake. "Because it didn't *go* anywhere. It was a fucking *failure*. And that's not what I wanted her to see."

Wendy put a cool hand on his wrist, soft as a snail flesh. "You're in love with her, aren't you?"

"The thought crossed my mind."

"Me too."

"You think so too, or you love her too?"

She squeezed his wrist. "Both. Is that okay?" She gave one more squeeze then pulled her hand—vulnerable, slinking back into its shell—across the table.

"Sure." His coffee had grown cool enough to drink without blowing on it.

Walking barefoot into the kitchen, a T-shirt hanging to her knees, Shawn wanted to know where he'd been last night.

"Passed out on the sand."

She rubbed an eye with a palm heel. "The sand, huh?"

Logan was tilting back in his chair, leaning on two legs, trying to balance himself without holding onto the edge of the table.

"Have some respect for the furniture." Shawna walked around behind him and tipped him back.

"Whoa!" His arms flew out, but she backed the chair with her thigh.

Wendy giggled.

Shawna went to the other side of the table, put her hands on

Wendy's shoulders. "Stay away from them." She lifted her chin at Logan. "Hazardous to your health."

"Men? Oh I do." She smiled. "You know I do."

"Gotta be a few of us who meet with FDA approval," Logan protested.

"Nah." Shawna wrinkled her nose. "You're all alike."

Logan looked down. "Certain equipment seems to be standard—I'll give you that." He was paying more attention to the way Shawna was massaging Wendy's shoulders than to what she was saying.

Shawna reached for the hem of Wendy's shirt, while Wendy held her arms up like a child being undressed by her mother. The terrycloth top came away inside-out. She had on a pink bathing suit top underneath.

His eyebrows went up. He was beginning to wonder whether he was the butt of a joke. He didn't trust the gray morning light or what was happening in it. Any minute now those wallpaper leaves were going to come floating down around them like big flakes of red snow. Or the rooster-shaped clock above the stove was going to crow.

Shawna's fingers kneaded Wendy's back and shoulders. They were like the brown hands of a gardener who loved earth enough to root around in it without gloves. Only the polished white nails, tipping her fingers like the lacquered insides of a seashell, seemed to have anything in common with Wendy's creamy shoulders.

It had seemed impossible, just a few minutes ago, that Wendy could be comfortable half-dressed in the kitchen. Sensing his confusion, maybe, Shawna winked at him.

He smiled lamely.

Wendy's head came forward until her short hair flopped on the table.

Territoriality asserting itself, Logan pushed out his chair, leaned over a corner of the table, and kissed Shawna, *Maybe we are all alike.* The kiss sent a strange feeling through him, invited him deeper to a place he'd never been.

Shawna tugged on him with one hand, pulled at Wendy with the other, each of them knowing where they were going.

Logan just watched at first.

Her legs thick, her haunches spreading like butterfly wings from her tail bone as she bent forward on her knees, Wendy was ghostly white on top of Shawna.

He reached out, put a hand on one of Wendy's plump cheeks as if he were breaking some tribal taboo. Wendy's head moved rhythmically between Shawna's legs. Shawna grabbed a fistful of sunny hair and pulled down as she arched, forcing Wendy's head up. Her thumbs denting Shawna's thighs and shoving them back, she moved her head in tight rapid circles. Shawna moaned, and let her head roll back so that all he could see was the underside of her jaw.

He stripped off his underwear (the last of his unwillingness). Tentatively, he put a finger just below the button of Wendy's anus. She seemed not to notice. He slid an experimental finger inside her. She moaned softly. Beneath her, Shawna's breath was raspy and urgent. Through Wendy, he felt Shawna come.

Shawna was still holding Wendy's head, but she was looking at him.

It wasn't so much that he wanted to fuck Wendy as he wanted to make his presence felt. Holding himself in his fist with one hand, he held on with the other to her hip and eased into the soft pink of a conch shell.

He couldn't tell from her groan whether she liked it or not. Grabbing both hips to steady himself, he tugged Wendy to him, the bed smacking into his knees. Reluctant to be separated from her, Wendy pulled Shawna. Tightening his grip on Wendy's hips, he watched himself sink deeper between her moony cheeks, felt her recoil.

"Easy." She turned to look at him. "I'm not that big, and you're not that small."

He eased into her again.

"Better."

Wendy was different from Shawna—the way she moved, the feel of her. He managed a rhythm with her, pushing deeper as she got wetter. By the time he was all the way inside her, she was ramming herself against him, and he had to hold on to her waist to keep his balance. Moaning the whole time like she was about to come, she would probably come and go, and he'd never catch on.

Wendy looked back at him, whispered harshly, "Like *that* ... slow."

This, he realized, was the only way she could make love to a man: she had to be looking at a woman, holding on to her, her face pressed between a woman's thighs, the briny smell of a woman in her nose.

Digging her fingers into Shawna's legs, Wendy let out a slow, tapering cry that broke into short, ragged breaths. Unable to hold back anymore, he pulled out, pressed himself against the seam of her rump and spurted on her back.

Wendy reached behind her, smeared the milky fluid with a hand. "Christ, I'm drenched."

"Hey!" Shawna threw a pillow at him. "You were supposed to save some for me."

Sitting up on her knees at the edge of the bed, Wendy began stroking his half-hard cock—still slick from being inside her—as if she owed him something. Leaning over, she braced herself with an arm on his hip, and took him into her mouth. Her mouth smaller than Shawna's, her thinner lips like eraser rubber, she sucked hard. He stiffened again. She started bobbing her head up and down furiously, wispy hair flying. *A lesbian?*

"That's enough you two." Shawna slapped Wendy's ass.

Shawna pulled Logan onto the bed and climbed on top of him. He put his tongue in her mouth, and she kept it there. Reaching down and guiding him in, she let go of his tongue, and her breath flooded his lungs as he entered her. Something inside him that was not his body, but needed his body, burned. He didn't remember her ever being quite so wet, didn't remember her ever coming so soon, crying out so suddenly, so sharply he thought at first that he'd hurt her.

"God I'm fucking jealous." Wendy slapped Shawna's ass.

Shawna tousled his hair, which was sticky with sweat. "So, how'd you like your birthday present?"

22. Slam-Dance Payback

Bored, Logan looked up at the four tv screens behind the bar. Tube #1 was white doctors in dirty smocks grimly desperate over children with overlarge heads and brown skin stretched over their skeletal bodies. Next to that, a singer in a music video hurled himself up and down, his long hair flying. Women wearing little more than lingerie and mascara that turned their eyes into black caves trailed him. While he stuck his powdered face into the camera and twisted his mouth to exaggerate a good time he'd in the back seat of a car, Third Worlders kept dying. Flies crawled around the eye of a boy too weak to swat them away, ringed a mouth stiffened open. On Tube #3, a middleclass house wife served up a plate of rice that wasn't too soupy but didn't clump either. He didn't bother with Tube #4.

Where the hell was Paul?

He'd been a little depressed since coming back from Long Island. The city was too cramped, too noisy, too crowded. Even Pam's apartment. Stumbling off the couch this morning, he'd banged his knee against a corner of the coffee table. Still hurt if he touched it.

At his elbow was the Geraci novel. He was still gnawing its dry pages. A way of procrastinating, maybe, because he was afraid to call Aris. Would Aris turn him in? Half of him said *maybe*; half said *no*. But he was afraid of everything that had to do with Upstate University, wanted it as far away as the star homes of the *katsinam*.

Over a shoulder, black-light teeth flashed purple, but the surreal smile wasn't Paul's.

The stool Logan had picked at the bar was some oversized machine part; he couldn't even guess what kind, but they'd put down a cushion to make it ass-friendly. Other stools were made from different pieces of scrap metal. For tables they'd stood cable spools upright (a chair at one of them had a Towaway Zone sign for a back).

The bar counter was glass seamed with metal. Through it he could see the hose of the bar gun, liquor bottles, glasses, electrical work running out to sockets. All bathed in red light. He was reminded of the transparent man they used in biology class—stomach, intestines, liver exposed.

A wall of natural stone behind the bar looked damp enough to grow moss. It was decorated with assorted objects: a motorcycle's gas tank, a mirrorless frame studded with unlit bulbs, an outdated welder's mask like the trophy head of a rectangular-eyed cyclops, a Mets hat, a tragedy mask (but not comedy), costume jewelry like pirate's booty, and a sign that read *Back From The Dead? So Soon?* Maybe apocalypse had come and gone, he'd slept through it, and they'd used junk left over to build this place.

"Blackfeather, my *man*!" The Black Cat was striding toward him, T-shirt hanging out of his jeans, a leather vest over it.

They slapped hands and hooked thumbs, pulled at each other's bent fingers.

"Good to see ya."

He hadn't realized how happy it would make him to see Paul, to see Paul so happy to see *him*.

He pointed at Logan's bottle. "Slam that down—enda round one." He leaned his elbows on the bar, pulled out his wallet.

He'd gotten his afro trimmed, but he still reminded Logan of a darker Jimi Hendrix.

"Yo, sweetheart! Sweetheart! Right here!"

A row of drinkers leaned over the bar, but Paul had gotten her attention. A platinum blonde with short spiked hair.

"Since we ain't got girlfriends with looks like yours—" The splayed fingertips of both hands touched his chest theatrically, elbows flaring out. "—we in need of a couple beers to drown our sorrows."

She smiled in spite of herself, pulled bottles out of a refrigerated chest.

Paul put one in Logan's hand and took a stool next to him. "Now what we got goin' on *here*? That a long face I detect? Whatsa matter, Blackfeather? Ain't been gettin' in Pandora's box lately?" Paul stripped laughter from the insides of the noisy bar. "You know that bad bitch a yours is just usin' you to get to me."

"She took me out to the Hamptons last week."

"The *Hamptons*! If I'd known that, I'da let *you* throw down for the beers."

A man squeezed between them, his chest in Paul's face, his back—a ghostly skull painted on his black T-shirt—in Logan's.

Paul stood up. "I already *got* two shoulders, so you can get that one—" Paul pushed it slowly away from the bar. "—out my face."

The guy, hair colors clashing, glared at Paul.

"What's that look for?" Paul's spread his arms as if he were tied to a cross. "Ain't nothin' between you and me but the air and opporTOOni-TEE. If you feelin' like a frog, *leap*."

The guy shook his two-toned head and moved down the bar.

Paul looked at Logan. "Must've been feelin' like a dog—he walked."

Logan sat back down.

"You know the problem with the white boys in here? They got no color. Like they ain't seen the Sun since the Beatles busted up. Now, I was gonna do him a favor." He lifted his fist. "Add some black and blue to his ugly mug." He took a long drink of beer.

Logan watched his Adam's apple bob. "Almost got into a fight today myself. Taxi driver tried to run me over, and I tried to haul him out of his cab." Logan shrugged. "He took off."

Paul leaned forward to facilitate a healthy burp.

"Hey, you remember Linda? The one I used to go to the movies with ...?"

Paul put a hand on his shoulder, and his long fingers sank into muscle. "Did herself in, bro. Couple weeks after you cut out."

Logan blinked.

"Found her in that brook on the far enda things. Cut herself up." He lifted an arm, slid two dark fingers along his wrist.

"*What*? Where'd she get a razor?"

Paul shrugged. "Found it, looks like. Rustin' in the grass."

"But she was ... they were going to put her in Transitional."

"Don't beat yourself up, man. Nothin' you could've done." Paul's hand tightened on him again. "When the lease runs out, it's out."

Logan swayed a little in his chair, nodding, afraid he was about to topple over and shatter on the floor. She'd talked about taking off her shoes, wading into the cold water when staff wasn't looking. Rubbing his eyes, he tried to forget what he'd never seen. "How 'bout Jack?"

"The Relic was doin' all right when I left. Even found himself a job—skinny vegetarian was bussin' tables at that diner up the road."

Logan nodded absently. "In the brook ...?"

"Some people use a bathtub." Paul shrugged.

Logan looked to his bottle as if it were some kind of votive object he could leave at the feet of a god who could take back what had happened. "You? You back at work?"

"Back to computers, back to ridin' the bus into the city every day from scenic Paterson, En Jay."

Logan lifted his hand and searched his palm for the place where, two worlds ago, he'd pushed the point of a butterfly knife against bone.

"Always liked it here." Paul pointed to pipes that ran along the ceiling. "Used to be a basement. Clientele changed, though. Bunch a spaced-out peckerwoods with starched heads these days. They think they into some kinda tribalism, shavin' they heads like your cousins."

The last of the Mohicans was white.

Paul sighted along an extended finger. "Check that dude out, with the home-made tee."

"Erase the sixties—buy punk?"

Paul nodded. "Hippies fucked it up for 'em. They tried redesigning cities—a temple of love on every corner—bringing altars into college dorm rooms, burnin' candles and incense, tyin' flowers in they hair. If you can't be with the one you love, love the one you with, right? But then utopia was a no-show. Kent State poisoned the flowers. MLK got taken out. Communes closed down and New Age shops opened up. The war ended but nobody felt like celebrating."

Not as old as Jack, Paul was probably in high school when Jack was already done with college. Catching the fringed end of commune living in the seventies, he got lost between what had gone before and what was coming to be.

"At least Jack and his pals meant it." Paul glanced around the room. "Not like these raggedy-ass em-effs. Doin' themselves up in leather and chains like they tough. Why you think that dude backed down so quick? All show."

"Lucky for you."

"*Me*? Shit. I'da trashed that no-account fool like last week's garbage. Collapsed him like a cardboard suitcase." He grinned big and wouldn't let Logan pay for the second round. "Don't sweat it, man. I'm makin' good money. They even put up with my epee-sodes. Know why?" He yanked on one side of his vest. "'Cause I'm the baddest ass in Silicon Valley."

Logan knew nothing about computers.

"Yea though I walk through the Valley of Silicon," Paul intoned, "I shall fear no artificial intelligence. Because one tug on the plug and those bad boys are just real expensive toys— batteries not included." He patted his stomach, burping himself. "I'da been out on my ass if it weren't for my one-of-a-kind mind."

"A regular Einstymie."

Paul backhanded Logan across the chest. "Omma let you get away with that 'cause we friends."

Logan could see he was trying not to laugh.

Music filled a pause and both of them drank.

Paul had once told him about a manic episode that made him feel like there was no computer program he couldn't create, nothing he couldn't figure out. "Man, you like the goddamn Silver Surfer, vibratin' to the tune of every atom in the universe, glidin' way above everything. Like gravity's just some theory in a dusty book somewhere and you already quantum leaped it. Problem is, before you know it, the dudes in white suits bag your ass and send you Upstate."

There was the problem: how to separate the solid from the illusory.

Paul had moved on to a different problem.

"Fool punks. Keep turnin' up the volume cause they just about deaf. Now you take Jack … sure he's fucked up, but even Jack's holding on to *something*."

Third Worlders were still dying on Tube #1.

The place was packed now. Smoke bothering his eyes, Logan stood up—he didn't want another beer—grabbed the Black Cat by the arm and pulled him off his chair.

Some punk song, all driving beat hammered out way too fast, blared out of the speakers and a skinhead in combat boots and Army fatigues started jumping around in the middle of the floor, ramming into people and spilling drinks.

Logan stared. Yeah, it was him. No wine bottle this time, but Logan remembered the way he'd grinned as he'd gotten into the cab with Shawna and Pam.

"Yo!"

He almost slam danced into Paul.

Logan took a step forward, felt a hand clamp onto his shoulder.

"Hey, man, don't pay him no—"

Logan shrugged off Paul's hand. "I *owe* him."

"You *know* this dude? All right then."

Logan waded into the center of five or six punks banging off each other like bumper cars and shoved the skinhead hard enough to send him flying over an empty chair. Cheers went up from the dancers.

Combat Boots, who looked like he might've recognized Logan, charged with his head down.

Logan brought his knee up. There was a soft explosion in the joint, pain shot up his leg, then there was an eerie numbness. The skinhead fell to the floor, ass-first, as if he just meant to sit there for a moment, take stock of things, except Logan could see from the way his head wobbled on his neck that he could barely hold it up. Blood poured from his nose, and there was more enthusiastic shouting.

Logan limped out of the bar, leaning on Paul.

"Damn! My *knee*!" The same one he'd cracked this morning against a dresser.

"Your *knee*!" Paul shoved him up the stairs, past the bouncer, who was making purposeful strides toward the commotion behind them. "You see his *face*?"

They pushed and pulled each other into the balmy night air. The sidewalk was crowded, and Logan—still limping, a hand on Paul's shoulder—drew stares.

"Shit, that was *mean,* Blackfeather. You busted his nose."

They turned the corner. Not quite so many people on West Third.

"Payback, Washington." He compressed the incident in SoHo into a few sentences.

"Well I think you all even now." Paul handed him the Geraci novel. "Left this on the bar."

Logan took it from him. "Thanks." He was standing on his own now.

Half a block up, Paul stopped in front of window ringed with light. "Who needs a cooler when we got all-night delis?"

He ducked inside while Logan sat on the curb rubbing his knee.

Paul came out after a few minutes, tossed a 16-ounce can of beer at Logan. "No more bars, we's air-conditioned gypsies." He trotted ahead, waving Logan on without turning around. After a few long strides, he stopped to harass a bum propped against a wall. "Sorry man, I threw out all my spare change last week. It was makin' this biiiig ugly pile on the dresser—where were you then?" He spread his arms in a gesture of futility before taking off again.

Logan limped behind him, pausing at the corner of Sullivan to pull off his sneakers and socks.

Paul, who'd waited at the light, stared.

Logan answered the question written into his face: "Air-conditioned gypsies, right?"

Paul smiled, started untying a sneaker. "Know why white folks made up technology?" In the flamingo position, he almost fell over.

"So computer nerds like you'd have a job?"

"Invented tee-*vee* so they don't have to get too close." One foot exposed to the night air, he got to work on the other. "Got artificial *colors* so they don't have to look at it. Put on *shoes* so they don't have to feel what they doin' to the planet." He held up a black sneaker as if it were Exhibit A in a court case.

Logan barely remembered the car ride—wind rushing through Paul's 280ZX, the T-roof off, being swallowed by a light-infested tunnel that took them to New Jersey. As they careened under the river, he wondered whether Linda had taken off those little high-top sneakers of hers, whether, when they found her, she'd been barefoot.

Suddenly they were out of the bright tube, and the city loomed on their right, a small mountain range of crystals, darkly sparkling.

Paul drove along highways lined with brightly lit gas stations, late-night diners, motels.

In Paterson he parked near a tavern he said was more than a hundred years old ("Got a bar shaped like a question mark").

His apartment was hardwood floors, richly colored rugs, lots of plants. A cluster of incense sticks in a tarnished copper holder sent up coiling smoke. The swirling gray seemed to hang together, like another plane of existence between ceiling and floor.

Paul lit a joint, held it out to Logan.

He shook his head. "Burns my lungs, makes me stupid." Lying on the couch, he looked up sideways at a woodcut print of an African woman. "Who made that?"

"*I* did, mothafucka." Paul was sitting in an armchair. Something cushiony, like a puffed-up throne. The joint held delicately between forefinger and thumb, he tilted his head back and blew smoke toward the ceiling.

Stretched out on the couch, Logan slipped into a dream about the bare-breasted African with long earrings and tall hair. Somewhere in the dream, she metamorphosed into Shawna.

23. Love Always

He saw her at the end of the bar. Scorched by sun, wearing something vague as mist. A shade of a color, lavender maybe. Hard to tell in the Crow's faulty light. An ankh dangling from an ear glittered reddish gold. She looked hard as the gleam off brass beneath the breathy dress. A feeling curled through him like cigarette smoke.

The men in the bar dragged their eyes across her, trolleys groping for contact with the overhead wires.

Her pinned-up hair, wound tightly on the sides, was a loose tangle of coppery curls on top. "Hi." She leaned toward him; their lips slipped in pale gloss.

A rippling undercurrent in her face told him something was wrong.

She reached for her drink; bracelets clinked together. Her dimpled smile held him as though it were his sarcophagus.

One of the waitresses walked past, dragging Shawna's scent with her, a tropical smell that reminded him of their weekend at the beach.

"What's in the bag?" he asked.

It hung on a hook under the bar.

She shrugged. "An album. Wendy said I should pick it up."

He took the plastic bag off the hook and peeked inside. Even at that steep angle, he recognized the cover, fought back a smile. It died when he looked at her again.

Lifting his beer bottle, he got suds. Pam wasn't behind the bar tonight, just that half-pint fill-in, Arab or Gypsy or something, his dreadlocks like dead black snakes. Wearing an old King

Crimson shirt, red with a snarl of gray in the center. He always wore that King Crimson rag, like ritual.

Medusa Man grabbed Logan's bottle without a word.

Shawna reached out, pushed aside his leather vest. "Sweating."

I'm glad you came he wanted say. If he could just close his hand on her shoulder, he could communicate this to her. But he was trapped in the sea-dark of the dusty oil painting at the bottom of the stairs. The schooner had somehow shanghaied him, shoved him in with a rough crew on a voyage through a gloom where ocean and evening mingled.

She reached into the still-life moment, took his hand. "What? Why are you looking at me like that?"

The never-knowing of this other person confused him.

The grip of her hand shifted. "Logan …?"

A woman next to him laughed loudly, a shelf of glasses sliding to the floor.

"Look, I came down here to see *you*. I mean, what are we *doing*?"

"Huh?"

"Where is this going?"

"Where is *what* going?"

"What are we doing together on weekends? On Thursday night when you're not working, and … that's it?" She lifted her hands, delicate metal rings sliding down her arm.

"Hey." He put a hand on hers. "Hey."

Her mouth shaped something that he sensed might split bone, but she shook her head, looked away.

He had never, he was sure, seen her this beautiful. A thought flashed, got lost in broken circuitry.

She leaned forward him and kissed him.

Confused, he didn't kiss her back.

She pulled away, studied his face. If she'd been a cobra, the blunt wings of her hood would've been spread.

He should *say* something.

She stood up, a cotton jacket sliding from her lap into her hand. "I have to get out of here." She grabbed her purse and bag and hurried away, heels punishing the floor.

Something inside him was tugged away with her. He turned to look at the empty stage, looked back at the door as she went out.

Again.

Again.

But he didn't move from his seat.

The signs across storefronts, over bars and restaurants, were smeary glows of color in drifting mist. An afterimage of rain, she thought. Every step was a photogenic frame: simple, empty of people, full of the things people had made.

She thought of her family, 3,000 miles away, which was about as near as she wanted them. Except for her father, who was the sweetest man she knew. But even he wouldn't understand. He'd hold her and let her cry and try to understand, but he wouldn't.

She considered buying a pack of cigarettes. Pain was one way of changing the topic.

She thought about going back to apologize. She thought about the hot orange tip of the cigarette.

The wet sent a shiver through her. Summer wasn't supposed to be clammy. She hugged herself as she walked, her hair heavy with gathered mist.

She wanted him to *say* it.

She looked at herself as she went by, a translucent reflection in the windows of closed shops. She'd begun to photograph him that way, which was the way he liked to be, she thought, nearby but out of reach. If you tried to touch him, you just banged into glass. Other times he was like a child his need to be held was so strong. She could feel it in their lovemaking. It was as if their bodies were in the way.

Logan had become a silhouette with a light source behind him, and nothing about him was clear or definite. Nothing was reliable. They were still strangers to each other.

And what if he said it? Would it matter? Sometimes the same words didn't mean the same thing. We signed letters and cards *love always* but took on new lovers, lost interest, pursued job openings across the country.

She remembered wiping herself after sleeping with him the first time. She'd flushed what had been left of their lovemaking. He was right. Things didn't fit into the boxes we made in our heads to hold them. It wasn't neat at all.

Why couldn't he say he was in love with her? This was the one certainty she needed from him. Why couldn't he give her that? Why couldn't he have said something to keep her from leaving? Why didn't he grab her by the arm or chase her out? He was so fucking *weird* sometimes. His soul could be ditching his body, and he'd watch it go, amazed that some effort on his part was actually required. If it were his life she was walking out of, would he still have let her go?

When she closed her eyes and tried to picture herself without him, she didn't see anything.

All that was left now was the man with the beard and the

Hell's Angel jacket walking toward her, the café with its empty chairs and tables scattered on the sidewalk, and the pyramid of illuminated drizzle beneath a streetlamp.

She passed little shops that sold souvenirs of the after-midnight Village: earrings, bracelets, black leather glinting with studs, sunglasses, postcards, movie posters, prints of famous paintings. We surrounded ourselves with images hoping that some of their posed perfection would rub off on our messy lives. They'd all been made to catch the eye, like those fishing lures that spun and flashed. That woman lifting an earring while she watched herself in a mirror didn't realize that, just like the fish that wasn't getting a meal, she'd still be hungry after she walked off with her new earrings, and tomorrow night she'd be out looking for something else to buy.

Shawna's own infatuation with galleries and museums was probably no different. There was a bareness she couldn't help seeing. And maybe all we could do was hang pretty things in the emptiness. *Art,* she'd heard somewhere, *follows from the friction between us and the world the way a pearl follows from the irritation of the oyster.* Something like that.

She rarely admitted to anyone she needed anything, and she wouldn't admit it to him either, but she needed him. Just for tonight. Tomorrow she'd be fine. If he would just be there—just until morning came and stopped the colors and shadows from bleeding into each other—everything would be fine.

Jazz floated out to her from a bar. Candles burned on tables. The glow on faces and foreheads, on hands resting on those round tables, reminded her of paintings by the Dutch masters. Music clung to her like mist.

The sidewalk she looked down on was cracked. Nothing

lasted in this city, nothing stayed clean. The city used things up until all that was left was an ugly residue. Which got into everything—the air, her lungs, even the sidewalk. People got used up too. Day after day you held off the disaster of uncertainty with an office job until one morning you woke up and realized you hadn't gotten very far. You were divorced for the second time, and you'd managed to seep into the seams between the floor tiles in your office. What was left was running off the sidewalk with grayed rainwater and disappearing into sewers. And there was no way of knowing what was solid enough to hold on to.

Standing on a curb on Sixth Avenue, she was glad her family couldn't see her now. She didn't have to hear her mother's *I told you so*. She didn't have to listen to one of her brother's lectures. She didn't have to look at her sister, who wouldn't have anything to say. It was as simple as that—they'd never figured out how to reach each other.

She coughed into a fit of crying that sucked her stomach in so hard it hurt. Wobbling back across the sidewalk, she leaned against a corner of brick to let it go. She pulled a pack of tissues out of her purse and blew her nose. Tucking the wet tissue in a pocket, she pushed off the brick.

Her gauzy white jacket had soaked through. She pulled the zipper up a little higher and stood there being rained on in the weakly lit Village, an oversized canvas with its colors running.

She just wanted to know that something would still be left, something besides a grimy film. Some kind of afterimage. When something was still there after the original was gone, you knew that the original mattered in the first place. Didn't every great city leave its ruins?

She stopped at the corner of MacDougal and Third. All she was doing was circling the Copper Crow.

She stepped off the curb, splashed the edge of a puddle. The reflected world quivered.

She wanted to get out of this city, but since she couldn't—not yet—she wanted to be uptown. Direction was enough for now. For the eternal, we are always in it, *now*.

For some reason the familiar stone of her building wasn't comforting.

A little farther uptown was a Gothic cathedral so tall the windows at the top were tiny slits. When light shone in one or two of them, it seemed the cathedral with its tower was still in the Middle Ages, and a spell had been cast so she could see it from the 20th century. She wondered whether someone lived up there. She pictured a monk who'd renounced the traffic and shut himself up in a room lit by standing braziers and hung with blunt iron crosses. Maybe he made do with nothing but a bed, a table, and a chair.

"Hey."

She jumped. A shadow backlit by a streetlight stood in front of her.

"Jesus, you scared me."

"Sorry."

He took a step forward. His white shirt, unbuttoned at the top, clung to his body.

"You must be soaked to your underwear. How long have you been standing there?"

"Years."

"Oh stop."

His face was as much in the dark as in the fragmented street light. For all she knew, he'd stepped out of time, just like that cathedral. "Well, don't just stand there, make yourself useful." She threw the keys at him. They *chinged* as they bounced off his chest into his hand.

He wanted to take her hand, she thought, but she kept both of them on the bag she was holding.

He unlocked the door—wrought iron over glass, set in marble—and held it open for her.

Her shoes made a hollow echo on the granite stairs. She heard him padding behind her in his sneakers. *Elevators*, he always said, *are evil*. He said the same thing about escalators.

He unlocked the apartment door.

Light exposed the Greek urn on its black pedestal, the Butterfly Maiden with her eyes behind slits, the antique table that was her pedestal.

"I can't believe how wet you are." She pulled off one of her shoes. "It's not even raining anymore. Whaddid you do, run here?"

"Yup."

An inch or two shorter now, she faced him from a few feet away. "You *ran* here?"

"Manhattan's not that big."

"I can't believe you." She hugged him with so much momentum she almost knocked him over. "I'm sorry I flipped out on you."

Clinging to her, he steadied himself.

"It wasn't about *us* or where we're going. It was about *me*, about where *I'm* going." She put the fingernails of one hand into the back of his neck, pressing just hard enough to lay her claim. "You're awfully short on words tonight."

He rubbed his cheek against the side of her head the way cats do. "Can't buy the groceries anymore."

She pulled her head away from his shoulder to look at him. "Why not?"

"Unemployed."

"No!" She pushed him away and held his arms with both hands. "Why? Because you ran out on your set? You've gotta be kidding."

"I am."

She batted him on the chest with an open hand. "I should've known." She struggled to get away from him. "Probably ... didn't ... run here ... either."

He tried to kiss her, but she turned her cheek. He laughed. He kept her close and pressed his face into hers until she finally kissed him back.

"God you're wet." She pushed him away.

She took the album out of the plastic bag she'd left on the coffee table and held it up. "Cool cover, huh?"

A stylized raven's profile—the eye the most prominent feature—circumscribed by a full moon. Huge and silvery. The handiwork of a Kwakiutl artist. He smirked. "Go ahead, play it."

She used a fingernail to slice the cellophane wrapping and put the record on the turntable atop her component system.

The smirk broadened to a grin as the first song began to play.

Confusion wrinkled her brow. She held still. As if moving would upset some delicate equilibrium. "Isn't that ... that's *you* singing!" Just as suddenly as it had come to her, she doubted the whole idea. Her head tilted as though she were a forest animal cocking her ear to the sound of a twig snapping. Her face, made of grains of sand, slid into a scowl. "Why didn't you *tell* me? I walk into a record store in the Village, buy one of *your* albums and you don't even *tell* me you made one?"

"I told Wendy."

"You told *Wendy* but you didn't tell *me*?" She stalked back and forth across the room, too mad to touch him or even look at him. "Do you *sleep* with Wendy? Does *Wendy* put up with you and your weird moods?" She walked up to him with her arms folded across her chest. "What is it? Why do you have to put things between us? Why is there this … *distance* you won't let me cross?"

"It's not that …" His mind had gone blank as a cold television screen.

"Why were you waiting for me in the rain?"

"I felt like … like if I didn't find you, I'd lose you. For good."

Her arms were still crossed over her chest as if protecting some vulnerable spot. "But you knew I'd come home sooner or later. You didn't have to *run* here. You didn't have to stand outside getting wet."

He shrugged. "When I was running after you, I kept thinking I'd catch up to you on the street. So I just kept running. Till I was here." *The electric magic of the subway was too noisy to invoke.*

With one arm she reached out, undid the buttons of his shirt.

He pulled at her other arm, which seemed to have cramped against her chest.

With both hands she peeled the shirt down over his shoulders. It flopped in a wet pile on the Navajo rug. She flattened herself against him. "Sometimes I don't know what to think about you."

She bit his chest hard enough to make him pull back. "You're hard to deal with, you know that?"

While he rubbed his chest where she'd bit it, she put one hand on each of his shoulders and pushed him off balance. She backed him again with her palms, tugged him when she wanted him to turn. He watched walls go past, the apartment recede, saw the Raphaelesque head explode before the bed struck him just below his knees and he fell onto it.

As if they were together for the last time and the night wouldn't last long enough, there was nowhere she didn't touch him, no part of his skin she didn't cover.

He sank into something viscous. His ears stopped up with fluid or the rush of his own blood, he thought he heard her say *I love you,* but submerged in that murky clot, he was too far from the surface to answer.

It wasn't until after he began to feel his own weight again, to realize how cumbersome his body was, that he heard her say it again.

"Me too."

"How fucking romantic." She dug her nails into his back and bit his ear.

"Ow!" He jerked back. "For a while now. I just ..." He cleared his throat. "I just couldn't say it."

"Don't tell me—you told Wendy."

"Uh … yeah."

"You're *such* an asshole."

She tightened her arms around. He thought she was going to bite his ear again, but—four long fingers on the back of his neck holding his head down—she whispered. A question.

He wanted to play a song for her. Without words. She'd have

her answer by letting the music stream through her like fresh blood. She'd feel it—from the tiniest capillaries to the fat padding the backs of her eyeballs. She didn't even need the song. If she was paying attention, if she just translated the way he held her, she'd know. *Yes.*

24. Counterlives

Yes, he'd moved up to 111th Street, but he was getting out of bed for the same reason he had at Hank and Pam's: goddamn beeping horns. Same stink of exhaust fumes too. Shawna didn't like air conditioning in the bedroom, so a humming fan drenched him with warm air.

Sounds rose from the floor underneath as though litter swept by an updraft, rained down from behind the ceiling like trash tossed out a window. This morning, instead of the guy upstairs taking a leak, Logan heard quiet jazz. Most likely, their topside neighbor was at work and had already uncorked his wineskin.

One day, thumbing through one of Shawna's oversize books, Logan had heard—blunted by the wall—a phone ringing. It'd gone unanswered. Like a church bell chiming in an empty town. When it was quiet like that, he could hear a tap turned on in one of the other apartments. Generally, though, it wasn't so subtle—furniture being rearranged to make a room look bigger, a nail being hammered to hang a photograph of someone forever smiling on whatever you were doing, a hole being drilled to secure a new mirror that would fold space out like a screen.

Cubes of space instead of acres of land. They'd taken to shelving the air, cutting up the sky into slices. Stacked on top of each other like shoeboxes, each apartment was storage for what had been hoarded. A place to drag everything, like those webbed tunnels into which wolf spiders pulled struggling insects. All kept safe behind a chained, bolted, deadlocked door.

Cramped as a crab in its underwater cranny, life in Manhattan had to carry on bent over. Last week in the Village, he'd seen two guys get into a fight over a parking space. A pair of glasses went flying, skittered on the asphalt. Knees crumpled. The guy who'd thrown the punch looked at Logan, decided maybe he'd done enough, and drove off. If they'd had guns, it would've been a shooting.

He didn't understand how people did it every day—beeped and shouted and fanned themselves with magazines on trains too crowded to read on, sweated underneath suits and dresses picked out to clash with the boring décor of the office. There should've been more glasses cracked into the street by fists, more stabbings, more shootings.

Sometimes, alone in the apartment, he stood next to the wall wondering whether there was someone just on the other side. Who translated into a subtle pressure on one of the senses that wasn't among the famous five, dented perception's skin the way a water strider's feet made tiny dimples in the surface of a pond (pricking shadow in the water's shine).

Remembering how, as a boy, he'd used a magnet under a table to move a paper clip across the wood, he wondered whether he could use the gravity of his body to position someone on the other side of the wall. Maybe, if he and Shawna had been next-wall neighbors, she'd have moved him up and down the common divide as if he were a chess piece.

It was still hard to believe he was living with her, especially because he hardly ever saw her.

He got up late because he came home late—later now that he'd started staying after hours at the Crow (Pam loaned him a key). Those dark early-morning hours were his favorite time, when the city was a body mostly shut down. Like the soft electric static the dreaming mind gave off, the city had its own mellow glow, which diluted the sky, obliterated all but the brightest stars. He and Shawna, who had to be in bed early, led counterlives.

While she was at work, he traded glances with the Butterfly Maiden, her masked expression placidly indifferent. Sometimes he felt as though he lived in a museum: He couldn't touch anything without feeling guilty. Shawna got irritated when he left something—usually a book—on the coffee table, the kitchen table, a dresser. *You never put anything back, you know that?* She'd slide the stray into its designated spot on a shelf. He'd have gotten around to it if she hadn't gotten there first. He just didn't see the rush. Now he did: not aggravating Shawna.

25. The Loop Lounge

"When are you going to tell him?" Pam tugged on a short leather skirt with one hand, tried to keep a glass of wine steady in the other.

"I don't know."

"You don't know?" Wendy was sitting on the couch, one leg crossed over the other.

"I never see him." Shawna made her wineglass ting by tapping it with a fingernail. "I *live* with him and he's never around. Or I'm not around. What's worse, sometimes we're together, and he'll just sit there and not say a word." Sometimes he'd just tap away on the coffee table with his fingers or a pencil or a fork. She didn't like the way he could tune everything out, including her. *Stop that would you?* Bewildered, he'd look at her as though they didn't share the same language. She didn't like being left behind. She wanted to be with him, wherever he was.

"Oh come on." Pam tried to muster a stern look. "You're procrastinating."

"Yup." Wendy backed her up.

The doorknob turned, and the conversation ended as if a stray word or movement would keep the door from opening.

"Hey." He smiled. "Look who's here." He bent down to give Pam a hug.

Wendy gave him a quick kiss on the lips.

"Where you've been?"

He could hear the contrasting tones in Shawna's voice: glad he was home but a little peeved he'd kept her waiting. "I was at the park, but then on the way home I stopped on Amsterdam."

"What for? To dig a subway token out of the tar?"

"No, I was just … looking."

"At mannequins in a shop window?"

"Just looking."

"Well you better not have eaten dinner …"

He sat down on the couch as she went to the kitchen. The notebook Shawna had bought him was on the coffee table with a little note on it: *Try not to leave it here. Try to take it with you. S.* He smiled.

Wendy sat down next to him. "How's the music going?"

"Not bad. Getting a little more of a crowd in the bar."

"Oh, Mr. Modesty." Pam turned to Wendy. "He's getting a *lot* more of a crowd. And if his album weren't out of print, we'd be selling them like them 50-cent beers."

"Okay, kids …" Shawna clapped her hands once, loudly. "Everybody in the kitchen."

In each of four plates was a lobster tail. The shells didn't even have to be cracked; the fluffy white meat was already blooming out of them like cauliflower.

The first mouthful reminded him lobster tasted to him more like bland rubber than anything else. If it weren't for the butter, it would have hardly any flavor at all. "You know, I don't even like lobster all that much."

"Well why didn't you say something *last* time we had it?"

He shrugged. "I don't hate it, it's just …"

"*Logan* …" Wendy put a hand on his. "There are some things you just *don't* say to the chef."

"Especially when you *live* with her." Pam rapped his knuckles with the back of her fork.

He'd always had a gift for mouthing some stray thought that turned out, for somebody, to be like sitting on a cactus pad.

"Guess what I did?" Wendy was grinning, maybe a little drunkenly.

"What?" Logan said it as if he were answering a knock-knock joke.

"I talked my boss into a leave of absence."

"Goin' somewhere?" Pam leaned forward on her elbows.

"Australia?" Logan wiped his greasy fingers on a napkin.

Wendy nodded rapidly. "That's the plan."

Shawna lifted her chin toward Logan. "He's been all over the country, everything he owns fits in a duffel bag, and can you believe he wants to go back to Kansas?"

"What's in Kansas?" Wendy looked genuinely confused.

"We don't have to *move* there—"

Shawna rolled her eyes up and tipped her head side to side as she spoke: "Toto. Dorothy. Auntie Em ..."

Lobster shell cracked loudly between his fingers. "You've never even *been* to Kansas."

"Oh look at him, he's pissed."

"Maybe he doesn't like it when people make fun of Auntie Em." Pam covered her smile with a hand.

"You know how it is with us tribal people and our aunts."

"You wanna go half way across the country to shack up with your aunt?" Shawna asked.

"I wanna go half way across the country to get away from you."

Shawna lifted an eyebrow. "What's stopping you?"

"Please, *please* don't tell me I'm going to regret introducing you two."

Logan turned to Wendy. "You want a little company in the southern hemisphere?"

"Yeah, but not unless you bring *her*."

"Gang-up-on-the-guy night, huh?" He nodded. "Okay."

No one said anything, and every clanking fork, every snap of pulled-apart lobster was too loud. He shifted uneasily in his chair. The floor underneath it seemed to sag. There was something depressing about the lobster he didn't like. About tonight, which couldn't repeat the charm of the first time she'd surprised him with an extravagant dinner.

His lobster half-eaten, he stood up. "I gotta use the men's room."

"We don't have one of those," Shawna said. "We have a bathroom, with an actual bathtub in it."

"Whatever."

"Wash your hands when you're done," Pam called after him, "or you can't pass me the salt."

Wendy giggled behind him.

Shawna took a deep swallow of wine. "Why does he have to be so god damn sensitive?"

"Maybe he's just in a bad mood."

"You two are having a pride war." Wendy sipped wine. "As soon as you give up the big egos, you'll start communicating better and work things out."

"That's it, huh? A little pride war? One of us just waves the white flag, and we move to Phoenix and live happily ever after? I mean, what am I going to *do*? I already got the transfer. I already agreed to *go*."

"Maybe you both need a little time off. You know, he could go to Kansas for a while then meet up with you—"

"That's *not* what I want. I want us to see *more* of each other, not less."

Wendy shrugged, turned her eyes down. "I don't know ..."

"What the hell is taking him so long?"

"Was that the bathroom door or the front door a minute ago?" Wendy looked at Shawna then at Pam.

"You heard a door?" Shawna jumped out of her chair and stalked out of the kitchen.

"Logan?" The bathroom was empty.

"Logan?" So was the bedroom. "God *damn* him!"

She walked back into the kitchen with her arms over her head and let them fall and slap against her sides. "He left!"

Pam stood up. "Only one thing to do—go out, get obliterated, take out our frustrations on the nearest guy."

"I can't *stand* it when he pulls shit like this. It's like hanging up your face."

"We-ell ..." Wendy drawled the word out as two syllables. "Talk to him about it."

Shawna threw her hands up. "I'd love to! He's not here!"

"I meant ... you know, later."

"Yeah, well. We'll see how he likes it when his fucking key doesn't fit the lock."

"You and the old lady sparrin', huh? You know she ain't gonna appreciate the fact you hopped a bus outa the city and left her high and dry." Paul took a drink. Like he deserved it for the wisdom he'd just laid out, free of charge.

Logan grunted. "Hadda get out."

"Shit. Don't work like that, bro. You in the modern world

now. She gonna kick that habit, get herself a new addiction don't give her so much shit." Black leather vest, no shirt, Paul's shoulder glistened like oiled wood.

Logan took a drink of beer then set the bottle down on the small round table between them. Wearing only a red tank top, he was sweating. "She says she loves me. If she does, she'll get over it. If she doesn't ..." He shrugged. Even as he said this, something in his stomach rose to argue the point.

Paul was shaking his head. "E.R., man. Plenty more where you came from—'specially with a bad one like you got.

"Emergency room?"

"Eminently replaceable. Babe like yours got a fan club. She just snaps her fingers and, yo, she got her pick."

Logan scanned the crowd, wondering which guy Shawna would take over him. You could never tell. And there was nothing you could do to change the way she felt, no spell you could cast, no shaman you could bribe who could reach into her heart and tamper with its workings.

"I hear you," he said, "but staying would've made things worse. I'da just stood there with about as much to say as this table." He rapped it with his knuckles "Just can't talk sometimes."

Paul nodded. "I know how you get." He smiled. "I lived with you for a while too."

Logan glanced around. A steer skull with glowing red sockets glared back. Illuminated bone. It was hung over the bar across the room. The curve of the horns like a crescent moon cupping stars.

"Where'd you say we are?"

"The Loop Lounge. Passaic, En Jay." Paul smiled. "Never no dress code."

Which was why Paul had no shirt under his vest.

Paul sipped from his bottle. "How you makin' out otherwise?"

Logan shrugged. "City's a little too much sometimes." He tapped the wooden table with the heel of his bottle. Three times. *There's no place like home.* "I'm glad I'm here."

Paul slapped Logan's back, tipped his head toward a woman next to their table. "Eddy Munster's date."

Black lipstick, white Kabuki makeup, and mohawked hair that peaked over her head and fell to her nose.

Logan nodded weakly. He lifted his bottle and took a good pull. Cool as it went down, it puddled warmly in his stomach.

Maybe they'd given up on angels here. Maybe why their looks took after demons. Summoning them up with the dusty magic you can get out of a cosmetics case. Calling them down on the crushing weight of the everyday (evil energy better than none at all). They could dress the part in the Loop, dance, keep metal-to-metal contact, burn without turning to ash.

Paul's head dropped toward the table, and all Logan could see was spongy hair trimmed down since the hospital, squared off.

Logan tried to imagine Angeldusted Jack in the Loop Lounge. "You think Jack's out?"

"Probably."

Jack and Paul and he had seen things that weren't there. Or that no one else could see.

A woman had jumped up on the bar in front of the glowing red steer skull, swiveling her hips. The bartender, in leather overalls, clapped for her.

Over the stereo system, David Byrne sang *Same as it ever was. Same as it ever was. SAME ... AS ... IT ... EVER-WUUZZZ.*

Logan slapped a ten-dollar bill on the table. "Why don't you get us a couple more?"

"What you gonna tell me next? Sit at the back of the bus?" Chair legs scraped against the wooden floor.

"Hurry up, Washington."

"Iza goin', Iza goin'."

Paul went through a door to the front room because the bar under the eerie-eyed skull was packed. The girl dancing on it, hugging herself at the waist, drew gazes and cheers.

Logan slid out from between the chair and the table. Over the doorway was a pterodactyl skeleton suspended from the ceiling. Dull red light shone through the ribs, exposed coils and twists of cigarette smoke, stained them with color. Turning away from the bones roasting in crimson light, he made his way to the dance floor.

A thought flashed like a strobe light: *How could I have left?*

A painting on the back wall was hard to see because everything was so dim. He maneuvered between people for a closer look. A woman, naked except for cowboy boots and elbow-length gloves, was lying on her side, erotic and surreal. Colors were hard to make out because the intrinsic tones and hues had been sabotaged by the way night was reconstructed inside the club. The large eyes reminded him of a cat's. Her mouth was open and down-curving, miming a call to pain or an invitation to ecstasy. He recognized the artist—Rita Massengill—because Shawna liked her work.

Rita, Shawna had told him, painted on a black canvas to make the colors hum.

Night, he thought, was our black canvas.

Reality—the empirical one—had been renovated inside the

Loop: a Greek column bobbed in the darkness, a neon clock, tiny stone gargoyles, dinosaur bones, a neo-Expressionist painting. Some things as new as yesterday next to reminders of what had disappeared so long ago they were petrified rumors.

"Hey." A hand fell on his shoulder. "You supposed to be savin' our table."

To one side Logan could see the steer skull, the blurry red eyes like aging stars. The light in the skull didn't go with death, as if the Lakota had been doing the right thing when they'd turned buffalo skulls west to face the setting sun.

"Now look what you gone and done." Paul plucked their beers from the table.

A woman with spiked red hair and a nose ring looked repentant. "Oh, were you sitting here—?"

"No babe, I always supply empty tables with full beers."

The song thumping out of huge speakers, vibrating in his chest, was one he and Shawna liked to dance to, singing to each other as they made themselves into blurry arcs.

We have the Sun in our hair, Moon in our eyes, we just don't give a damn ...

The redhead started to get up, but Logan put a hand on Paul's back and pushed. "Fuck the table." His mind suddenly felt clear as a sky scoured by a thunderstorm. The smell of electricity in his nostrils, he realized what it would be like to lose her: in his gut he'd feel a kinship with every scar—curving or straight or jagged—that ever marked him.

"I gotta go back to the city."

"*Now?*" Paul held up the beer bottles in silent protest.

The Black Cat drove his 280ZX recklessly, the T-roof open, warm air rushing past. Half way to drunk, Paul laughed about near hits, passed illegally, waved and smiled at drivers who gave him the finger. The bridge, as they approached it, was a bright rectangle, a huge gateway studded with bulbs like an immense actor's mirror.

"You know I'm goin' way outa my way here, right?" Paul had to yell over the wind roaring between them. "Coulda just gone through the tunnel and let you take the subway home, but, nah, here I am driving you over the GW—droppin' you off at your door."

"You're all right, man."

Logan looked up at the enormous cables that hung down from the sky like smooth vines that Jack might have climbed to get to the giant.

"My next project, I'm gonna write a program that does a find-and-replace in every hard drive I can slimjim my way into. You hear that George? You history! The Paul Washington Bridge from now on!"

At the 125th Street exit, the 280 went bumping over cobblestones.

Paul cruised up Riverside Drive, slowed to a smooth stop in front of Shawna's building.

"When you gonna set me up with that little redhead?"

"Pam? Can't. She lives with her boyfriend."

"You didn't see the way she was lookin' at me in Bill Bailey's?"

"She got a thing for black guys."

"Yeah, an' I got just the thing for *her*."

"She *lives* with him."

"A'right, a'right ..."

They hooked thumbs and Paul took off with an arm raised, waving through the space in the roof where a glass panel had been removed.

Logan hovered before the door, beneath its stone arch carved with leaves. Pulling his keys out of a pocket, he wondered: *What's the worst she'll do?*

Inside, he bounded up the steps two at a time until he came to the seventh floor.

Turning the key in the lock of 7D, Logan pushed on the door but it jerked to a stop. A chain stretched between the door and the jamb. "Shit." He let the door hang open, and stared at the chain. He heard Shawna coming.

"I shouldn't even let you in." She closed the door, unhooked the chain, opened it again.

"You're drunk."

But he wasn't; she was. Her cheeks were flushed, her breath winy, her eyes balls of glass.

"You're lucky I didn't stay at Wendy's or Pam's." Wearing a pair of cut-offs and a T-shirt, she was barefoot. "Why do you have to do that? Go running off when things get a little hairy?"

"I'm better now."

"Well maybe I don't care now." She took him by the straps of his tank top, banged her knuckles against his chest, almost knocking him over as she emphasized each syllable. "*I ... was ... so ... pissed.*"

He grabbed onto her neck to steady himself. Then he pulled her close, kissed her behind the ear hoping that she'd missed him too. "I'm sorry."

"You're not getting off that easy."

"I'm *really* sorry."

She might have believed him if he hadn't stuck his tongue in her ear.

"Cut it out." She twisted her head away.

He pulled her back and kissed her neck.

"Stop it!"

She pushed against him, but he locked his arms around her waist and picked her up.

"Oh you're such a jerk! Put me down!"

He carried her past *Raphaelesque Head Exploding* and into the bedroom. "I wanna peach."

"No peaches for you."

"A fuzzy peach." He fell onto the bed with her, trapping her underneath.

"No!" She tried to shove him off her, gave up with a groan, and bit him.

"Hey—!"

Her teeth left marks on his shoulder.

They struggled out of their clothes.

He was always amazed by the peculiar change that came over her face as he pushed inside her, at the way her mouth opened—as though holding an operatic note—but no sound came out. The lines of her face going liquid was enough to a weight from his body. He watched her expression become desperate, as if death were a finger-length away and nothing mattered but holding off that finger-length a little longer. Constricting him suddenly, her body pinned him in its convulsion. Slowly, still prone to soft spasms, she began to relax. Loops of sweat-soaked hair stuck to her cheek like embroidery.

She slapped his chest, the sound of it sharper and louder because he was slick with sweat too. "I hate you."

He grinned down at her. "I hate you too."

26. Woman, Blue

The voices that usually filled the Copper Crow had deserted it. Logan had gotten used to rubbing up against the emptiness, to nights drawn out—like notes struck and held—until early morning. Drifting toward the nocturnal, he spent half the day sunk in sleep and dream, felt no more solid in Shawna's apartment than a thought roving among memories that didn't belong to him.

Alone at his instrument, he hadn't touched a key for ... five minutes? Ten? Half an hour? The light was barely a smolder, hardly enough to show the cracks running through the ancient oil painting at the bottom of the stairs.

In the silence—a desert he could transform simply by switching on the house stereo system, putting his finger to the keyboard, opening his mouth—he heard his grandfather's voice. Dry as the chafing of cicada wings. Saw his father's face etched with an intricate labyrinth of swirls and dots (the fingerprint of the underworld), his features indistinct like the shadows cast by natural formations. One eye glimmered with a mottled full moon, the other a crescent. He saw Cal, his head tipped crookedly to one side, a gleaming *fuck you* still in his eyes. Trapped in the eerie amber of memory, certain details were fine as insect hairs; others were blurred, hard to make out.

It was always with him, this lump of amber, though he couldn't always see it. It wasn't there when traffic was loud and the streets were crowded. He had to wait until darkness arched itself like a bridge and the city emptied itself out. Then it was right there in his hands, a chunk of honey-colored glow gone solid. Murmuring, whispering.

Sitting with as little enthusiasm for movement as a saguaro, he remembered the cold desert night stretched all around him, lonely stone towering in the distance, calling to him. He struck a note on the keyboard to answer. He joined hands with ghosts that had gone the sepia of old photos. He was even willing to open a hand to Uncle Cal, whose blood he'd smeared on himself while Cal's eyes were becoming balls of opaque glass.

Cal never got up to grab hold of the chances thrown his way, never used those oversized hands of his to save himself or anyone else. Mostly, he'd sat in the middle of his life like a hermit in a decrepit house, the air thick with dust, musty and damp with decay, sun never making it through the drawn shades. He sat there while the front porch rotted through, walls began to lean, ceilings sagged. Until it finally came down on his head. He'd wanted it that way, his last act of will to kick out a couple of the supports.

Logan made his peace with Uncle Cal. With Indian-hater Tom too. The feel of his hand hot and slippery with blood, the blade sunk as far as it would go. Because he'd been in the soft part, no bone to stop him. Trucker Tom, whose good luck charm had failed him.

The echo-murmur of their presence was held together by the notes he played. The keys tempered his stifled howl, tamed it in measures. Strangely, it was Linda who stayed with him the longest. Her face gone white, whiter than he'd ever seen it, all the blood drained out of her. Like Cal.

Logan imagined her walking along the brook, plunking pebbles as she went. Taking off her shoes and socks, wiggling her toes in the cool grass. But the water was so cold it made her pull back. Another Eve, aware for the first time that pain is also allotted to the body.

Then she got used to the iciness flowing around her ankles. She sat on the bank with that rusty razor, her feet soaking, and worked at her wrists with the deliberation of a painter recreating a landscape down to the blur of a dragonfly's wings. It *hurt*. The pain sharpened her concentration, and she pressed harder, sank the blade deeper.

She bent close to his ear now, told him how the pain dissolved in the cold water and the red life flowed out of her. More life than she'd ever known she'd had.

Girlishly small, her sneakers lay stranded in the grass, laces undone.

She let her blood mingle with the clear water, she said. Watched it unwind in red ribbons, spread into cloudy plumes, stream away in the running water. She'd never been so happy. So happy she began to float. Above the water flooding her veins, washing away the medication, the years she'd added to her age, the inky memories scribbled in hidden diaries. It was all clean and running now. Out to a blue lake.

They hadn't known when they found her in the water—such a pale white, so stiff and cold—that she'd died a peaceful death. With no anger toward life, no love of death. Water rushing over her body, around her face, she looked as if she were sinking into sleep. Her eyes half open, glazed a milky blue, the beginning of a dream still held in her pupils. The dream had caught her gaze as she lay in the cold water, worked its hypnotic magic on her, dissolving a cloud twisting restlessly past, the flight of a distressed bird, the sky itself. *What* is *that?* she'd wondered, staring more intently, and in the midst of her curiosity, drifted free of her body. A gentle dip and she was off somewhere else.

The calm shores of a blue lake.

Her face became alabaster set with the filmy blue of her eyes and the grayer blue of her lips. Her hair waved behind her like tawny sea grass. A leaf or two from an overhanging tree tangled in the strands and—what else? Flowers, Paul had told him. She'd tied flowers in her hair she was in such a good mood about what she'd decided to do. Daisies probably. They grew near the hospital. Tiny yellow moons spreading white halos, blurry beneath the running water.

She lay with an arm behind her head as if to pillow it, the other across her stomach. Her shirt was still tucked into her jeans, and a bare foot was half buried in sand—something he'd never seen but would never forget.

He wiped away sweat. Played. Started over. Played again. Fingers separated clumps of wet hair, nails raked his scalp. He heard laughter. He smelled the grass from the night they'd made love on their clothes. The breeze came through the walls of the bar, raised goosebumps on his skin.

Fingering music, he sang softly to bring her back. The skin of her arms see-through down to blue veins, liquid eyes a melancholy shade of sky. She took on this color too readily, bruised too easily—a shortcoming she'd inherited from her mother, she said, a weakness they shared.

Whatever hand had tied Linda together as a bundle of sinew and a puff of breath hadn't done a good job of it, and she undid the knot herself. What was left—what *was* left? Nothing he could hold, nothing he could take to the movies or lie next to, nothing to warm him or ward off loneliness.

Drained, he stabbed a plastic button with his finger and shut off a tape recorder. He took out the cassette, labeled Side A *Woman, Blue.* Tucking the tape in a back pocket, he snapped off the lights. The snaking neon, silently echoed in the mirror behind the bar, went cold.

He closed the door behind him and locked it.

A shiver ran through him. The warm night air was cold where sweat had soaked through his shirt. West Third was empty. His eye held what little light there was the way ore locked away a mineral's shine.

He glanced at the old firehouse next to the Crow, an artful mix of brick and stone. Two red bulbs glowed through wire cages on either side of the garage door. He'd almost forgotten the incandescent coincidence, this displaced element of the hospital where he'd been living only months ago. Except those bulbs had been blue.

Darkened shop windows reflected him, the street, a fire hydrant.

He walked past the Blue Note's elegant metal silhouettes jazzing it up over a marquee shaped like a piano, the brass poles holding it up doubling as piano legs.

The tears that had gathered while he played in the Crow had dried without falling. The pain of Linda's pain had broken inside him like a storm. The veins in his hands were swollen. He held his fingers out, expecting to see a ghostly light around them, to see beyond them an avenue of telephone-pole crosses and sagging wires aglow. In Kansas the horns of cattle sometimes burned blue at the tips just before a twister touched down. Maybe there was nothing to see because he was at the wrong end of it: the twister had come and gone.

Silently he asked Linda to forgive him. For letting her wade out into an emotion he couldn't return. For being in love with being able to walk and listen and breathe. He had no doubt that the Earth, which had taken her back, had a soul too, something you might hear rustling among stalks of wheat where even a crow could see that a paralyzed farmer, leaking straw, lacked the breath moving through the field.

His steps slow and buoyant, he might've been wandering an underwater city, the now-and-again breeze a current. If a brick were to shake loose from a building, it would cut an odd, jerky path, take its time coming to rest at his feet. A cracked lamp set out for trash took on the bearing of an ancient urn. He could see the pitting left by rust on a wrought-iron railing, understood that its hard spirals signaled there was a route the dead could take to return.

Crossing the near-empty avenue, he thought he saw those two musicians, the ones with straight black hair who looked more Indian than he did. All he could see now were the backs of their heads and instrument cases that needed some bodywork. *Hey*. His lifted itself, but he didn't call out. He wanted to talk to them. They turned a corner, one of them glancing back and … smiling? Was it they? In their fraying suits, the brown rusting away, leaving a trail of brittle flakes for him to follow? When he turned the corner, he was alone. He stood scanning the night-blurred street, but he had no idea which way they'd gone.

Giving up, he dropped down the dirty stairs of a subway entrance that smelled of electrified grease and stale urine.

The graffiti on the train cars looked more like Arabic than English. People who had nothing better to do complained it was done by people who had nothing better to do. Galleries in SoHo might be deadened by canvases turned into color swatches, but the subway was still breathing.

He jumped off the train a stop early, bounded up the stairs.

The sky was a dark window onto more of creation than anyone needed to see. The space between stars was a coolness he took in with his breath. The Moon had taken on the pale orange of a distant fire—a constellation burning to cinders maybe. Or a single star collapsing into nuclear embers. The Moon seemed extraordinarily solid behind a sky full of silent motion—gray clouds driven by winds too high to feel. The clouds came slowly apart, shredding on invisible shoals.

Anything added to this night—one more homeless man against the curb, one more Styrofoam coffee cup, half-eaten hot dog, candy wrapper flapping past his feet, would make it trickle over.

He turned the corner, hopped up the marble steps of Shawna's building. A minimalist angel illuminated the corner. He glanced back at the haloed aluminum pole as though it were a lover he was leaving.

Inside the apartment, his outstretched fingertips brushed against a wall for guidance (he didn't bother with lights until he got to the kitchen).

The woodgrain patterns on the kitchen table seemed strikingly clear—his fingers went wonderingly over the polished surface—as if his pupils had enlarged and his eyes had become more sensitive not to light but to detail.

A triangle of light widened on the floor as he opened the refrigerator door. He pulled out a bowl of macaroni salad, peeled back cellophane as thin as the city's dreaming, and stabbed with a fork. He knew he shouldn't eat it all, not before bed, but he also knew—as the fork clanged more and more often against the glass bottom—he was going to.

"Why don't you sit down when you eat?"

Startled, Logan turned. Shawna was standing there in a T-shirt and panties. "What're you doin' up?"

Arms folded over her chest, she shrugged.

"Something on your mind?"

"You."

He pulled out a chair and sat down. "C'mere." He patted his lap. The chair groaned with the weight of both of them. "What about me?"

"I've been watching you."

"Oh yeah? How do I look?"

"Like you're headed somewhere."

"Because a few more people are comin' to the Crow to hear me?"

"Stop trying to make me feel better. I'm tired Logan. Tired of New York, tired of my job—they take too much out of me. And I'm not going anywhere."

Standing up, she took a pack of cigarettes off the table. "I used to … when I really hated everything, I used to get so high I didn't care. For a while that was the only time I felt alive. You don't know how lucky you are that way. You *are* alive. You don't question it, you just are."

He watched her light a cigarette. "Is that what you think?"

"It comes off you. Even when you're sleeping next to me. I mean, I know you doubt yourself and get depressed and all that, but you've got your eyes on something." She exhaled smoke. "That's how you get by in the world. That's why you look through people. Even me sometimes."

"You don't smoke."

"Oh really?" She took a deep drag and tilted her head back as she sent a blue-gray plume toward the ceiling. "I'm sick of all this—the morning commute, living a wall away from strangers, the tar and concrete everywhere, these buildings I can't see past, the crowds ... "

"So come to Kansas with me."

"Oh that's your answer to everything. I'm not like you, Logan. Everything I own doesn't fit in a duffel bag. And even if I bring it all to Kansas, what do I do *then*?"

"Take pictures. Same as here."

"It would be hard enough selling my work here, where I could actually exhibit it. In Kansas ... I can't imagine anything but cloth backdrops and kids who won't sit still."

He stood up, ran his thumb down her neck, along the spine.

She stubbed out the cigarette. "And don't tell me I should quit my job. You think we could afford this place on what Dave pays you? We couldn't even get a hole in the East Village. You get to stay up all night working on songs at the Copper Crow and fuck around all day because I go to a job every day."

"Yeah ..." He nodded. "I know."

"I'm sorry." She put her arms around his neck and squeezed. "You didn't deserve that."

He kissed her ear. "Couldn't you do it on the side for a while? Show your stuff to what-his-name, Trevor, the guy who runs those art shows?"

"I feel like I need to get out of here. I feel like I can't breathe."

For the first time it occurred to him that she couldn't stay in one place either, that something inside her was struggling to split open its chrysalis.

"What do you think about Phoenix?" She raised her eyebrows. "My company has an office out there. Suppose I get a transfer …?"

"Does it have to be Phoenix?" He didn't want to drive past the run-down barrio he'd started off his life in or stop at the intersection of dusty streets where his father had been killed.

"We'll talk about it tomorrow." She let her arms slip from his shoulders. "Let's go to bed."

"Hey …" He grabbed one of her wrists and exposed the underside of her forearm. A fresh sore, as round as a sucker's mouth, glared from a cluster of dark circles. All about the same size.

"What? You never saw a cigarette burn before?"

"Not on you. Why didn't I ever notice these?"

"Amazing what a little makeup and an absent-minded boyfriend can accomplish together."

He remembered her in the Hamptons, wearing a long-sleeve shirt out to the beach. "When did you do *this* one?"

"Tonight."

Logan thought of Upstate University, of Jack and Bible Mike and the rest of them. "Why?"

"*Logan* … my *wrist*." She pulled back but he held her.

"Why?"

"Let … *go!*"

She yanked her arm away so hard she almost fell when he opened his hand.

"To see how it would feel. Now. Tonight."

"And?"

"It didn't help, okay? Neither did trying to break my wrist."

"I didn't mean to—"

"Do you love me?

"I love you."

"Then forget about it. I won't do it again." She hung her head over his shoulder and pressed up against him. "I'm glad you're home."

"Just give me a couple minutes to wash up."

"One, not two."

"Deal."

When she left the kitchen, he pulled Aristotle's card out of his wallet and reached for the book of matches she'd left behind. He lit the card at a corner, watched the flame blacken the coppery letters. It fell from his hands into Shawna's ashtray and curled in on itself like a crab dying on its back.

27. Sleep Talk

"Who's Buddy?"

"Buddy?" He looked at her, eyebrows lowered, forehead wrinkling.

"You were talking in your sleep last night."

"Whaddid I say?"

She shrugged. "I couldn't really understand what you were saying except *Buddy*."

He grunted. He didn't remember anything after he went to sleep last night. "I used to call my father Buddy. I guess I was dreaming about him." Only he couldn't remember any of it. It was lost, gone to wherever dreams go.

28. Believeth All Things

She treated each wall as if it were a canvas with its own composition. She'd chosen prints that complemented one another, hung them at measured distances: a café in cobblestoned Paris by van Gogh, the stars like overlarge snowflakes; one of Monet's cathedrals, imposing though barely solid in morning mist; a Dutch still life whose diffuse glow brought objects—a dusty lute, a leather-bound tome, a pewter pitcher—out of an abiding gloom. Her own black-and-white photos of the desert and New York were here and there among them, rectangles of gray evening where the dream of color had begun to dissolve.

His favorite was still that night scene, the clean lines of a corner diner with glass walls and a single customer—an old man in an overcoat hunched over his table. On the street, smudged with shadow, a man and woman were wrapped in a kiss as though breathing depended on closing the last of the distance between them. The photo was perfectly balanced, settled between a universe running down (that fire hydrant was a monument to rust) and one that eternally renewed itself (crab grass had sprouted up around its base). Go ahead—touch, laugh, walk the narrowest, the darkest of places. Thy hand and thy countenance comfort me. The light of the diner is enough to see by. The old man is an inescapable destiny though it might never be reached. The city is sprawled all around, edged in brick, but this embrace makes it bearable. Endureth all things, beareth all things, believeth all things.

29. Ghost Dancer

Buildings defaced by tears of dried soot, their profiles hard against what little sky there was, threatened to eclipse the Sun permanently, make mornings extinct.

He'd never seen her cry before. Had sat there in the Copper Crow at an awkward loss.

She'd promised they'd talk about it, but she'd already taken the transfer. It was a done deal. He was on the bus or off the bus.

He didn't want to go back. To a city where storms brought dust instead of rain. A city sinking a little more each year to feed the lawn sprinklers and fountains and swimming pools. A city flanked by barren mountains, their slopes pitted and lunar. A city sprawling farther into the desert. Concrete and asphalt and rusting cars wavering in the heat.

He'd never told her about how he'd once followed movement as if nothing else existed. How wind had whistled through the hollows after his sense of who he was had eroded. He knew if he wasn't careful he'd turn into one of those mesas in the distance, wearing away a little more each year. Even if he had told her—but he couldn't have told her because he didn't know anymore, because what was left was the ashes of a memory. What he could tell her now was that he wasn't ready to be so close to what had almost rubbed him into oblivion beneath a thumb as empty and unavoidable as the sky.

"Why does it have to be Kansas?" Her voice had hit a pitch like the squeal of brakes on a subway train. "I can't work there. What the hell are *you* going to do in Kansas?"

He had a house out there—well, it wasn't his, but Jim Lee kept a room for him. Jim Lee's front porch was almost as big as their apartment in the city. There was even a darkroom Jimmy had put together in the basement. He'd take her to abandoned filling stations and ghost cafés, show her all the stopped clocks in the Midwest.

But she wasn't ... no she just couldn't. She kept shaking her head as if that gesture alone would convince him. She knew people in Phoenix, a friend with a gallery out there who would help her get started. She'd be able to keep her job and freelance on the weekends. They could rent a house in Phoenix, a whole house to themselves.

"Why don't I come later?"

"When later?"

"After ... when it's right."

"What does *that* mean?"

"I have to be home for a while." He repeated *home* as if it held charm enough to swing from the end of a gold chain.

"And just how long am I supposed to wait?"

"I'm not sure."

He still wasn't. It was just that whatever it was that told him it was time to move on, to go back, was telling him now.

"Look, this is so much all at once—do you have to make it harder? I know I've never been to Kansas, but Phoenix ... things are going on there, and ... don't you understand? *That's* where I have to be right now, *that's* where I see myself, *that's* what I need right now. I don't see why you can't just come with me."

"I just need a little time."

"A little time. A little space." Her voice was contemptuous. "I've heard that before."

He reached for her hand but she twisted away.

"This isn't working."

His stomach collapsed. As if it'd always had a vacuum at its center and had finally given in to it.

"You treat me like I don't exist when I'm in the same room with you. You take off whenever things get a little out of hand." Although hardly anything in her face changed—no involuntary trembling at the corners of the mouth, no racking sobs—her eyes reddened and began to tear. As if she'd been resolved to the decision for a long time and there was only one part of her she couldn't make abide by it. "You should go now."

She went into the ladies' room to wipe away smeared mascara, cry in private, get away from him.

He wandered from the Copper Crow without paying much attention to where he was going. In front of him now was the marble monument on which Washington's faces—one on each side of the arch—had cracked as finely as skin wrinkles. The jagged lines were dark with grime.

Night settled.

The marble span was thick and wide, columnar. There to support, some vague notion of cultural pride.

Paul Washington Square Park.

Those who'd already staked a claim clustered together around music (he heard bongos and a guitar) or smoke (the breeze smoldered with pot). Always a center things crystallized around. A strange tension held it all together. He glided over it like a water strider moving with its own reflection. Tonight, he might be the only killer among them.

"Hey …" An index finger bounced up and down. "Don't I know you?"

The weathered face in front of him was handsome in a rough way. Eyes the blue of a northern evening looked at him expectantly. A little taller than Logan, he was older too but not old enough for the way his crown had gone smooth. Looking at the blond ruff, which curled above a thick neck, Logan couldn't help thinking that, had he lived about a millennium earlier, he could've been a Viking.

"Almost didn't recognize you with that buzz-cut."

The wrinkly flesh of a scar grooved the Viking's jaw. "Bruce."

"Right." His smile pushed a golden biker's mustache a little higher. Bruce put out his hand. "What was that? Two, three years ago?"

Logan took hold of a hand as rough as tree bark. "'Bout that." He figured their grips to be about even.

Bruce closed his eyes, put his forehead into an open palm, pressed it there. "I know you got an Indian last name, kind of an unusual first name ..." He looked up with his finger pointing and a smile on his face. "*Logan*."

Logan nodded. "Yeah."

"How long you been here?"

"Few months."

"Whaddaya think?"

"A lot packed into a little space. Too much maybe. I think I might've liked it better ten years ago."

"Yeeaaaaaaah." Long and low from Bruce. "Ain't what it used to be. Gettin' hard to operate around here. Even the park ain't the same. Used to be people were just waitin' to be friendly and talk to you. Now, it's more like they're waitin' for you to make a mistake. Doin' the wrong kindsa drugs for the wrong reasons." He shook his head. "No code."

Bruce dug three fingers into the front pocket of a denim vest that had been a jacket until someone had cut the sleeves off. It looked too small to button over his hairy chest. His fingers came up empty. He jerked his thumb at a punk with orange hair. "They hate us because we let 'em down. The Establishment won."

"The Establishment?"

Bruce nodded. "I used to be a longhair. Beard too. Almost wound up in Vietnam." He grinned mischievously. "Burned my draft card instead."

"Didn't believe in the war?" Logan asked.

"*Believe*? That war ruined everything America stood for."

Logan supposed he didn't look surprised because Bruce shook his head.

"See, this generation can't understand. They grew up *expecting* the government to lie. Wasn't like that 20 years ago. This was the greatest country on Earth." Bruce patted his chest. "*We* were the good guys. You ever heard a the *Pentagon Papers*?"

"Uh-uh."

"Read 'em some time. The U.S. stepped in right after the French got their asses handed to them in '54 and signed the Geneva Accords. What you have to understand is there *was* no South Vietnam. Or North."

"No North Vietnam?" Logan glared skeptically. "Who were we fighting?"

"That's just it—we *invented* the whole war! Vietnam was *one* country. The *accords* divided it. It was just a line in the sand to give the French time to get their kicked asses out. But then the U.S. installs a puppet regime in the south under a guy named Diem and blocks the elections promised by accords *we* signed too. See, everybody knew Ho Chi Minh would win by a landslide. Meanwhile, Diem's secret police torture and murder thousands of rice farmers who don't know communism from a coconut."

"You ex-CIA or something? Floating around the country, dodging the feds?"

"Me? CIA? *Hell* no. I used to recruit protestors."

"Kennedy was going to pull out, wasn't he?"

"Exactly! But then he's assassinated in '63 and a few days later Johnson signs a memo calling for a secret war in Vietnam. Yeah … *secret*. Then he runs against Goldwater as the *peace* candidate! Once he's voted in, he lands Marines at Da Nang. And I *voted* for the fucker!" Bruce threw a slow punch at Logan's shoulder, pushed at him with his knuckles. "Ah hell. I'm not gonna bore you with old news. Whaddaya say we roast a bone?"

The bit about the bone took a couple of seconds to click.

"Come on, meet somma my friends." He put a hand on Logan's shoulder and began walking him. The arm was bare except for the carpet of hair that tickled Logan's neck.

"Bruce …" She was sitting against a fence of iron bars hardly waist high. "You brought company."

He jostled Logan with his arm. "Road warrior I met on my travels."

She was on a kind of platform, a truncated circle made of brick. He and Bruce went up four steps to join them.

"This is Logan."

Sprouting from beneath the red skullcap of a bandanna, her dark hair fell in curls. Bracelets hung with charms jangled as she took his hand. "Sybil." Worn denim shorts exposed thighs thick with muscle. Her black T-shirt had something written on it. *Kein Mitleid für die Mehrheit.* German? Below it, in red letters: *No Pity for the Majority.*

"That's Batman." Bruce pointed. "He only comes out at night."

Batman lay on a bench overhung by a low branch, the foliage dense enough to hold off a light rain. He lowered a newspaper to his chest and raised an arm without bothering to get up. He was wearing fingerless gloves and enough chains to sink a body in the Hudson.

"Oh Christ," Batman moaned and shook out the newspaper. "Yankees lost again." His voice sounded like a yawn. "The Pentagon is worried about a new missile the Russians are developing. And the highest rate of poverty in the country is on the Pine Ridge Reservation in South Dakota."

"Highest rate of suicide, highest rate of alcoholism, highest rate of poverty—all on the rez," Logan said. "Leave it to the Indians to bring home the gold medals nobody else wants."

"Sorry, I didn't—"

"Don't pay any mind to Batman." Bruce waved a hand. "He's a professional bum."

"Bruce is just an amateur. Not to worry—he's working his way up."

Sybil was looking at Logan. "You might jazz up the vestments with a little leather."

"She's an interior decorator." Bruce gestured in her direction. "She likes to decorate *exteriors* too." The stubble on his face glistened like wire bristles.

Sybil's dark skin had a creamy quality to it. Puerto Rican? Maybe a mixed-blood like him.

Bruce lifted a booted foot. "Here's *my* leather. Nothin' like a broken-in pair a shit-kickers. Like walkin' on feathers."

They looked like he'd never taken them off.

"Hi ho, Silver." Batman rustled the newspaper.

If Bruce was the Lone Ranger, that made him Tonto. Too much insult, not enough joke to mention.

Flame shot past the joint in Batman's mouth. When the stiletto-thin lighter clicked off, the roasting bone made its way around to Logan by way of Sybil (jangle, jangle, joint). His face twisting into a demon's grin, he cauterized his lungs. He heard a boombox playing somewhere. A Doors song. He exhaled.

She was going to Phoenix without him.

Come on baby, light my fire …

Kansas, she said, will always be there.

Come on baby, light my fire …

He took another hit, held it in.

Try to set the night on fire …

His eyes began to water.

Shit.

"Does that song have to be playing *now*?" The song he'd played the first time she'd seen him at the Copper Crow. The band he loved. The keyboard player he loved more. Shawna pressed her fingertips in a semi-circle under her eyes, probably smudging her eyeliner again.

"The world is like that," Pam said, "inconsiderate, insensitive, and pretty much indifferent."

"You sure you're not talking about the guy who just dumped me?"

"We all have our moments. I'm sure you'll straighten things out." She speared Shawna's drink with a straw, clicking past ice cubes.

"It's ironic. For once he doesn't leave, and what do I do? Tell him to piss off."

"Did you call the apartment?"

"Twice."

Shawna stared at the cracked painting near the stairs. There was so much dust the ship was a gray silhouette on the brink of vanishing. She wondered whether it had gathered the way tree rings did—a year of drought left the ring a little deformed. If you studied the painting, would the layer of dust from the year the United States boycotted the Olympics be finer or grittier? Leaning more toward silvery or gray? What about the day—it was night really—he walked into her life? And what about when he walked out? Would it be a sooty black closer to volcanic ash?

"He'll show up. You two'll kiss 'n make up and live happily ever after in Arizona. Leaving me to my own vices in a city *full* of people to encourage them."

Shawna pushed the drink away and stood up. "I'm going." She squeezed one of Pam's small, warm hands. "You're my best goddam friend, you know that?"

"My work here is done. I can go to my grave with a clear conscience."

She squeezed harder.

"Ow!"

"I'm serious."

Pam freed her hand and pressed herself against Shawna. "I wanna visit you guys in your desert abode and pick cactus needles out of my money-maker while I sip tequila on the patio."

"You better get back to work before Dave takes it out of your paycheck."

"I'll take it out of his *ass*. I got enough dirt on him to bury him where he stands."

Shawna hugged Pam again.

There wasn't a light on in the place. Disappointed, she dropped her purse on the couch. Pressing the toe of one foot against the heel of the other, she got out of her shoes. Her feet felt suddenly cool beneath their veil of nylon.

In the bedroom she slid open the closet door. His bag was still there. She covered her heart with a hand as if following a script. He never went far without that ruin of water-stained leather. *It's been to Maine, Spain, Spokane, an' a couple a cow-callin' contests in between.* The third time he said it, it wasn't cute anymore.

She checked the answering machine: two calls from her, one from her ex. She shut it off.

Reaching under her skirt, she hooked the waistband of her pantyhose with her thumbs and peeled them off her legs in a sweeping motion. Tired and sweaty, she decided a shower was what she needed. And some music. In fact, *his* music. The water would get to work on her muscles and tired feet. His voice would soothe the ache under her ribs.

As the windy sound of a flute drifted out of the speakers, she stepped into the shower. When Logan began singing, she felt suspended—just for a second—and thought about pirouetting to the slow swirling she felt inside.

Why the hell wasn't he home?

The evening began to unravel as the warm water ran down her body. It was mainly the expression on his face when she'd asked him to leave that she remembered. He looked hurt and bewildered. She was glad about the hurt part. It meant that he cared. It meant that he wasn't invulnerable and that *she* was one of his weaknesses.

The phone? She leaned out of the spray of water to listen. It rang again. She slid the glass door open, grabbed a towel as she ran out. She picked up the phone just as a ring ended. "Hello?" It had already clicked. "Hello?"

He'd hung up. She knew it had been him. She slammed the receiver down. "Dammit!" Her recorded voice filled the room. She picked up the phone, the answering machine sliding off the dresser with it, and threw it against a wall.

"D'jew make your phone call?"

"Nobody home."

"Ah well." Bruce opened his hands and turned them up like *what can you do?* "Batman's got another log on the fire. Might as well hang out."

Logan nodded. From somewhere closer to the middle of the park, maybe from that dry wading pool, he could still hear bongos but no boombox.

The lit end of a joint turned Sybil's high cheekbones, straight nose, and angular jaw ruddy. He reached for the joint, but she took his hand, pulled it closer. He took the loosely rolled joint with the other hand. While he sucked in, she blew out. Her fingers went over his palm then his knuckles and fingers.

"You got a mean streak in you, don't you?"

He winked at her. "Might could be."

"Sybil's a witch," Batman said. "Turned me into a tiny, hirsute, flapping critter once. That's how I got my nickname."

"Logan …" Sybil tossed his name out as though plinking a stone in a well. "Logan what?"

"Blackfeather."

"Logan Blackfeather." She had a voice that reminded him of a draft finding its way under a door.

"We're gonna have to change Batman's name to something more accurate," Bruce said. "Johnny Jobless maybe."

"And you can be Herman Homeless." Batman was still lying on his back along the length of a bench, newspaper cast aside, ankles crossed over one another.

Laughing, Bruce handed the joint to Sybil and leaned heavily on Logan's shoulder. His blue eyes had the gnawed shine of ancient glass. "His real name's Battista," he whispered to Logan, "John Battista. That's why we call 'im Batman."

The joint came back to Logan, only now he thought they were lying about Batman to make him look stupid. He passed it on to Bruce without taking a hit. His head had begun to feel like a wide-mouthed sewer pipe, words blowing through it like dry leaves. What he hated about pot, he had to scurry around looking for thoughts, couldn't figure out the right order, then forgot what he was trying to say.

Smoke curled from Sybil's half-open mouth. The sight evoked déjà vu. The same faraway look in the eyes of a woman he'd seen in a dream or an hallucination, the same tilt to the face, the same dangling earrings (as elaborate as the headdress of an Incan priest).

His hand tightened into a fist but closed on nothing. They

hadn't been able to hold onto Shawna, and he despised them for their uselessness.

"So you're Indian, huh babe?"

The question, travelling a great distance, took a long time to get to him. He nodded without bothering to admit to the white part.

"Now they knew what to do with names," she said.

"Got your name the old-fashioned way in those days—you earned it." Bruce's face was cheery.

Somethingorother *Witko*. Crazy Horse. *In-Mut-Too-Ya-Lat-Lat*. Chief Joseph's real name. Thunder Traveling Over The Mountains. Logan Feather Of The Eagle Hidden From The Sun.

Bruce sat next to Sybil and put an arm around her. "This here's my cowgirl."

"The Stoned Ranger," Batman joked.

"Only we …" Logan stuttered. "We were here first."

The playfulness drained from Bruce's face, and the expression that remained hovered somewhere between wariness and confusion. "Who was where first?"

"Indians." Logan aimed a finger at the bricks under his sneakers. "Here." He felt his face arrange itself in a cocky half smile as if he knew hundreds of things they didn't.

Bruce scratched his chin. "No problem. There's plenty a room."

Logan shook his head. "Not even on *two* continents." He laughed without knowing why.

"All the crime gets blamed on spics an' niggers." He laughed again, out of place (*inappropriate affect* they called it Upstate). "But two ripped-off continents … there's *your* gold medal."

Logan stopped talking because he'd put Bruce in a bad place.

Bruce had given him a ride, cooked dinner for him, shared his beer and his pot.

He heard Sybil's drafty voice offering a change of subject. "So where do you come from Logan Blackfeather?"

From Upstate University. My real name's Crazy Horse.

"Wounded Knee Creek. I'm a ghost dancer." He loved the power of his lie.

Batman sat up. "Whatsa ghost dancer?"

Logan looked at his feet. Those were moccasins that were his sneakers.

He closed his eyes to see across a century-wide canyon, through its snowy space. No, not snow. The swirling flakes were the grains of an image that refused to emerge. It must've been hours before he came up with "Someone ... caught between worlds." He closed his eyes again, a long blink. "One that's worn out, better than half way to dead. One that's new, still on its way." He blinked again. "You dance. And you keep dancing until you get a vision. Of what the World Coming is going to look like. You dance until it shows up."

It'd gotten colder. Logan folded his arms across his chest, goosebumps rising on his arms.

They didn't really understand what had happened at Wounded Knee. He wanted to tell it so that they got it right this time. Historians were always distracted by the obvious, all those bodies in the snow. History was full of massacres. This one was different.

He didn't feel stupid from pot anymore. He felt like something supernatural had hit him with its invisible fist and swelled the sun eye shut. Everything in the moon eye was black and white but clear.

When he started talking again, they weren't in the park anymore. It wasn't summer's end.

It is winter, 1890. The Great Plains are covered with snow. The wind cuts through the rags you are wearing, sings bitter and cold in your ears. And it never stops. Can you feel it?

The goosebumps on his arms hardened in the wake of a spasm snaking through his body.

You have to eat horsemeat because there are so few buffalo left. But there's not even enough horsemeat to go around.

Your mother died two weeks ago because her body had been weakened by hunger and cold.

Your father died when the Blue Coats attacked the village. He wasn't able to save your sister. You wouldn't let your mother see the body of your sister because of what the Blue Coats had done to it. Your mother had to wail and keen without seeing her daughter for the last time.

Last winter your wife did not survive the white-scabs disease. You leaned over her while she lay stretched on the ground. Your baby was curled and frozen in the round hill of her belly. Your son, your daughter—you will never know which—never came into the world.

You are what is left of your family, and you are soon to die.

If you look up, the sky is empty. The clouds are still there, but the voices that sometimes spoke to you are quiet. Once you saw the eagle circling above the Earth and knew that the wind carrying him was your own breath. You don't hear the voices of the eagles anymore. The four-legged animals have nothing to say either. The music between the stars has been stilled. There are no more signs to follow, and you haven't seen the Sun for days.

What's left of your band is called the No Clothes People by the tribe you joined. Your village was burned. Your tepee and the buffalo robes that would have kept you warm were also burned. In dreams you hear the crack of the soldiers' guns while you run away. All is gray above you as if the sky were filled with the smoke of all the villages ever burned, and it will be gray forever.

The Lakota chief Red Cloud has said there is no hope on Earth, and you believe him. Other chiefs have whispered that the powers that protected the tribes have abandoned them.

You send a prayer as you walk through the snow, but you have heard of distant tribes that have been completely wiped out by soldiers, by starvation, by the white-scabs disease. Their languages, their ceremonies, their lives are gone, and there will be no more children.

The No Clothes People are almost gone too. The people around you are not your own. Even the great Lakota war chief Tashunke Witko is dead. So are your parents and your wife and your unborn child and the warriors of your tribe. Custer's ghost is laughing at you. In-Mut-To-Ya-Lat-Lat, Thunder-Traveling-Over-The Mountains, has said that he will fight no more forever. And you believe him.

You have nothing left but the emptiness in your stomach, the cold in your body, the bitter wind singing in your ears. This is what makes you Indian like all the rest although you don't speak the same language—your numb fingers, your frostbitten toes, your skinny legs, your weak arms.

If the Indians die out, surely the Earth will die too. The ceremonies will not be performed. The Sun will stop rising. The Earth will no longer be fertile. The fur that once covered the sacred buffalo holding up the Earth, fur that used to roll across his back in dark brown waves, is almost gone. Three of his legs have dropped off. The end of the world is just over the next ridge.

Then you hear about the coming of Christ to Earth as an Indian. His name is Wovoka and he has promised that everything will be renewed. The Earth will roll up like a blanket and take with it the fences and the railroads, the forts and the telegraph poles. Underneath will be the old Indian Earth. The white man will be swept from the land. Only the Indians will be saved. The world will end, but a new one lies underneath it. The buffalo will return. The ghosts of your ancestors—all the dead—will live again. The horses will be numerous, and there will be plenty of grass for them to eat. This is what the Indian messiah has said, and you want to believe him.

A new world is coming,
The eagle has said so.
But you must dance.
A new world is coming,
The eagle has sent word.

Dance the dance of the ghosts, and you will see your mother again and speak with your father. Your sister will come laughing to you, and you will sleep in your wife's arms again and watch your child grow. The white man will be extinct, and your tribe will live as it lived before his coming.

Only you must dance the Dance of Ghosts.

You dance to renew the Earth, to be free of the white man, to see your family and your tribe live again. You fall into a trance on the frigid earth, your face against grass pounded flat, but you do not feel it. You are in the spirit world, and when you awake, the other dancers tell you to paint what you saw on a shirt.

This will be your Ghost Shirt. You have seen some of these shirts hung with feathers and strips of rawhide, even thin tails of human hair. They are painted with eagles and hawks and crows with outspread wings, with colorful two-headed birds and buffalo-horned beings, with five-pointed stars like those on the flag the Blue Coats wave or a red daybreak star. Others are decorated with constellations, crescent moons, circles divided into four parts, streaks of red lightning, feverish spots. Wovoka has said that the bullets of the soldiers cannot harm you when you wear your Ghost Shirt.

You hear the voice of the eagle again. The Earth sends dreams of the land as it used to be. There is music between the stars. The old ways have returned.

The whites see that your backs are not bent and your heads are not hung. You are dancing—dancing! They want you to stop.

The Blue Coats come to take away the leader of the band you have joined. They take away the last of your guns even though most of the warriors have died and there are twice as many women and children as men. Even though the guns are used to hunt the last of the buffalo.

One man among a hundred refuses to give up his gun. A new, many-shots rifle that cost him most of his wealth in horses and hides. It is all he has left to show that he is still a man.

And they fire.

They fire not only with their rifles and pistols but with new guns that echo like thunder and flash like lightning. These new guns, which leave great holes in the Earth, are turned on the tepees where women and children are huddled against the cold.

Men who are not armed are shot like deer who forgot to run.

Women carrying children are chased down. They are stabbed with bayonets, and their bodies are left in the snow. They are not worth a bullet.

Old men who cannot run are beaten to death with the butts of rifles. They are not worth a sharp blade.

You try to run, hoping you won't be killed, but the bodies of children beside their mothers tell you you will.

It is 1890. The Great Plains are covered with snow.

A new world is coming, the eagle has said so.

You walk among the bodies, whose limbs are frozen in strange positions. The bitter wind blows as it always has.

The Indian nations shall rise again, Wovoka said. It will be like old times. You believed him.

(The Ghost shirts did not protect you.)

Our ancestors, our loved ones, all of the dead will be reunited with us, it was said. The white man shall perish utterly from the face of the Earth. You believed this too.

(The Ghost Shirts did not stop the bullets.)

The hunting will be good again. The buffalo will return, and the land will be fertile. We will roam the Earth as we did before the coming of the white man.

The Ghost Shirts are dark with blood. And now you don't believe anything.

30. THROUGH A TUNNEL

Daylight distinguished a window from a wall. He was waking up so there must've been a time when he'd fallen asleep; he just didn't remember it. His mouth pasty and dry, he pulled himself into a sitting position. He was suddenly aware of the pain and stiffness spreading up his back. The couch had been too small for him.

His last day in New York.

Bruce was asleep in a room separated from his by a sheer white curtain only half-pulled. Face-down, one of his thick arms hung over the side of a narrow bed. The forearm was brassy with hair, the hand bent backwards against the floorboards.

Logan left a note thanking Bruce for taking him in again and sneaked out the door.

The hallway was covered with grime as if it'd been used as a chimney. By the time he reached the last flight of stairs, there was no banister, just holes in the plaster where it had been anchored.

A whole street of soot-streaked brick dark with damp. Warehouses mostly. A corroding industrial sector.

The rain had begun by the time they'd left the park. Now the sky was an unbroken sheet as blank as cigarette smoke. Crossing the street, he saw himself go by in a puddle dark enough to be a leftover patch of night. At the western end of the street he could see a small strip of the Hudson like a shred of tarnished metal. The shine had rubbed off this city, and he was left with its straight edges, the smell of exhaust fumes, and a silvery taste that reminded him of the boyish time when, out of curiosity, he'd put a quarter on his tongue.

A raindrop spattered on his wrist. Another brushed the tip of his nose.

A crow took flight from one of the black wires sagging between telephone poles.

He walked quickly, desperately hungry.

Turning onto the avenue, his face hovered in shop windows like a trapped ghost.

The rain suddenly grew loud against the sidewalk and street, a rush of sound like a stadium crowd reacting to a big play.

He walked faster.

He saw rain bounce off an umbrella tilted against the wind. He guessed from the legs and feet that a woman was walking toward him.

Even if he'd had an umbrella, he wouldn't have opened it. Stepping down rain-darkened cement (the terraced gullet of a subway entrance), he was disappointed to have escaped the storm so easily. Water reformed into drops, slipped down his scalp and face, the back of his neck. Tricklings of the torrent he would need to cleanse him. To dowse the city, scour a layer of grime off it, and send the filthy water streaming along curbs until it was waylaid by sewers and resounded in hollows under the streets.

The concrete platform on which he waited floored a space that held the dull echo of metal colliding with metal somewhere down the tracks. The entire city could be sheared off at its foundation, and, tucked away in this tunnel, he'd be among those who emerged unharmed, shocked at all the open space and exposed sky.

A block or two west of where he stood, the surface of the Hudson was being pricked by raindrops into a new texture, which would last as long as the falling music.

A train took him noisily uptown.

He spent the morning in the apartment narrowing his life down to what money he'd managed to save, a few books, two tapes of what he'd been working on at the Copper Crow, some clothes. Lifting his two-toned boots, his hands felt heavy and cumbersome. As if they were reddish lead, as if they'd taken on weight to slow him down, to protest what he was up to. He kept his sight whittled down so that he couldn't look past the moment, past his leaden hand loading the boots into the leather bag he'd picked up in Mexico, lumpy now, like a stomach taken out of an enormous animal after it had gorged itself.

In the kitchen he reached for a frame Shawna had hung. Bending staples back with his thumb, he removed a photo Wendy had taken of them on the porch of the beach house. His hair was a mess from the wind and the sea. Hers was caught up in a breeze. Her green eyes held a glint of the water. He notched his nail, then ruined it altogether. He replaced the snapshot with a note he'd written.

His bag already strapped over one shoulder, he had one last thing to do: call. If she answered, he'd unpack his bag, lie down on their bed, and read a book until she came home.

He knew, as he dialed her office number, that he was loading the deck—where else would she be? It was too early for lunch—

"Modern Associates, can I help you?"

"Extension 47, please."

"Certainly, sir."

He felt his heart rattle inside his chest, like something a

shaman shakes to drive away an unhealthy silence. Each time the line rang, he anticipated her voice, felt easier that he could just put his bag down, put his things away—

"Ms. Madrepearla is away from her desk. Would you like to leave a message?"

He was so surprised the voice wasn't Shawna's he almost forgot to answer. "No. Thank you. I'll try again later."

When he left, he knew better than to look back.

Once he was outside, he kept himself in motion. Stopping would give him an excuse to think. If he started thinking, his limbs would stiffen, the iron in his blood would solidify, and there he'd be: human to the eye, as inanimate as a table to curious fingers.

If only she'd been at her desk.

Port Authority was a squat cathedral of reddish girders and glass, of rushing people and raggedy, evil-smelling men putting out their hands for money. As the wind shifted, rain danced on the windows.

He got in line to buy a bus ticket to western New Jersey.

"They're sayin' on the radio it's gonna rain for two days straight ..."

The man in front of him was old, had to lean on the ticket counter to hold himself up.

"I heard they might close the tunnels because of flooding."

Logan watched the old timer shuffle off, his head down as he counted his change, a peacock feather in his fedora like another shiny eye keeping watch for him.

Ticket in hand, Logan's stomach insisted he was making a

mistake. Still, he took an escalator up, found the bus already running in a cavernous garage. As he boarded, trying not to breathe in the diesel stink, he was more certain of his mistake.

Why hadn't she been at her desk when he'd called?

As the bus pulled out of the gloomy cement belly of Port Authority, the drumming rain made him feel like he was inside a rattle while the little beads were on the outside.

They rounded a sharp curve, and he could see the twin mouths of the Lincoln Tunnel. Another two days of rain would flood them. He imagined being washed away and later identified as an artifact that had mysteriously drifted a couple thousand miles east of a mesa top.

When the tiled tube ended in a huge puddle, which the tires churned into spray, it was hard to convince himself he hadn't emerged into another world entirely: Manhattan was gone. Gray sky spilled over him as if it had leaked out of a cracked egg big enough to hold a solar system.

He looked back at the tunnel, a receding black hole. To his right was an empire of glass-faced towers, the tops of the tallest obliterated by a sky that had lowered itself, its edges ragged with clouds dragging rain-swollen bellies. Impressive. Even if it were to collapse in the next second.

A couple of miles down the highway, he saw New Jersey's Meadowlands—a plain of tall reeds—through the rain-dappled window. (On another plain, soldiers dug a mass grave to bury the frozen dead.) He listened to the drone of the bus's engine, the wet sound of its tires over the road. He saw dull steel tracks cutting through the sun-burnt reeds, careening bravely toward the bend of the Earth. And he remembered how beautiful Shawna was.

"Hey, I'm home."

But he wasn't. *Still.* She didn't have to poke her head in every room; she recognized the empty feel of the apartment. She sighed, checked the machine for calls. The red light wasn't blinking. She went into the bedroom and saw an envelope with her name on it pinned to the corkboard. She yanked the envelope and the tack flew off, landing softly somewhere in the carpeting behind her. She knew what she was holding even before she dug a fingernail into the flap and tore it open.

She read it three times before the tears came.

To make herself believe what she'd read, she slid open the closet door. A fist tightened around her stomach when she saw the space his bag used to take up.

No matter what his letter said, she knew he wasn't coming back. He was running away, the way he did every time she wanted him to stay. The way he had all his life.

"I'm not chasing you!" She wanted the echo to carry out of the apartment. She wanted him to hear it wherever he was. "I'm *not.*" She wrapped her arms around herself and began to cry.

She couldn't stand herself when she cried. She couldn't stand feeling like she was unravelling, but trying to stop made it come out in chokes and coughs.

"Dammit." She used her arms to straitjacket the sobs. "Dammit! Dammit!" When the tears slowed to a trickle, she tilted her head back and took deep breaths. The ceiling was a white blur.

Wiping at her eyes with the back of her hand, she went to

the bathroom. She kept one arm across her chest as if without something to dam up her insides she'd start leaking tears again.

She blew her nose and pulled a few more tissues from the box. Pressing with a finger, she wiped the bottom of her eyes then fixed her hair in the mirror. She spent the next five minutes relining her eyes and touching up her makeup.

She went to a window in the living room. It was pouring outside. Even though it was only September, the trees lining Riverside Drive were shedding in a fierce wind. A scattering of leaves blew down the sidewalk. They disappeared on the same gust that had swept him into her life—and out again.

She thought of Rockefeller Center lit up for Christmas and the smell of smoke from the vendor carts. Fresh tears ran down her cheeks because he wouldn't be here for any of it. Then she remembered that she was going to Phoenix and felt stupid.

Walking briskly through the living room, she went out the front door and slammed it. It wasn't to satisfy her anger so much as to close herself off from a life she was leaving behind.

Rain pelted Shawna's umbrella. Hardly anything in the Village looked any different. There were fewer people out than there should have been, but the young Asian standing in front of a wall of earrings, his arms folded across his chest, was the same one she'd come to know by sight. They never said hello to each other, but this time he had something curious in his half-awake eyes, as if he *knew*. It wasn't until he looked away that she realized she was staring.

What was it, she wondered, as she walked past densely packed, neatly arranged merchandise, that kept us reaching for a new pair of sunglasses or earrings that had been hung out as if to dry? What was it that kept us looking in shop windows and boarding planes for places with names like Istanbul, Corsica, and Damascus? Why do we keep going to art shows and museum exhibitions and gawking at painted canvases? Why do we come home with new prints or old photographs bleeding yellow? Why do we pick up something as trivial as a new shirt when we've already got a closet full of shirts? Probably for the same reason that we push on the doors of badly lit bars: we want to fall in love again.

At the bottom of the familiar little flight of stairs, she collapsed the umbrella. She stood there for a moment looking around for Pam and hoping at the same time she looked like everyone else, like a drink and a little idle chatter was all she had on her mind.

Pam came over, wiping her hands. "Uh-oh. *Somebody's* having a bad day."

Just the distraction of talking to Pam soothed the nausea sending twiny fingers into her insides. "He left a letter." She said it as if it were a fact easily detachable from her life.

"Oh he *didn't*."

She nodded.

"A fucking *Dear Jane* letter? Next time he orders a beer I'm going to piss into a mug."

Shawna coughed into a laugh.

"He'll be back. He's fuckin' crazy about you. You wanna know the truth? He's scared. He's 24, in love for the first time in his life, *and* living with her. He'll be back."

"Yeah?" Shawna felt a smile bend her lips.

"You should see him in this place. You know how many phone numbers he gets in his tip jar? You know where they all go? I find them on the floor when I'm sweeping up."

"Yeah, you told me."

"This one woman, this pure unadulterated slut? Kinda cute, heavy-duty pair of lungs—she kept trying to buy Logan a beer, and he kept telling her to put the money in his tip glass. Finally, she says, '*When* are you going to let me get you something from the bar?' And he says with this Kansas accent and a totally straight face, 'Huh-nay, when the Moon turns t'cow shee-it'."

The odd mix of emotions made Shawna cry through a smile. "Maybe you're right. I mean, he said he just needed some time to work a couple of things out. He wanted to be home, where he grew up. Like he's a goddamn salmon or something. But he said he'd come back."

"Told ya."

A wave of anger swept away her optimism. "Oh, and I'm supposed to wait around while he's out fucking around in the cornfields? He doesn't leave any phone number or address. He says he doesn't know how long he'll be gone—"

"Trust me, he can't live without you."

"Well, he better learn."

BOOK IV

TUWAQACHI

1. Sotuqnangu

The rain was beginning again, big drops that splattered hard against the windshield: plak! Plak-*plak*!

He slammed the door shut. The air in the cab was warm, smelled of oil and old leather. Maneuvering his bag onto the floor in front of the seat, he put a leg on either side of it.

"Got you just in time."

The rain was hitting the glass with such force it seemed they were under attack from the sky. So fast the wipers couldn't keep up.

Gears shifted and the rig jerked forward. The trucker took a thick-fingered hand off the steering wheel and offered it. "Burt Hauser."

"Billy John." Burt's hand was heavy, the grip friendly.

"Good to meetcha Billy John. Is that a first name or a first and a last rolled into one?"

"Rolled into one."

"Solid grip you got there."

"From swingin' a hammer, I guess."

"Carpenter?"

"Framer."

"Good trade. Sometimes I wish I'da picked one up. But here I am with 18 wheels under me an' a shitload a space in front." He shrugged. "Ain't a bad livin."

There was a loud crack followed by deep rumbling. The rain banging against the window washed down it in waves.

A spring in the seat had worked its way through the padding. Too many asses in the same place. He shifted his weight.

"Whooooo-eeeee!" Burt leaned forward because it was hard to see anymore. "Looks like this one's been brewin' for a while."

Billy John stared out his window. "Looks that way."

The rain had stopped, but the sky was still sheathed in clouds. Mist clung to the windshield before squeaking rubber wiped it away. The truck's headlights cut a hazy pyramid of light out of the waterlogged dark. He smelled grass and wet earth on the air rushing through the window. The land, wide and sprawling, hosted there an occasional farmhouse. Some squatted beside silos so big they looked like they might have intercontinental range.

The pelting that the sky had given the Earth had softened the land. The silence was deeper in these rain-washed spaces, reminded him of the stillness after a ceremony had ended and the fires burned low. The ground showed where feet had pounded it through the night, and in the quiet you knew—smoke lazily adrift, hardy bothering to rise—that nothing as solid as earth had been reshaped.

The truck's engine numbingly loud, the wind through the window a howl in his ears, he tried to place himself in the quiet of the fields they were passing.

"It gets to you after a while ... truckstop eatin', sittin' on your ass all day—packs it all right here." Burt slapped his gut. "But it ain't a bad livin'."

Smiling and age had creased Burt's squarish face, lines that deepened or flattened depending on the expression that went with what he was saying.

"Tell you what else—I seen this whole country from one end

to the other. I ain't driving a Mercedes, but them people don't get too far. They turn off a couple exits down the highway." He brushed back bristly brown hair with a hand, every hair snapping right back up as soon as his palm had passed. "Drivin' a rig all day's got its drawbacks, but what the hell?"

"What the hell?" It fit like a cap on a bottle, and he went back to studying the lay of the darkness on the land.

Burt kept his eye on the road, his hands on the wheel. Because tons of truck were guided by the little hub, by the little man holding on to it. And Burt didn't even have to think about it anymore; he knew it all by instinct. He shifted gears while he had a hot cup of coffee on his mind, trusted to side-view mirrors to see what was behind him.

"You get to live on this stuff." Burt blew on steam rising out of the Styrofoam cup in his hand. "Gets into your blood."

Burt had offered to buy him a cup, but he'd shaken his head. Something else was keeping him awake.

Not even the caffeine got Burt through the whole night. He pulled over to a rest stop, apologizing about the room in the cab, but Billy John said he wasn't tired anyway and got out. His boots came down on the tar hard enough to shoot a fuzzy pain up the bones of his legs. His legs were stiff, and his ass was sore where that spring had been pressing.

A diesel haze surrounded the truck. It was lined up with a bunch of other rigs, their engines running. He couldn't abide the stink.

Taking long strides, his boots made the sound they always did on hard surfaces.

Then he didn't hear them anymore. He looked down and saw the scuffed toes darkening as they swished through wet grass.

A field spread out before him like the first darkness. Only the silence then had been unbroken, perfectly symmetrical, like motionless waters without an island or so much as the distant shadowy suggestion of land to ruffle their glimmery surface.

In perfect silence a breath is a symphony.

In perfect stillness there is no time.

And no direction. there's something ... terrifying. to listen to the silence and be the only listener. to be a thought moving upon the stillness, the one thing in motion though there is no motion.

The thousands of buzzing, whirring insects infesting the night made the difference. As if their gathered hum were incubating the world.

On a night like this, he'd heard it glide across the skin of the darkness. A hum leading to a song that had begun in the canyon in his grandfather's chest. He hadn't seen him, but it had to have been *Qua'ah*, perched on a bit of stone wall under open sky. Up on the mesa. A song he sang quietly, just above hearing.

He stayed awake, listening. Though he understood none of the words, something inside him quivered at the same low pitch.

Far away and faint, he heard the deep rumble of thunder.

In a roadside field of corn, wearing a traveler's shabby clothes and a scarecrow's hat, a hitchhiker whose face was etched with intricate tattoos.

A shiver ran through his body.

In his dream the mouth of the hitchhiker had never opened, but in it was a syllable. That would break the symmetry like a new day.

(His grandfather, his father, his uncle were all dead. He was a son, a grandson, a nephew far from them all.)

He hadn't seen *Qua'ah* before they buried him, but he

imagined him asleep, his face peaceful. The evenly spread calm of a lake. He hadn't cried. He believed in the stillness that had overtaken his grandfather, believed in the finish of the marathon his grandfather's life had been. Over parched terrain that loved to prick or bite, loved to sting your eyes with wind-whipped grit, caked on your scalp so that scratching at a fresh idea your fingernails had to dig around in dirt. He'd earned that rest, which would outdistance the last clock built to tick off eternity.

The ceremonies had been *Qua'ah's* axis, his heart, the star in him. Donning the kilt, the sash, the spruce ruff, the mask, pouring himself into a body made of drumbeat and rattle and dance step and the eager belief of mesmerized children. Dancing kept the Earth properly balanced, brought on rain, quickened crops. The dances what they needed in New York, their masks reserved not for peering into another realm, the way a diver does, but for delivering a sales pitch, for a board meeting, for a sit-down with the boss.

He'd never been initiated in the kiva. Never participated in a dance or worn a katsina mask. He'd seen a handful of ceremonies in different parts of the country, only one or two on the mesa. Sitting on his grandfather's lap, on a rooftop near the plaza, the Sun just breaking the faint curve of the horizon. The dancers rose with it, emerged from below the mesa chanting in a language he'd never been initiated into either.

Burt had taken to the name Billy John easily enough, but it hadn't fooled the hitchhiker. The grinning shadow standing on the edge of this field.

They'd banned alcohol on the reservations, but it was a joke because everybody just drove off the rez to drink or brought it back with them. You could see in their eyes they didn't believe in anything anymore. Not all of them but too many. The same look he'd seen in the eyes of a Vietnam vet. *I will fight no more forever.*

The insects went on singing their nightchant.

If only the Mayflower had sunk. Or the Indians hadn't been so trusting.

On the outskirts of the field, the hitcher—his clothes rain-faded, his hat wind-blown—was pointing. Up. His gray face cuneiformed with tattoos. The hitcher wanted him to look up.

A rider as red as the dawnsun. nightblack slashes across a face that has never smiled. his mount the color of deepening evening, shocks of white in the flying mane, flecks of albino across a chest made of muscular dusk. silent as a running cloud he shakes his lightning lance rides like the incendiary edge of a swelling star. the circle of his shield circumscribes unnamed constellations. his mouth opens to shiver sky. His eye—it has no pupil—is split by jagged light.

The grass soaked through his dungarees, left wet spots on his ass. Trying to follow horse and rider, he'd fallen over. The hairs on the back of his neck were still raised, the veins in his hands swollen as if he'd just played music for a host of katsinas.

Some don't see and still they believe. Some see and still they don't believe.

The stars had dissolved nearly to the last although the sun was not yet up.

What had he heard?

He kicked dew off the grass as he shooshed through it, the fronts of his boots soaked now.

(The rider had used darkness for war paint.)

He was going back to Kansas. But it was a drier, hotter place he'd been born in. The ancestral home of the Anasazi. Great-great-grandparents of the Hopi. Their history written in petroglyphs, cliff dwellings, pottery. Riddles now. Horned beings and floating shapes so unearthly rampant imaginations had posited space travelers as an explanation. Space travelers maybe, but no space you could aim a telescope at, and no fusion-powered engine had brought them here.

None of this would matter if there'd been no Emergence.

He looked up from the ground (tar-covered again), tried to pick out Burt's truck. Yes, that one, a pale yellow nearly white, a tear-shaped splotch of bird shit on a fender—a little blessing they'd picked up along the way.

Qua'ah had tried to tell him. About the Emergence. Some of the words were new and strange, so he kept them by their sounds, like exotic birds in cages.

"This isn't the first world with people in it," *Qua'ah* said. "It won't be the last. But it'll be here a long time after we're gone."

The first world had been *Tokpela*, Endless Space.

But before that, there had been only the Creator, Tawa. With no cosmic scrap heap to crib shapes from, no flotsam of exploded suns or nebulae ghostly with starlight shining through to steal from, the Infinite brought forth from Himself.

He came up with a nephew first, Sotuqnangu, His contractor. A rolled-up copy of the blueprints for Endless Space tucked under an arm, He was to lay out the universes in the order conceived by his Uncle.

(He too was an instrument, a flute with a katsina's breath flowing over him, music coming out of the hollow part of him.)

Sotuqnangu got contracted to put together this world and a bunch of others besides, not just a condominium complex. So it shouldn't be surprising that he wasn't too keen on going it alone, any more than Tawa had been, and created Kokyangwuti, Spider Woman. Who, upon waking, asked the inevitable question: *Why am I here?*

Being in the presence of a supernatural, she got an answer. "Well, look around you." Sotoqnangu waved a hand. "We got this Earth solid enough to stand on. We got directions laid out, but isn't a thing moving far as the eye can see."

She caught on quick, having a woman's instinct to create. She gathered up earth, mixed it with her saliva, and molded the mud into two shapes. Covered the shapes with a veil woven of her woman's wisdom (on what loom he'd have liked to know) and sang the Song of Creation over them.

In the beginning was song. A grand, quivering flaw that had unperfected the silence, had been incubated for an eternity in a darkness that was scheduled to suffer one blight after another—stars, fires, candles, kerosene lamps, incandescent bulbs, fluorescent tubes, neon signs.

When Spider Woman uncovered the War Twins, she told them their names: Poquanghoya and Polangawhoya. She sent them off in different directions to travel the world and call out so Earth wouldn't revert to mush, so mountains would vibrate with solidity when someone yodeled across their peaks, so even caverns deep underground would resonate like kettle drums being thumped. Even now, when you strain your voice and hear it come back to you, that's Poquanghoya or Polangawhoya answering. To them the universe is an instrument to be played, an array of vast depths to be sounded, and all sound carries back to the Creator, who set this world spinning marvelously on its axis.

And those who'd seen Creation on its first wobbly legs, what must they think now? Of the cities swelling like tumors and spreading like plague, of the thundering machinery stripping the Earth, spewing it back out in sterile black heaps beside deep gouges waiting to be filled by rain?

He looked into the sky. The Sun still hadn't risen.

It was a time like this, an incipient moment, when Spider Woman gathered earth of four colors—white, yellow, red and black—and made mud with her spit. The light in the sky grew as her tireless hands squeezed and pressed and patted the mud into four new beings. This was the time of the dark-purple light, a dawndusk when luminescence was evenly balanced against darkness.

These first four beings were men, who would soon enough get around to hacking at each other for territory, fighting amongst themselves over food, would most likely kill themselves off if left on their own. The next four were women, each a different color.

But it wasn't until the time of the yellow light, when the Sun had risen above the horizon, that the soft spot on their heads hardened, and they stood, finally, in the time of the red light, fully formed. Without being told, on plain instinct, they knew their father was the light in the sky that warmed them, their mother the Earth they walked and slept on.

One who had a flare for flashy entrances, Sotuqnangu appeared amidst a rushing wind as if a visiting god were a rising storm. He stood before the first People and told them the world was theirs (how generous gods are), that though it was no plaything, it'd been made for them (maybe this was just a pitch and they'd been made for *it*), and all that was asked of them was that they respect Tokpela as if they'd created it themselves, that they honor and respect its Creator, that they walk a path that would keep them in harmony with the infinitely intricate, ultimately impenetrable plan of the Creator. For although they might not always see it, His hand was at work even in the fall of a sparrow. Bestowing a different language on the People of each color, Sotuqnangu sent the four tribes wandering, each in a different direction.

He too had wandered off but without finding any particular direction or color that suited him. (He rubbed his eyes because when he hadn't been looking, the Sun had finally risen.) Hopi Red, Chinese Yellow, German White (what difference if he was Korean Yellow and Norwegian White?), he was made of rainbow mud rather than carefully segregated earth.

He'd tried to keep it open, his *kopavi*, the skull's unglassed skylight, which let the soul climb aboard at the time of the yellow light, let dreams lodge for the night, let the spirit guide come by with his medicine bundle and tinker when it knew you weren't doing what was right and proper (maybe too adjust the gaps between neurons, a mechanic spacing spark plugs). If you put your fingers to it, the *kopavi* felt closed. Until death, anyway, when it let the soul go like a weighty sigh. It was one of the five centers Tawa had put there to help people navigate the world (He was right in figuring they'd need at least that many).

Things beyond hearing echoed in each center.

He'd tried to use the open door to find his way but doubted the confusion he'd made of his life could be any worse, and now all he had left was a homing instinct. He felt this in the fourth center, which beat regardless of what the rest of him was up to. Sleeping, it beat. Eating, it beat. Running from or running to, it beat (faster). And it reminded him when the second center, the overrated one between his ears, was more confused than usual.

Looking skyward, he squinted and turned away.

Burt, he guessed, was still hibernating. If he wanted to wake him up, he could use the third center, the one in his throat, shout in his ear. No doubt the Twins would be amused. They were particularly fond of this center, the one he needed to be a singer, the one he used to tell Shawna he loved her.

He was surprised the fourth one—and the third for that matter—hadn't been paralyzed by his stupidity. He should've been dizzy, wobbly on his feet after leaving her. Most likely the centers had told him one thing, and he was doing another. He'd gotten mixed up about what was coming from where.

Once upon a time people had been able to see without prisms. Attuned, they had known how to use their centers.

Listen, there is more.

His name was not Billy John. He started walking toward a low brick building.

The first humans did not endure forever. Tokpela, the first world, was not eternal.

Listen.

He went into the men's room, pissed in a tiled trough. It would find its way back to him, maybe rain on him some summer day when he was too lazy to duck into the house.

On his way out he almost bumped into Burt.

"Hey there, Billy Buck." His voice was rough with sleep, his eyes bloodshot. "You been up all this time?"

He nodded.

"Shit, you look better'n I do."

He smiled.

"Well, soon as I take a leak an' throw some water on my face, we'll get rollin'."

He nodded as he angled past Burt.

The day had gotten bright, and he lifted a hand to shield his eyes. He would've looked the Sun in the face if he could, atone for his sins by having the bad in him burned away. He looked down at the tar. Something about it—the sun-grayed black, the vague creosote smell coming off it—brought him back to the Smiling Aztec, the way Trucker Tom's eyes bulged, seeing something Logan had never seen. Logan's one consolation that sharpened steel could harm only the body (though that was plenty for any court).

He climbed into the cab, slammed the door, that spring prodding his left butt cheek. He shifted over toward the steering wheel, got it to hit him just at the base of the spine, where the pressure was almost comforting. He tilted his head back and closed his eyes.

There is more, listen.

The driver's door opened and Burt got in. He was wearing a cap this morning, like the one that had gone flying when he'd snapped Tom's head back with a fist.

"Don't know how you do it." Burt started the rig, the engine rumbling into life before settling into a smoother rhythm. "I think that tank a yours runs on air and water."

The voice came from far away, somewhere behind clouds soaked red with dripping sunset.

"The body of a man is like the body of the world." *Qua'ah,* who'd lived on a mesa overlooking the distant past, understood these things. "Through each runs an axis." He ran two of his bony fingers up his grandson's backbone. "This is yours."

His grandfather told him again how the five centers vibrated and echoed when properly tuned. The fifth was the solar plexus, the true origin of a gut feeling. You get kicked there, it's like somebody pulled the breath out of your body, and it's not coming back. The pit of the stomach knew this or that, all right, but didn't say a whole lot unless you were paying attention. Squirming or knotted up, simmering in its own acid, it was a mute hunchback bell-ringer with no way to get things across to you but to bong furiously.

It was probably a day like this, sunny and near cloudless, that Sotuqnangu announced that He was going to put an end to Endless Space.

The people had lost the good sense their Creator had given them—hell, the way *Qua'ah* told it, their disrespect was so great, if they'd had spray cans back then, they'd have been doodling all over Creation.

Three more worlds followed. Each had its own direction, its own mineral, its own color, its own totemic animal. For Tokpela the direction might have been west (he sometimes mixed them up), the mineral gold. A bird fond of eating fat and a big-headed snake—he'd never known the English names and long ago forgotten the Hopi ones—were the mascots. And a plant, a little one with four leaves that grew near the mesa. The color, he thought, was yellow.

Everything had been hunky-dory at first (isn't it always?). The first People hadn't minded roaming the Earth bare-assed. Nobody got sick, nobody got so hard up he was ready to take on a goat. The ceremonies held in the plazas, in the kivas, were as faithful as the seasons.

Ever so slowly the people began to forget they were supposed be in harmony with Creation. They began to use their centers for earthly purposes. They got to mistaking lust for love, coveting the neighbor's pottery, his rugs, her husband. They got bogged down with grabbing things up.

Now any god with any gumption wouldn't let this go on forever, but Sotuqnangu was a bit harsher than some. He decided to destroy First World.

The obliteration of Tokpela was beyond contemplation even for a shaman, let alone a husband getting on with the business of planting beans or a wife grinding corn to make *piki* bread. But a dark figure sitting at the edge of a mesa, sprinkling corn meal whisked away by the wind, seemed caught up in just such a reverie. Chin tilted toward the late-evening sky, it was he, Logan. He didn't how it was possible to see himself from a distance and still be himself, half asleep in a rig hurtling down the highway, but that's how it was.

Retreating from the edge of the mesa, he felt an ache when he thought about his village. He knew he would have to leave it—the kiva where he'd been initiated into manhood, the land he'd helped farm, the broad plaza where the dances were held.

He'd had a dream that hadn't left him since he'd woken from it. The fear in the pit of his stomach was like none he'd ever felt before. When he spoke of his dream, he was told to clear his heart of bad feelings. No one wanted to hear of his vision of a red sun too swollen for the sky and a moon the color of fire even after it had lifted itself far above the horizon.

He became more afraid when he found someone who'd dreamed the same dream.

Having walked a good distance from his village, he stood with sweat making little trails in the dust on his skin. Many people had come. A few were from his village. All of them came without understanding why.

The Sun had gone down and the first star was a sparkle.

A gust of dry wind made him feel empty inside.

The wind grew stronger, and he had to shield his eyes from blowing sand. As suddenly as it had arisen, it died.

Standing in their midst was a being too perfect to be a man. He wore a white kilt trimmed in beige. Sage ringed his ankles. There was no sweat on his bare chest, and his skin was as clean as if he'd just bathed. The eyes behind his mask were as deep as the nighttime sky.

The people, he announced, had gotten too far away from their original purpose. Endless Space had become World Out Of Balance. It would be purged by fire. His words kicked up a breeze as he spoke.

He tried to imagine his village turned into a heap of black ash, and the lands he had farmed scorched away.

This must be what it means to be a god, to create and yet not be a part of Creation. Sotuqnangu hadn't farmed the Earth He was going to destroy. He hadn't laid a father to rest in the Earth. He didn't live in the villages He was going to burn.

"You will go to a certain place. Your *kopavi* will lead you. You will see a cloud, which you will follow by day, and a star, which you will follow by night. Take nothing with you. Leave tonight."

It was their first lesson in detachment.

He looked at the few stars glimmering overhead and wondered what held them in place. How many nights had he stared into the sky, which sometimes seemed to him a dark desert inhabited by glowing spirits, and thought it indestructible and always?

The god in his white kilt was gone.

He looked to the mesa in the distance where his village lay. It would be as if it had never been.

Walking alone into the evening, he heard the voices of children at play. *So they will die too?*

He stopped when he saw a white-haired woman. Her face was furrowed but not shriveled. Though there was a bright moon overhead, she cast no shadow. Robed in white, her eyes had the glitter of polished turquoise and the depth of canyons. They'd seen creatures raised up from the dust. They had seen silences populated and deserts brought to bloom.

Her eyes changed. Now they were like the mist that lies in a valley after a rainstorm.

They stood looking at each other across a distance. It may have been the distance that separates a man from a goddess or maybe between the living and the soon-to-die. She pulled the white garment higher on her shoulders. If he were to die on the spot, her spit could restore him to life. When she turned and walked away in silence, he didn't follow.

The next day many people walked with him, following a cloud that moved against the wind.

By night they trailed their star.

The Moon had become a floating lake reflecting a vast fire.

Cloud and star stayed ahead of them for four days and four nights.

When dawn broke on the fourth day, the clouds were as orange as flame. The Sun, angry and huge, threatened to swallow the sky.

His band joined with other bands. There were men, women, children, even infants. They were all going down into a great mound, the hill of the Ant People.

He looked on the red daylight a last time and was afraid of the Sun-Father who was so angry with his children.

Climbing down a ladder, he welcomed the darkness. But this was a place of endless night. Dreaming was no different from waking. He began to forget what life had been like before he'd come to the home of the Ant People. All life, he came to understand, began in darkness.

A time came at last when his limbs ached as if afflicted by the blunt pain brought on by winter's deepest cold, and his joints rubbed together like stones. Memories danced in his skull like katsinas in a great kiva. He saw a woman with silvery hair who was wrapped in a bit of cloud and evening light. He saw fields of corn being washed with rain like grateful children. He saw firelight on the faces of the men in his village and sparks drifting toward the sky like newborn stars. He remembered the Sun, red and terrifyingly huge. Blinded by the dark, he saw these things while he felt his way along narrow passages of cool earth and stone.

Something as fine as a spider's thread waved in front of him. He reached for it but missed. Now he was on a ladder, reaching for a silvery strand of hair floating lazily above him. The wetness on him was sweat.

He climbed.

He and hundreds of others, below and above him. With his hands on the ladder, he climbed toward the tiny hole of light.

A cool wind blew across his body, raised bumps on one of his arms. The sunlight made him blink and look away.

"You awake there, Billy John?"

He grunted, squinted in the brightness, and sat up straighter to get the sun out of his eyes.

"You about ready for somethin' to eat? I'm starved."

His stomach felt tight, unbearably empty. "Yeah." He nodded. "I am."

Eating was one of those things reserved for the living.

2. Call

At first she thought it was just her clothes. She'd pull on a pair of panties that were supposed to be pink, but they looked like they'd been pressed out of tarnished lead. Or there might be a T-shirt that hadn't come clean in the wash. When she held it to her nose, it would have a flowery fragrance, but its white would be dulled to a powdery gray. She put a dish in the rack to dry and listened to the faint tap of dripping water. When she'd bought these plates, their white centers had been rimmed by a pattern in brick red. Now the red had drained out, and the white had darkened to the hue of an old filing cabinet.

She really wouldn't mind if he strolled through the door right now. Not that he deserved her, but she'd be willing to give him another chance.

"At least call," she said aloud. "Just call if you can't turn around and come home."

She cocked her head. The phone? She shut off the water and listened. No, it was the phone in the apartment next door. Her shoulders relaxed.

He wasn't coming back. And somehow he'd managed to drag color with him.

It was all gone now, faded to the same gray that got tapped into ashtrays. The gray of a foreign cab driver's teeth. The gray of a subway train. The hushed gray of secrecy in a doctor's office. The tedious gray of waiting.

She put a glass in the rack. The city was so filthy she couldn't see that it mattered. Even the sky looked like it had been exhaled from a car's tailpipe. The water was gray too. It was gray coming out of the tap. It was gray as it swirled into the drain.

Just call, would you? Call from the diner in Jersey where you stopped for a bowl of soup. Call me from the weedy gas station in the middle of Ohio. Call me from Jim Lee's front porch. Call, you selfish bastard. Just pick up the phone and dial.

One of the photos in the frame she'd hung was missing, and his I-love-you note filled the blank. The note wasn't composed of perspective or lighting. It had nothing to do with arrangements (unless you counted the arrangements of letters and words). So much depended on how one thing fit in with another—he must've felt it too—how two or three or four things on up to infinity fit in with everything else. How even a table in a café with a petite spoon and a coffee cup on it, an ashtray holding a few stubbed-out butts, a tiny pitcher for milk, could all seem as immovable and immutable and deliberate as a scaled-down Stonehenge.

Thoughts like this seemed ridiculous now—like combing your hair before getting it cut. She envisioned taking her pictures one by one, setting fire to the corners, and letting them shrivel and blacken as she dropped them out a window. From another window she'd watch them waltzing on the wind like the flaming remnants of color. She wouldn't mind doing that today.

The phone startled her. "Please, please, please ..." She walked so fast she bumped a doorway with her hip.

"Hello?" Her mouth had gone dry.

"Hi, it's me, Brian ..."

She fell three stories. "What is it?"

"Hey ... I just called to say hello."

She wondered whether the prick had somehow found out that Logan had walked out on her. "And?"

"Take it easy will you? All I want to do is talk. I called the office and you weren't there. I just wanted to know how you're doing."

He was probably glad Logan left. And now he wanted her to carry on as usual, go to the office like nothing had happened. "I'm fine. I just don't ... I don't feel like talking right now."

"Shawna—"

She hung up.

She unplugged the phone and walked to the bedroom with the same urgency with which she'd answered its ring. She glanced at one of the photos she'd hung up after their trip to the Hamptons. She'd left all the reminders of him right where they were. A few months from now she might toss them all into a shoe box and in a few years she might hold one as if it were a religious relic and rub it between her fingers to get a trace of how she'd once felt. Hiding everything wasn't even a half-assed solution—she thought of him wherever she went, whoever she was with, whatever she did.

3. CAYUGA STREET

"St. Louis, Billy John!"

Night had fallen and there it was, a city piled against the bank of a river. He watched the phalanx of skyscrapers and the illuminated steel arch pull up beside them then fall behind.

"We oughta make Kansas City before morning." Burt shifted gears and the rig jerked forward.

They'd lived on the Kansas side of Kansas City after Cal had moved them out of Arizona. Didn't last long, though, and they'd gone south, to Frontenac.

The desert had disappeared.

The city had disappeared.

One wall of his small room on Cayuga Street had been covered with stars, planets, comets, nebulae, distant moons, a neutron star burning the white of fired iron. A celestial oddity of such density a piece no bigger than an ice cube weighed as much as a mountain peaking in clouds. Denser still were black holes, whose gravity was so crushing light was drawn into the invisible gullet like anything else unlucky enough to be nearby. Lying on his stomach in bed, his desk lamp aimed at the pages of the book on his pillow, he'd read that if Earth were reduced to a black hole, it would be the size of a golf ball. All the meters and gauges in his head broke when he tried to imagine an invisible golf ball that weighed as much as a planet.

And just who the hell gives a shit? Cal answered half the questions you asked him that way.

The universe was expanding. *Space* was expanding.

Who really gives a god damn?

If you could travel at the speed of light you'd stop aging.

Cal turned the page of the newspaper. "You ain't gonna start payin' the bills around here 'cause you know so much, are you?" He shook his head without looking up.

"Gettin' chilly, ain't it?" Burt rolled up his window up some.

"Little bit."

Fall coming on.

"I tell ya, Billy John, I ain't what I used to be."

"Tired huh?"

"Hell yes. My eyes got more red lines than a road atlas. Couple more miles and I'm gonna stop for a large black."

"If I could drive a rig, I'd give you a breather."

"Oh that'd be the life, I tell ya. You drivin an' me drinkin' coffee." He gave his head a jerk to one side. "Whadid you say the name a that town is you're headed for?" Burt asked.

"Frontenac."

"Small town?"

"Yup."

Burt was from a small town himself, back in Ohio. He talked about people he'd known, people he'd met, people he'd heard about. He knew more about people, he said, than those guys who wrote books. Whatever kind of a rig they were driving, they didn't get around enough.

Logan wondered whether Burt knew that he'd be able to tee off with the Earth if it were a black hole.

There was another thing about black holes. Once inside the event horizon, the edge of the hole, nothing could escape. Just outside it, though, hovered light that could neither escape nor was drawn into the hole. Only light could come so close without actually being drawn in. Anything remotely as sluggish as ordinary matter (a man for example) would be pulled in at frightening speed. This was what had happened to him. He'd passed too close, been crushed down to the buzz of a wavelike particle, and drawn into her. All that was left, just outside the event horizon, was a ghost in the image of the light he'd once reflected.

4. Purdah

It would make more sense to call for an appointment, but she preferred the necessity of making the trip and constructing an appearance. Most of all of leaving the apartment. Staying at home, two days in a row, wasn't a long-term solution.

She dug through a drawer and pulled out a pair of graying jeans with a stain on the thigh that—thank God—actually looked yellowish.

She pinned up her hair, washed her face, and decided that she'd do without any makeup. If she could have made herself even less noticeable, if she could've covered herself in black and veiled her face like a Muslim in purdah, she would have. She put on a pair of sunglasses instead.

The subway station—floor, walls, bystanders—was gray, a *dark* gray thanks to her sunglasses. That's what the neon was for, to pretend there was something else. But underneath and in between was the same nondescript color, the background everything returned to. The train that showed up was covered with graffiti, which proved someone else was tired of the creepy sameness.

As she dropped onto a plastic seat, she thought of Brian and regretted having been so brusque yesterday. When she got home, she'd call and apologize. She sighed. That was just a stone thrown in the ocean of things she needed to do. She had to make *changes*. She got a hot flash thinking that she was wasting her life. She should've gotten out of her rut in New York and gone someplace else. She should be *doing* something else.

The heat inside the clacking train got worse because she couldn't start soon enough. The thick subway air, which was always hotter than the air above ground, made it hard to breathe. Beads of sweat formed on her chest and soaked into the neckline of her shirt.

Why had she waited so long? She'd been procrastinating and making excuses and fucking around, and now it was too late to change her life fast enough.

She stood up because she couldn't sit still anymore, but she couldn't hang onto the overhead strap without shifting weight anxiously from one foot to another.

A drop of sweat from under her arm trickled down her side.

Lurching forward, she clutched the strap more tightly as the train came to a squealing halt.

She plunged through the doors without checking the stop.

At the top of the cement stairs, a breeze cooled her. The buildings around her looked as if they'd been drawn in pencil then thickly shaded with the sides of the lead point.

A shoulder bumped hers surprisingly hard and she glanced back. She should have known: a loser with a bad haircut that made him look like some kind of imitation Indian.

Stopping in front of an office building, she caught her own dark reflection: She looked like a chrome shadow on the glass door. Tugging the handle, she watched the glossy image of herself slide past. She didn't want to be here again. She didn't want to admit she couldn't handle this on her own.

She got on the elevator and pushed a button. When the doors shuddered open, she stepped into a carpeted hallway and pushed on a door that rang an electronic bell as she opened it.

The receptionist was a round, fiftyish woman with a pleasant face. Shawna didn't recognize her.

"Can I help you?"

"I'd like to make an appointment to see Dr. Manolakos."

5. Jim Lee

The wooden floor against his back was uncomfortable, but it was the cold that woke him. With his body mostly shut down, a hooded sweatshirt wasn't enough. Reaching up for a windowsill, he pulled himself to his feet. Wood creaked. His fingertips came away black with grime. The floorboards were covered with plaster, broken glass, boxes, splintered wood, spilled papers, and a few one-of-a-kind items: a headless doll, a sneaker without a lace, a hand-held mirror jaggedly divided by a crack.

He picked up his bag, deeply dented where his head had rested, and crunched debris under his boots. Sunlight streamed through a miraculously intact window, illuminated dust motes milling around like aimless souls.

The pale light he moved through was the only thing besides his sweatshirt keeping off the cold.

He turned a rusty knob and pushed the door open. There hadn't been much point to closing it—most of the windows had no glass—except maybe to deter a curious coon or possum from sniffing at him while he slept.

The damp breath of the earth reeked of manure and freshly cut hay, familiar smells as comforting to him as his child's hand disappearing into his father's fist. Even when they'd first moved to Kansas, he'd never minded barn odors (the manure of an animal living off grass somehow cleaner than a meat-eater's).

Burt, headed farther west, had left him on a gravel shoulder outside Kansas City.

He stood facing north, the direction from which he'd come, and one of the two directions in which the road disappeared.

The light in Kansas was different, seemed to come from farther off than it did in Manhattan. The slant it came in on wasn't the same either. Blue sky surrounded a few billowy white islands. Which was it he wondered: the place that altered the light? his memories that altered the place? or the light that altered his mood?

Autumn was falling ever so slowly, a month-long evening.

He started walking, looking back at the house he'd just slept in, at its graying clapboard. The paint had been weathered away a long time ago, and weeds crept as high as the windows. They were all over the Midwest—hollow tombstones whistling the story, when the wind was right, of how the last grown child had come to close the door for the last time.

He imagined the smell of coffee coming out of one of those busted windows, imagined a kerosene lamp lit at night while he turned the pages of a book, the skin of his hands just like that clapboard—the natural oils weathered away while scraping snow off windows, burned away by the summer sun—the hands themselves hanging bitterly on to some sense of purpose all year round. Would the old memories stop by to visit? Would they get a groan out of the floorboards as though someone were shifting weight from one foot to another? Maybe show up as an unexpected wavering in the lamp flame?

How long would he be able to stay he wondered. Would it happen on some mellow evening, with his back against a peeling wall, the insects a soft ruffling in the dusk, and thousands of dry words held in his idle hands? Would the glaring red of the sheriff's car bring him to his feet to hear the sermon of how he couldn't stay there? *No, nobody's usin' the place, but that don't make it legal.*

It wasn't the sheriff giving him the boot now but a pull as unfathomable as what dragged a baby out at the end of nine months. The fields on either side of the road opened like the sea beyond a strait.

He put his thumb out and caught a couple of rides that only got him 10 or 15 miles. Finally, he hopped in a pickup driven by a guy—"Name's Lester"—headed all the way to Joplin, Missouri. Logan pushed aside some empty bottles and dropped his bag on a greasy rag.

Although clean clothes didn't seem to be high on Lester's list of priorities, he was friendly enough, apologized for the mess, and threw a wrapper of some kind behind his seat. If you emptied his pockets you'd probably find nothing but a tobacco pouch, rolling papers, a driver's license, and a few dollars.

"You from around here?"

Logan nodded. "Frontenac." It surprised him how good it felt to be able to say that. How good it felt that it wouldn't be a foreign word to Lester.

"You all had a good football team when I was in school. I come from Arma myself."

An old rivalry. So there was some football talk though Logan had never played high school ball. They moved on to a news item that came up on the radio, Lester shaking his head as he lamented the loss of the space shuttle and its astronauts. "They still ain't figured out what blew it up. Somethin' about O rings is all they come up with."

Maybe a chance collision with a tossed-overboard angel. Maybe with a katsina on a detour from the mesa.

The ride was over sooner than Logan expected, and Lester pulled off to the side of Highway 69. Jim Lee's house was set back about a half mile. Before he got out, Lester shook hands with him as if they were old friends. "Glad t'be of help." His smile showed teeth brown around the edges.

After the sound of Lester's truck had faded, Logan could hear a dog barking. Maybe to buoy up the Sun, keep darkness at bay.

The grass covering Jim Lee's fields waved. Just below the roots, generations lay piled on top of one another. No fluted columns, no kingly monoliths, no grand temples, just bones and a few arrowheads. Just beneath the waving grass.

A few horses were penned up near the barn: a muddy palomino, a paint, and a gray Quarter Horse that looked to be the best of the bunch.

His boots crunched gravel. A barking dog came out to meet him. Looking vicious but backing up with every step, it abandoned the bluff and ran off.

Skirting the huge front porch held up by squared-off columns, Logan made his way around to the side. He saluted a steer skull that stared blankly at passing ankles (the Loop Lounge in New Jersey came briefly to mind). When he opened the door—it was never locked—another dog came out barking.

The screen door hissed to a close as if calling attention to the end of a season.

The floor creaked as he picked his way among the clutter: Indian pottery, kerosene lamps, Mexican blankets, riding tack, antique glassware, German beer steins. It was a marvel that what Jim Lee collected hadn't been buried under some collapsed barn or broken up and put into a potbelly stove. *Ain't worth nothin' to nobody, but it's priceless to me.* Only a few oddballs like him would want an old Sears catalogue, a weather-faded Coca-Cola sign, a miniature table with a round top and three bowed legs. He sold, traded, and bought, but there never seemed to be any more or less of it. Visitors would prod Jimmy to at least sweep up once in a while. *Would if I could find the floor.*

Out of the corner of his eye, Logan saw wind broom leaves off the side porch and set them dancing in the air. The movement was silent behind closed windows. Why didn't Jimmy open them? Maybe he wanted to be sealed off, like an ant gone into a deep chamber, abolishing time, waiting out whatever the world was going to inflict on itself.

There was something almost miraculous in being in the old farmhouse kitchen, in knowing that he'd aimed from better than a thousand miles away and managed not to miss. Although there had been the fear that he'd find only a foundation, the rest carried off by some natural disaster. Or worse, he might've found the place empty, abandoned like a roofless shed in the fields. The fact the farmhouse and its contents, give or take the odd item or two, were as he remembered them reinforced the unexamined belief that the farmhouse stood somewhere outside the laws that governed the rest of the universe and that, while galaxies pushed farther out toward the edges of existence and ancient cities eroded into mounds of earth, Jim Lee's place would go on creaking and rusting and leaning without ever falling into ruin.

Logan stopped in the doorway between the kitchen and the living room. Sitting in a reclining chair, wearing Ben Franklin half-rims, Jim didn't bother to look up from his book. "Don't you know any better'n to knock when you enter a man's humble abode?"

"I oughta knock it *over*. With a dozer."

Jimmy sat up straight, snapping the chair closed. "Well I'll be slapped naked." He dropped the book on a table. "If it ain't the ghost a Christmas past."

6. Grace

Aristotle checked his watch and looked up. A page of newspaper flapped past his feet. Guardrailed by the curb, it looked like a blind thing finding its way down Columbus Avenue. The breeze pushing the old news along carried with it a thick summery bouquet that was an amalgam of the season's own rampant scent, the upscale cooking of nearby restaurants and, underneath, a trace of uncollected trash.

He still hadn't quite gotten over the surprise of finding Shawna in the waiting room of his office. Although she'd shown up in old jeans and hadn't been wearing any makeup, an interest he hadn't realized was there had flared. It'd been a couple of years since they'd last seen each other, and he didn't recall having had anything more than a few wistful thoughts about her. They'd passed without inspiring so much as a phone call.

Instead of an office visit, Shawna had suggested a therapeutic dinner. "No business," she'd said, "this is strictly personal."

Of course, the personal *was* his business.

They'd begun seeing each other when, a few months after she'd wrapped up her therapy, they'd bumped into each other at an Upper West Side New Year's Eve party. "This is it," he'd told her, "you won't be able to resume therapy with me again." It wasn't a legal boundary; it was his own.

"I don't think I'll be needing therapy anymore." Her accompanying smile had been uniquely debilitating.

He wasn't sure why it hadn't worked out, but if nothing else, he was interested in where her life had gone since they'd lost contact.

A cab pulled over to the curb. He was almost surprised to see it slow to a stop in front of the restaurant. He'd temporarily forgotten what he was doing at summer's end standing on the sidewalk in a silk suit, traffic whizzing past him as if he were a statue of the explorer after whom the avenue had been named.

He opened the door for her as decorum demanded, but after she stepped out, he almost failed to push it closed. Her hair fell loosely about her shoulders, and the fluttery gown she wore, as light as the overripe breeze, was a yellow so pale it could have passed for a shade of white. Her eyes weren't shadowed but dusted to a buttery iridescence. With her angular face deeply tanned, she couldn't have been more startling if she'd been wearing a dress made not out of sequins, but from their twinkling reflections.

He cleared his throat and managed a compliment about the subtlety of her outfit's palette.

"Well thank you, doctor, you're not looking so bad yourself. But there's something ... your hair. I really like what you did with your hair."

He'd left the curls on top but had smoothed back the sides with a gel that gave his hair the consistency of a credit card.

"It makes you look five years younger."

"I knew there was a reason you used to be my favorite patient."

"Because I butter you up?"

"It helps."

He opened the door and followed her in.

"*Kalispera*, Dr. Manolakos." The maitre d' had a thick black mustache and one of those faces that always needed a shave. "This way."

The ceiling was two stories above the floor, and fluted pilasters ran up the walls to meet it.

Wearing a black tuxedo with a satiny yellow cummerbund, the maitre d' led them up a stairway to the second floor where tables were lined up along a wrought-iron railing. He stopped beside a table as if he were a guard at Buckingham Palace who'd been recently re-assigned.

After the maitre d' had pulled Shawna's chair out for her, Aristotle nodded and he quietly withdrew.

"You're not afraid of being stereotyped?"

Aris shrugged with his face. "Can I help it if I happen to *like* Greek food?"

A bus boy carried a basket of bread and a pitcher of water to their table. In a mild panic he filled her glass too quickly, and the ice hit with loud clunks. He walked off in a hurry, his feet padded by the carpeting.

"Look what you did to the poor boy."

"He'll get over it."

Shawna pointed at what looked like huge fragments of ancient wall that had been imported and hung around the restaurant. "They're so pretty." Each piece held part of a fresco, one of which depicted elegant blue monkeys in a rocky landscape that sprouted reeds and long-stemmed flowers. The flat perspective reminded her of Gauguin. "The originals were dug up in Crete, weren't they?"

Aristotle nodded. "Crete and Thera."

An ice cube knocked against her front teeth as she took a sip of water. She ran her tongue over the cold spot. "So, um …" She looked the table over. "Where's the menu?"

Aristotle was busy unfolding a napkin as heavy as sail canvas. "No menu."

A waiter arrived at their table pushing a silver cart filled with plates.

"Ah," she said, "a la carte."

"Whatever you like, just pick." The waiter opened his hands and spread his arms as if introducing a magical act.

"Oh, let me see ... what's this, moussaka? I'll have that. A salad ... aaand ... the stuffed grape leaves."

Aris saw strands of freshwater pearls wound around her wrist when she pointed. Matching clusters dangled from her ears. "*Dolmades*. That's what we call stuffed grape leaves."

"*Dole-MAH-dase*," she repeated in a mocking tone.

The waiter transferred the cold dishes to the table.

Aristotle took a salad and ordered grilled sea bream.

The waiter dressed their salads using bottles of vinegar and olive oil that had been standing at attention in the center of the table. As one waiter trundled off with the cart, another brought a bottle of wine. He opened it and offered the cork to Aristotle. Aristotle poured just enough into her glass to line the bottom.

Shawna drank it without holding the glass up to the light or fussing with the bouquet. "Wonderful."

The waiter nodded and said something to Aristotle in Greek. The single word she got out of it, repeated several times, was *Americanos*. "What was that all about?" Her voice was edged by mild irritation.

"He wanted to know whether you're Greek. American I told him. Not 'American American,' he said. No, I said, Italian American although I know that's not exactly accurate. He couldn't claim you for the Greeks, but he's happy knowing you're Mediterranean."

She took what had bordered on rudeness as a compliment.

"So tell me about your life these days."

"Well, I'm still with Modern Associates, still single. I had a boyfriend for a while, very sweet but not really my type. I met someone else. By accident really, but ..." Her face crumpled.

"What happened?"

Her fork hung in the air. The lettuce on its tines was ragged and gray. "He left."

Aristotle's jaw tightened. "And you're still in love with him."

She nodded. "Of course."

He smiled to reassure her. "What are the chances of getting back together?"

The feta was a sodden lump in her mouth. "He *really* left. He's probably a thousand miles from here now."

Logan had come from a long way off, someplace she'd never been, and now he'd gone back—not to Kansas or Arizona, not to a city or a town, but someplace she'd never been able picture. He'd somehow taken the distances he'd traveled inside himself, used them to keep himself separate from her, and now he was lost in them. He lived in the cavernous place she'd sometimes seen behind his stare. His eyes told you that, no matter how you tried, you couldn't keep him here, *you* weren't enough. You were a temp, a fill-in. He knew he was asking too much, and that's why he'd learned to look through you—he was still looking for what you couldn't give him.

Maybe this was what made him an obsession: the constant challenge to be enough for him, to satisfy the demands he made on her, to make him trust her. And for a while, he had, curling himself up beside her like an exhausted little boy. For a while.

"I'm sorry," Shawna apologized. "I've been staring at my plate."

"Take your time."

"Right, well ..."

"How did you meet him?"

"He was staying with a friend." She decided to skip the part about blowing him off at a nightclub. "I should've known it wouldn't work. He was kind of a drifter, never in one place too long. And a musician. Bad combination."

Aristotle swirled wine in his glass. "A musician?"

She nodded."He was different—a little weird maybe. Okay, a lot weird sometimes. But I never met anyone I could talk to like him. Except you."

"I feel complimented somehow."

She picked up his tone: soft sarcasm mixed with a need for reassurance. "You should. Anyway, here's a guy who's got a great mind, he's fun to be with, he's a talented musician, and we get along great. Most of the time. Spaces out once in a while, but so what?"

"What do you mean, spaces out?"

"I mean one morning he asks me if he went out for a walk in the middle of the night. I was asleep, how was I supposed to know?"

Aristotle nodded. *The odds,* he thought, *have to be astronomical* ...

"Yes, I know I can live without him. I just can't go back to way things were before I met him."

Aristotle looked up. "You mean you won't."

"I mean I *can't*."

"Why not?"

"Because I don't see things the way I used to. I mean, Brian? The other guy I went out with? He was Mr. Mainstream. I was becoming *Mrs.* Mainstream. I got so settled in my job, I barely noticed it had stopped being interesting *two years* ago. I hardly ever thought of getting rid of it. I just accepted it the way you accept Monday mornings—you get up because the weekend is over, and it's time to go to work. You *expect* to be at work Monday morning. You *expect* not to like your job. And you settle in to your expectations after a while, and you don't want them disturbed because that's what your life is made of now."

Despite the fact that Aris seemed curiously half-attentive, as if he were listening to a conversation at another table while trying to follow what she was saying, she gathered momentum.

"That's what it is, Aris, you get distracted. You become a stranger to yourself because you're busy trying to fit into this city—you need to be *this* size or *that* shape—until you come home one night and you realize you let things get away from you. And then you *want* to be distracted, you *want* to go to happy hour and talk about meaningless things and eat dinner out all the time. You don't want to deal with that sense of loss." She put down her fork. "Is that all you can do? Nod?"

"Sorry, I'm still in listening mode."

"Well do you see what I'm trying to say?"

"It seems clear enough."

"Well that's it. My life has fallen thirty stories and it's all over the sidewalk. I mean he left me with a job I don't like, a city I don't want to live in, and an insecurity complex that could be fatal."

"Have you—you didn't start burning yourself again, did you?"

She held her arm out. A spot a little smaller than a dime had been paled with makeup. "Just once. Don't worry. I'm over it."

The waiter appeared with their entrees, placed them on the table, and exited gracefully.

The smell of grilled fish rose like steam, but he ignored his plate. "Okay, so let's put things back in perspective, insecurity complex first. You're still a young woman—what? Twenty-seven? Twenty-eight?"

She picked up her fork and stabbed at the moussaka. "Twenty-eight."

"You're exceptionally attractive, independent, and you have a talent for succeeding in whatever you put your mind to. You practically *forced* your way into the firm you work for and squeezed money out them for a degree. Let's face it, you're pretty irresistible when you want to be. Men consider themselves lucky to be able to sit across from you at dinner, myself included. What is there to be insecure about?"

"Looks are half my problem, Aris. Most men can't get past them. You can, you're a shrink. Logan could, he was different."

A strange buzzing began at the back of Aristotle's head; he raised his voice to be able to hear himself clearly. "I wasn't talking about your looks, but let's stay with that. You feel that because … because Logan got past your looks and didn't stick around there's something missing?"

"I guess that's part of it."

"Well, as your former shrink and as your friend, I can't believe he left you for some shortcoming on your part. If we talk about the relationship a little more, I'm sure we can figure out what the real problem was."

"Well, Logan—"

"What was his last name?"

"Why? Is that going to help you figure out the problem?"

"No." He cleared his throat. "Just curious."

"Blackfeather. He's half Hopi."

Aristotle drank some wine to slow his heart. "Tell me about your relationship with Logan."

As Shawna talked about the problems she and Logan had as a couple, Aristotle began to feel at ease again. Then she stopped in mid sentence.

"Do you *know* him?"

Realizing his hesitation had given Shawna her answer, he nodded.

"That's *bizarre*." She took a deep breath and shook her head. "It figures. A guy who can't remember what he does in the middle of the night is bound to have a shrink. But for God's sake, how could he afford *you*? And why did you sit here without saying a word? Unless he never mentioned me."

Aristotle was still trying to decide how much to tell her. "He never came to my office. I met him in a hospital. The end of January or so."

"He was *committed*?"

Aristotle nodded, wondering whether he wasn't intentionally telling Shawna something that would make her lose interest in Logan.

"Unbelievable. Mr. Right turns out to be a closet psycho."

"*Shawna ...*"

"*Please.*" She held her hand out like a stop sign and turned her face away from him. "This a lot to take in over dinner."

"If I recall correctly, one of your best friends was hospitalized for a while."

"Wendy, yes." She sighed. "It's not just that. It's the idea you *know* him—that *you* met him before I did."

"Well, I was his fourth shrink. No one up there made much progress with him. Wasn't I your second or third choice? As a therapist."

"Third. The first was an idiot and the second—never mind."

"So it's not so quite so coincidental. If you weren't both difficult in your own inimitable ways, I'd never have met either of you."

"I suppose."

Aristotle put his fork down, a chunk of sea bream impaled on it. "Legally, I'm on shaky ground here, but I'm going to talk about Logan in generalities and in more or less clinical terms. Nothing he confided, nothing specific about our sessions. I still may wind up stepping over a line here or there, but I think you're entitled to know certain things."

"I appreciate that."

"Right. So, as I was about to say, Logan retreats ... into silences, distances, books, music, himself. You ... you mark yourself up. Remember your punk phase? You shaved half your head and dyed the other half Crayola colors. You added five or six piercings. And, of course, the cigarette burns. You and Logan have sort of opposite ways of handling your discontent—he withdraws from the world; you spit in its face—or your own."

"I never thought of us that way, but I guess you're right."

He hadn't intended to push her back into thinking of herself and Logan as an *us*.

"So how crazy is he?"

"He didn't belong in the hospital. In fact, it made him worse."

"Then how did he end up there?"

"Well, he did have a kind of breakdown. *Epistemological trauma* is the textbook term."

"Can't wait to hear the translation."

Aristotle nodded. "Basically, something happens—an event that so completely undercuts what you thought to be true that you lose faith in yourself, in your ability to make decisions and relate to other people … ultimately, in your own sanity."

"Wow. What did *that*?"

"He left before we quite got there. In fact, I might've been able to get him released before he took off, but I wanted to … I guess I wanted to play Virgil, guide him through that last trip of his. Whatever he found out or *thought* he found out is related to the last time he experimented with mescaline."

"So he's not psychotic."

"Not at all. Although he was terrified that he might be. Aside from the epistemological trauma, which was a one-time thing, he makes unrealistically high demands on himself, and when he doesn't meet those demands, he experiences anxiety, sometimes panic attacks. In other words, somewhere out there is a perfect Logan, and the real one doesn't measure up. Of course, there *is* no perfect Logan. He just can't accept himself as he is."

"Basically, he's neurotic."

"Not pathologically."

She sipped her wine. "Okay but why can't he accept himself?"

"You know about his father?"

"He died when Logan was six."

Aristotle nodded. "He told you about his uncle?"

"Cal? Yeah."

"So, when it came time for Logan to choose a role model—obviously not Cal—he could have looked for someone who'd measure up to the idealized father. But instead of settling on a father figure to emulate, Logan set up an idealized self-image to which he's always trying to measure up."

"But he can't, and he takes it out on himself."

Aris nodded. "He also goes to great lengths to cover up perceived flaws or failures."

That's *why his album was an embarrassment*, she thought.

"But dissatisfied as he is with himself, he's even less tolerant of others and their shortcomings. He expects too much of himself, so he demands too much of the people around him."

"That's my guy."

"He tends to rebel against authority because he doesn't realize that, with his uncle out of the picture, his constraints are mostly self-imposed—he's projecting them onto the outside world. His life is ruled by *should*—he *should* do this, he *should* be that."

Logan had been acquitted of murder on a plea of self-defense, but Aris wondered which one he'd been defending—his actual self or the idealized one?

Shawna nodded. "So how about some doctorly advice?"

"Well, what would you do if Logan showed up asking for forgiveness tomorrow?"

"Have a nervous breakdown."

"Doesn't sound promising."

"Well, I'm not counting on his coming back. And if he does, right after my meltdown it's like, hey ..." She waved goodbye to an imaginary Logan. "Don't let the door hit your ass on the way out."

He hadn't expected her to be so definitive. "I guess that leaves you with a job you don't like and a city you don't want to live in."

"Well, I've been offered a transfer to Phoenix."

"You always had a thing for the Southwest, didn't you?"

Shawna nodded. "That's why I asked for it. But they pushed back the date, so now I'm not even sure they're going to let me go."

Phoenix was a long way off, but objectively—he was trying hard to be objective—it was probably best for her. Only now that her departure seemed imminent, he felt a keen sense of loss.

"You know, I knew I was in for trouble the night I met him. He just had a *way* about him."

Aristotle nodded. "I know what you mean. He's off-putting and somehow habit-forming at the same time."

"Yeah." She smiled as her gaze dropped. "Well." She smiled again but didn't waste this one on her plate. "I'm glad we talked. I feel better about things. Right now, anyway. I know I've got a sleepless night or two ahead of me, but at least I don't feel so desperate."

He gave her that fatherly smile of his. "Glad I could be of some use."

"Oh for Christ's sake, Aris, you make yourself sound like a can-opener."

He laughed.

"So what do you say after dinner you drive me home? I don't feel like being alone just yet."

"I guess this is my chance to prove I can do a couple of things a can-opener can't."

"Gentlemen's night: dollar well drinks, 75-cent drafts. What'll you have?"

"You have sweet vermouth?

"Actually, I think I do."

"How about a Manhattan, no cherry?"

"Ah, a man who likes to spend his money."

Although the apartment wasn't exactly the way he remembered it, it retained the ordered beauty of a Japanese flower arrangement. A pair of Navajo rugs brought Logan to mind. A Greek urn done in the Attica style rested atop a black pedestal. A plant with leaves like slender spear tips had been given equal billing on a tiny table, and the walls were a collage of framed prints and photographs.

"Chilled, no cubes." She handed him his drink. "So, Mr. Headshrinker, now that you've poked around in my more personal areas, tell me a thing or two about yours."

"Like what?"

"Like how come you never got married?"

"Just never felt that way about a woman."

"But you don't seem very concerned."

"If it happens, it happens. If not ..." He shrugged.

"It doesn't have anything to do with avoiding a commitment to something other than your work ... or maybe a certain unwillingness to open up?"

"I admit I like living my life the way I want to—I don't have to call a two-person conference every time I make a decision.

And it's not that I haven't met exceptional women—my hostess tonight for example—"

She frowned skeptically.

"It just never ended in marriage."

"I think you get off on being a savior."

"You mean with my patients? Yes, I suppose that's true." Shawna had a habit of saying things, without the least introduction, that left him unsure of how to answer. "My only saving grace, I guess, is that my omnipotence complex doesn't seem to do anybody any harm."

"Except you. No matter what you say, you're peak experience is lonely."

"I have my moments."

She sipped wine. "Ever use it against someone? Psychology?"

"How do you mean?"

"Were you ever vindictive about it? Crack someone open like a safe?" She lifted one bare shoulder as though too indolent to shrug with both.

He tipped back his glass, felt the bourbon warm his insides. "When I was younger, yes, I did something like that."

"Would it be a breach of ethics to tell me?"

Shaking his head, he swallowed another hot mouthful of whiskey. "Happened at a party. A hockey player in his twenties. He told me that psychology was a lot of bullshit, a 'pseudo-science' as he put it, full of 'pseudo-technical terms' so we shrinks could sound like we know what we're talking about."

"That must've got you going."

"He challenged me to change his behavior or tell him something about himself he didn't already know. So I sat there for about an hour drinking with him, listening to him talk about himself. He'd had kind of a rough childhood … a heavy-handed father, two older brothers who kicked him around a bit but from what I gathered, no extensive physical abuse.

"His big thing was hockey. He was a goalie—good enough to be in the minors with a shot at the pros. He kept saying, 'It's all I think about, stopping pucks.' One time he added, 'I love to protect the net.' The word *protect* made everything fall into place. 'The net,' I said, 'is *you*, the self that was vulnerable to two older brothers and a hot-tempered father. By protecting the net, you're being your own father, your own big brother—the ones who *should* have shielded *you*.'

"He just sat there and looked at me. The rest of the night we hardly said another word to each other. I think I ruined his love of the game. At least for a while." Aristotle shrugged. "At the time I didn't care. I just wanted to prove him wrong."

Shawna sat down next him on the couch. The hem of her dress pulled back over her knee as she crossed her legs.

He lifted his glass, but there was nothing in it but a dribble of liquor.

"Here …" She stood up and put her hand out. "Let me get you a refill."

"Make it straight bourbon this time …?" He took off his jacket and laid it over the back of the couch.

When she sat back down, she was closer than when she'd gotten up.

A song was just ending.

"Who are we listening to?" he asked.

"Grace."

He gave her a confused look.

"Grace *Jones*."

"Oh. I'm more used to seeing her than listening to her."

The next song coaxed Shawna off the couch. "*This* is why I bought the album." She started a slow dance on the Navajo rugs, her shoes off—he hadn't noticed when—and her arms crossed over her stomach. Making a serpentine motion with her body, she looked at him expectantly.

He stood up and pressed his palms against hers. A bent arm's distance away from her, he tried to follow her lead as she moved them around the living room—purposely bumping the coffee table with the back of a calf to move it closer to the couch—her feet sure and bare but for sheer nylon, while his were shoed and a bit awkward.

Grace and Shawna were both speaking in French, most of it lost on him because he was concentrating on keeping up with her.

She let go of his hands and stepped chest to chest with him.

A courting dance, he thought, that would end with the song because somehow propriety would take over without the music, and the moment would be lost.

He slid his hands down her back and pulled her closer. When he looked at her, she kissed him. A surge of blood ended in a rush in his head.

Her breath was hot and sweet with wine.

He brought both of his hands up along her sides feeling the hard bumps of ribs and then, softer, of breast. She adjusted her position to make it easier for him. The strap of her pale dress came away. His hand slipped between bra and skin. Her nipple was firm, and his balance came into question.

He broke off a kiss. "I ... uh ... I don't think this is a good idea."

"Who's talking ideas?"

"No, really."

She arched herself against him, ground her hips into his. "Really, Aris, sometimes I wonder whether you're human."

"Well it's not that I wouldn't love to, it's just … I think we'd be very uncomfortable in the morning. In fact, I happen to know that regret sets in way before then."

"You're not doing my ego any favors, you know."

"You're doing wonders for mine."

"So why don't you stay?" She hugged him closer.

"Well, uh, because it's not really me you want. I'm, uh, just standing in for Logan. It would be taking advantage of you at a very vulnerable time. If I stayed, it … wouldn't be fair to you."

"You know what I really hate?" She pushed herself gently away from him. "You're right."

It still stabbed a bit to hear it.

She pulled the strap back up over her shoulder.

A remarkable sadness in her face made him suddenly regret having denied her.

Leading him back to the couch, she kissed him lightly.

He picked up his jacket.

"Thanks for the evening. It did me a lot of good. It could have done me *more* good …" She looked at him with one eyebrow raised. "But thanks."

"Well, if you're not busy this weekend, why don't we meet up? I'll cook dinner if you promise to help me with the dishes."

"What a bargain." Her laugh was short. "But, yeah, okay, sounds like a plan."

The record player clicked off, calling an end to something and leaving behind a silence too large for the room.

He stood at the door, his jacket draped over an arm. "I'll call you tomorrow."

She opened the door for him. "You better get going. Leave me to my misery."

"I'll call."

Their kiss goodbye was more than friendly but less than passionate.

In Aristotle's absence, she felt Logan through the Navajo carpet he'd walked on barefoot. Instead of Grace Jones's liquid voice, she heard his windy one. She'd changed the sheets on her bed, washed the pillow covers, but she sometimes still caught his scent—or imagined she did. She was glad Aris had had some presence of mind. She took a deep breath and thought of Kansas, of the endless flatness where she imagined even the wind could get lost. As she unhooked a cluster of pearls from an ear, she wondered whether he was thinking of her.

7. The Mathematics Of Fishing

The bed was bouncing up and down, tilting him backwards and making it difficult for him to sit up or get his bearings. It stopped suddenly, leaving him disoriented. *Kansas doesn't have earthquakes …*

"Get up you heathen." Jim Lee, standing at the footboard, eased the bed down. "We're going fishin'." He gave a knobbed post a shove with his knee, a half-hearted effort to straighten the bed out.

"Fishing?" Logan peered out a window; the Sun was still a ways from coming up. "What the hell time is it?"

"'Bout five in the mornin', give 'r take an hour. Prime time for lunkers. An' I can't go it alone. I need a harpooneer, preferably a pagan like yourself. Otherwise I got no one to treat like an inferior. You comin' or what?"

Logan threw the sheet off, the skin of his bare legs quickly going bumpy in the cool air. "I guess *some*body's gotta change your diapers."

Jim Lee clumped out of the room, but his voice ricocheted up the stairs. "Had a dainty dinner last night outa pure consideration."

Sliding off the bed, Logan opened the window half way. The crickets got loud and cool air came in like a moist exhalation from the fields. The sky was deep blue, the clouds trails of ghostly vapor lying flat on the horizon. No place better than Kansas to spread your life out, take a good long look.

In New York you could have an empty apartment, but you had to step out into an overstocked city. Where you ran the risk of being buried by noise, grimed by the streets, bombarded by the overflow—T-shirts, stereos, records, tapes, books, cameras, incense, jewelry, sunglasses, leather vests, boots with wings on them, sneakers autographed by a machine. Sold in shops, department stores, boutiques, tables, or blankets on the sidewalk, out of vans, car trunks, bags held open like shabby little Santa Claus sacks.

Horns and police sirens wailing, jackhammers breaking up the streets, motorcycles rattling windows as they passed, car stereos concussive with thumping bass, diesel-powered machines digging up sewer pipes—the shimmery cacophony kept up until you vomited gold necklaces, platinum chains, quartz watches, and your voice came out of a tinny speaker (you had to turn a knob to adjust the volume of your own words).

He pulled on the jeans he'd worn yesterday. Tight as bow strings, his legs were shot through with the sweet ache of overworked muscles. Yesterday he'd taken Raincloud, the gray Quarter Horse, out for a ride.

He grabbed a shirt and dropped down stairs that whined at different pitches like an out-of-tune instrument.

The stove was covered with cast iron pans. The yellow of eggs Jim Lee had failed to gouge out stuck to the bottom of one; a dark mirror of grease stood in another. Jim had piled the scrambled eggs on a plate, fried some sausage and a mound of home fries, toasted bread. Buttoning his shirt, Logan ignored the puppy attacking his ankle.

"I can tell by the look on your face— 'bout the same one Joan of Arc pulled before somebody lit the match—that you're as excited as I am."

Logan yawned.

"Haddaya like that little feller?" Jimmy lifted his chin in the puppy's direction.

"What's 'is name?" Logan was looking at Jimmy while his hand toyed with the dog, cupping his head, squeezing lightly, feeling his puppy skull underneath the fur, then letting go.

"Broonzy."

"Why? Does he sing blues?"

"Only when I don't feed 'im."

"Teach 'im anything yet?"

"Yeah. He's learnin' to latch on to door-to-door salesmen. Jumps up on a leg before they even knock. Makes it kinda hard for them to pitch the Encyclopedia Britannica."

Jimmy's wavy hair was as intractable as ever. No gray among the black, but there were dark rings under his eyes. While his paunch had shrunk, so had his arms.

Broonzy ran to Jimmy when he heard the pellets rain against his plastic bowl. He was so eager to get at the food, Jim hit his nose with a stream of milk. Broonzy flinched and sneezed.

Logan sat down to breakfast.

Ignoring a full plate, Jimmy was still talking, trying to warm him up to the prospect of the trip. Cranked up, Logan decided, probably been up all night. He'd stay up two days in a row then sleep 18 or 20 hours. His record was something like 78 hours straight. He might've made it to 79 except that, driving back from town, he'd seen a lobster the size of a freight car cross the road and decided it was time for bed.

This morning Logan planned to live the way Jim Lee did, treat his body like a furnace that'd burn anything, belch out black smoke if he happened to down some old tires. To celebrate the decision, he poured sausage grease from a pan onto his toast.

He filled a cup with coffee and soaked the dryness out of a corn muffin. The yellowy clouds of egg were oily with butter, salty with cheese, spicy with sausage.

"Who took an' Innernational Harvester combine to yer head, anyway?" Jimmy scowled. "Can't get used to that haircut." He stabbed at a mound of eggs with his fork.

"It's growing out now." Logan lifted his chin. "What's that pad in your shirt pocket for?" He'd already cleared half his plate.

"I'm writin' a book."

Logan took a sip of coffee. "You?"

Jim Lee nodded. "The layman's guide to makin' it big in this land a endless opportunity."

"What's it called?"

"*When to Lead, When to Follow*." He swept a hand across the table. "And then in smaller, fancier type: *Who to Know, Who to Blow, and When to Swallow*."

"I see you've grown in sophistication and shrunk in manners."

"Used to have the moral fiber of a goat. Now I rank with, oh, a crawdad."

Logan pushed his plate away. He was so full he could feel the coffee—a creeping warmth—running down the sides of his stomach.

Jim Lee stood up. "All we gotta do now is drag the boat outa the garage." He crushed down his unruly hair with a fisherman's cap sewn with patches advertising various lures, reels and tackle shops. "Brings me luck."

"All bad."

Logan went out the screen door but stopped to lean over the porch railing. The Sun had come up, and the sky was clear. The air had the snap of good leather in it, turned his breath to fog.

Jimmy batted the screen door open and led the way to the chicken coop he'd converted to a garage. Logan caught the gleam of the '74 Cougar he'd bought for $500 a few years back.

"Still runs," Jimmy said.

They took an aluminum rowboat down from a wall, walked it over to The Hog, and slid it—scraping noisily—into the back of the truck.

Logan pushed a stack of UFO magazines toward the middle of the seat. Even through his jeans he could feel how cold the leather was.

Every time they hit a bump or a dip in the road, the boat rattled and scraped.

They turned onto an empty highway.

The solitude and sprawling fields greased Logan's gears, kept them from grinding.Cruising into Frontenac, Jimmy slowed the truck. After a few blocks of streets without sidewalks, he took it off the pavement. The Hog tipped side to side on the gullied road, the boat knocking against the bed. Weeds shooting up from the road's center bulge made it look like it had grown a Mohawk.

Just past the trees to his right, Logan could see ponds that had once been strip-mine pits.

"Led many a bigmouth by the lip through these waters," Jimmy muttered.

He stopped at one of the bigger ponds. The engine barely rattled to a stop before Jimmy was tapping out a line from a creased square of paper. He snorted it off his wrist. "Just a tad, m'lad."

"You're a bad habit, Jim." A hard one to kick as it happened.

Logan found a bandanna shoved into the crevice of Jim Lee's seat. Once white, time and sun had yellowed it. He tied it on. With the silver hoop in his ear, he probably looked like a Halloween pirate.

"As captain a the Peapod—this fully pond-worthy an' only just short a mediocre rowboat—I designate you first mate. Which means you don't have to take orders from nobody but me."

After they pulled the boat out of the truck, the aluminum scrape running a cold finger along Logan's spine, Jim Lee stood with his hands on his hips looking at the sky.

"Fishin' is a highly scientific, quasi-superstitious pursuit." He seemed to be addressing the tops of the trees, maybe the clouds. "Good catch depends on the position a the Sun, the barometric pressure, and the angle a my cap." Which he adjusted. He wet his finger and pretended to test the direction of the wind.

Logan kicked him lightly on the ass, leaving a dusty boot print on his denims. "Let's get this tub in the water."

They turned the boat over and settled it on the pond's surface. The bow floated—magically light—while the stern caught on rocks embedded in the mud. Jimmy got in first. Logan pushed the boat and jumped in behind him. Sinking the blade of an oar into the gravelly bottom, he pushed them away from shore.

"You unnerstand, of course, that as first mate you're entitled to row."

Logan set the oars in their pivots.

"Pull there, Mr. Blackfeather, *pull*."

"Shut up, Jimmy." Logan rowed hard and evenly. He let the boat glide to a stop in what he judged to be the middle of the L-shaped pond.

"Drop anchor, Mr. Blackfeather." Jim Lee lit a cigar and threw the match at the bottom of the boat as if he were casting out a rebel angel.

Trees were sparse, the land lacking the will to make a forest proper.

Jim Lee knotted and pierced a worm with a hook. He threw the line out, clicked the reel over and let it sit. "The lazy man's way to success." He leaned forward to get into the cooler, pulled out a beer. "Want one?"

"Too early."

Psss-sssst. Jim Lee twisted the cap off. He took a sip and got another line ready. "Keep me busy while the other one's doin' nothin'."

"You're a talent," Logan said. "Smokin' a cigar, drinkin' a beer, fishin' with two rods."

"Stick with me, pardner, an' you'll be wearin' diamonds big as horse turds."

Zzzzzzzzzzzzzzzzzz, plunk. The line went out.

Jimmy tugged on the visor of his cap. "Now the reason this fishin' thing works is 'cause fish have not yet produced a great mathematician. I can see by the look on your face—'bout the same one on Sir Isaac Newton when he was tryna figure out the laws runnin' the show—you expect an explanation. See this lure?" Jim Lee reached for it: a tuft of fur hiding the hook and a dangling oval of pale gold that spun in the water. "Doesn't look like an insect, doesn't look like another fish. Underwater, though, spinner is shiny, vibrates some, and the lure moves along at a lazy man's pace. Now, see, fish math goes like this ... movin' equals alive, *alive* plus *small* equals *edible.* Edible gets a hit. They forgot to add in the vast array a lures as variables to their equations, see? Soon as a catfish Pythagoras or a perch Descartes comes along, fishermen're done."

"You been up too long."

Exhaustion had left dark thumbprints under Jimmy's eyes, deepened lines to furrows. His face had the look of a tilting barn—a good rainstorm might finish the job. Times like this a smell came off him, something like leather soaked in horse sweat and left in the dark to grow a coat of smooth green (behaving like anything else cut away and dead).

"You ain't been sleepin' so well yourself, I noticed. The other morning you looked like something a wolf ate and shit over a cliff. That gal you left back in New York?"

Logan nodded. The spell cast by Jim Lee's banter and being home had worn off.

"Well why don'tcha giver her a call?"

"I will." He'd called last night, got her answering machine. At four in the morning, Eastern Standard Time. She hadn't spent the night at home.

A bend in one of Jimmy's rods got his attention. He gave the line a tug, reeled in a few clicks but put the rod down. He re-lit his cigar and settled back. Smoke curled hesitantly from his mouth as if terrified of spreading into nothingness. He had that deep-set stare going as though he had to look through murky water to see Logan, as if he were focused on something on the bottom of this strip pit.

"You're gettin' old, Jim Lee."

Jim Lee held out a hand, flexed his fingers. Logan was probably a distant voice to him, coming from the treetops maybe, nothing he had to answer directly. "Nah." He turned his fist over as if it were a chunk of coal given a different meaning each time light hit it at another angle.

He looked over at Logan, and Logan saw his best friend was back.

"Now it's true I ain't what I used to be. Not too very long ago, in my junior elder years, I could take on a bull barehanded."

"That a fact?"

"Blindfolded if need be."

Logan's rod tugged.

"Shoelaces tied together for good measure."

"I got a hit Jimmy."

Logan cast again, trying to land in the same spot. His rod bent then straightened.

Jim Lee shook his head. "Snagged the hook on the bottom."

The rod bent into a sharp arc, and Logan reeled in. He gave Jim Lee a satisfied smile, let out some drag so he wouldn't snap the line. Reeling in when the tension eased, he waited for the fish to tire. A patient angler, Jim Lee liked to remind him, could catch a 10-pound fish on two-pound test.

A tail flipped water a few yards from the boat.

"B'lieve I caught sight a the varmint," Jimmy said. "Wrinkled jaw an' a crooked brow on 'im."

There was a flash of white underbelly through the brown water. Logan let the fish take out more line.

Jim Lee picked up the net, leaned over the side of the boat. "Got about as much chance of gettin' away as the First National Bank had of gettin' a deposit from Pretty Boy Floyd."

The net dipped into the water, came up sagging and dripping, an elongated lump twisting in the mesh.

"It ain't the record-breaker I got on my wall, but it's a keeper."

Jim Lee unhooked the lure then slipped an angular steel loop—open like a safety pin—through the fish's mouth, closed it when it came out the gill. The chain sawed noisily along the aluminum side of the boat as it went overboard.

"I don't think I'm even gonna throw my line out again." Logan loosened his bandanna, retied it higher on his head.

Jim Lee took what was left of his cigar out of his mouth and spat into the water.

"Don't look now, but I think you got a nibble, Jim."

Jim Lee turned around in time to see his bobber go under.

"Yessir, Blackfeather, this is a big'un."

"Probably a turtle."

The line went slack when Jim Lee flicked his wrist to set the hook. "Damn." He took the line in, but there wasn't enough worm left to get stuck between his teeth. Jimmy pointed at himself. "About the same look on Nixon's face when the polls closed in 1960."

"The look you're gonna have all day."

"I'm just gettin' warmed up."

"You ain't even room temperature."

Smoke rings floated lazily up, some strange eddy of gravity holding them together until at last they wavered, shredded. Jim Lee was on his back, his jaw making timed mechanical movements, his mouth a tight circle as he puffed them out. The Sun was high now, its brightness bouncing off the water. Insects whirred lazily. A few birds chirped.

When Jim Lee threw out his line, the boat bobbed gently and settled again. Logan would've liked to learn the boat's trick of lying on the stillness, of drifting effortlessly. He'd come back to Kansas to toss a few things overboard, whittle his expectations down to something that fit comfortably in his hand. Scatter the shavings on the water, let his ambitions turn into tiny islands connected to nothing. Easing himself back into the rhythms here, he was learning to overhear idle-hour conversations in The Round Up, watch for the reddish brown caterpillars whose appearance foretold the coming of a cold spell, listen to Jimmy and Larry tell stories that'd been watered with nothing-better-to-do beers till they were greener and taller than they'd ever been.

Jimmy reeled in his line. The skewered worm, untouched by any fish, was pale, sodden, dead, Jim Lee its Pontius Pilate.

Toying with his balisong, Logan flipped the blade out between the handles and flicked it closed again. "Remember Bill Tarp, the guy who taught me how to use this?"

"I remember Tarp. Dangerous fucker. Moved up to Kansas City."

Logan held the knife up. "Used this in a fight once."

"Cut somebody?"

"Worse than that."

Jim Lee's face—all of it—seemed suddenly to give in to gravity. "You're shittin' me."

Logan shook his head. "Self defense, though."

"Jesus."

Like a magician practicing sleight of hand, Logan flicked the blade out again. "Spent some time in a hospital too. The kind for people whose elevator don't go to the top." He could see it was an effort for Jimmy to keep quiet. "Left without sayin' g'bye. The law might be lookin' for me."

"Well go on …" Jimmy gestured with a hand like a conductor instructing the brass section to drown out the rest of the orchestra. "Tell me the whole story."

Logan talked for a long time, flinging his line out every now and then. Just enough distraction to keep him focused. Jim Lee got a nibble or two, but he ignored them, shifting

uncomfortably from time to time and making the boat slide a little left or right.

When Logan had finished, Jimmy lifted his hat and wiped away sweat on his forehead. "Yeah, you've been through something." He settled the hat back on his head. "A lifetime or two in a year or two." He scanned the pond's shimmering surface. "You oughta call that shrink, straighten out that legal business."

"If he doesn't turn me in."

"No he won't neither. Besides, he don't know where you're calling from."

Why did it sound so easy when Jimmy said it?

"Another thing—when you were talkin' about that gal a yours, you had about the same look on your face as Dr. Zhivago when he rode off with the Red Army at bayonet point."

"I don't think he was ever in the Red Army."

"Never mind that. You oughta straighten things with her too."

Logan nodded.

"Truth be told, I been lookin' forward to seein' a little Blackfeather runnin' around the farm for some time now. I like the sound of Uncle Jimmy."

"Something wrong with your sperm count?"

"I'm allergic to diapers and bottles that don't say Budweiser on 'em."

"That allergy a yours wouldn't happen to have a twin brother named Lazy, would it?"

"Might could be some resemblance between the two."

They went home with two fish. Jim Lee's wasn't as big as Logan's, but it was good enough to grill.By the time they pulled into the long gravel drive, the Sun was flattening out in the west and the temperature had cooled. For a moment, they both stood beside the truck listening to the chorus of humming insects. Never stopped this time of year, night or day. You were always surrounded (all the ghosts crowding the planet, you were always surrounded anyway). The crickets, hoppers, cicadas, whatever other bugs buzzed or chirped, scraped wing to leg or vibrated feathery mouthparts letting you know they were there. As constant, as lasting, as the shivering of starlight.

8. Art Deco Angel

"So what's up with the hot doctor?" Pam dumped a shot of amaretto in her cappuccino.

The café they were in was a peninsula of sorts. Surrounded by the opacity of walls on three sides, they could watch the city glide by through the glass front. A soft drizzle slanted past a streetlamp and phosphorescent jellyfish seemed to undulate around the bulb. The interior of the café had been wallpapered with yellowed copies of *Le Figaro*.

Shawna shrugged. "I'm going to Nyackfor the weekend."

On her way here, near the corner of Thompson Street, she'd stopped to look in the window of a chess shop. One set arrayed Mayan deities, with their almond-shaped eyes and the fabulous headdresses, against one another. Another set consisted of tall, elegantly robed Chinese figures. There'd also been an Egyptian set with Osiris and Isis as the king and queen. She hardly ever played chess, but if she'd had the chiseled profiles of Nile gods at her fingertips, she was sure she would have found more time for it. The pieces were wood, malachite, marble, camel bone— even fossil and coral. There was a devoutness implied in the hand that had shaped the austere mouth of Osiris. There was a lifetime of patience suggested by the fine black line of mascara around the tiny god's eyes.

As she moved along the front window, she gradually became aware of how long the shop was. Then she saw that it wasn't just a shop, there were men—only men—playing one another at tables for two. There must've been a dozen games going at once. Some of the players moved with contemplative slowness while other pairs made frenzied strikes and exchanging two or three pieces in the space of a few seconds. Silent behind glass, they were also silent behind their eyes. No matter the fireworks going off in their heads or the grinding of their mental strategies, their faces were as impassive as Osiris's.

"This is … what? Like three weeks in a row you'll be seeing him?"

Shawna nodded a little absently, listening to the soothing voice of a French singer whose name she couldn't recall. Just the thought of music was enough to upset her. "I hate him." Pam didn't hear her. Shawna hated him so much she wished he were sitting next to her.

"He's the best-looking guy I ever saw you with."

"Looks were never my thing."

"Yeah, I know. But it's kind of a nice bonus, isn't it?"

"We can talk about anything—really, *anything*. Right now that's better for me than all the hot guys in New York rolled up into one big scorching ball."

"Yeah, okay."

Maybe, it occurred to Shawna, she needed something like those chess players she'd watched. If the walls of the shop had fallen away—rain beading on the boards and pieces, speckling their glasses, running down their faces—the sky wouldn't have gotten more than a glance before they went back to their strategically arranged little armies. Maybe those pieces weren't carved out of camel bone or wood or jade at all. Maybe if she picked one up, what was in her hand would weigh the same as distilled belief. They believed in that two-dimensional board as much as the rest of us believed in the contoured world at our feet.

"You know something else? I don't know about this transfer to Phoenix. Maybe I should stay. Maybe running away isn't the answer."

When she went grocery shopping, she still bought things she knew Logan liked as though she expected him to be back by the time she got home.

"Well, you know I'll support you either way, but, selfish bitch that I am, I'll support you more if you stay."

Shawna wondered whether his music had changed, whether she showed up in it. Had she slept beside him and made love to him and shared enough of herself with him to make him want to? Worse, what if she *had*? What if he could make that come through the electronic guts of her radio? What would she do then, with him as far away, as impossible to press up against as a foreign city?

Looking at Pam's expectant face, she raised her cappuccino but put it down without sipping. The white cup sat there, reflected in the glossy finish of the table. "Please Pam, could you order me a beer?"

"Sure, hon." Rather than flag down their waitress, she got up.

Shawna probably should've come out tonight wearing the darkest sunglasses she could find, a hat, and a heavy jacket. But it wouldn't have been enough. She'd still have had to confront waitresses and the looks of pedestrians. She'd still have had to deal with car horns and guys leaning out of their windows to yell that they were they were going to write her a ticket because she was a moving violation. And those were the creative ones.

Pam handed her a draught in a heavy glass mug.

Shawna took a sip and closed her eyes as the beer went from a cold fizz in her mouth to a mellow warmth in her stomach.

"This is better." She smiled at Pam. "This is nice."

Pam reached over and took one of Shawna's hands.

Shawna had begun to enjoy the soft melody and the French singer. Jill Caplan? This was all she wanted right now: to be next to someone who wouldn't make her do anything she didn't feel like doing. She just needed this for now. Tomorrow she'd start again.

Over Pam's shoulder she could see an art deco print of a woman traced out in glowing yellow. Composed of clean, simple lines, she was reclining: One hand propped up her head while the other held a fan. But there was no floor in the print, no walls, or any background. She floated in a rectangle of black.

Shawna thought she might enjoy that, looking down from a comfortable height and drawing respectful—above all, respectful—stares, without ever being approached. *There* was our angel, outlined in yellow, sent to comfort us. You dimly hoped she'd be fleshed out, that you'd bump into her at a party or in a café, but you didn't expect it. You just let this face, hauntingly beyond human, liven up your movements. Even if you prayed to your angel, you didn't expect a reply. Why should a vision of divinity bother with you? But there's no end to hoping.

Although Pam was still holding her hand, she wasn't looking at Shawna. "You're staring at that Asian guy, the one with long hair over by the window, aren't you?"

Pam smiled. "What else?"

"You're so bad."

"I know but it's not my fault. The doctor says I have a hormone imbalance."

Looking down, Shawna saw how pale Pam's freckled hands

were next to her own. "You're lucky Hank doesn't know you like I know you."

"Welllllll …" Pam idly rubbed Shawna's hands between her palms. "Hank's not going to have to put up with me for much longer."

"*Pam*! What are you saying?"

Pam shrugged. "Just look at us. I mean, sure, he's ten times better than most guys I meet, but I've been kidding myself about long term. We're *so* different—"

"Well, we all wondered what kept you two together."

"Exactly. We lead completely different lives, we don't like the same music, we don't like the same clothes, we have different friends—"

"If you had been faithful, you probably *wouldn't* have stayed together."

Pam twisted up her mouth and nodded. "I'm already seeing someone else."

"Who?"

"Logan's friend, the one we met at Bill Bailey's."

"Paul?"

"He makes me laugh. All the time. He likes to go out, he likes to dance—all of that."

Although Shawna could see how Paul and Pam were a better fit, she couldn't think of Hank and Pam separately. In her mind the two of them had merged into a single person.

She looked around the café, and just as her eyes settled on the man by the window with long black hair and an Asian face, he looked up. A little embarrassed, she dropped her gaze. *There's no end*, she thought, *no end to it at all.*

9. The Place Of Disappearance

The front porch faced west and took in Highway 69 maybe a half mile distant. No screening, it was open to the slightest stirring—a field mouse given away by a wobbly line of disturbed stalks, the ruffle of dragonfly wings, the occasional sigh let go by the fields.

Feet on the card table Jim Lee kept out there, Logan had a beer in one hand and a stubby cheroot in the other. Jim Lee's front porch was one of the few places where he could sit and watch the slow shifts in light, eavesdrop on the chirped prayers of insects (every now and then, they picked up the pace as if they'd gotten an answer), think hardly at all. Sure there was the aloofness of the mesas or the eroded beauty of Chaco Canyon, stretches of desert that could hold him in a fist of magnificent space, but none of them was home.

He felt a twitch in his stomach as he brought a match flame to the tip of the cigar. He'd looked for some fruit this morning, found nothing in the refrigerator drawers but some crumbly onion skins, stalks of withered celery, and a couple of wrinkled carrots. Unable to come up with something he wanted to eat, he wound up going all day without anything but a couple slices of toast.

Smoke bit his tongue as he inhaled. Tobacco was a cagey plant: you didn't need to pull the smoke into your lungs to feel it dissolving in your blood.

He tipped his head back and closed his eyes. Maybe he'd worked out the boat's trick of weightlessness, after all. Reason enough, all by itself, to come home.

Letting smoke go toward the sunset, he watched the breeze derail it, carry it south. The clouds were bright as fire just above the horizon but—slate-dark on top—looked too solid to be part of the sky.

He sipped his beer and tried to fill his chest with dusk. But something was different. Something had unsettled him.

"Jimmy?"

He turned when he heard the screen door open behind him.

His father was standing there.

Logan stared for a second but turned away before he could be convinced that the half-cocked smile, the feet spread in the stance of someone used carrying things pig-a-back, the hands tucked loosely in the pockets of his jeans, belonged to his father. Looking away, he squinted at the blush of life the sky had left.

He closed his eyes. When he opened them again, his father was still there, the face a lot like his own except that it was wider, creased at the corners of the eyes, a hardness etched into his mouth as if a chisel had been used to turn it down slightly at the corners.

"Well? Ain'tcha gonna ask me if I want a beer?"

Logan put his cigar in an ashtray of black Bakelite and stood up. His father moved away from the door to let him pass. Afraid to touch him, afraid he'd make his father waver like road heat and disappear, Logan didn't so much as brush against the T-shirt advertising Soapy Smith's Bar & Grill—the shirt he'd died in. While Logan hovered in the doorway, the screen door in his hand, it occurred to him that something about his father wasn't right.

"You're shorter than I am."

His father's grin broadened. "Hardly taller than Cal. How

'bout that beer?" His father pulled a chair up to the table, put his back to the sunset.

Logan left him with his big hands folded on the table like a well-mannered kid, made his way around Jim Lee's junk into the kitchen.

He reached into the refrigerator for two beers and let the door close on its own. Boots clumping against the wooden floor as he hurried back, he knocked over an empty hurricane lamp. *Probably gone by now.*

But he wasn't. He even had the thin line of a scar under his right eye from the time he'd gone hunting and the bow's string had snapped, whipping the bow against his face. He'd come back with stitches, a doll with a badly sewn seam. It had gone white, the spindle of a scar beneath an eye that belonged to a man who was at ease with himself, whose body took up a rhythm when he moved the way rain did when it fell.

"You're shorter than me?" As if this were as hard to take in as the resurrected dead.

His father nodded.

Logan watched him twist the cap off the beer bottle—quite a feat for a man who'd been dead for 18 years—his eye keen on the subtle interplay of bones beneath the skin, the vein that seemed to wiggle across the back of his hand. Everything his father did, every sound that came from him—his voice, the groan of the chair under his weight, the rustle of his clothing— was miraculous. Logan wanted to put his hand next to his father's mouth and feel the heat of his breath. He wanted to smell on it the last thing his father had eaten. Wanted to see his father swat a mosquito, see the bead of drawn blood and know that his father was still vulnerable to the thousand shocks flesh was heir to.

Feeling a little weak, he sat down.

"I stayed around for you, you know." His father's shoulders hunched forward a little the way Cal's had, crowding the bottle like a looming mountain.

"Buddy …?" Logan wasn't sure whether he was talking to himself or not. "Are you dead?"

His father nodded.

"Am I crazy?"

His father shook his head. "No more'n the rest of us."

"You been around the whole time?"

"Pretty much."

"Why didn't you come before?"

His father smiled. "I came. Lotsa times. Last time, you were livin' in New York, and you'd already forgotten by morning." The smile straightened out. "But this is the last."

Logan nodded. He was on the brink of something—not about to fall but about to become something else for which flight would be a genuine possibility.

His father took a long drink, the bottle looking small in his mason's hand. Logan was taller all right, but he'd never have hands that could palm a cinderblock, never have hands as heavy as that cinderblock, either.

"You look a lot like me," his father said. "Don't think like me, though. I'm not bad with numbers, but you got me in the smarts department for sure."

"What about …?" Logan started to ask the old question, a tumorous swelling that had grown heavier every year he'd lived without his father, but now that he had the chance, he couldn't voice it. All he could do was push it like a lump over the edge of his need to know. "Cal...?"

His father nodded. "I was drunk that night. I shoulda known

something was wrong. Cal never bought so many rounds, not since the day you were born. He just kept buying. When I'd had enough, I asked him if maybe it'd be better if he drove us home. 'You ain't that drunk,' he said. 'Besides, what kinda Indian can't outdrink a white man then outdrive him too?' I was never a big drinker and Cal knew it. Anyway, he just about pushed me out the door. Now, it was a fool thing to go drivin' around like that, but at two in the morning, who was gonna be on the road? Home wasn't that all far, Buddy. I just never figured on that kid runnin' the light. If I'da been sober, maybe I coulda braked in time."

"I knew it. I *knew* it."

"Don't be too hard on Cal. He wanted me outa the way, sure, but he didn't really think it would happen. I mean, without that kid to help things along, I coulda drove home like that a couple dozen times without dentin' a fender. Besides, you know how Cal ended up."

"Why did Mom have to take up with him?"

His father shrugged. "We were no Romeo and Juliet, you know. We got married 'cause you were on the way." His father tipped back his bottle and drank deeply.

Logan looked at the floorboards to see whether beer was spilling onto them, but they were as dry as before his father had sat down.

"Least I didn't run off on 'er."

The math was obvious enough, but it had never occurred to him that the best man at his parents' wedding had been a shotgun.

His father started to smile, an apology of sorts. For having conceived him through a slip-up, for not being able to help with his homework, for having died and left him alone with Cal. He looked over his son's shoulder, southward, as if something was headed their way from that direction. Then he fixed his eyes on Logan.

Logan looked away.

"Saw the moon eyes again, huh?"

Logan nodded. One had been full, the other a crescent.

"No sun eye where I am now. Nothin' here to see with it." His father was smiling at him.

"Is it cold, Buddy? Where you are now?"

His father turned the corners of his mouth down and shrugged. "Hard to say." Then he nodded. "Cold is a way of putting it. Don't know that I'll ever be warm again, but I'm ready to move on."

Logan nodded, hurt again where he thought he couldn't be.

Roughened by calluses, the hand that came across the table wasn't much kinder than a sidewalk is to a shoe. It could hold you up, the hand on Logan's wrist, the whole weight of you, as easily as come down on you and break bones. It was the first part Cal had never learned.

His father said something to him, but whatever it was, it was drowned out by a thought rushing through his mind like a gust kicking up before a twister: the hand was real and no one had the right to take it from him again.

His father seemed to read his thoughts: "Things can only be what they are and no different."

Logan nodded, a distant part of him locking this away, keeping it for a time when the rest of him would need it.

His father stood up, took a long swallow of beer, the sliding white foam visible through the clear glass. The heel of the bottle hit the table with a clunk. "You're what's left of me here." His finger tapped the table. "Remember that."

Logan stood up.

"G'bye, Logan."

His father put his hand out the way he might for any of the masons he'd worked with, the day done, the foundation laid, the week over. Logan was surprised to find his grip not so far behind his father's although Logan was squeezing for all he was worth. His father put his other hand on Logan's shoulder, put some firmness into it, and smiled. "Don't worry about me anymore, okay?"

Logan nodded.

He didn't realize he'd done it, didn't remember the quarter second or so it'd taken to let go, but he must have because his father was walking down the stairs. Logan saw that there were now four feathers, all of them white, tied to his wrist. And the black T-shirt, somehow or other, had gone white.

He watched his father head across Jim Lee's land toward the highway. It took a little while before his father crossed 69, used a wooden post to vault a barbed wire fence, and kept going. Logan could've sworn his jeans had been replaced by a white kilt. Didn't matter. His father was only visible from the waist up now, diminishing to a speck that, like distant thunder, couldn't be traced to its vanishing. After a few minutes, there was only darkening sky and tall grass swaying in the breeze.

Logan had seen the scar on the back of his father's neck where it'd been scraped by a cement block. A shallow wound but an ugly mark. His father had been walking the concrete floor of a foundation when it happened. A careless driver backed a truck into scaffolding, sending two or three blocks into the basement, one leaving a blemish even death hadn't managed to erase. An inch the other way and he might've died sooner. Logan's hand went to the back of his own neck, remembering the barn doorway that could've had him following his father and Cal both.

Staring at the empty fields, at a grassy spot he'd marked as his father's final place of disappearance, Logan wondered whether missing his father the way he did all those years had kept him rooted to a place worse than cold. The body gone—he didn't know where his father had borrowed the one he was walking around in—how could it have been cold he felt? It must have been like being born inside a lump of iron, metal the only touch you know, a silvery taste in your mouth, your spirit too weighed down to do much of anything, too uncomfortable to be at peace.

He was glad he wouldn't see his father again.

"I promise," he said to the place of disappearance.

He hadn't saved Linda. He hadn't stayed with Shawna. He'd all but abandoned his mother.

He said it again: "I promise."

Hardly aware of what his hands were up to, he lifted the beer bottle and took a long drink.

He wondered whether he could change his nature, shift his center of gravity just enough to bring himself to give up the idea of looking for the unbreakable in human beings, who were, after all, neither physical laws nor katsinas—dust collected on them, they sweated, they sometimes failed in what they'd set out to do. The people in his life, even his father, had all been allotted more time here than a desert bloom. You had to be thankful for that because who knew? Maybe, after they died, some of them would not return again, even as a ghost or a sprinkling of rain on the mesa.

10. Memory's Ghost

The evening air carried the smell of burning wood, reminded him of cold nights in northern Arizona. Probably a trashcan fire.

He was in New York City. Again.

Rain had fallen and the streets glistened. The city had refined fire to cool light—bright, colored, scripted. Mist scattered the illumination, obscured the tops of taller buildings (where once he'd seen them stomp and dance, flash like lightning at the dusty core of a desert storm).

Memory was a glow fading on the edge of the city.

His boots rapped at the sidewalk; there was no answer.

Unsure of his direction, he stopped, his hands trapped in the pockets of a leather trench coat.

The season made his breath visible.

He was on West Fourth in the West Village.

A black man walking toward him looked him up and down. "Sharp, man, sharp." He tugged at the lapels of his own coat, rolled his shoulders forward as he walked by.

Styles flickered and faded in the city like a firefly swarm on a warm Kansas night.

He turned his eye inward and saw himself coming up the steps of a basement bar with Shawna, walking city streets near dawn. Remembered never feeling alone, even when he was.

He should've gone straight to her apartment, but he was afraid she wasn't home. Or that she was but wasn't alone.

Before leaving Frontenac, he'd gotten in touch with his manager in L.A. Surprisingly, the news was good: LowKey records had picked up the rights to his album and rereleased it. Sales were almost respectable. The label's owner was throwing one of his penthouse parties, and Logan had been invited. Harvey told him he might as well go back to the hospital if he sat this one out.

Logan hadn't come half a continent for a party; he'd come for Shawna. He just had to wait one more night.

Three punks, two of them men, stood on the corner. Faces milky as if they lived on an island that was always cloudy. Brits maybe. Twenty-four dollars' worth of trinkets dangling from the woman, her bleached-white hair in a state of shock. Caked-on makeup to put back something that centuries of *pip pip cheerio* had washed out.

He stuck his hand in a pocket, felt a folded wad of bills. No rent to pay, no real expenses, he finally had a little spending money.

He kept walking.

A couple dragging each other by the waist sharpened an ache. He was so used to it now he didn't remember what it was like not to feel it.

One night she'd looked at the kitchen floor as if she'd caught sight of the underworld below the city. *We go from image to image*, she'd said (or something like that), *we keep looking for one to help us remember or orient us or*—something. An image of loss—flash-frozen light and shadow—a déjà vu that wouldn't flow away like another twilight.

The air was getting colder.

He saw the marble arch of the park. Like the humped back of something fossilized. The two Washingtons—one hatless, the other wearing a tricorner—flanked the opening. Eroding guardians, they could only watch, grieve for the 13-year-olds wearing too much eyeliner, already learning to turn the heat between a man's legs into money. For the bearded junkies who'd gone gray shivering under park benches. For the elderly man who—out walking his dog—had been beaten to death with a pipe for the five-dollar bill in his pocket.

It hadn't been the city's sooty breath that had left their marble faces rife with—deepening, blackening rifts—no, grief had left them longing to crumble away, to be swept up some Sunday morning by a coveralled groundskeeper.

A stiletto slipped into the hazy side of the night left it to the moon eye to stitch it closed.

One more day.

A burly man coming from the park walked toward him. Old jeans and sneakers, woolen cap and worn bomber jacket, a wire-bound notebook under an arm. Did Logan know him from somewhere? Had he seen before the grayish-white hair and matching beard? He looked at Logan briefly through rectangular glasses (wondering, maybe, whether he was worth a jot in his notebook, deciding, finally, no), turned, and walked past, a deep arch to his back as if there were a spear point dead center of it.

The night ran parallel to the sun eye's perception of it.

He began walking toward 23rd Street. It was still early.

He tried to call up a memory of Shawna, but all he saw was the blankness after a camera flash, a bright ghost that made him blink.

11. Baroquen Wings

The place was lit about as well as the far side of the Moon. What light there was, was mostly purplish, deep and soft. A dab of it came from a glow globe on a metal stem, a pearl enfolded by the bruise-tinted dusk. In spite of the marble floor, he felt like he was walking an ocean bottom. Where vision dissolved and the things around him gazed with eyes the size of manhole lids, were bloated, half-finished forms. That standing lamp might be a bit of bioluminescence dangled as a lure. To a mouth that opened like a tunnel.

"Take your coat, sir?" The butler showed up well because his tuxedo, his skin, were white. Eyebrows lifted expectantly, he leaned slightly toward Logan.

"Sure." Logan let the unbuttoned leather slide down his arms.

The butler—he'd never seen one before—disappeared with the trench coat draped over an arm.

Cavernous enough to be haunted by echoes, the penthouse looked to stretch over the entire top floor. The floor itself was covered by black tiles veined with white.

For a whole minute he stared. At the ceiling that converged on a dome supported by four marble columns that belonged in a cathedral. At the arcs of water flung from the brass fountain beneath the dome. At the oversized double doors that swung inward to let you pass. At the labyrinth of walls—partitions really—he couldn't decipher. A series of semi-rooms, they took up all four corners and three walls.

Against the fourth wall, behind him and to the right of the door he'd just come in, was a bar big enough to service a nightclub.

The eerie sounds drifting through the place, Logan realized, were whale songs overlaid with synthesizer music—a touch of the artificial (but familiar) superimposed on the voice of the alien (but natural). Sounding out the shape of the space they were in. He couldn't recall the name of the band. Sunk. Just beneath the waves of memory.

He moved to his left, closer to the long-stemmed glow globe. The "room" it was in had the cut-away feel of a set in a tv studio. It was about twice the size of Shawna's living room.

A penthouse mansion of many New York City apartments.

On a chest-high table of black glass—was it really a table? Most of its polished surface was at a steep angle, was mitigated only by what amounted to a shelf jutting out parallel to the floor. No straight edges but not evenly scalloped either, simply curves that avoided symmetry. On the shelf was a piece of sculpture that reminded him vaguely of a heart, complete with truncated arteries and veins. One of these tubes held a birch branch, glaringly white. There was also a sort of pouch in the shelf filled with water, on the surface of which floated a single leaf. The veins of the leaf inspired him to lift a hand and examine the back of it.

Beyond his hand was a painting, a globby abstraction as brightly colored as a kid's crayon drawing. The kind of thing that said less to him than a puddle of spilled milk.

On an opposite wall was a Picasso, a circular entanglement of human forms and visual puns (a foot was part of a head; a toenail doubled as an eye).

A tv set with an enormous screen presented a montage of movie scenes: the Motorcycle Boy using his namesake to break up a rumble; Chief Bromden's neck cording as he tears a water fountain up by its plumbing roots; a pair of hippies with their eyes hidden by modsunglasses crisscrossing the country on choppers; Citizen Kane shuffling in bathrobe and slippers through a palatial mansion empty except for statues, who stand like old friends betrayed by his Medusa touch; Dorothy fleeing a Kansas funnel cloud.

His host, Harvey had told him, was Erik van Loken. Standing on the threshold of the room he was in, Logan tried to pick him out, but no one looked like he owned the palace. *Place*, he corrected himself.

Drinks were held like Holy Grails. A sip followed a remark; a gap was filled by a long swallow. A woman gazed into her glass as if a pearl at the bottom shone through the dark wine.

Everything he came across in the first suite of semi-rooms was shiny plastic or gleaming metal. In one, a synthesizer sat on a spindly stand. There were a couple of vinyl blobs in case you wanted to sit, but nothing he'd call a couch.

"Quite a setup, huh?"

His graying hair perfectly groomed and the flesh around his eyes puckering, he was probably somewhere in his fifties.

"Mr. van Loken …?"

"Me? Oh no. No, no, no. Not that I would *mind*—the kind of money *he* has? It's no wonder everybody goes off to see him like he's the Wizard of Oz."

"Is he giving it away?" Logan asked.

"No, but … well, he does consulting—art as an investment, antiquities as a tax write-off, hedge funds to avoid, that sort of thing. But he's not just some financial hierophant. He owns things—LowKey Records, a couple of magazines—*New Psychologist* is his—and he writes art criticism, music criticism." He shrugged, lifting the shoulders of his elegant suit.

"What about you?" Logan asked.

"Me?" He leaned forward with a hand against the breast of his jacket.

Logan had meant to add *what do you do?*, but now he wanted to hear the answer to his misfire.

"I like a good party just like anyone else. And these are the best." He swung the flat of his hand through the air as though it were a blade. "Your first time?"

Logan nodded.

"Well, you'll see then." He held up a glass with nothing in it but ice cubes slicked with purple light. "Off for a refill."

As if in exchange—one leaving, one arriving—a white-gloved, tuxedoed butler held a silver tray out to Logan. Logan took a baked clam. The butler remained until he returned the tooth-scraped shell to the tray.

The whale voices had dropped out of the music, leaving only a synthesizer-sustained melody.

Logan circled back to the birch branch. Wasn't an object, any object—a leaf lending texture to water's placidity, a toy bank turning mechanical tricks, a bit of sculpture that could be a heart magically melted down and recast, a key pressed into the asphalt—a tiny moon? One face in the light, the other veiled in dark? The bright side you could see, finger, scent (if it rubbed off when your nose scratched), but the hidden half you could only intuit. A nebulous surfacing from somewhere below thought. Well, maybe he made up the last part.

Separated by a partition from the display of modernity was a completely different suite. In this one were a couch with curved legs and puffy cushions that looked like they might've been leavened with too much baking powder and recently pulled out of the oven; a drawered table—overwrought with polished brass—that served as a scenic overlook for a magnificent urn out of which sprouted a leafless tree branch; a chandelier suspended from a blocky beam, light from its cups of frosted glass so mellow it might have been produced by flames running low on gas.

Beside the urn was a white porcelain bowl rimmed in gold and filled with water that held the room's shallow light. A maple leaf stared up at him from the illuminated water like a green five-pointed face.

Most startling of all was a marble fireplace, glowing infernally. It belonged in a mansion of grand staircases and balustrades, French doors and latticed windows, a manor complete with cellar, attic, study, library, drawing room, alcoves, walk-in closets the size of East Village studio flats.

"Hors d'oeuvre, sir?"

This butler was in a silk vest that looked like it came from a costume ball, the kind of tie Logan thought might be called a cravat, a white shirt with cuff-linked sleeves. Logan took a slice of kielbasa.

On the mantle of the marble fireplace was a row of worn leather-bound books. Heat growing on his thighs as he drew nearer, he picked up a poetry collection and opened it to a page marked with a narrow strip of velvet.

Not till the fire is dying in the grate

Look we for any kinship with the stars

He re-shelved the slim volume. He thought (playfully): *It is a fire, after all, one wants to come home to. More efficacious than brandy, it's just the thing to take the stiffness out of one's joints and melt the chill lodged in the backbone. To dull the sharpness of winter's breath, dissipate the chill gloom of a sodden eve, brighten windows, which can be seen even at a goodly distance, and offer invite to the lodgeless passerby. If one seeks to make yet more comfortable one's high-backed and well-stuffed reading chair, a robust fire is unsurpassed.*

He wondered whether the marble framing the fire was genuine, decided you had to rap with your knuckles to know whether the guy throwing this party was a van Loken or a van Neer.

Logan wandered into the gravitational field of a painting: a woman on her back, mostly submerged but fully clothed, in sluggish water. The image was striking. For the eerie look on her pale face, as though she were entranced by a dream some magic let her peer into. For the superb rendering of the overgrown riverbank—each leaf, each flower, an accomplishment in itself. For the brushstroke, unlike van Gogh's or Cezanne's, as invisible as the Holy Ghost. For the flow of the golden red hair around her head and shoulders. For the dress, a murky cloud just beneath the surface of the water. Ophelia? He couldn't even guess at the artist.

And there … He recognized Monet's *Sunrise over the Thames*, which had gotten Monet laughed out of the Salon. The numbered Pollock of its day. The one before him now, the texture of the paint discernible, was not a print. A copy …?

Van Gogh's sunflowers, flawlessly forged as far as he could tell, were as astonishing as the lanky blooms themselves.

"Mr. Logan Blackfeather."

It was an observation, not a question.

He turned around.

Tall, studious-looking, horn-rimmed glasses, black. He wore a doubled-breasted jacket, padded at the shoulders, tapering at the waist. A toned-down zoot suit. Plum-colored.

"Tiby." He shook Logan's hand. "Your travel agent so to speak. Here to help with the itinerary. Although I see you started in room number one and moved on to two all by yourself."

"Van Loken sent you?"

Tiby lifted his chin slightly as if he were peering over a sentence taller than most. "He likes theme parties." He pushed the glass he was holding toward Logan's chest. "That's a happening jacket."

"Thanks." Black crinkle leather, lighter than it looked, more comfortable than Logan had guessed before trying it on. He took a drink to cool off. "He goes all out for these, huh?" Logan used his eyes to circumscribe the penthouse.

"Part of his psychology background, I think. A weird hobby almost."

"An *expensive* hobby."

Tiby shook his head. "He never loses money. After this, he'll rent the space out to some wanabe oligarch until all this …" He swept an arm in an arc. "Pays for itself.

The chandelier, hissing softly, wasn't throwing off enough light. Everything seemed suspended in the same embryonic state. Including Tiby, with his curls stiff with gel, his modern haircut, his outmoded hornrims.

"Psychology, huh?"

"Consciousness is a whole, Erik likes to say. Figure out the shape and you can make a key."

Key turned *whole* into *hole*.

Tiby gestured. "This way ..."

They went through a doorway.

Except for a bench, the piano was alone in the room. Sheet music open and waiting.

"Can we get a beer?"

"Bar's over here ..." Tiby took the lead.

No charge, of course, but the bartender wouldn't even take a tip. For once, he had the money.

As heavy as a stout and slightly sweet, the beer had a rich taste vaguely reminiscent of coffee. He savored another mouthful as smoke drifted lazily toward him from a censer of tarnished brass. Four smoldered on the bar. The domed lids had star-like perforations through which the spiced smoke seeped. A hot fragrance not unlike cedar singed the back of his nose.

Looking around, he tried to spot Harvey, who (allegedly) was flying in from LA. Instead, he saw, near the brass fountain, a six-man band of South American Indians wearing colorful serapes. Bolivian? Peruvian? They played Spanish-inflected music heavy on flutes and Pan Pipes. Listening to the windy harmonies, he could almost believe that their mountain home, their ruined city overlooking the curvature of the Earth, was the tip of heaven.

Near the brass fountain he thought he also saw—battered instrument cases at their feet—the two musicians who'd been following him since the days he'd played in Phoenix bars. Still wearing reflector sunglasses and their rusty Salvation Army suits. Couldn't tell what instruments they were toting around, but before the night finished its disappearing act, he was going to find out.

"Champagne, sir?"

Logan turned to the bartender. "From that?"

It looked as if it had been underwater since the Beginning. Crusted over with barnacles and whitish veins of something shell-like. As thoroughly and lumpishly covered as if the bottle had collected the drippings of a dozen tall candles.

Tiby lifted a glass. "Rumored to be from the S.S. Disaster."

Logan remembered the underwater cameras exploring the sunken hull (*hell?*), zooming in on a chandelier that could have hung in Poseidon's cavern. They were still talking about raising it. He wondered whether the carbonated wine really *was* an undersea relic, never mind the implied pedigree.

"To icebergs." Tiby looked toward the diminishing back of the bartender. "More proof that white is not to be trusted— especially in large concentrations."

Rims *ting-tinged* together.

The champagne was light, crisp.

Behind the bar was an ice sculpture, fresh and sparkly, just beginning to sweat. An owl with wings outstretched. Mist came off its glittering contours in slow swirls. Smoke floated across the graven image from a censer—what was left of the incinerated Second World, from which the owl had taken flight (or had that one been drowned by flood?). Once light enough to glide silently across the night's surface, the bird had been petrified into a purple-tinted fragment of cold chisel-work.

Logan cast a glance to his left. Beyond the bar and its glistening mascot, the double doors majestically unfolded. New guests were arriving in groups of three and four.

"See somebody you know?" Tiby asked.

"Maybe." He picked up his champagne. "Be back in a few."

As he walked, he glanced up at the dome—smooth as the inside of an eggshell—and looked for a hole. A tingling sensation rose along his neck toward his scalp.

"Hi." She smiled.

"Not yet." He hadn't seen her since the park. With Bruce.

"Cute." She leaned back to look him over. "Nice outfit. Told you you needed leather."

The tingling had become a numbness in his neck. "You know him too? Van Loken?"

Her skin, adjusting for the light, was a golden shade of brown. Her gown tarnished gold or burnt honey or something like that.

"I've done an interior or two for him."

"This place?" He remembered she had a psych degree.

"Suggestions really. Mostly his idea."

The band had gotten closer to the bar, a serenade that returned him to a mesa top.

"You wanna drink? On me."

"I can think of better things on you." She smiled.

"How you doin', doc?"

He looked vaguely familiar. "I'm sorry, have we—"

"We met at the launch for *New Psychologist*. I work with Mr. van Loken." Tiby clasped his hand warmly.

"Oh yes." *With* Mr. Van Loken, not *for* him.

A woman wagging a finger at him came between them. "You wrote that book about self-destructive personalities, right?" She was wearing a low-cut black dress, perhaps too low-cut. She held a wine glass out in front of her as if it were lighting her way.

"Pegged you, doc." Tiby grinned.

"I knew it." Her blond hair was short, and she had aqueous eyes of such a light green they looked yellow.

"You're … in psychology?"

She shook her head. "Genetics. Why do you look so surprised?"

"I guess I never pictured a scientist … in a dress like *that*."

"That's a stereotype, not an archetype."

His ears warmed along the tops.

Tiby introduced himself, put out a slender-fingered hand.

"Joyce."

"And you know Dr. Manolakos."

"Aris is fine."

"So which is it?" Tiby asked Joyce. "Nature or nurture?"

"Well it's both, isn't it?" She had a high-pitched voice.

Tiby mocked a frown. "Playin' it safe?"

Joyce shrugged. "Genes come with their limitations. I mean, if you're a painter, you can't get music out of the paint, especially after it's dried on the canvas. If you're a musician, you can't *visually* depict anything. The medium has inherent limits. So, you could look at genes as, say … clay. And the environment as the sculptor. There are certain things clay simply won't do. But there are numerous ways it can vary within its given set of restrictions."

Aristotle was thinking about his distant cousins, the guardians of the Hot Gates, who were among the earliest practitioners of genetic weeding: sickly newborns were left to die on a slope of Mount Taygetus. And then there was Plato's *Republic* and his myth of the metals: the gold men were paired with the gold women to keep it all pure. And, of course, the silver men were to reproduce with silver women, and so on. Like went with like, raising homophilia of a different sort to an ideal.

Joyce finished her wine and hooked Tiby's arm. "A room, a room, my research lab for a room in another era."

Aristotle followed, reprehensibly enough watching Joyce's muscular rump shift beneath her dress as she walked. The hot tingle of what might have been a controlled substance was spreading across the back of his head. Could the pH of his wine be somewhat acidic? No, Erik was a prankster, loved the unsanctioned experiment, but he wouldn't risk that kind of liability. It had to be something mild, something that would wear off relatively quickly.

The absurdly ornate furniture in the room Joyce tugged Tiby into was, he supposed, rococo. Inside were the kinds of gilt pieces you might see in the Rijksmuseum or the Palace of Versailles. Candelabra provided most of the light. There was a certain resemblance between the bowed leg of a buffet and a melting candle: the leg had been carved in a teardrop pattern that could've been inspired by dripping wax.

"Well look who's here. Logan, my man, I want you to meet—"

"Yeah, I know him." Logan's hand went out. "How are you, Aris?"

"It's good to see you again. *Really* good."

Aris seemed his usual, polite self, but Logan sensed a nervousness in his smile. "You're not going to rat me out, are you? For skipping out?"

Aris smiled as if he were a frat brother who had a copy of the math test Logan was studying for. Every time he moved, light rolled like mercury across the surface of his suit. The metallic sheen gave the look of ultralightweight armor, a stylish new fabrication, and Logan wondered whether there was a helmet to go with it.

"You thought they were looking for you?" Aris shook his head. "You passed—everything. After you took off, I just signed off on the paperwork. You shaved maybe a week off your official release. Maybe less. And probably gave yourself a few unnecessary nightmares."

So he hadn't needed to dodge cops, after all.

"You know I heard 'Wind Rock' on the radio? It's good. *Very* good."

The suite they were in, displaying an overflow of opulence, reminded Logan of an opera house. Aristocratic souls, he decided, would've withered on a mesa, would never have befriended an eagle or a cloud.

Hopi mesa, to Heaven up-piled
Of rude access, of prospect wild,
Where, tangled round the stony steep,
Strange shadows o'erbrow the canyons deep.

A niche in a wall had been given a gilded, overwrought frame featuring a carved cherub—hands pressed together—at the bottom. It held a Chinese vase, which in turn held a bare branch. On a lacquered table beneath the niche was a water-filled ivory bowl, a leaf floating in it. Elm?

A waiter appeared in an embroidered coat from whose sleeves protruded frilly white cuffs. His white wig ended in a tail tied with a bit of black ribbon. Knee-breeches and stockings completed his outfit. The tray he carried held an assortment of raw vegetables.

Logan pushed his glass toward a canvas. "Awful."

If the cherub carved into the niche degraded angels, the rosy-cheeked baby-faced heads with wispy suggestions of wings and vague hints at bodies melting into clouds suffused with lemony sun were outright humiliations. A family portrait of Mary, Joseph, and the baby Jesus, he guessed, barely worthy of a greeting card. Jesus as blond as a Viking, white as Santa's beard.

Aristotle lifted his glass as if he were toasting the artist. "Watteau, I think. *Flight into Egypt* or … *Flight of the Holy Family*. Something like that."

Logan put a hand on the slope between Aristotle's neck and his shoulder. "Let's walk."

On the polished tile, his boots and Aristotle's shoes made sounds nearly identical in timbre.

Logan craned his neck. "This place makes me feel like Marco Polo. I mean … a *fountain*?" Gathering the glint of sunken coins and the brass railing that ringed it. "Look at this … a Greek inscription. Can you read it?"

Aristotle frowned and put a knuckle in his dimpled chin (probably because he had no pencil).

Below the threshold of hearing, neurons whirred and clicked like the gearworks of a clock assembled from a swarm of microscopic parts.

"*I am a child of Earth and starry Heaven, but Heaven … but I am born of Heaven.* It's not modern Greek, but I think that's it. Here …" He moved along the railing. "There's more. Uh … *Quick, give me refreshing water to drink from the Lake of Memory.*"

"So you know this guy, van Loken?"

"I met him a couple of times—he owns one of the magazines I've published in—but no, not really."

Logan pulled a quarter out of his pocket, tossed it underhand. Gone with a *plink*. "My old man always told me never look right at the Sun."

In Teotihuacan, just outside Mexico City, the stairs of the Pyramid of the Moon were tall, encouraging you to approach obliquely the deity to which it was dedicated.

"Bad for your eyes," Aristotle agreed.

In the old days his Lakota cousins waited in a pit for four days. Nothing to eat, nothing to drink, no sleep. Until they got what they'd come for. Sent by What-Gives-Motion-to-What-Moves. A name old as language. What-Gives-Motion was not enthroned as ruler of the empyrean, was, instead, a nebulous presence. In the blind root groping into damp earth. The breath of damp earth that rises as the season warms. Breath itself. In the water stain surrounding a rock-stranded leaf after an old rain. The rain itself. The lightning that unseams the sky. The echo of your footsteps along a canyon floor. The sizzle of meat on the fire. The lowing of buffalo not made meat. To be certain What-Moves was there, you needed only look up. Sky was His other name.

"That last trip of yours, what happened?"

Javert still pursuing his Jean Valjean.

The Lakota hunted the buffalo and knew it was themselves they hunted, sacrificed hide and meat and horn to awareness. Alone in a pit for four days, they cried for a reminder.

"You did it alone," Aris said.

No guide or interpreter. No tribal shaman.

Logan closed his eyes, saw clearly that he was nothing more than a shape honed by humming wind. "I guess that's why I'm still putting things back together."

What if, Humpty Dumpty, nothing would hold?

Water gurgled.

Images of heaven, warned a pop song, *can lead you to hell.*

The night waxed stranger.

The wax melted into a mathematical description of events. The form it filled out could be bent by thought, curved like light in a field of gravitation. By intent, desire.

Aristotle wiped sweat from his forehead. "I think there was something in my wine."

Logan nodded. His scalp was electric. Probably there was a halo dancing over his head.

He put a hand on the back of Aris's neck, pulled him closer. His sweating shrink became a greasy-haired trucker. Although it wasn't road dirt darkening the creases of his neck, not sourness coming off his body but the fading blue freshness of cologne. And it wasn't oblivion Logan wanted to send along his nerves—he wanted to wrench Aristotle open, expose the wound to the cold rush of seawater. "What about you? You ever had a night like I had?"

"I think maybe I did."

The tenseness in Aris's neck eased, but Logan's grip didn't.

"It wasn't because of a drug," Aris said, "although for the record I was doing acid and mesc when you were in grammar school. I mean, I came out of college in the '70s. My roommate had died. My best friend through four years of high school, four years of college. It was our senior year."

Logan relaxed his grip, pulled back, smelled moist leather in a rush of hot air forced past his face by the movement of his jacket.

The mysterious moundbuilders. Death a bird symbol. Was that it, Uncle Cal? Your tattoo? Flight of the soul after a lifetime of gestation? Flesh cast away like shards of eggshell?

"I just sat there after I got that call, and … okay, a joint, I smoked a joint."

Feathers spring from Logan's skull, his arms stretch across sky, span daylight. Nose elongates, curves, hardens into a beak. Bones shed their weight, fill with airy space. Weary flesh sloughed, a sacrifice left in a heap of folds.

"I sat smoking and watching tv till the pot was gone, and the screen was full of snow. I kept watching, listening to one of his jazz records trample the tv snow. I watched that fucked-up bluish light buzzing in my eye until … I just drifted. Until dawn, I guess."

Logan remembered bare-chested dawn-runners in New Mexico, breechcloths flapping, bodies white-washed and dotted with red, breath steaming in the cool air, remembered wanting to claim his Indianness then, renounce the ways of the white man and his jealous god. Hold hands with spirits who smell of earth and corn, not brimstone and fire. They rise like wind on a spring day and don't mind drinking a beer with you if you're buying. What-Gives-Motion-To-What-Moves in the growth of a blade of grass. Every blade of grass. In his grandfather's voice.

But you must dance. And not stop dancing.

Maybe Wounded Knee had been the end of the Fourth World. Apocalypse had come and gone.

The dancing goes underground.

Where they were waiting to emerge. A navel in the earth. Onto a new Earth. Under a different sky.

They will come again.

Aristotle moved and purplish light rolled over the surface

of his suit. "I faced everything I had to face about myself that night. Or at least I felt like I did."

Embrace your fears like family. Sweat. Bathe in your sweat. Sit in a desert—any emptiness will do. Or sameness. Accept the monotony. The smell in a room goes away after a while. After enough time the desolation is populated by dancing ghosts. They make offerings you didn't know you'd understand. You are not the same when you come back.

He and Aris walked on. Until they were distracted by an argument just outside the suite beside the Rococo Room (they'd walked in a circle). Two men in suits and ties couldn't agree on whether a motionless figure was a woman or a mannequin. A mermaid, gold-scale dress glittering, blond hair dusted with gold, skin stained a shade of amber. When neither man was looking, she winked at Logan. He expected at any moment she'd open her mouth, utter a sound so inhuman that his terrified soul would take flight, be caught in her golden fist.

Tiby had moved down a room. This one had a domed foyer held up by pairs of columns, slim and fluted. The dome itself painted with a falling angel—

"Icarus," Aristotle murmured.

Eyes wide with fear, mouth downturned like a Blakean ghost in despair, one hand in the limbo beyond the circular frame of the foyer's ceiling, the other disproportionately large (in deference to perspective), fingers outstretched as if to grab you who looked up at it. Grab at anything at all.

Logan stepped back through the doorway just in time to see one of the two men arguing over whether or not the golden-skinned mermaid was a mannequin swing a knife in a downward arc. Before he could raise his voice or a hand, the knife thumped into … plastic? Or some other dead material.

Logan laughed. A performance. They'd replaced the winking woman. Hadn't they?

He disappeared again between fluted columns. He took off his jacket, felt the cool against the small of his back where his shirt was wet with sweat. He draped the crinkle leather over an arm. A beautiful Persian carpet spread outward from his feet.

The room had been lavishly architected, its space contoured with furniture and sculpture (he recognized Daphne turning into a tree just as Apollo slid a hand over a hip, her upswept hair branching and sprouting leaves). Paintings had been hung in gilded frames so large they could've collared elephants—the spirit of an age that swept up your attention like an untethered kite, tossed your perspective around up there, left you trembling inside like Phaeton as the chariot spilled him.

The weight on Logan's arm got lighter. The wigged butler who'd taken his coat was looking at him inquisitively, a waiter silently asking whether he was through with what was on his plate. Logan nodded.

Aristotle was standing in front of a painting, grinning at Logan. "Rubens. *Raising of the Cross.* I know these are all copies—no signatures—but …" He nodded emphatically. "Really *good* ones."

A triptych. Brawny backs, arms knotted with muscle, a Christ who looked to be at the center of a tug-o'-war though the men raising his cross were supposed to be working together. An expression of surrender written into his features as if there were nothing in his spirit to counter their brute limbs. A horse in the panel on the right was not like any other horse. Nostrils flaring, it blew out a febrile gust—Logan almost leaned closer to Aris to ask, *Do you feel it?*

Aristotle looked to be in the throes of a hallucinatory ecstasy, the oil colors prying his skull sutures open just enough to let themselves in. Clothing, hair, bodies. And movement along with them. Form itself quivering with the effort to persist. That pallid Christ—his hair golden brown—a feeble eye in a storm of uplifted arms and raised voices (Logan heard them). Jesus' left side was shadowed, yes, but if you looked closely, you could see that Rubens had treated his body almost like a light source, a tube of dull fluorescence or a fallen fragment of moon. Had subtly subjugated realism to get at something else.

"Is that a harpsichord?" Aristotle: a piece of sculpture that had miraculously found a voice.

Logan nodded. "Vivaldi."

The penthouse was a domed netherplace, an enclosed nebula where each of the harpsichord's struck strings sounded the creation of an elementary particle then, as the note faded, its disappearance.

There *was* an actual harpsichord in one of these "rooms" (a stall, really, with three sides). Never an instrument so crawling with the ornate. As if the paths of particles spiraling from smashed atoms had been traced out in gilded, overlapping arabesques. More complex even than Ptolemy's scheme of cycles and epicycles to go on explaining the impossible movement of the planets around the Earth.

Desire, the engine of human movement, ended in Paradise. Our original home. The second-oldest myth was of the savior who'd lead us back or magically transform our wasteland into a land flowing with silk and money. Exile and return. The third, the ordinary man or woman led on by an insistent longing. The Promised Land, Xanadu, Kansas, a rock garden created in the image of the Far East (where she'd never been).

Lost children that we are, we look up to our father who art in heaven and hope he's watching, listening, there.

On womb-dark seas, Odysseus spent ten long years making his way back to the rock slag where his mail showed up.

Our patron saint is the Unhomed Angel, the Dispossessed Demon.

I, you, Logan, still wandering, looking, hoping.

The cover of the harpsichord was propped open like the hood of a stalled car. On its underside a painted landscape: the piercing blue of a cloud-swept sky and a ruined castle atop a hill raised against it.

Logan sat down to the two rows of keys and tried playing, stepping on the Vivaldi. Getting the feel of it, he listened to the instrument loan to one of his own songs a confectioner's refinement, a powdery sweetness.

"Not bad." Aristotle nodded.

Logan gave his head a shake. "Not right."

Somewhere behind him Tiby said, "Whose calendar you goin' by?"

Abandoning the harpsichord, he reached for the splinter of conversation as though it were something that had washed ashore.

"I mean, the Mayan calendar … a whole different measurement."

The world spinning on another axis.

"You're right. It's not even a solar year. I don't *think* so anyway …"

Sun and Moon circling each other like old foes. Like separated lovers.

"It works in cycles. It's complicated." When Tiby smiled, his mouth held a candelabrum of hot light.

"On the old Roman calendar, the year begins in March. It makes sense—spring, when the Earth renews itself. Someone should set it right. October shouldn't be … I mean, it's right in the name."

It's all timing. *Oral genesis. Ordained* "A time of *syllable rising on the rim of* disequilibrium …" Tiby *an eclipsed disc,* again. "Out of joint. *repeatrepeatrepeat chorus.* Before things can *Orbit: a circle recalling* return to— *harmony and proportion.*

The tension strung between a feather drifting on the current and a star. Orphic strain on a lyre. Bird omen. Dilation and compression. Spiraling softly downward. A galaxy aswirl in the dark. Out of the dark, an emergence.

"—normal, something has to precipitate out."

Disastrous twilight shed on half the nations. A time of cultural distortion, fallen idols and broken conventions, inner-city drug addicts amerced of Heaven, alcoholic Indians whose faces deep scars of thunder had intrenched, radical hippies from eternal splendours flung, retrogressive negative punks looking at the world through empty skull sockets. An old myth—excess of glory obscured, usefulness exhausted—abandoned, a new one drawn into the vacuum.

"Sometimes art is … a measure of disorder mostly." Logan raked fingernails across his scalp. Sparks fell. "Another kind of nacre. The more difference between what is and what should be, the more music there is to be made."

"Ohhhh, Mr. Blackfeather? So glad to run into you. What were you saying?"

It's a nice day for a ghost dance.

"I love your new song—oh. I'm sorry go on ..."

Why shouldn't Jesus return as a Paiute named Wovoka? A Lakota? A Hopi? He was no Viking, no Earl of Shropshire.

"If it hadn't been for Roman oppression and taxation without representation," Tiby said, "Jesus would've just gone on the with family carpentry business, Joseph 'n' Son."

"I don't think I follow," said Logan's new acquaintance.

Tiby shook his head. "Nobody would've been listening to him. The society, as a medium, wouldn't have propagated the ripples and made them into waves if he hadn't been a Jew and the Jews hadn't been under the sandals of the Romans."

A windfall prophet.

Hitler too anointed by desperation. A whole nationful.

The weak, the whupped, the losers, seek change.

"You're saying Christianity is a crisis cult ...?"

Christianity, punk, Nazism, the Ghost Dance, all of 'em.

"It's not *my* idea but yeah. When the shit hits the fan, people turn to the nearest savior. "

Wind howled, bent back the grass of Wounded Knee, where something—he wasn't sure what—had ended. But somewhere else the ceremonies went on. Masks made of dusk, syllables germinating like seeds. A rhythm of footfalls destined to bring back the buffalo world.

It was still happening.

Listen.

The sound of thumping feet the Earth's heartbeat.

Listen, there is more.

The walls were stone blocks now. Chipped, pocked, worn as if in a previous life they'd been part of a castle. Logan rapped with a knuckle. Real fucking stoned. *Ow.* Stone. With tapestries to warm the dull roughness. Hunting scenes embroidered in the cloth. Hamlet's shield—no—*helmets*, shields, a pair of enormous swords. The floor coarse stone, grayish brown (no more smoothly polished tiles). And torches. Those butlers, dressed like wandering minstrels, carrying pig ribs and goblets of whatever, probably had to change them every so often.

"Why didn't we stop in the Renaissance Room?"

A piece of ironwork identical to the ones securing torches to the walls held a single oak branch. An oak leaf floated in a stone basin cupping water beneath it. The basin, decorated with a frieze of monks or priests in some kind of procession, reminded him of a birdbath.

The wall niches held Christ, Mary, weeping saints. Carved in wood. Logan came nose to bloody foot. Christ's head drooping, encircled by a wreath like barbed wire. Candles on long brass sticks lighting his misery. Eat of this body, drink of His blood. And the Jesuits called the Hopi, whose religion of dance and song they outlawed, barbaric.

Sybil took him by the hand. "Some fans want to meet you." She pointed. "Over there, with Tiby.

Fans?

Somehow he'd lost Aristotle. He had to tell him about a rider galloping across the stars, katsinas stomping on the roofs of brick towers, the return of the gray-skinned hitcher.

There are more things in heaven and Earth. (Not to mention the sea's lightless depths.)

Tiby lifted his free hand as if to indicate something that had just been unveiled. "This is Roselyn Krantz …"

She giggled. "I'm a surreal estate broker."

"… Bob Marwick …" Tiby continued.

Bob's smile held a cigarette. "Quantum mechanic. I can fix anything that leaps."

"… and Gil de Sterne."

Gil affected a short bow. "Deconstruction worker, sans hardhat."

The three of them laughed, mouths open, teeth glinting.

Logan was vaguely aware that he needed to go to the bathroom.

Gil de Sterne jumped into a blocky chair carpentered from dark wood, high-backed, like a throne. "I am friend to the king and sit upon his royal ass's resting place with impunity."

Roselyn applauded.

All the furniture straight and crude and unfriendly to the human form. The Victorians showed more balance, softened the blow of the hard-edged empirical with a cushiony dream of comfort.

Out of the chair now, Gil tested the point of a sword with his finger. "Is this thing real?"

Logan didn't like him—or Roselyn Krantz. "Let's just say if I swung it at you, you'd need a real shield."

"Where does van Loken come up with this stuff?"

"I'm not disagreeing with you, Tiby …" Bob Marwick was in the midst of lighting a cigar. "I mean, is it any surprise Born-

Again Christians are reborn right after they've crawled from a bed covered with their own vomit?"

He offered a cigar to Logan, which Logan took, and the flame of his lighter, which Logan did not. Bob flipped the lighter closed and shrugged. "Desperation is the mother of religion."

"And ignorance is the father."

The sacred lost between them.

Disequilibrium. Art the measure. Fallen angels with baroquen wings. The smell of singed plumage and a sky streaked with bright tears that promise a retinal scar for those who watch.

Tiby made the natural connection between desperation and slavery. "Sometimes you sing when you're happy." He looked at Logan through his horn-rimmed glasses. "Sometimes you sing to let people know there's something that can't be chained."

Stone walls and iron bars do not always a prison make; sometimes they comprise a castle.

Was it the beer or the champagne that had been spiked? Tiby the travel agent. The trip was in full swing now, the wooden Christ dripping sap instead of blood. One of those serving minstrels should've brought him a goblet that he might drink a measure.

Indians in the old days died when you put them in prison. Autopsy couldn't pinpoint the cause. Aristotle—was that Aris's voice?—was explaining what Logan was thinking.

"The future became unimaginable to them—not unseeable, which it is anyway—they couldn't even *imagine* it anymore."

There was something wrong with Aris's voice. As if it'd been recorded and the tape crinkled up. Syllables creased, stretched, lopped off.

"A bull assumes all walls are solid. Even one made of sheets.

So they don't charge. The Indians, in captivity … time became … days stretched all the way to forever."

Their dreams went colorless and iron. As the crown of a poor king. Sleeping and waking grew together like twisting vines. Something let go, slipped away unnoticed.

"Has anyone seen Mr. van Loken?"

"Mongst theyr number eke ther was a Jewe,

Who much was wont to give his lust free reyn,

And from woman's charms much pleysure drewe

But alas they from hym little had to geyne.

Seyeth one wench to hym to make this pleyne,

"If love's art yow master not by and by,

Shoorly your Messiah shal come ere I!"

Tiby was laughing, really in hysterics. He put an arm on Logan's shoulder to keep from doubling over.

"I've been meaning to tell you," Roselyn Krantz was saying, "your music—"

He stood there looking at her—she had on too much dark lipstick—thinking about how he needed to piss. His mouth opened, but the sound came out of hers (thickly outlined with color).

"And your *voice* …"

"You play anything, Roselyn?"

"Excuse me?"

"Flute? Guitar? Harpsichord—"

"Me? Oh, I *wish.*"

"What the hell makes you think you can play *me*?"

Roselyn looked at her sidekick, Gil. "Did I say something … wrong?"

To pee or not to pee? That is the question.

A hand squeezed his. Sybil?

"Well, I've taken up enough of your time ..." Roselyn was looking for an off-ramp.

Though Logan couldn't see it from a stained-glass window that came to a gothic point—as if it were necessary to indicate the whereabouts of heaven—he knew the owl was still melting behind the bar. Drops of water dazzled golden slipped down smoothing curves. He thought about the beauty of the sculpture as it melted, different than if it had stayed frozen—

"You look different." Sybil was smiling like an enchantress.

Maybe she was just a wood nymph's lascivious tendencies melted into a dress. Then he saw that she'd changed too. The change—his mind wasn't traveling at the same speed—had evaded him until now. "The light ...?"

A mellow amber. Aged in a venerable cathedral, maybe, before van Loken had it piped in.

Speaking of pipes ... he'd seen organs before, in churches that he'd wandered like a tourist, but he'd never sat down to play one.

Bob Marwick lifted his chin toward the instrument. "Give it a try."

Logan depressed a key experimentally. The note clashed with the sequence broadcast by speakers, sounded as deep and sonorous as a whale call. Logan let his right hand wander, smiled at the way the pipes resonated. So what if he was squashing ... Machaut? *Mass of Notre Dame*? God dame it, was the music following him around?

He sat down, let his booted foot find the brass petals and improvised a riff. As his fingers adjusted to the unfamiliar keyboard, he enjoyed immensely obliterating the Machaut recording. He stayed among the lower notes, composed something gloomy and doomy for the revelers. A wind instrument made to echo in the cold, stony space churches created in the soul. A chorus of flutes at the command of a single pair of hands. A flue into or out of this vale of tears to which we cling because it beats the vacuum, a void that won't carry a note—not a single weightless note will it support.

"Where's the soul come from anyway?" somebody asked.

"I heard Navajos think the whorls of the fingertips—pretty handy when criminals need to be caught—trace the path it took coming into the world," somebody answered.

No two paths, souls, snowflakes, the same. But *whence* came they?

"Very nice." Sybil clapped.

For the music.

A few others did too.

He got up.

Sybil hooked his arm. He wanted to go to another room, but they didn't get past a woodcut of Adam, Eve, the Tree, the serpent. Adam and Eve looking skeletal, a kind of medieval minimalism.

"There were no apples in ancient Palestine." Bob blew a plume of cigar smoke. "It was a quince or a fig—probably a fig since they wound up using fig leaves to hide their guilty loins after they got down to business."

"That's from the Vigilianus Codex, isn't it?" Gil de Sterne was standing next to Logan. "Ninth or tenth century?"

Eden the place where mind first looked at itself.

And saw that everything had suddenly, irreversibly split in two: saw that everything had suddenly, irreversibly split in two: male, female; ignorance, knowledge; good, bad; conscious, unconscious; soul, body.

As above so below.

A fearful symmetry uncovered.

A church steeple penetrating the sparkling turquoise above, a kiva opening into the damp earthdark below.

He recalled a distortion of spacetime by Escher, a man in an art gallery looking at a painting, and—here's the rub—he's *in* the painting he's looking at.

"Nobody with a rational bone in her body goes for that original sin silliness. I mean, you can't take Adam and Eve *literally*. It's a metaphor."

"For what?" Roselyn Krantz looked offended.

"Come on, it's obvious, isn't it? It's a perfect little story about how we woke up one day a little more than animals—that's why we can't talk to them anymore. That's why we're full of angst all the sudden. Somebody disconnected the autopilot."

Logan pointed at Bob with the cigar he'd given him. "Instinct?"

"Of course, yeah. Now that we have to fly the plane ourselves, we make up a control tower in the sky that never answers—"

"That's insulting, Bob, calling Christianity a myth? And God a control tower? Like those fables about Zeus throwing around thunderbolts and turning himself into a bull or a swan just to—"

"But that's what it is." Bob shrugged.

Apple, fig, quince, didn't matter, the fruit growing on that tree was autonomy, choice, free will. The train jumped the tracks, and to keep it from being a runaway, we concocted myths as sign posts then put up religions as guardrails—salvation *this* way.

That's how we got outside the circle, Jack Be Quick. A divine bouncer with a burning pool cue tossed us out of the Paradise Lounge, and we've been drinking ourselves into oblivion ever since. Forgetfulness ain't quite bliss, doesn't quite replace ignorance, but it'll do in a pinch. It's a lot easier than trying to follow some eight-fold origami path to get to a dry establishment called the Enlightenment Inn.

He was at the center of a strange moment, everything spinning out from him. Ah, the way Tawa must have felt, whirling and flinging off bits of His Infinite Self—stretches of desert, hunks of mesa, chunks of belief, souvenirs sparkling with beads made in Taiwan, an old shoe without a mate, the wail of a police siren changing pitch as it passed—Doppler downshifting on its way to the High Times Lounge in Flagstaff, where a Hopi woman was stabbed to death in the parking lot by her Navajo ex-boyfriend.

Bundles of shrivel-dried peppers as dull as old blood, sheaves of corn and husks, silvery mysterious glass tubes from a television set (the light has rubbed off), a woman's compact to signal the Sun.

Something inhuman pushed its face through events. The human beings it glowered at just one more attempt to mirror the unbearable sadness of infinity taking an eternity to die of entropy.

A black hole in reverse, Logan was giving back everything he'd sucked into himself, everything that had been crushed down to form a dark unutterable core, a surge of regurgitated matter.

Lost fathers, dead uncles, broken katsina dolls, the head of a hammer, watches with cracked crystals still ticking time.

Memories had fallen into the hole he'd become and disappeared in the night covered over by his ribs, gone from the event horizon, arising only in nightie-night dreams, never again to be seen in the escaped light of what had so long ago been set in motion.

There was some kind of slow erosion, though, the edge of the whole was fuzzy, was full of quantum randomness: things slipped away as if memories siphoned off by Alzheimer's.

Cinderblocks, the railroad-tie lintel he'd cracked his head against, kerosene lamps, fizzled filament bulbs, electric cords ending in a sudden wreckage of gleaming copper wires.

The Smiling Aztec incinerated, Upstate University iced in, New York washed away in a deluge, and he'd come out through a legal loophole, through a skunk's burrow under the fence, through a tunnel named after a president.

The four distillations of matter thrice performed do not resolve the universal confusion, the atom of chaos at the heart of spacetime. Though we assign seven metals to the seven planets spread across the four heavens, it must be remembered: That which thou sowest is not quickened unless it die first. Only then can the disorder that incinerates meaning be reassembled on another plane, flight number 74, for it can neither be created nor destroyed, only quantumfied and put past us at the speed of light when we're not looking. It has altered nothing but its form yet in our inability to keep up with the alchemy of change we're stupefied into believing something was lost. At the dark heart of the black hole—that sunless nadirland—the energy debt has been called in, the balance restored, the rottenness in Denmark rectified.

It never felt better, emptying himself, dying, shrinking, and each thing returned to its original place.

A man with a cane and a wig of white doddered through one of the rooms.

("How old is he?"

"Let's put it this way—when God said let there be light, he screwed in the bulb.")

Sybil asked something, but he felt too good to answer. He had the sun in his hands, knew instinctively how to handle it. Light glowed capillary-red through his fingers, sliced out in luminous planes from the cracks between them.

Krishna or jehovah or osiris or allah or tawa or skan or vishnu or odin doesn't matter because time and place experience and language are the limitations within which He had to work and the medium changes the appearance of the message though the song remains the same. in the beginning a cosmic egg rested on the primal waters78888uy88888882212q like a drifting continent. the oldest form of divination deciphering the cracks in animal bones, in tortoiseshells cast into the fire. I ching you ching we all ching. The Zuni Bar on route 666. a bus ticket purchased for 30 pieces of silver. 60606 and the wholly bible in Jim Lee's farmhouse opened to the same page. revelation 13 tattooed on Cal's arm. Bible Mike impressing revelation 21 on him like a tattoo: and i saw a new heaven and a new earth, for the first heaven and the first earth had passed away. *the moon eye a casino dealer with a tarot deck the empirical as interpretable as dream, myth, text, delusion, painting.*

The crook of Sybil's elbow tugged him as if he were a hooked fish. "Ah, the Greco-Roman Room."

Aristotle stood beside a fluted column.

Logan handed him a folded-up note, a long description in small, neat letters of the plague of hallucinations that had visited him since he'd left the hospital.

Bob Marwick was running his hand over a striking bas relief— the marble immaculately white—of a man being torn apart by women. "Poor bastard." He was still puffing the cigar he'd lit in the Medieval Room. "Wandered into a pack of Maenads while they were ... a word like *enthusiasm* falls flat now, but it used to mean *full of god*. Something like that."

We no longer identify with heavenly beings do not dress their parts in the ceremonies, we sit back in our stiff sunday clothes and have the bible read to us. no new visions, waking nightmares, revelations, reveries are added to the good book no shaman interprets your dream no katsina guides you through the lower realms. the native american church was barred from holding your hand through a night of prancing peyote phantasms and if you stand out there in an open field inviting lightning to strike you end up like the psychedelic relic you wind up in the parking lot of the Burning Aztec, knife in hand.

"You know what that is?" Tiby, hands in his pockets, was standing next to Logan.

It was an odd-looking contraption, taller than both of them, with multiple backbones of pipes—larger ones on the left (bass), taller on the right (treble).

"A hydraulos?"

Levers instead of keys, filled with water to keep the air in the pipes under pressure, the flow even.

"You know your shit."

"Right now I gotta piss."

Tiby pointed. "Turn that corner, you oughta find what you need. The only door in the Classical Room."

A narrow door at that. Behind it, a hole—about the right size to squat on without falling in—in a kind of marble step. That was all. He took his long-awaited pee, heard the stream hit water he couldn't see, and was relieved.

On his way out, Orpheus was scene again, its relief figures raised not only on marble but on his skull. A blind woman could read the myth with her fingertips.

"Yeah, they ripped him apart, but his head kept singing." Bob was still smoking his cigar. "They threw it in the river, it was washed out to sea, then it got caught on some rocks on some island—"

"Lesbos." Aristotle glanced at Logan. "Where it was buried."

"Right. But they all came back, Osiris, Adonis, Attis, Tammuz, Dionysus, all resurrected fresh as daisies in the spring."

The ice sculpture was still melting, blunting, losing definition, the newest testament to entropy as it spread into a homogeneous puddle somewhere behind the bar on the far end of this pleasure dome decreed.

"I'll be back." Sybil melted into murk striated with topaz.

Was he ever going to light this cigar Bob had given him?

Turning around, spinning on his boot heels, he bounced lightly off someone several inches shorter but decidedly heavier. "'Scuse me..." He stared for a moment. At the gray-white hair and glasses and gray-white beard and skin not even as dark as his own, and somehow he knew. "Mr. Geraci? Daniel C. Geraci?"

"Mmm." He swallowed a sip of wine. "Yes. But if we're going to be on friendly terms, you should call me Chet. That's what the C stands for."

Chet? This was so odd to Logan, he wondered whether it was a joke. *Chet*? He didn't look like a Chet anymore than he looked like a Biff or a Chip.

Logan hesitated as if meeting for the first time the father who'd put him up for adoption, from whom he wanted so much, about whom he knew so little. "I was hoping I'd run into you."

"And you are ...?"

Seeing the hand extended, he took it. "Logan."

"Logan ..." Geraci rolled it on his tongue. "Scottish, isn't it? But *you're* not, are you?"

He shook his head.

"Didn't think so. Believe it or not, I am."

"You?"

"If you go back to maternal great-grandparents."

Mixed breeds, both of them.

Geraci smiled pleasantly, and it occurred to Logan that he was, behind the glasses, beneath the beard, a handsome man.

"I read *Grendhal,* and I—something I've been wanting to ask you—if you were ever in a mental hospital?"

"I *hope* that's not the kind of question you generally confront people with at parties."

Chet's smile showed large teeth (slightly gapped) and something of an overbite.

"I ... no. Just you. Because ... I guess I know something about you from reading your book, but it's all mixed together, what's you and what's other people ..."

"That's *at least* part of the point—"

Logan Blackfeather, part Indian, part white, wondered which part was which.

"I was in a hospital for about a year. Just north of the city."

Geraci sighed sympathetically. "Oh dear, yes, I know the facility. Well, to answer your question, yes, I was in a hospital when I was about 24. In fact, I'm engaged in an autobiographical project at the moment, and when it's published, that question won't take anything more than a trip to the library to answer." Geraci's voice surrounded each word like clear water.

"Then your narrator's ... sort of a doppelganger."

"In a very loose sense, yes—emphasis on *very*." Geraci reached out to stop a man in a toga bearing a silver tray. "Have you tried these? They're very good."

"Sure, why not?" Bread stacked with feta cheese, a slice of tomato, an olive, a toothpick skewering it all together. Why had he ever imagined himself as a reflection in the mirror of an author's mind?

"The works of art in your city, the fictional city in your novel, none of them real."

Geraci pushed the black-framed rectangles of glass on his nose a bit higher. "They didn't need to be. The point is that art organizes the space around it. Time too." His hands were moving like those of a conductor trying to call up nthrough the music a Mephisto and a cloud of brimstone. "Art has a way of making the wilderness no longer quite as wild—or alien. Making it *us*. We need that."

Subdue silence and fill emptiness with a vachuuman.

On the flipside of the coin, let instinct loose in the neighborhood.

All hail the conquerors of spacetime. Fourteen billion years rising up to meet this moment, *now* (is, was, always will be), the peak of the heavenly mountain, the growing tip, the latest, breaking this is *it*, and we were all in it till death do us part.

"But what about the void ..." Logan began. "... surrounding art? Have you ever read Gass? His essay—?"

"Oh, right. A work of art is surrounded by the void."

"Yes." Logan aimed an index finger like a lance. If he's right, if art doesn't spill over, then why ... I mean, if you take the promise of an afterlife away from a Christian, he may have the will to go on, but is he still a Christian? How do you press on in the face of that? No soul, no heaven, all ends final?"

Glass of wine in one hand, Geraci tugged on his long whitish beard with the other. "I think Gass meant *physically* ..."

"Physically?"

Geraci sipped and nodded. "Art is a material reality after all. It doesn't have any extension beyond its borders except in terms of our *subjective* response to it. When you say that a work of art controls the time and space around it, or at least textures it, it doesn't do anything *directly* to spacetime. It does it via our perception. And that, I think, is what he's trying to point out."

Entering the sun eye to emerge through the moon eye.

"Ahhhhh, I see."

Geraci tugged on his beard a bit more, a kind of Odin trying to uproot something and trade it off for a hair-fine thread of wisdom. "As I say, art has an extension in actual space, but—"

"The echoes are in here." Logan tapped his head. Out of one continuum and into another. The thing to remember that the sun setting in one can rise in the other.

"Well look who's here."

Sybil's gusty voice.

"You know, um, Chet?"

Sybil and Chet shook hands, Logan realizing they did *not* know one another.

"Daniel C. Geraci, the author, right? Big fan of *Grendhal*."

"Oh, well, thank you ..."

Sybil turned to Logan. "But that's not who I meant." She lifted her chin. "Over there, by the Assyrian Gate." She guided him by his shoulders.

He almost reached out behind him for Geraci, thought how unfair Sybil was being, how rude.

Geraci held up his wine glass as if in salute. "I'll catch up with you in a minute. I'm just going to poke my head into the Chinese Dynasty Room."

Mammoth winged bulls with human heads flanked an entrance that could've accommodated a dump truck. The walls the aeronautical bulls dwarfed had been built out of long flat bricks. Beards, like armor woven of ringlets, hung to their chests. Visible through the entrance of this, the second-to-last room, an Egyptian obelisk towered over the flat-brick partitions, rose above even the grand headdresses of the plumed man-bulls.

Van Loken—it had to be him—stood next to one of the bulls. His white hair, tinted gold by the light, was pulled back into a tiny tail. The Silver Surfer. Way back when he'd been out with Shawna and wondering. Tonight in a shirt that might've been the color of red sandstone with a simple design on the pockets like an inlay of silver, rust-colored denims, and brownish red, snake-skin cowboy boots. A small hoop of silver pierced one lobe.

"Very good to finally make your acquaintance." He offered a smile and his hand. "Erik, your host."

Logan guessed him to be over fifty. The features of his face sharp, Scandinavian. Logan smiled back. A hard hand, a warm shake. "Good to be invited."

"Chet …" Van Loken took Geraci's hand. "Good to see you again."

"Hello, Erik."

Van Loken turned to Logan. "You're enjoying yourself?"

Logan swept his eyes over the place. "How could I not?"

White, white hair and ... blue eyes? Hard to tell. Yes, he remembered them as blue. Then he remembered the two of them—Geraci and van Loken—facing off at that gallery opening. Mercurial when the light was fluorescent in SoHo, van Loken looked strangely less so now that the light had gone gold.

Geraci turned to Logan. "If you'll excuse me for a few minutes, I *will* catch up with you. I really *was* enjoying our conversation."

"Sure."

"Tell me ..." Sybil hooked arms with Geraci. Beside the graying author, she was a lamprey latching onto a giant manta ray. "What are you writing these days?"

"Shall we?" Erik gestured toward the winged man-bulls.

The room, badly lit by braziers, was as hot was wine-warmed breath. Two hung from chains but most were standing. The smoke was spiced, as it had been at the bar, but stronger, a different scent.

"That ... harp." From the harp's sound-box sprouted a golden bull's head possessed of a long beard of ... lapis lazuli? That showed up dark but fiercely blue against the gold foil of the bull's face. "It's not ... from Sumer?"

"Look just below the bull's head ... perhaps the world's oldest such painting. The bearded figure is Gilgamesh. A reproduction, of course."

It was a goofy-looking Gilgamesh, squeezing, in the crooks of his elbows, the necks of two bulls on their hind legs, their faces human. It looked like a Three Stooges skit.

The music being piped in had been composed on a lyre or a harp, something Middle Eastern but somehow not Arabic. The notes as delicately held together as a clump of cigar ash.

Logan laid fingers on the bull harp, tried to pluck to the

music playing, failed miserably, laughed, then ran the backs of his fingernails across the strings as if drawing a knife across the throat of a sacrifice.

Erik pointed at a tall, slender figurine, a man with spindly arms and legs and a squared-off head. "Elamite. Four thousand years old."

"Looks like a Giacommetti." Shawna had shown him photos in one of her art books.

"*L'Homme qui marche?* Yes, you're right."

African masks, Picasso, the moderns broke up form. As if form were Orpheus, Osiris, Dionysus. (The soul, like water, takes the shape of its container. And when the form is destroyed …?)

"There's no going forward without going back," van Loken said. "At some point anyway."

The journey isn't complete without return.

Without descent there's no emergence.

Returnally.

You're not ready for the light till you've been washed in darkness.

The unconscious was a horse the rational mind had to learn to master. And sometimes got its head cracked against an old barn doorway. The two had to be balanced as Aris, good Pythagorean that he was, must've told him a dozen times. Harmony and proportion. Neither moon eye nor sun eye should hog the sky.

"Four thousand years ago the moon eye had the upper hand. To mix metaphors." And body parts.

"The moon eye?"

Logan nodded. "It doesn't always see clearly. Sends impressions, not precision, to the gray mud behind the retina—"

"That's just it, isn't it? Any freshman in philosophy knows you never see the thing itself. It's already wrapped up for you in preconceptions—social conventions, religious dogma, tv commercials, bad books, good books, films … the mind can't reach for anything without wearing a glove of preconceptions. Anything it handles, the feel is already muffled by the glove, some thicker than others. Wear the glove down enough …"

By spending four days in a pit with no food or sleep or water.

Holed up in a cave on the island of St. John.

Chewing peyote until you meet Grandfather Saguaro.

You invite the lightning.

Too much glove gone too fast with no tribal mother around to hold your hand, with no tribe to take you into its bosom, you wind up covering the wound with a sunny myth of your own device, and they send you to Upstate University to relearn the straitjackets you'd spent your last ounce of energy shrugging out of.

The branch in this room was bare like all the others. The reddish bark made him think it might be cedar. To satisfy the sun eye, he moved close enough to sniff the wood. Yes, cedar. He stood back and closed the sun eye. In the twists of the branch, he saw petrified the desperate desire to live.

In the center of the room, a towering obelisk.

"The hieroglyphics on the tree—"

He said obelisk, *but I heard* tree.

"—tell the story of Osiris." Van Loken patted it with a hand on the third finger of which glittered a ruby ring. "Which is a Greek name, of course. Here, look. It's not as difficult as you might think." Three of his fingers folded over, the ring disappeared, and he pointed with the one that remained extended, held out the thumb for balance. "This tiny sarcophagus represents the coffin his brother Set lured him into then nailed shut and sealed with molten lead. These wavy lines represent the river—he was thrown into the Nile ..."

Ah, brotherly love.

"Isis, veiled in morning—"

Van Loken wasn't trying to be poetic, he realized; the goddess was wearing black.

"—veiled in mourning, wandered in search of the body until she found it in Byblos, on the coast of Phoenicia. Here you can see the tiny sarcophagus has ... well, a tree grew around it, enclosed it. The king of Byblos, who had no idea what the tree contained, had it cut down to use as a pillar in his palace.

"He later granted Isis's request to cut open the pillar. After removing the coffin, she returned with it to Egypt. But one night she left it unguarded in a marsh, and Cal, hunting boar by moonlight—"

He said Set. Not *Cal.*

"—recognized the body of Osiris and tore it into 14 pieces, scattering them about as he went." Van Loken shrugged. "It was like sowing seeds."

Or like the waning Moon, losing another piece of its luminous body every night until, 14 days after being full, it was absent from the sky.

"Isis sailed up and down the marshes in a papyrus boat ... see this glyph that looks like a tiny boat? Collecting the pieces."

The waxing moon: Isis restoring the god a piece at a time.

Van Loken's hand was still on the obelisk, while his eye seemed caught by the sparkle of the ring on his finger (the warm luster of the metal or the cool fire of the gem? And which of his eyes was it holding?).

The room was too hot, the light from the smoldering braziers like flames beneath a pan of his blood. The smoke spiced, spiked, *something*. With myrrh or sage or mescincense, he didn't know, but he was sweating and light-headed.

At the entrance Logan put his hand on the cool stone belly of a bull-man, traced a hard vein with his finger. He saw the carved ribs rise and fall. He laughed. Aristotle should see this. Hooves resting on a floor that was breathing too.

He turned around to face van Loken. "Hey, are they your scouts? Those two musicians? They look Indian. Maybe even Hopi. The guys with the reflector sunglasses …?"

No sweat on van Loken, his clothing without a crease—why was there no rush of wind when he entered a room? His brow wrinkled, lowered. He looked confused.

"I saw them earlier … in those antediluvian suits?" Logan gestured with his hands to take in his own outfit. "Carrying instrument cases."

"Here? Are you sure? I have no idea who they might be."

Ghost riders, katsinas, the nightmare hitcher, phantom musicians. Where was Aris when you needed him?

"Maybe not …" Logan let it drop.

"So … music. Why not something else?"

The belt van Loken was wearing matched his snakeskin boots.

Logan's shrug was half-hearted. "It got to be the way, I guess, to harmonize what's in here—" He tapped his chest with four fingers held like a farm tool used to turn earth. "—with what's out there." Heal the breech. Even if some wounds never really healed. Not Christ's, not Lancelot's, not Linda's.

Van Loken nodded. "I used to think of the artist as a little Dutch boy, his finger in the dyke, delusions of holding back entropy in his head."

In the unbroken stillness there was only silence in Endless Space.

On the wall opposite, a bird-headed man with wings watered a tall vine. The detail in the musculature of a forearm was astonishing. An Assyrian katsina maybe. No, a carved relief of a djinn (later to be mistaken for an angel by captive Hebrews).

A note sounded over the desert quiet, a freight-train warning on tracks through Arizona, the hunt for what vibrates insistently within.

"Entropy?" Logan asked as if its definition eluded him. "Too impersonal."

The spectrum played on the human ear tiny compared to the universes of sound above and below the threshold of hearing. All he had to rummage around in.

"Do you think your second album would've been much different if your first had been a success?" Van Loken switched his wine glass from one hand to the other.

Harvey must already be pitching it. Where the hell was he anyway?

"I pushed myself harder, I guess. Tried to make it impossible to say *no* to the music. Why?"

"I'm thinking about what happens when you put something under pressure."

Logan turned the corners of his mouth down. "Breaks or bends or … gets squashed flat."

"Or transforms itself."

The People of the Red Willow observed the Festival of Saint Jerome during the day, put on a show for the Spanish missionaries who watched through two sun eyes. At night they held the old ceremony in the kiva.

Break me open, van Loken, you'll find a katsina who's been hiding behind a human mask.

Logan suddenly twigged. "You heard my album when it first came out." His mouth knotted into a smile. "You could've bought the rights, hyped it, got it on DJ lists—*then*." Instead of a fucking *party*. Now.

Erik laughed, water trickling down smooth rocks.

Under a stately dome, pleasures measureless to man. Long, long way from Kansas. Jimmy got to watch the god of wheat turn brown in the afternoon sun. Osiris a Greek name for an Egyptian divinity. His name in English might be Ed. A god was a god. And whether it was Set or an International Harvester combine, he'd get cut up all the same. And come up in the spring.

"Haqumi?" *asks the questioner.* Who's there?

"Pnu'u," *answers the katsina.* I am I.

Sybil looked different again because the light … was different again? Red bleeding through the glow of the braziers.

"Where's Geraci?"

"He went off looking for you …"

The last room wasn't a suite but a cavern. From outside it looked like a mountain sloping down to meet the great wall protected by the Assyrian bull-men, its opening more a misshapen mouth than a door. It couldn't have been real stone, but it felt like it. Light from a fire pit. Throwing flickering shadows. You had to go down, it all sloped down.

Paintings in ocher or maybe desiccated blood covered an

entire wall. Bison, horses, mammoths, woolly rhinos, aurochs. Another wall crowded with Aboriginal rock paintings. A third dedicated to Anasazi rock art: ghostly forms without legs or feet, floating gown shapes or tapering triangles. Some with horns, others with circles drawn around their heads like halos. One with a perfect *O* of a mouth.

The Aborigines too had painted ghost faces, bulbous heads without noses or mouths, flat as medieval paintings but haunting, the eyes black pits that tunneled into the darkness every soul is born in, eyelashes raying like starlight from the emptiness they rimmed.

Logan pointed. "*Wandjinas*—Aborginal katsinas. Weather *wandjinas*, I think. Or storm *wandjinas*. Something like that."

Aris slipped on the rough stone floor, almost fell, the note Logan had handed him flapping in one hand.

Another set of *wandjinas*, these with noses as dark as their eyeholes—rendering them more skull-like—had been painted sideways. All of their heads haloed, aura-ed, aglow.

Aris was at his side now. "These visions of yours ..." He held up the note.

Choose a wall, change a continent: Europe, North America, Australia.

Logan stared blankly at Aristotle.

"You never had them until you moved to New York, where you felt hemmed in, cut off. You never learned Hopi, and you went to ... what? One or two dances on the mesa? When you were a child, right? The visions are ... waking dreams, I think, a kind of compensation for cultural loss."

His mind out on its own, without easel or brush, projecting on the canvas of the city, on screen of the sky.

Logan nodded. "Very maybe."

Figurines all around them—in shelves of rock, stuck into the floor, carved into a wall—naked women with buttocks like pumpkin halves; sagging, melon-sized breasts; sausage-like legs; indistinct faces. (A blue period, a rose period, a period of oversized women.) Most were freestanding, but one or two sat on crude thrones of stone. Sprinkled with rust or dried blood.

The surrounding images unframed, adrift in their rough backgrounds, as natural as seepage staining rock.

A painted lioness with eyes as round as coins. They seemed to reflect the firelight. What was so odd … was that her head formed the hump of some other animal. He shivered, recalling a foot that was part of a head, a toenail that outlined an eye, a returnal trope.

Was that a katsina laying a log on the fire? It looked up at him, slits for eyes, a short tube for a mouth. Color smeared on the bare upper body.

Logan moved to the Anasazi wall. He wanted to stay among images a people kin to his own had left behind. Footless, ethereal, benevolent. Could he quilt a blanket of the faintly drawn images? Throw it over his shoulders to stay warm in the desert night?

Sibyl had taken his arm.

There was a collective *"Aaaaaaaaaaaaaah …"* As if they were at a fireworks display.

The darkness beyond the mouth of the Neolithic Room was complete.

Sybil tugged at him. "Let's have a look."

Cigarettes were sparks floating in a black void. The music had faded to a low ground hum, like drumming muffled by cottony distance, the hum of the Earth itself, maybe, the one scientists say is there when it shouldn't be, when faults are holding, volcanoes quiet, nuclear weapons safely tucked in their silos. The music reminiscent of the break of day and distant chanting, an occasional gust of wind that might've been a flute call.

"Bet he blew a circuit with all the power he uses."

Voices drifted in the darkness.

"Maybe the whole city's having a blackout."

"Maybe the Russians are coming."

"To arms! To arms!"

All the king's horses and all the king's men won't be able to put us back together again.

"The world is run by a bunch of precocious children with apocalyptic toys. The point isn't to take away their toys, it's to make them grow up."

"Yeah, but it's easier to take away their toys."

Faintly, as subliminal as his own breathing, he heard music, the opening to a song from his second album. Damn Harvey.

"*Ooooooooooooooooo.*"

Chinese New Year. A big bang to announce an arrival.

He looked up and saw what had stirred the voices around him. There were stars on the dome in the center of the ceiling, a black-and-bright planetarium sky. He looked for a dawn-red rider with floating hair, a horse with flecks of albino across a muscular chest the color of dusk.

"Hey, isn't that the Big Dipper?"

"That ain't even a little one."

"Those aren't constellations at all," Geraci said.

A false sky.

Geraci was just in front of him, his head tilted back and his hair making his head look a little like a dandelion that'd gone to seed. Maybe, Logan thought, he should try blowing on it. Chet was right—no familiar constellations. Scorpio conspicuously absent. No crab. No grainy bits of beachwashed light traversed the oceans of space.

"It *looks* like a horse though, doesn't it?"

"We'll call it Horse."

"No, look. Those could be wings."

"Pegasus."

The angst of uncertainty, life resting on the abyss of the unknown. Each of us a moon reflecting light—but what is the source?

His fist had gone through. A window when he was seven years old. Looking for … the source?

"It's all secondhand."

Used clothes.

Sometimes the light is twice diluted: a dark lake holding a wavering image of the Moon.

"Forget about van Loken's parlor tricks." Aris, lit like a Roman candle (or maybe Greek fire), guided him toward the Neolithic Room. "That night out on the desert … you got an answer to one of your questions, didn't you? It wasn't the mescaline. It's what you figured out—believed you'd figured out—wasn't it?"

Logan felt struck, as if he were made of brass and a steel hammer had *kranged* against the middle of his back. He tried to answer but wasn't sure whether Aris could hear him above the quivering metal.

"Your destructive tendencies …" Aris preambled. "I wonder whether, whether part of you is trying to break up the world around it, shatter the mirror it sees itself in. And then … then put it back together, but differently so you get a different image. One you've had out in front of you all your life."

Like a carrot. For every action.

Consciousness—not angels, not Humpty Dumpty—had a great fall.

From the walled garden.

Orpheus re-membered.

Osiris resurrected.

Form (the figure) disintegrates.

Would you stick needles in your eyes to hear what you could not see?

There's sanity in a neatly trimmed lawn. (And pathology.)

The soul is a bird of iridescently beautiful plumage, but it can die of loneliness.

The sun eye deals in surfaces and instruction manuals, conventions held in empty halls.

The moon eye is cataracted over with religious platitudes.

Start again.

The many-colored dome of glass shattered, Shelley's white radiance unstained.

The light, returning now, was a weak red, a sun just up seeping through closed eyelids.

In Kansas wheat grows like ripening time.

The symmetry of silence, the perfectly smooth monotony of nothing, the vacuum-bitten desert of infinite distances. Until its flawlessness shifted, broke, set sound and time in motion.

In Eden a unified beasts-of-the-field symmetry cracked when the first woman, the first man thought to use a mirror, *became* a mirror, reflected, speculated, were *in* the picture they were looking at. Smacked two stones together and made music.

Oh yes, it was coming back.

They were in the Neolithic Room—he and Chet and Sybil and Aris—among the shaggy beastshapes, horned and tusked and antlered (tree branches rooted to animal skulls). A leaf floated in a huge gourd filled with water. A fig leaf, he guessed.

The world founded not on this rock hollowed by a cave but on the insects cloud around a streetlight, the seasonal circling of planets around a sun, the steps of body-painted dancers around a fire.

"They're all still, these images." The arc Logan's hand traced took in a wall. "Even the movies in the modern room … only the illusion of movement."

Only—

The last time he'd seen the *katsinam* dance, he'd been five or six. Sitting in his grandfather's lap, on a rooftop overlooking the plaza. He heard the dancers coming—gourd and tortoiseshell rattles, voices lifted in song—before he saw them. The Sun just breaking the shallow arc of the horizon, the dancers rose with it from below the edge of the mesa. Chanting, wearing sashed kilts and spruce ruffs, faces blanked out by masks impersonal as elementary particles. Eagle feathers fluttering in the wind, they shook their rattles, drummed the earth with their feet, blended into a single entity. The ground of rootedness. A unity of things we stopped seeing a long time ago.

This penthouse party, which could, in a single night of squandering, sustain the reservation through four seasons, had no dancing. A three-dimensional still life.

Dance to keep the world aspin. What separated him, you, all of us from the mesas in the distance. What-Gives-Motion-To-What-Moves (God's real name). The fish of the sea and the fowl of the air, every living thing that moveth on the face of the Earth.

He stopped before the petroglyphs and rock paintings, understood they were merely seeds.

Understood that the fountain was a tree, watery-limbed, alive.

The stone had called to him. The cold metal of the car he'd been leaning against shape-shifted. The grandfather of all saguaros. Blunt branches reaching into the sky, its deepest root lodged somewhere near where the Earth's core had gone liquid with heat. Nerves skewered on the needles.

In perfect silence a breath is a symphony.

In perfect darkness, a candle a sun.

Sterility the nature of perfection. Nothing can change. By definition.

"Heat death, you're talking about heath death."

Yes, heat death at the end of our gasoline rainbow.

"What's heat death?"

Time is finally a word without meaning.

"Well, it's when … when there's no more energy left. None at all—anywhere. Nothing can happen."

Change and time Siamese twins: one dies with the other.

The universe is never, not since its creation, still. never quiet. stars hiss and fizz in their self-centered orbits, dizzy in their own din, send electromagnetic fuzz to fill the space between stations on the radio dial. fountains of sound. the earth too atremble and aquiver. even between quakes and nuclear tests conducted by top brass in subterranean corridors it hums. unlike starsong no one knows where the earth's voice comes from, why it never dies out. unless it's the oceans breaking against the edges of continents unless it's a palpating field of atmospheric pressure unless it's the war twins (one at each pole) sending shivers up the Earth's backbone with their calls unless it's thousands of years of feet drumming the earth treading it down patting and pounding it over and over while circling a burning pile of wood that sends sparks aloft like newborn stars.

Hearts thump, breathing rasps, electrons whiz, atoms buzz, quartz watches vibrate, birds twitter, leaves rustle, stalks of wheat stir, wind moans unseen in dark caverns howls against mountain slopes whispers over sand.

Heath death is silence.

Unbroken.

Perfect.

In perfect stillness there is no time. and no direction. there's something ... inhuman. to listen to the silence and be the only thing listening to be the one thought moving on the stillness the one thing in motion though there is no motion to be behind the first motion to invent time. sound. worlds. to set the ghostly life of the universe to music.

"The nothing I believed was out there turned into the nothing in here." Logan tapped his sternum as if he were beginning a song.

"Ahhh." Aristotle nodded, sweat on his forehead glowing orange.

Logan Feather-Of-Coot. Logan Earthdiver.

To plumb the acoustics of emptiness you set your wishbone thrumming like a tuning fork (only there's no sound in a vacuum).

Part of our blueprints, maybe, to crave perfection. A kind of (heat) death wish. Was the universe that cleverly built into us? Were we *helping* to bring time to its end? Our bodies were programmed to die after 70, 80 years—why not psyches programmed toward one entropic telos?

The moon eye riseth now in my desert firmament.

There in that desert underworld, his back against a hallucinated saguaro, he'd grokked that you can't swallow the vision whole. Orpheus or Osiris or some sacred rodeo bull cut up for fertilizer. Reborn through a tree or wheat or a brass fountain. Some giant named Skyrmer hacked down from his beanstalk and they capped the sky with his skull.

Logan saw the two of them standing by the wall scrawled with Anasazi images. So alike in their fraying suits they could have been twins. One held a wooden flute; the other, a drum and a stick.

The drummer rounded his mouth into an uncovered manhole. It filled with hot light, stabbed his eyes. Not a sun but a scorching wind rising from the twin's throat, tugging at Logan's hair, straining it at the roots. He turned away from the bright breath. Stricken, a blind cave-thing, he lowered his head but the song scalded his crown.

"Are you all right?"

Geraci's voice.

Is my hair ... burning?

"Yes," Logan answered.

"For a minute I thought you were—"

He smiled. "No, I'm all right."

"I was thinking about your first name. I seem to recall it's from Scottish Gaelic ... isn't it a—"

The fear, he'd tried to tell Aris, that behind it all was nothing but Newtonian mechanics. *An   a   lyze.* Break up. Bite-size lysosomes. So that all these gods getting cut up were nothing but the impersonal mechanics of comprehension, the mind dissecting to understand, analyzing to apprehend—all dressed up in anthropomorphic clothes, just-so stories told to children facing a forever-and-a-day sleep in an unending night. A fabric braided out of fiction to cover the vacuum underneath. Everything. The order—all of it—ours. Artificial, arbitrary. No dimensions but three, no fire escape out of the Burning Aztec. The only certainty that you're a bit of skin and nerve bounding a silence. Through which no sound will stir, no music can move. How easy it was, worlds ago, to drop a man's life into this emptiness.

One of the musicians pulled up a trapdoor beside the fire pit, disappeared into a navel in the floor.

I've scene this before. in the same red.

Stars fall from the dying sky. For you and I.

Where there's nothing but cause-and-effect determinism, there's nothing to pray to. No song, no ceremony. (What else did the bloody Ghost Shirts teach their wearers?) In the parking lot of the Smiling Aztec, he killed a man who meant nothing to the nothing inside him, to the nothing around him.

"—hollow?"

Nothing, Chet, is a moment just before Creation.

Scorpio aflame rises in my desert firmament near the place where dawn is a collection of hammers falling on lumps of bright bronze

Runaway moons whirl in a Kansas twister

Wandering stars

suspended as ornaments from the sky's elongated earlobes

Sweatshined bodies dance a ghost dance above the night

Feathers drift downward

A fire-orange swarm in the darkness
It can be neither created nor destroyed
They dance
binding the wounded the fragmented the outofkilter.
An emergence
out of the remnants
(but there was)
it has altered nothing but its form
on the cusp of the latest world
a slow-coming arc of light
Into a star
you have cast yourself
into a newly risen
rhythmnmn.

BOOK V
FIFTH WORLD

1. The Pyramid Club

Day was a subtle change in the tone of the room, grains of light surrounding pools of dark: one of three dawns. Later than the purplish twilight, when color has begun to edge the dense black. More likely the time of yellow light, when something as momentous as a new planet is being forged just below the horizon, its surface as unblemished as a ball of mercury. To be followed by the ruddy final phase, when the Sun is bisected across its center: half in the lower realm, the source of dreams; half in upper, where we can wave a hand in front of our faces, light a cigarette, change the channel.

A building cut him off from the sky (he could only guess that the Sun was up), its brick blackened by soot from a century when the city was fired by coal, the fallout drifting like dark snow through long winters. The sky, which somehow trapped only the blue out of the spectrum and hid a vacuum behind it, now seemed a remote possibility, a clear turquoise memory he'd imagined to cover this eroding city. Wherever you go, you have to look up.

He was on a couch, still dressed. Only his boots were off.

The pale light seeping through a single window made him feel as though he were deep below the Earth's surface, locked away in cool silence. A place of fermentation.

A Chac Mool, a flat-headed stone idol from Mexico that might still bear the ferrous stink of old blood, sat on the coffee table. One of Mexico's blunt gods (no mystery to what they demanded). A silver necklace hung on the Chac, making the deity a two-bit valet.

He got up, walked through a curtain of beads as if it were a dry waterfall.

"You're up early." Sybil was sitting on the edge of a bed.

"I'm a bad sleeper."

She wore a white T-shirt that reached to the middle of her thighs. "So how much of last night do you remember?"

"How much of last night *is* what I remember?"

She sighed. "You have someone to go back to, don't you?" She smiled in a way that made him feel younger than he was and a little foolish.

He nodded.

"Sometimes I see her reflection in your distracted iris."

"That obvious?"

"To me. Don't worry. You were a good boy—a bad take-home date but a good boy."

"I should get going." There was a blade beneath his ribs, and whenever he moved, it hurt.

He was in the East Village, the day cool and sunny. There was a reassuring familiarity in the brick tenements, the narrow streets, the smell of smoke (a fireplace left over from the days of burning coal?).

The Pyramid Club hibernated during the day, its façade hidden behind sheets of corrugated steel. A huge Egyptian sun disc, spray-painted black, spread its wings over the ruffled metal. Clumsily, he'd once reached out to touch a tiny sun disc of red gold Shawna sometimes wore, thinking to enter her affections through that bit of jewelry. Could he do that now? Put his hand dead center of the cold sun hovering above the club's entrance so that she felt him trying to become a shape at her throat?

He touched the back of his neck, felt the scar he shared with his father.

His heels cut urgently at the sidewalk.

The brick walls hemming him in were layered in graffiti. Fliers and posters had been pasted over each other, left white paper scars on the walls where they'd been torn away. A yellow smiley face bleeding from a bullet hole in its forehead had been the wave a while back.

Another, a skull with a hammer and sickle in one dark socket, warned: *Run, comrade, the old world is behind you.*

Was that what he'd been doing all this time? Making music to dance with ghosts? His father and grandfather. A song to set Uncle Cal free—and to free him of Cal. Linda doing slow pirouettes on the surface of a blue lake. Others he'd never known swarmed his veins, flowed out with his blood though no doctor had ever noticed them in his glass tube. Maybe, though, if he donated a pint, somebody else's veins would be haunted. Or maybe he was giving them a blood transfusion through their ears. Those who listened anyway.

A row of photocopies covered the bricks now. Shades from another continent, from a time before he'd been born: shaven-headed, hollow-faced, the blueprints of their bones showing painfully through. Buchenwald, Treblinka, Lodz. *The Old World is behind you.*

He descended the stairs into the subway.

He stood in front of the door to her building with his heart slamming against his ribs. He reached into a pocket for the key, tried to imagine what he'd say to her, what she would say back.

He took the granite stairs, heard only the lonely sound of his boots on the smooth stone.

He turned down a hallway he'd walked a hundred times before. This time felt like the last.

Trying to drain his face of expression, he knocked on the door (he had no right to use his key).

When he heard footsteps, a fluttery swarm rose in his stomach.

The door opened but jerked to a stop, a chain taut across the opening. The face of a man appeared in the narrow space. "Can I help you?"

A wave of cold sank through his body. "Is, uh, Shawna around?" The words stuck to the roof of his mouth, and his voice sounded boyish and thin.

"She the one who moved out? I just moved in. Haven't even opened most of the boxes."

Smiling, he fought a desire to embrace this man. "Thanks."

Feeling immune to disaster, he dropped down the stairs at reckless speed.

2. The Storm Katsina

He gripped the steering wheel to keep from slipping. Down and away into the soft dark.

Yesterday, she screamed something in a dream (his name?), but there was no sound. Just the O of her mouth.

His musty '74 Cougar was finally out of storage. The wind across his face was dust-dry, hard enough to scrape stone. Its heat a gift from a burning star hidden behind the horizon.

His headlights tracked a stretch of asphalt scorched almost white. The radio off, he heard the drone of the big engine, the dum-*dump* after some break in the smoothness of the road, the wind rushing in from both windows.

Beyond a certain point, his memory lay in ashen drifts.

At some other point no compass needle could fix, his memory consisted of the brick shadows of a city he'd deserted, the hollow of a cheek below a green eye marbled with darker jade, the slant of light falling through endless space.

Behind him the Sun was rising. Before him, a storm.

If New York was ancient light-hindering forest, its floor littered with fallen logs, the leaves of long-past autumns, new undergrowth taking root in loam rich with decay, then Phoenix was sod laid down over the sandy earth, irrigated by sprinklers on timer. Here the storms carried scraped-up grit, dust left over from the mythical Red City of the South, from Uruk, whose heavenly mountain rose above the swampy plain where civilization had first fingernailed its name in wet clay, from Hiroshima and Nagasaki, from the scorched Cities of the Plain.

* * *

Obscuring the sky with mountainous black clouds, the storm loomed.

He ran.

As if he would always be running. His T-shirt soaked with sweat, heavy enough to slap against his stomach.

If the Cougar's rods and pistons had been built for anything, it was to get him to a city before the new day caught up with him, to heal the distance he'd opened between him and her.

He didn't hear the fan belt snap, didn't know it had until white billowed from under the hood. He'd left the Cougar smoldering on the highway's gravelly shoulder like something cast out of a higher realm, blackened by its fall.

He took nothing with him.

The twinkle of the city before him was like a scattering of stellar debris across the desert floor, stopped at the feet of a few half-grown mountains.

Driving the interstate all night, he'd tried to keep the road from turning into something else, keep himself from being carried on weightless wings off to sleep. He looked to the Moon, still and bright above the night-charred landscape, hoped a bit of advice might blow in on the tepid wind.

The Moon remained distant, silent.

He ran.

Inspired by the iron in his blood, he gauged direction by a pull that had skewered him through two chambers of his heart. Nothing clouded the opening through which pale starlight shone. Not anymore.

Overhead, lightning flashed: the storm katsina grinned. After a brief space, thunder rumbled: he laughed.

The road was gone.

The earth through his sneakers was pebbled, the scrape of brush and burned grass muted by pliable soles. Now and again there was the squish of a cactus pad, and he slipped, arms lunging out for balance. He regained his stride, settled back into a rhythm of breathing, loose-fisted swinging, digging at the face of the Earth with the heels and balls of his feet. Nostrils flaring, he sucked at the dry air as if it held no oxygen. He lost moisture with each spent breath. It didn't matter. Inertia alone would carry him as far as the city.

He smelled dampness on the wind, like a dew-soaked tombstone in early-morning Kansas. Above the sound of his own breathing, the thumping footfalls that jarred his bones and scrambled his hearing, he heard rain.

The first fat drops splattered against his face. Puffs of dust rose where they hit the ground.

The katsina's laughter rumbled overhead.

Without breaking stride, he pulled off his shirt, clenched it in a fist.

His father or his uncle or Linda or a katsina or just a storm or all of them and a thousand more, lightning smiles flickering.

He lifted his face, bared a ghoulish grin to the sky, daring the lightning. The storm reminded him. Of the infinity out of which both of them had come. Carried by its careless force, swept up in its overarching strength, he used the storm the way a gull's wings caught the wind. The only way to master the storm was to align himself with it.

Running wasn't a replacement part for his abandoned car; it was the beginning of something.

The rhythm of the seasons in his legs, the drift of the clouds in his blood, he knew how the Moon felt to have the Earth at the center of its being.

Rain ran down his body, mingled with sweat. Alive to the touch of this wet blessing, he and the land both. As only those on speaking terms with extinction could be. He licked his upper lip gratefully, tasted diluted saltiness. Now he knew what it felt like to come into the world by a clean birth, spit out by the black night, already formed, hardened, tempered.

Weight fell away from him like shed clothing until he was the lightness of his bones, wind singing through his ribs. Until he was a spiny feather whirling inside a dust devil across the hard landscape.

Direction was inside him, was all around him.

Knowing that he'd fallen in with his destiny as surely as his destiny existed, he ran.

She was somewhere in the bird-named city. And though he would fail at something tomorrow and the day after and the day after that, he would find her. His father gone for good this time, what he must do now is run.

All of him gathered up in the movement, he and the running and the storm katsina and the ground his feet slapped over and over and over didn't exist separately, couldn't exist except through each other. He needed no mask, no kilt, no sash, no rattle. While the storm katsina shook the sky, his feet fell like rain, heightened the Earth's everlasting hum.

Head pushing forward as if to break some invisible barrier, arms punching upward, he felt himself swelling the sea a single drop more, his movements the movements of birds flocked in formation, of tides and circulating blood and revolving planets. Long reaching strides that quivered along the Earth's spine, sustained its spin, defeated stillness. The mask and the face had merged. He knew who he was, inhabited a place older than words, Hopi or Anglo. Was the storm katsina itself—and a hundred others. Was the dance, circle after circle, was the song that washed over silence, was a whirling beyond the reach of watches and clocks and calendars, was this motion and nothing else, nothing but this running—above all he must run. Must Dance. And not stop dancing.

In 1991 my Philadelphia-based agent received the following letter of decline from Michael Pietsch, a New York–based editor:

> *Dear Mary Jo,*
>
> *I was very impressed by the subtlety and loveliness of Vincent Czyz's writing, and by his ability to bring a large cast and several distinct settings to life. But for all the author's skill, Sun Eye Moon Eye strikes me as a very difficult novel to sell. The story unfolds at a very stately pace, and Logan is a tough nut to crack. It will get good reviews, but I can't foresee selling many copies. So I won't be offering for Little, Brown.*

Mary Jo and I were encouraged. Our mood, in fact, was celebratory. If we'd come so close with Little, Brown, we reasoned, surely it was a matter of months, maybe a year, before we found the right editor for the novel. (Five years later Pietsch would acquire David Foster Wallace's *Infinite Jest.*)

Mary Jo, however, was overly optimistic, and I was hopelessly naïve. After half a dozen more declines that praised various aspects of the book but raised similar concerns about sales, I overhauled the manuscript, cutting nearly 300 pages and restructuring the rest (the manuscript Pietsch had rejected was over 800 pages.)

That ought to do it, we thought.

In 1994 I was awarded a grant from the NJ Arts Council on the basis of a chapter from *Sun Eye Moon Eye* but a publishing contract wasn't even a speck on the horizon.

Two years later Mary Jo quit the business in frustration and disgust—it was too much of a *business* for her.

Unagented, I tried the smaller, independent presses. One of them, Persea, sent a scribbled-on form rejection: "I regret that we cannot take this on. Gorgeous prose; you are a real spellcaster. K. Russell."

The novel, it seemed, wasn't commercial enough for the larger houses, while smaller presses balked at its size (even after revisions, it was still upward of 550 pages) or it just didn't suit their tastes. In 2009, for example, an editor at Dalkey Archive recommended it for publication but was overruled by the editorial board: "Several editors have considered your submission, and while we found many remarkable things in your work, it unfortunately did not meet with the response necessary to move forward."

In retrospect, I can see it really *wasn't* their kind of work. I'd trained my sights on a visionary novel—ambiguous a classification as that is—but Dalkey was more interested in discursive metafiction, Sadean subversion, and, among other literary approaches, Menippean satire.

I kept an ever-fattening folder of declines in a filing cabinet. At some point, editors stopped sending letters and began rejecting the novel via email. I saved those too.

I was discouraged, of course, but one of Rilke's letters to

a young poet had persuaded me that I needed to be patient: "There is here no measuring with time, no year matters, and ten years are nothing."

In 2011 a chapter of *Sun Eye Moon Eye* was the basis for the Truman Capote Fellowship at Rutgers University. Excerpts were published, beginning in 2014, in a number of journals. One was a finalist in the Jerry Jazz Fiction Contest.

As digits on the chronological odometer continued to click over, I began to doubt Rilke's advice—or at least to suspect it didn't apply to me. I thought it increasingly likely the manuscript would never see print, and I subjected it to yet another round of revisions with, as ever, an eye to cutting the page count. I trimmed it down to 515.

When the offer from Spuyten Duyvil finally came, I didn't see it for 17 days: I spotted it, purely by accident, in my spam folder.

Here, at the end of a 32-year odyssey, I can only hope that you found the time and attention you set aside for this book well spent.

Vincent Czyz is the author of *The Secret Adventures of Order*, an essay collection, *The Three Veils of Ibn Oraybi*, a novella, *Adrift in a Vanishing City*, a fiction collection that received the 2016 Eric Hoffer Award for Best in Small Press, and *The Christos Mosaic*, a novel. He is the recipient of two fiction fellowships from the NJ Council on the Arts and the W. Faulkner-W. Wisdom Prize for Short Fiction. The 2011 Truman Capote Fellow at Rutgers University, his stories have appeared in *Shenandoah*, *AGNI*, *The Massachusetts Review*, *Tin House*, *Tampa Review*, *Georgetown Review*, *Copper Nickel*, *December*, *Southern Indiana Review*, and *Skidrow Penthouse*, among other publications. He spent a total of nearly a decade in Istanbul, Turkey before settling in Jersey City, NJ, USA.

www.ingramcontent.com/pod-product-compliance
Lightning Source LLC
Chambersburg PA
CBHW061849310726
48972CB00004B/943